Praise for the

THE BOOK SPY

"The walled-off feeling of loneliness in a crowd pervades the pages of Hlad's piercing historical thriller. Based on a fascinating and little-known true story of World War II . . . Hlad's immersive portrayal of wartime Lisbon and its inhabitants, of the loneliness caused by the terror that anybody at any time could be an informant, plus his captivating thriller/romance tale make this a must-read, especially for fans of Kate Quinn's *The Rose Code*." —*firstCLUE* (starred review)

CHURCHILL'S SECRET MESSENGER

"Hlad does a nice job of intertwining the romance and action stories, treating both realistically and largely without melodrama. The early parts of the novel, detailing Rose's work in the below-ground War Rooms and her encounters with Churchill, prove every bit as compelling as the behind-the-lines drama. Good reading for both WW II and romance fans." —*Booklist*

THE LONG FLIGHT HOME

"Hlad's debut snares readers with its fresh angle on the blitz of WW II, focusing on the homing pigeons used by the British, and the people who trained and cared for them. . . . Descriptions of the horrors of war and the excitement of battle are engaging, and the unusual element of the carrier pigeons lends an intriguing twist. This story will speak not only to romance readers and WW II buffs but also to animal advocates and anyone who enjoys discovering quirky details that are hidden in history." —*Publishers Weekly*

"I've always been fascinated by homing pigeons, and Alan Hlad makes these amazing birds and their trainers shine in *The Long Flight Home*—a sweeping tale full of romance and espionage, poignant sacrifice and missed chances, uncommon courage and the ongoing costs of war. A compelling debut told with conviction and great heart." —Paula McLain, *New York Times* bestselling author of *The Paris Wife* and *Love and Ruin*

Books by Alan Hlad

THE LONG FLIGHT HOME

CHURCHILL'S SECRET MESSENGER

A LIGHT BEYOND THE TRENCHES

THE BOOK SPY

FLEEING FRANCE

Published by Kensington Publishing Corp.

FLEEING FRANCE

ALAN HLAD

John Scognamiglio Books
Kensington Publishing Corp.
www.kensingtonbooks.com

JOHN SCOGNAMIGLIO BOOKS are published by
Kensington Publishing Corp.
900 Third Avenue
New York, NY 10022

All Kensington titles, imprints, and distributed lines are available at special quantity discounts for bulk purchases for sales promotion, premiums, fund-raising, and educational or institutional use.

Special book excerpts or customized printings can also be created to fit specific needs. For details, write or phone the office of the Kensington Sales Manager: Kensington Publishing Corp., 900 Third Avenue, New York, NY 10022. Attn. Sales Department. Phone: 1-800-221-2647.

ISBN: 978-1-4967-4556-9

ISBN: 978-1-4967-4557-6 (ebook)

First Kensington Trade Paperback Edition: August 2024

10 9 8 7 6 5 4 3 2 1

Printed in the United States of America

For the fallen in the fight for freedom

PART 1

THE PHONY WAR

CHAPTER 1

PARIS, FRANCE—SEPTEMBER 12, 1939

Nine days after France and Britain declared war on Germany for invading Poland, Ruth Lacroix—a twenty-year-old American nightclub singer—entered a crowded dressing room of a cabaret named Bal Tabarin. Music, coming from the orchestra that was warming the crowd, resonated through the backstage changing area. Female dancers put on can-can dresses layered with colorful ruffles and frills, and Ruth slipped into a sleek black evening gown. The entertainers—crammed inside the room with costume designers, make-up artists, and hair stylists—were preparing for the evening show.

"You're giving Parisians an escape from their worries of war," Ruth said to her friend Lucette, a statuesque dancer with toffee-blond hair.

Lucette's eyes filled with gratitude. "You are, too."

"That's kind of you to say," Ruth said, "but we both know that patrons are here for dancers, not singers."

"Clientele adore you."

"*Merci*," Ruth said.

"I wish I had a dulcet voice like you."

"Would you like me to teach you to sing?"

"*Oui*," Lucette said. "That would be lovely."

Ruth slipped a faux diamond bracelet over her wrist. "With a few lessons, you'll be warbling like a goldfinch for France's victory celebration."

Lucette smiled and buckled the ankle straps of her high-heeled shoes.

Bal Tabarin—home of the French can-can—was a palatial cabaret on Rue Victor-Massé in the 9th arrondissement of Paris. The lounge, large enough to seat a few hundred guests, was a towering space with an elevated parquet floor stage that jutted into the audience like an oversize runway for fashion models. Well-dressed patrons, who were seated at small tables covered with fine linen, sipped champagne and cocktails while being entertained by dancers. Each of the performances, which had elaborate themes and costume designs, were separated by brief intermissions of music and song. Bal Tabarin attracted some of Paris's best dancers, many of whom had attended ballet academies. Unlike the other performers, who'd been trained by professionals to develop their artistry, Ruth had learned to sing by listening to records on a wind-up gramophone.

Prior to arriving in Paris in 1937, Ruth lived at her parents' apple orchard on the outskirts of Lewiston, Maine. She was the only child of Sarah, a Parisian Jew, and Charles, an American Protestant. Her parents had met during the Great War, when her father, a soldier with the American Expeditionary Force, was stationed on the western front. Sarah—a volunteer nurse at a French Red Cross field hospital—had dressed a shell splinter wound to Charles's shoulder. During his recovery, the two became friends and soon fell in love. After the war, they were married in a civil ceremony and set sail for the United States to create a life on the Lacroix family apple orchard. A month shy of their first wedding anniversary, Sarah gave birth to Ruth, a six-pound-two-ounce baby girl.

Ruth's musicality came naturally. She could sing in perfect pitch by the time she reached kindergarten and, throughout her school-age years, her parents fostered her ardor for music by buying her a secondhand gramophone and loads of jazz records. She was a steadfast member of school and community choirs, even though she was dissatisfied that the repertoire was usually limited to folk songs. It's not that Ruth had an aversion to tunes of Americana, but their lyrics and melodies didn't feed her heart like jazz, swing, and big band music. Lewiston lacked jazz vocal teachers, so Ruth developed her craft by modeling her style, timbre, and vibrato to recordings by the likes of Ruth Etting, Ella Fitzgerald, Ethel Waters, and Lucienne Boyer. In her free time, she performed duets with the voices of famous singers flowing from her gramophone. However, much of her practice was *a cappella*—without instrumental accompaniment—while she completed chores of harvesting apples, making cider, pruning trees, and driving the farm tractor. She cherished her private rehearsals, but her fondest memories were of entertaining her parents, hunkered on the living room sofa with their family dog, a black Labrador retriever named Moxie.

"*Magnifique!*" her mother had cheered as Ruth finished singing a rendition of Billie Holiday's "What a Little Moonlight Can Do."

"Bravo!" Dad shouted, fending off Moxie's wagging tail.

Ruth's chest swelled with pride. She relished how music could bring people joy, and she knew, deep down, what she would do for the rest of her life.

Ruth's father—a pragmatic man by nature—encouraged her to attend nearby Bates College to obtain a teaching degree. But Bates, as well as every other university in the country, didn't have a curriculum for jazz studies. Besides, Ruth wanted to entertain for a living and the best way to make a go of a singing career, she believed, was to live in a big city with a thriving music scene. Places like New York, New Orleans, Los Angeles, Kansas City, and Chicago would have been fine choices, but ever since her first visit to Paris she aspired to perform at the Casino de Paris.

At seventeen years of age, Ruth made a three-week trip with her mom to Paris to visit her mother's sister. She'd forged a close relationship with her aunt Colette, uncle Julian, and cousin Marceau through the exchange of letters and family photographs. Also, she'd developed a sibling-like bond with Marceau, who spent most summers working on her parents' apple orchard. During their visit to Paris, Colette and her mother surprised Ruth by taking her to a show starring Lucienne Boyer, a famous Parisian singer, at the Casino de Paris. Boyer, in addition to being well known in France, was quite popular in the United States, given that she had made many recordings with Columbia Records. Ruth had never been to an esteemed music hall, nor had she attended a live performance by a prominent singer. Ruth's exhilaration soared through Boyer's performance, and she imagined what it might feel like to be on-stage, singing emotionally infused songs to a vast audience. And while Boyer took bows for her standing ovation, Sarah—as if she could sense her daughter's yearning—leaned to Ruth and said, "Follow your heart, *ma chérie*—I believe in you."

Ruth, her eyes filled with tears of happiness, applauded until her hands ached.

Upon returning home to Lewiston, Ruth, with the support of her mother, informed Dad of her aspiration to someday perform at the Casino de Paris, and that she planned to move to France to live with Aunt Colette. Charles was stunned by the news. But after much time and discussion—and Ruth explaining to her father that the Casino de Paris was a prestigious music hall, not a gambling house—he eventually accepted her decision.

After high school graduation, Ruth worked as a waitress and labored on the orchard through the fall harvest to earn money. She purchased a third-class ticket on board the SS *Champlain*, sailed from New York to Le Havre, France, and moved into Aunt Colette's and Uncle Julian's apartment in Le Marais, a Jewish neighborhood in the 4th arrondissement of Paris. Julian was a doctor and Colette was a nurse, and they worked together at Saint-Antoine Hospital. Her aunt and uncle, a sweet and benevolent couple, gave Ruth a spare room next to her cousin Marceau, who was studying chemistry at the University of Paris. Ruth adored her Parisian family, especially Marceau, whom she'd grown fond of when he selflessly worked a summer school break on her parents' orchard while her father recovered from an appendectomy. To Ruth, Marceau was more like a brother than a cousin. He looked after her like an older sibling by showing her around Paris, including the safest routes to and from the 9th arrondissement, where many of the music halls and theaters were located.

The first year in Paris had been difficult for Ruth. She failed three auditions at the Casino de Paris, and she had trouble landing singing gigs, except for an unpaid part in musical theater. Some of her rejections had little to do with her vocal capability, considering that more than one casting director had informed her that they were seeking a tall female singer with a voluptuous physique. Ruth—a slender, five-foot-two-inch woman with wavy auburn hair and childlike dimples on her cheeks—buried her resentment and resolved to continue with auditions. *Eventually*, she'd thought, exiting a theater stage, *I'll earn a role based on my singing, not the size of my cleavage.*

Although her aunt and uncle didn't charge for room and board, Ruth didn't feel right about accepting charity, so she waited tables at a *brasserie* to earn money to contribute toward rent and groceries. She auditioned, anywhere there were openings, and last autumn she landed a job as a cabaret singer at Bal Tabarin. She was elated, despite that the role paid little and would be limited to singing short pieces during dance intermissions. Things were looking up, Ruth believed. But soon after she began performing at Bal Tabarin, Hitler's drums of war began to beat.

Early in the year, the Nazi leader proclaimed in his Reichstag speech that European Jews would be exterminated if war erupted, sending a wave of fear and outrage through France. Soon after, the German military invaded and occupied Czechoslovakia, and thousands of young Parisian men, including her cousin Marceau, enlisted in the French Army. The city of Paris issued gas masks to civilians. Ruth's parents urged her to return home, but she declined, reassuring them through letters that she would be safe in Paris, like it was during the Great War.

The sound of music and clacking of high-heeled shoes grew from Bal Tabarin's stage.

A stout, middle-aged man named Serge, who was the show's stage manager, entered the dressing room and removed a cigarette from his lips. "Ruth, you're on in two minutes."

Ruth nodded. She applied red lipstick and made her way to a backstage curtain. Butterflies fluttered in her stomach. The cancan music stopped, the audience cheered, and dancers exited the stage.

"Good luck," Lucette said, brushing past Ruth.

Ruth smiled.

As clapping faded, a barrel-chested emcee wearing a tuxedo and top hat walked onto the stage. *"Mesdames et messieurs!* I give you Bal Tabarin's international, Franco-American songstress— Ruth Lacroix!"

The music conductor waved his baton, striking up the orchestra. The audience applauded and the emcee left the stage.

Ruth, her adrenaline surging, gracefully walked to a standing microphone. A scent of stale champagne and cigarette smoke filled her nose. Applause dwindled away and was replaced by a tender musical introduction, composed of a clarinet, xylophone, violin, and muted trumpet. She gazed over the crowd, most of whom were affluent, older men and women. *The young men have gone to war,* she thought, conjuring the mood of the piece. She drew a breath and sang the first verse of "J'attendrai" ("I will wait").

The song, inspired by the Humming Chorus of Puccini's opera *Madame Butterfly,* was a new addition to her repertoire. The lyrics of the piece depicted the yearning for a beloved to return home. Nearly every Parisian had a friend, darling, or family member who'd gone away to war, and Ruth—determined to give patrons hope of reuniting with loved ones—had convinced the show director to include the piece in her performance. As she progressed through the heartfelt lyrics, the faces of guests turned somber. Several women dabbed tears from their eyes with handkerchiefs. And as she finished the song, the crowd rose to their feet and applauded.

"Vive la France!" a man shouted.

Cheers erupted from the audience. The clapping grew louder.

A wave of pride surged through Ruth. She took a bow and left the stage.

Two hours later, after the dancers performed a patriotic finale in which they wore military-style uniforms with shiny metal helmets, the show ended with a standing ovation. The curtain closed and the dancers, as well as Ruth, made their way to the dressing room where they hung up their costumes, washed makeup from their faces, and changed into casual attire. Long after the patrons had left, Ruth and Lucette exited the Bal Tabarin to a dark Rue Victor-Massé with few pedestrians. The streetlights of Paris had been turned off as a measure against potential Luftwaffe air raids. Under a starlit sky, they walked together on the way to their apartments.

"I enjoyed your new song," Lucette said, her shoes clicking over the sidewalk. "You lifted the spirit of the crowd."

"*Merci*," Ruth said.

"Pierre should allow you to sing it for each show until our men come home."

Ruth smiled, feeling grateful for her friend's kind words. She buttoned her coat and turned her thoughts to Lucette's fiancé, who'd joined the French Army's 503rd Combat Tank Regiment. "How's Paul?"

"I received a letter from him yesterday," Lucette said. "He's well, and he informed me that there have been little, if any, skirmishes at the front. He thinks it's because most of the German military is focused on combating Poland."

Ruth felt horrible for the Polish people, struggling to survive Hitler's onslaught.

"Paul believes that the Maginot Line will deter any invasion by Germany."

"My uncle Julian told me the same thing," Ruth said, envisioning the massive concrete fortification along the French border. "He thinks that it's impenetrable to attack."

Lucette slowed her pace and clasped her arms. "Some of the dancers say that the war isn't real, and that it will all be settled soon. Even so, I can't stop worrying about Paul."

"I feel the same way about my cousin, Marceau." Ruth placed a hand on Lucette's shoulder. "We must have faith that the war will end, and they'll come home."

"*Oui.*" Lucette blinked her eyes, as if she were fighting back tears.

For the remainder of their walk, they discussed nothing of the war. They spoke in English, allowing Lucette to practice her excellent language skills, and they talked about Ruth's offer, partly

in jest, to give her singing lessons. Reaching the 4th arrondissement, the pair said goodbye. Lucette crossed the Pont d'Arcole
bridge over the Seine River toward her apartment in the Latin
Quarter, and Ruth continued her path through Le Marais.

Minutes later, Ruth entered a narrow, Lutetian limestone building next to a Jewish bakery. She climbed the stairs, the weathered
floorboards creaking under her weight, to a third-floor landing. As
she removed her key, her eyes were drawn to a glimmer of light
from under the apartment door. *They're awake*, Ruth thought, feeling excited to tell Aunt Colette and Uncle Julian about her performance. She entered the apartment, hung up her coat and purse,
and then went to the kitchen and froze.

Colette and Julian—with red, swollen eyes and disheveled,
gray hair—rose from their seats at the table.

Ruth swallowed. "What's wrong?"

Tears fell from Colette's cheeks. "Marceau is dead."

Ruth stepped back. "*Non*—he can't be!"

Julian's lips quivered and he began to cry.

Colette, her hand trembling, pointed to a torn envelope and
piece of paper on the table.

Ruth shuffled forward, and her breath stalled in her lungs as the
words of the telegram came into focus.

```
    It is my painful duty to inform you
that a report has this day been received
from the War Office notifying of the
death of Corporal Marceau Bloch, 32nd
Infantry Regiment, which occurred at the
German town of Brenschelbach on 12th of
September 1939, and I am to express to you
the sympathy and regret of the Superior
Council of War at your loss. The cause of
death was killed in action.
    Your obedient servant,
    M. S. Toussaint
    Officer in Charge of Infantry Records,
No. 2 District
```

A wave of nausea rose from Ruth's stomach, producing the urge to vomit. Her legs buckled beneath her, and she crumpled to the floor.

Colette and Julian kneeled and wrapped their arms around her. Ruth sobbed. Together, they wept until no more tears could be shed.

Chapter 2

Le Havre, France—September 13, 1939

Fifteen thousand feet above the English Channel, Flying Officer James "Jimmie" Quill of the Royal Air Force (RAF) peered through the cockpit glass of his Hawker Hurricane, a British single-seater monoplane fighter aircraft. Ahead and below his plane, a Blenheim bomber squadron was flying in a tight, Vic formation. The drone of propellers filled Jimmie's ears, and a mix of patriotism and disquietude stirred inside his chest. He was serving as an escort for the bombers of the Air Component of the British Expeditionary Force (BEF) that were being deployed to France to support British and French armies. But, after accompanying the bombers to their airfield, Jimmie wasn't returning home. He was going to war.

Jimmie—a tall, hazel-eyed twenty-five-year-old son of a shipbuilder from Portsmouth—had been given orders to report to his new post with the No. 73 Squadron, a unit of Hawker Hurricane fighter pilots that arrived in France earlier in the week. Unlike the other pilots of No. 73 Squadron, who were experienced and had flown together for quite some time, Jimmie was a raw recruit. Two weeks ago, he finished his advanced training on fighters at RAF Tern Hill in Shropshire. Although he had graduated near the top of his class, he was far from an adept aviator.

Prior to advanced training, Jimmie flew a Gloster Gladiator, an obsolete biplane fighter that was no match for a German Messerschmitt. The RAF expected the new Hurricane to be a more formidable opponent, given its light weight, maneuverability, and one-thousand-horsepower Rolls-Royce engine that could produce a top speed of 340 mph. Additionally, the Hurricane was heavily armed with eight .303-inch Browning machine guns, four in each wing. Jimmie, despite his rigorous training, was still getting acclimated to wearing a flying helmet with a radio set, as well as having his nose and mouth covered by an oxygen mask that contained a microphone. Also, the space of the cockpit was quite narrow, especially for a broad-shouldered man like Jimmie, and each time he turned to examine his surroundings, his arms brushed the sides of the compartment. He hoped that, with additional flight time, the Hurricane would begin to feel like an extension of his mind and limbs. But training was over, and gaining expertise in the Hurricane would likely need to be acquired in combat.

An hour after departing RAF Digby in Lincolnshire, England, Jimmie's adrenaline surged at the sight of the earth's crust that rose from the sea. As he gazed at the rugged Normandy coastline, the radio speaker crackled inside his helmet.

"Welcome to France," the bomber squadron leader's voice said.

Jimmie drew a deep breath and exhaled. He reached into the interior pocket of his flight jacket and patted his good luck charm—a small, tattered stuffed Piglet—which was a gift from his sister, Nora.

Minutes later, the squadron reached the Le Havre-Octeville Airport and was given permission to land. Jimmie circled the perimeter while the Blenheim bombers took turns touching down on an earthen runway. After the bombers safely landed, Jimmie lined his sights on the strip of smooth ground. He adjusted the control stick and cut back on the throttle, decreasing the airspeed. The pointers on the altimeter gradually lowered until the wheels of his Hurricane touched the ground.

The airport was primarily used as a French military airbase. It contained a large fleet of planes, most of which were outdated French aircraft. Much like Britain, France had been militarily complacent in the decades after the Great War, and the country had been scrambling over the past year to modernize its air force. At the far end of the field were canvas tents and aircraft of the RAF, identifiable by their painted roundel symbols. He taxied his plane to a squadron of parked Hurricanes on a grass-covered area and cut the engine. He unbuckled his harness, slid open the canopy, and climbed out of his aircraft.

A bespectacled RAF ground crewman, wearing a blue coverall and cap, approached Jimmie and saluted him. "Good day, sir."

Jimmie returned the salute and extended his hand. "Flying Officer Jimmie Quill."

The man shook Jimmie's hand. "I'm Corporal Horace Yates, your fitter."

A "fitter" was a technician who was responsible for aircraft engines, as well as loads of other mechanical parts. Although each of the ground crew—including "riggers" who fueled the aircraft, and "armorers" who loaded weapons—performed important roles, a cracking "fitter" could be the difference between life and death for a pilot.

"Where do you call home?" Jimmie asked.

"Southampton, sir."

Jimmie grinned. "We're almost neighbors. I was born and raised in Portsmouth."

"My wife, Daisy, and I were married in Portsmouth Cathedral."

"It's a grand church, and a short walk from my childhood home," Jimmie said. "Do you and Daisy have children?"

Horace's eyes brightened. "A six-month-old girl named Olive." He removed a small photograph from a breast pocket of his coverall and showed it to Jimmie.

"She's a darling," Jimmie said, peering at an image of a chubby-cheeked infant wearing a lace dress and bonnet.

"She takes after her mum." Horace put away the picture. "Do you have a wife and children, sir?"

"Not as fortunate as you, I'm afraid." Jimmie placed a hand on the wing of his Hurricane. "Until the war is over, I'm devoted to my bird."

Horace chuckled. "Of course, sir."

"You're welcome to call me Jimmie when we're not in the presence of officers."

"Will do." He pointed to a large tent with a British flag. "The squadron leader is expecting you."

"There's a duffel bag stowed away in the plane," Jimmie said. "I'll get it after I meet with him."

"No need. I'll have it placed in your barracks." Horace slid his cap from his head, revealing a receding brown hairline. "When you were landing, I noticed an oil streak on the belly of your Hurricane. I'll check over the engine to make sure there's not a leak. Also, the stain clashes with the camouflage and you might be spotted by the Luftwaffe. I'll have the aircraft touched up with some fresh paint."

"Thanks, Horace."

Jimmie made his way to the squadron leader's tent, its canvas flap door tied open. He stopped at the entrance and saluted a group of four RAF officers who were inside, standing around a table with a map. "Flying Officer Jimmie Quill reporting for duty, sir."

"At ease." A thin-framed officer with pale skin and chapped lips approached Jimmie and shook his hand. "I'm Squadron Leader Hank More. Welcome to Seventy-Three Squadron."

"Thank you, sir," Jimmie said.

Hank gestured to a mustached, pipe-smoking pilot, who was wearing a red, paisley ascot that was neatly tied around his neck and tucked into his tunic. "Flying Officer Gord Fernsby."

"Good day," Jimmie said.

Gord, his face stoic, gave a nod and puffed on his pipe.

An acrid scent of burnt tobacco penetrated Jimmie's nose.

Hank pointed to a pilot with a round, boyish face and unkempt, thick brown hair. "Flying Officer Newell Orton—his nickname is Fanny."

"Welcome." Fanny shook Jimmie's hand.

Hank gestured to the last pilot. "Flying Officer Edgar Kain."

"Everyone calls me Cobber," the pilot said with a New Zealand accent. He had dark brown hair, parted down the middle but slightly off center, and dark circles surrounded his eyes, like someone who suffered from insomnia. He approached Jimmie and shook his hand.

"It's good to meet you," Jimmie said.

Hank slipped a cigarette from his pocket and lit it. "Gord, Fanny, and Cobber are section leaders—each is responsible for two wingmen. They were about to provide me with their recommendations on your section leader assignment."

Jimmie shifted his weight. "Would you prefer privacy, sir?"

"No," Hank said. "In the Seventy-Three Squadron, we don't keep secrets and I expect my men to speak their piece—including you."

"Yes, sir," Jimmie said, feeling a bit surprised by the squadron leader's candidness, as well as his willingness to accept counsel from his men.

Hank took a drag and turned to Gord. "Tell me your thoughts."

"It might be best to assign him to me," Gord said, pointing at Jimmie with his pipe. "The lad will need a regimented section leader to break him from his cuddly toy."

Jimmie looked down to find Piglet's head peeking from his flight jacket. His face turned warm. He tucked Piglet away and said, "It's a good luck piece."

"Perhaps you should consider a charm more becoming of a fighter pilot," Gord said in a demeaning tone of voice.

Maybe he's testing me, Jimmie thought, remaining poised.

The squadron leader turned to Cobber. "What's your recommendation?"

"Assign him to me," Cobber said. "The vacancy is with my section, so adding Jimmie would be less disruptive to the squadron."

Gord adjusted his ascot. "Are you sure that you're the best mentor for a new pilot?"

"What do you mean by that?" Cobber asked.

"You've lost a wingman," Gord said, "and you've been disciplined—on more than one occasion—for performing aerobatic stunts at too low an altitude."

Jimmie's shoulder muscles tensed.

"What happened to Taylor was an accident," Cobber said.

Gord smoothed his mustache. "Of course."

"Enough," Hank said. He flicked ash from his cigarette. "Fanny, I haven't heard from you."

Fanny clasped his hands behind his back. "I have a few thoughts, sir. First, pilots are a superstitious lot. Most of us have good luck charms, and I don't view a cuddly toy as any different than a St. Christopher medallion, rabbit's foot, horseshoe, or a lucky ascot."

Gord furrowed his brow.

"Second, we haven't seen action," Fanny said. "Our missions have been to escort ships and aircraft on their route across the Channel, and many of the French pilots are saying that this isn't a bona fide war, and that a peace agreement will be signed before any major confrontation. Jimmie should have more than adequate time to get acclimated to our squadron before—"

"I was asking for your recommendation," Hank interrupted, "not a bloody speech."

"Yes, sir," Fanny said. "I suggest that Cobber take Jimmie as a wingman."

Hank took a long drag on his cigarette, as if he was contemplating the options, and blew smoke through his nose. "He's yours, Cobber."

"Yes, sir," Cobber said.

Hank dropped his cigarette and ground it under his boot. "Dismissed."

The pilots filed out of the tent. Gord walked away, and Cobber and Fanny accompanied Jimmie to his barracks, where his duffel bag had been placed on a cot. For several minutes, the three chatted while Jimmie stowed away his things in a metal locker at the foot of his bed. He learned that Fanny was from Warwick, England, and that he loved to play pinochle. Cobber was born in Hastings, New Zealand, and, unlike Fanny, who preferred a gentlemanly game of cards, he enjoyed a physical match of rugby.

"To fit in around here," Cobber said, "you'll need to gain the trust of the pilots and prove your worth as an aviator."

"Of course," Jimmie said.

"We're scheduled to conduct a patrol this afternoon over the Cherbourg Peninsula," Cobber said. "It'll give you a chance to show me and the men what you're made of."

Apprehension swelled in Jimmie's chest. "I look forward to it." He unzipped his flight jacket and placed Piglet into the foot locker.

"What's the story behind your good luck charm?" Fanny asked.

An image of Jimmie's younger sister—laboring to walk with steel braces strapped to her legs—flashed in his head. "My sister, Nora, was stricken with polio as a child. She was quite fond of the children's book *Winnie-the-Pooh*. That stuffed Piglet comforted her through dreadful times, and she thought it might do the same for me."

"I cannot begin to imagine what she went through," Cobber said, his voice turned somber. "How is she doing?"

"Better," Jimmie said. "She's able to walk when she wears leg braces."

He patted Jimmie on the shoulder. "Never mind what Gord said about a cuddly toy. You've got a proper good luck charm, mate."

"Indeed," Fanny said.

Jimmie closed the lid on the trunk. Feeling comfortable to speak his thoughts, he looked at Cobber and asked, "Do you mind telling me about what happened to the pilot named Taylor?"

"Were you told anything when you received orders for your post?" Cobber asked.

"Only that my assignment would fill a vacant position with the Seventy-Three Squadron."

Cobber drew a breath and rubbed the side of his neck. "Me and two wingmen—Taylor and Benny—were given an order to escort a BEF supply ship across the Channel. On our mission, we got caught in a severe rainstorm, and the visibility was poor, at best. With heavy turbulence and our fuel nearly exhausted, I gave permission for my wingmen to land ahead of me. Benny touched down safely, but Taylor descended too soon on his approach to the airfield. The left wing of his Hurricane clipped an electrical tower."

A chill ran through Jimmie's spine.

Cobber lowered his eyes. "He was killed in the crash."

"I'm sorry," Jimmie said.

"Thanks," Cobber said. "Taylor was a good airman."

"Undoubtedly one of the best in the squadron," Fanny said, looking at Cobber. "The lad merely made an error in judgment, and I would have done the same thing if I were in your shoes. When fuel is low, a good section leader orders their wingmen to land first."

Cobber gave a reluctant nod.

"You probably noticed that Gord is rather bitter toward Cobber," Fanny said to Jimmie. "Gord and Taylor were card mates."

"I see," Jimmie said.

"How about a cuppa?" Cobber asked, as if eager to change the subject. "We have an hour before our patrol, and it's best that Jimmie gets acquainted with the other pilots before he's put to the test of flying with the squadron."

Tension spread through Jimmie's shoulder muscles.

"Tea sounds splendid," Fanny said.

Jimmie followed the men out of the barracks. As they made their way to a mess tent, he saw what he believed to be regret in Cobber's eyes—the sorrow that filled him and the pain of ruminating over a decision that resulted in the loss of a man's life. *He feels responsible, despite that there was nothing he'd done wrong.* Jimmie buried his thoughts. He resolved to learn everything he could from his fellow pilots and fight, each day, to survive the war.

CHAPTER 3

LONDON, ENGLAND—SEPTEMBER 21, 1939

Winston Churchill, First Lord of the Admiralty, entered the Cabinet Room at 10 Downing Street to find Prime Minister Neville Chamberlain—a thin, seventy-year-old man with salt-and-pepper hair and mustache—who was reading a newspaper while seated alone at a long, green baize-topped table. Near the prime minister was an ornate ceramic teapot and two cups with saucers. Of the twenty-four Victorian leather upholstered chairs that surrounded the table, Chamberlain was settled in the only one with arms—the seat that long eluded Churchill.

"Good day, Prime Minister," Churchill said.

Chamberlain, his back to a large marble fireplace, put down his newspaper and gestured to a chair across the table. "Come in, Winston."

Churchill sat and placed his hands on his lap.

"Tea?"

"No, thank you."

Chamberlain poured a splash of milk into a cup, added tea, and stirred it with a silver spoon. "I suppose you know the reason why I summoned you," he said, his voice slow and deliberate.

Churchill clasped the lapels of his charcoal three-piece suit with a matching polka-dot bow tie. "My letters, I presume."

Chamberlain nodded. He took a sip of tea and lowered his cup, clinking onto its saucer.

At the outbreak of war, Prime Minister Chamberlain offered Churchill responsibility for the navy as First Lord of the Admiralty and a place in the war cabinet. Chamberlain's appeasement of Nazi Germany had failed, and he was pressured by newspapers and political parties to bring in Churchill, who was viewed as a strong military leader given his experience in the Great War. Starting on Churchill's second day in office, he began to send daily, prolonged letters to the prime minister that spanned all matters of the war.

"I appointed you to lead the Royal Navy," Chamberlain said, "not direct the entire war effort."

Churchill removed a cigar from the interior pocket of his jacket and held it between his thumb and forefinger. "My intentions are merely to aid you in your duties."

"I do appreciate your tenacity and vigor, Winston. But I intend to bring this conflict to an end. I have not—and will not—abandon my efforts to seek a peaceful European settlement."

Churchill lit his cigar and puffed smoke. A memory of Chamberlain's acceptance of the Munich Agreement, allowing German annexation of the Sudetenland, flashed in his head. He'd urged Chamberlain to tell Hitler that Britain would declare war if the Germans invaded Czechoslovak territory, but the prime minister had refuted his recommendation.

"Your pursuit for peace is admirable," Churchill said, "but there is no appeasing a barbaric dictator. Hitler's hostilities will not cease with Poland."

"He'd be foolish to attempt to annex more territory. He'd have Britain to contend with, and the French Army is a million strong with five million reservists. Further military advances by Germany would surely end in a long, drawn-out stalemate."

"Hitler has his Luftwaffe," Churchill said. "Allied aircraft are significant in number, but the French Air Force—as well as the British Royal Air Force—has fallen behind with modernizing its weaponry."

Chamberlain shifted in his chair. "Despite our declaration of war, there has been no British military engagement and little fighting by the French. The British Expeditionary Force remains in the process of being deployed to France and the Low Countries to dig field defenses on the border. Furthermore, the minor French offensive in Saarland, Germany, has fizzled out."

Churchill straightened his back.

"I received a report this morning," Chamberlain said. "General Maurice Gamelin has ordered his units to return to their original posts on the Maginot Line."

Churchill flicked ash into a crystal ashtray. "Gamelin squandered an opportunity to hold the Saarland. Poland's defeat is inevitable and, with time, Hitler will redeploy military reinforcements to the border of Germany and France."

Chamberlain slid his newspaper to him. "The Americans are calling it the Phony War."

Churchill eyed the article about US Senator William Borah, who was quoted about his views of the inactivity on the western front. He folded the paper. "It's not the Phony War—it's the Twilight War."

Chamberlain furrowed his brow.

"We are at the eve of Nazi Germany's quest to conquer Europe. We must be prepared to fight at all costs."

Chamberlain took a sip of tea. "I received word that US President Roosevelt has been in communication with you," he said, as if eager to change the conversation.

"A congratulatory note on my appointment to First Lord of the Admiralty," Churchill said, "and to share his willingness to personally keep in touch."

Chamberlain lightly tapped the rim of his cup.

"An escalation of war is unavoidable," Churchill said, leaning forward in his chair.

"I will continue to pursue tactics of diplomacy," Chamberlain said firmly. "In the meantime, I trust that you'll have the Royal Navy ready to be called upon, if needed."

"Of course, Prime Minister."

Chamberlain looked at him. "It's difficult not to like you, Winston, despite that you're usually mistaken and quite difficult to deal with."

Churchill, maintaining his composure, tamped out his cigar.

"I expect that you'll refrain from sending me more garrulous letters." Chamberlain refilled his cup with milk and tea. "That will be all. Good day, Winston."

Churchill stood and left the Cabinet Room. As he exited 10 Downing Street, determination burned inside his chest. He quickened his pace and made mental notes on war strategy to include in his next correspondence to the prime minister.

CHAPTER 4

PARIS, FRANCE—SEPTEMBER 21, 1939

There was no burial service for Ruth's cousin, Marceau. His body was not returned from the front, and the French Army provided no further explanation on how he perished. Newspapers reported that a French invasion of Saarland, Germany, had taken place during the week of September 7th but gave few details on the military offensive. Two days earlier, Ruth's aunt Colette and uncle Julian received a handwritten letter from a soldier named Léon, who had befriended Marceau. He informed them that Marceau fought valiantly and was among nine men of the 32nd Infantry Regiment who were killed during the siege of the German town of Brenschelbach. Although Léon's letter was brief and nondescript concerning Marceau's death, he did say that his regiment was ordered to retreat from the heavily mined German territory, and that he deeply regretted not being able to return Marceau to France.

Ruth had grieved with Aunt Colette and Uncle Julian for shiva, the Jewish seven-day mourning period. Neighbors and members of their synagogue congregated in the apartment to console them, and Ruth's friend Lucette—a non-practicing Catholic—stayed with them throughout each day, until she had to go to work at Bal Tabarin. Ruth was grateful for the comfort of her family and Lucette, but the week of mourning did little to relieve her sorrow.

After shiva was over, Ruth reluctantly dressed for her first day back to work from taking a bereavement leave from Bal Tabarin. She left her room and paused in the hallway near Marceau's closed bedroom door. An image of a land mine explosion flashed in her head, tears welled up in her eyes, and she prayed that Marceau did not suffer.

A door lock clicked and Colette and Julian, who'd finished their shift at the hospital, entered the apartment and hung up their coats.

Ruth wiped her eyes and gathered her composure.

"*Bonjour*," Julian said.

Ruth forced a smile. "How was work?"

"*Bien*," he said.

Colette approached Ruth. She looked into her eyes and gently placed a hand to Ruth's cheek. "I cried today, too."

"I miss him," Ruth said.

Colette hugged her. "Me too."

Julian wrapped his arms around his wife and Ruth. He held them tight and gradually relaxed his embrace.

Ruth slipped away. "May I make you coffee before I leave for work?"

"*Oui*," Colette said. "I'd like that very much."

Colette and Julian sat at the kitchen table while Ruth lit the stove and prepared a pot of coffee.

"Have you eaten?" Ruth asked, retrieving cups.

"*Non*," Julian said.

"I'll prepare something to eat."

"I'm not hungry," Colette said.

"The coffee will sit better in your stomach if you have some food," Ruth said. Her aunt had consumed little nourishment in the past several days, and she'd lost weight. Her dress hung loosely over her thin frame, and her once silky gray hair had begun to turn dry and brittle.

Julian clasped his wife's hand. "A meal will be good for us."

Colette squeezed his fingers. "I'll try to eat."

Ruth sliced the remains of a two-day-old baguette and slathered it with a bit of apricot jam to hide the bread's staleness. She served cups of steaming coffee and placed the plate of baguette slices in the center of the table.

Julian took a sip. *"Merci.* Your coffee always tastes better than mine."

Ruth nodded, feeling grateful for her uncle's efforts to make her feel special and distract them from their grief. She sipped her coffee, hot and bitter, and looked at her aunt and uncle. The wrinkles on their faces appeared deeper, as if the passing of days since Marceau's death had accelerated the aging process.

"Your *maman* sent me another telegram," Colette said, picking at a piece of bread.

"I'm glad," Ruth said.

"She wishes that she and your dad could be here."

Ruth slumped her shoulders. With the outbreak of war, it had become nearly impossible to acquire a passenger ticket for leisure transatlantic travel from the US to France. She could tell, from the string of her mother's telegrams, that she was heartbroken over not being able to be by her sister's side for shiva.

Colette lowered her eyes. "Also, your parents think it might be best if you search for a way to find passage to the United States, perhaps with a British or Canadian supply vessel."

"We've already discussed this." Ruth clasped her cup. "I'm not leaving."

"You'll be safe if you go home," Julian said.

"America may be my home, but my homeland is France." Ruth's shoulder muscles tensed. "Am I no longer welcome to stay here with you?"

"Of course not," Colette said. "I adore having you live with us. But I—" She drew a breath and her bottom lip quivered. "I've lost my only child, and your *maman* and I can't bear the thought of anything happening to you."

Julian blinked his eyes, as if fighting back tears.

"I will be safe in Paris." Ruth reached across the table and clasped hands with her aunt and uncle. "I cannot turn my back on the country and people I love. Running away is no way to honor Marceau."

They squeezed her fingers.

"When you were my age, you were fighting to save lives near the battlefront. If anything, I need to do more for the war effort—not less."

"She's right," Julian said to his wife. "We worked at a field hospital a few kilometers from the front line."

Colette looked to the ceiling, as if her mind was reliving memories of her service in the Great War.

Ruth released their hands. "When I get home from work, I'll write a long letter to my parents."

Colette nodded.

They spoke no further of Marceau or the war. After they finished their coffee and bread, Ruth washed the dishes, kissed them on the cheeks, and left for work. Outside the apartment building, she glanced at her wristwatch. With a bit of extra time, she decided to take a longer route to work to clear her head.

As she walked through Le Marais, she hummed her repertoire of songs that she hadn't rehearsed since the night she received notice of Marceau's death. She easily recalled the lyrics, but the pieces evoked no emotion. Her humming dwindled away and she wondered how long it would take to repair a broken heart. *A year. Two years. A lifetime?* She shook away her thoughts and traveled along a cobblestone street.

"Try it again!" a man's voice shouted.

Ruth turned. Across the street was a French Army truck that was parked in front of a warehouse of a canning factory. One soldier sat behind the wheel, while a second soldier peered under the open hood of the truck.

The engine cranked over but didn't start.

"Are you pressing the accelerator?" the soldier asked, raising his head from the engine compartment.

"*Oui!*" the driver shouted.

The starter grinded for several seconds and stopped.

Ruth crossed the street. She passed the bed of the truck, which contained crates of canned peas, and approached the soldiers. "Do you need help?"

The driver leaned his head out the open window. "We need a mechanic. Do you know of someone nearby?"

"You're looking at one," Ruth said.

The driver wrinkled his forehead.

"I grew up on a farm," she said. "We had an old truck and tractor, and I helped my papa complete all the repairs. Mind if I have a look?"

The soldier at the hood shook his head. "I can fix it myself, *mademoiselle*." He fiddled with the wire connections on the battery.

"Have you checked the fuel line?" Ruth asked.

"Not yet," the soldier said. He scanned the engine compartment and scratched his head.

"Want me to show you where it's located?" she asked.

"*Non*," he said. "I can find it."

"You've been tinkering under that hood for twenty minutes," the driver said to his comrade. "Let her have a look. If we ring the base, it'll take at least an hour before an army mechanic can get here."

The soldier shifted his weight and gestured with a hand to the open hood.

Ruth walked to the front of the truck, put down her purse, and peered at the engine compartment. From across the street, the truck appeared new, given its fresh coat of matte olive-green paint. Up close, she discovered it was an old, repurposed truck, given the layers of grime on the engine. An acrid smell of burnt oil penetrated her nose.

"Where are you headed with the peas?" she asked.

"Our base in Nancy," the soldier said.

"My parents were stationed near there during the Great War." She checked the fuel line, which was intact.

The soldier relaxed his shoulders. "Where's your farm?"

"Maine, United States."

"You speak like a Parisian," he said.

"My *maman* is from Paris." She glanced at him. "Was the truck having problems before it stopped working?"

"It usually takes several tries to start and, on the trip here, it began to lose power."

Ruth examined the connections to the spark plugs. "One of the cables is loose," she said, pointing.

"Is that it?"

She removed the connections. "No. The spark plugs are in bad shape and need to be replaced. I'm surprised you got here, considering the amount of gunk on them."

"Damn it."

The driver got out of the vehicle and joined them.

The soldier looked at his comrade. "We need to ring the base."

The driver frowned. "All right."

"I didn't say I couldn't get you back on the road," Ruth said. "Give me five minutes, then make your call."

She reached into her purse and removed a handkerchief and a small nail file. She wiped each of the spark plug heads with her handkerchief to remove as much grime as she could. Then, using her nail file, she gently scraped away soot from the heads of the spark plugs.

"Are you sure this will work?" the soldier asked.

"No, but it can't hurt." Ruth replaced each of the spark plug caps, making sure that they were securely connected. She tossed her nail file into her purse and wiped her hands, which were covered with oily residue. "Try starting it."

The driver got into the truck and turned the ignition.

The engine coughed and roared to life.

"You're a genius," the soldier said.

"*Non*," she said, closing the hood of the truck. "I'm a farm gal who knows a thing or two about keeping an old truck on the road."

The driver exited the vehicle and shook Ruth's hand. "*Merci beaucoup.*"

"*Je vous en prie*," she said.

"You should be a mechanic," the soldier said.

She shook her head. "I would rather drive a truck than fix it."

"Then you should consider joining the army," the soldier said. "They're recruiting civilian volunteers to serve as ambulance drivers."

She tilted her head. "Women drivers?"

"*Oui*," the driver said. "Near our base, there's a corps of women ambulance drivers stationed at a field hospital."

She stashed her dirty handkerchief into her purse. "If I didn't have a job to go to, I'd be first in line at the recruiting office."

The driver grinned. "May I ask your name and what you do for a living, *mademoiselle?*"

"Ruth. I'm a singer at Bal Tabarin."

"I'm Édouard." The driver gestured to his comrade. "And this is Yann. We receive a military leave in a couple of weeks and will pay a visit to Bal Tabarin. It would be a pleasure to hear you sing."

"I'll look for you." She glanced at her watch. "I better go or I'll be late for work."

"We'd give you a lift," Yann said, "but it's against regulations to allow civilians as passengers."

She nodded. *"Au revoir."*

The men climbed into the truck and pulled away. She watched the vehicle disappear around the corner and began her trek to Bal Tabarin. For the first time in over a week, her mind was distracted from the loss of Marceau, and she felt like she'd done something, albeit small, that supported France's fight for Europe's freedom.

CHAPTER 5

PARIS, FRANCE—SEPTEMBER 21, 1939

Ruth entered the backstage dressing room and was greeted with warm welcomes and hugs from the dancers who were putting on costumes for the show. A bouquet of white tulips, bundled together with pink ribbon and paper, had been placed on her makeup table.

Ruth picked up the flowers and held them to her nose, taking in a citrus, honey-like scent. She turned to Lucette. "Thank you for the tulips. They're lovely."

"You're welcome. It's from the dancers and musicians." Lucette adjusted her multilayered can-can skirt. "I'm glad you're back."

"Me too," Ruth said, despite a strange apprehension stirring within her. She changed into a black evening gown and put on makeup. Her hand trembled as she attempted to apply lipstick.

"Are you feeling up to this?" Lucette asked.

"*Oui.*" Ruth steadied her hand. "A small case of collywobbles. I'll be fine once I'm onstage."

Lucette adjusted her seamed stockings and put on a red-feathered hat. "What's that saying in America before a performer goes onstage?"

"Break a leg."

"I like it for a singer, but Parisian dancers will always say *merde*."

It made sense, to Ruth, that it would not be a good idea to say something to a dancer about fracturing a limb. But she wondered, although briefly, why French dancers—before going onstage—preferred an expression that translated to "shit," and it struck her that Lucette might have brought it up to lighten her spirits.

Ruth read over a list of three songs that she was scheduled to perform, all of which she had sung dozens of times. Soon, the doors to the hall opened and guests began to fill the seats. Waitresses served cocktails and fluted glasses of champagne, while the orchestra warmed the crowd with cabaret music. The dance hall lights dimmed, and the dancers began to exit the dressing room.

Ruth nudged Lucette. *"Merde."*

Lucette smiled. "Break a leg."

Ruth sat on a stool and listened to the opening can-can dance performance. The vibrant music and cheering of the crowd did little to brighten her mood. Usually, the beginning of the show sparked her enthusiasm to perform, even if it came with a few butterflies fluttering in her stomach. But everything had changed. Marceau, who was like a brother to her, was dead. French soldiers had perished in a short-lived invasion of Germany, and the Polish people were fighting to survive their invasion by Hitler's military. Despite rumors of a peace agreement, her gut told her that the conflict would get worse before it was over. Her mind drifted to her conversation with Aunt Colette and Uncle Julian. *I need to do more for the war effort—not less.* Muscles tightened in her shoulders.

A knock came from the door and the stage manager peeked his head inside the dressing room. "Ruth—you're on in two minutes."

Ruth nodded. She put on a faux pearl necklace and a pair of white gloves, and made her way to the curtained entrance to the stage. As the dancers gave their bows, her heart thumped against her rib cage. She took in deep breaths, attempting to calm her nerves.

The dancers, shaking their can-can skirts layered with colorful ruffles, exited the stage.

"You'll be great," Lucette whispered as she passed by Ruth.

"Oui," she breathed, despite that—perhaps for the first time in her life—she had no desire to sing.

The emcee stepped onto the stage and removed his top hat. *"Mesdames et messieurs!* Please welcome Bal Tabarin's international, Franco-American songstress—Ruth Lacroix!"

The crowd cheered.

Ruth put on a fake smile and walked onto the stage. The orchestra conductor gestured with his baton and a pianist and violinist began to play the introduction to a beautiful ballad, "Parlez-moi d'amour" ("Tell Me about Love").

The audience grew silent.

Ruth clasped the standing microphone and her eyes were drawn to a bit of engine grime on her fingernails. She discreetly placed her hands behind her back and gazed over the well-dressed patrons holding glasses of champagne and smoldering cigarettes. *How can we celebrate when men have given their lives for France? Why are so many Parisians oblivious to the war?* A childhood memory of Marceau, picking apples at her family's orchard, flashed in her head. Her mouth turned dry. She struggled to concentrate and missed her entrance to the song.

The conductor glanced at Ruth and guided the orchestra to repeat the introduction.

A cold chill ran through her body. She made her introduction on time and sang the piece, all the while struggling to hide her heartbreak. Her voice quavered during the high notes of the chorus, and she forgot the words of the last verse. She ended her performance with patrons whispering to their neighbors and a lackluster round of applause.

Between the dancing act intermissions, Ruth willed herself to sing her songs. Her last performance was not much better than her first piece, and she exited the stage with mild clapping, as well as some hisses and jeers, from the crowd. After the show, she washed off her makeup and changed into her casual clothes.

Lucette buttoned her blouse and approached Ruth. "It'll get better."

"Someday it will," Ruth said, "but for now, my heart is telling me I need to make a change."

"What do you mean?"

"I don't want to do this—not when there's a war and people are dying." She swallowed. "On the way here, I met two soldiers who told me that the army is seeking women volunteers."

"Nurses?"

"*Non*. Ambulance drivers."

Lucette's eyes widened.

The door to the dressing room swung open and banged against the wall. The casting director named Fermin—a hulking man with slicked-back hair, a manicured mustache, and fingers the size of sausages—entered the room.

The air turned silent. Partially dressed dancers stepped aside and covered themselves with their arms and pieces of clothing.

Fermin glared at Ruth. "What the hell happened out there?"

"I performed poorly," Ruth said.

"You've had over a week off from work to get things in order." He folded his arms. "If you sing like that again, I will terminate you from the show."

"There's no need." Ruth swallowed. "I quit."

Lucette's jaw dropped open. Eyes of the dancers fell upon Ruth.

The lines on Fermin's face hardened. "I know every casting director in Paris. If they know you worked here, they'll come to me for a referral. Who do you think is going to hire you?"

Ruth gathered her confidence. "The army."

He laughed.

"They're recruiting volunteer ambulance drivers," she said. "I have experience driving a truck, and I think I can be of value to the ambulance corps."

"You're a fool," he said. "Even if the army accepts you, the war will be settled by winter and you'll be back here begging for a job."

"I'm grateful for the chance to perform at Bal Tabarin," Ruth said, plucking her purse from a table. "But it's time for me to put the needs of France ahead of my own endeavors."

"Me too," Lucette said.

Ruth froze.

Fermin furrowed his brow. "You're not going anywhere, Lucette."

Ruth turned to her friend. "Please don't lose your job over me."

Lucette tucked her blouse into her skirt and raised her chin to Fermin. "I'm joining the fight."

He pointed at the door. "Out!"

Ruth and Lucette grabbed their things and left Bal Tabarin. They walked alone through the dark streets of Paris, its once glittering lights eradicated by the threat of Luftwaffe air raids.

"You're the best dancer in the show," Ruth said. "Why did you quit?"

"I feel the same way you do," she said. "Every night, I lie awake thinking about Paul and the sacrifice he made by joining a tank battalion. It's about time I do more for France than entertain wealthy patrons with my legs."

"Paul would be proud of you."

Lucette smiled. "Do you really think so?"

"I know so."

They walked, their shoes clacking over the sidewalk, and discussed plans to inform their families and visit the army recruiting office. Reaching the Pont d'Arcole bridge, they stopped and peered to the Seine.

"Do you remember telling me that you would teach me to sing?" Lucette asked.

"I do, and I intend to keep that promise."

Lucette clasped her arms. "May I ask another favor of you before we go to the recruiting office?"

"Of course."

"Can you teach me to drive?"

CHAPTER 6

ROUVRES-EN-WOËVRE, FRANCE—
OCTOBER 14, 1939

Jimmie, eager to begin his mock dogfight, adjusted the control stick of his aircraft to maintain his position in the No. 73 Squadron's Vic formation. He looked through the side of his cockpit window at Benny, a twenty-one-year-old Yorkshireman whose boyish, freckled face was hidden by his oxygen mask.

Benny raised a gloved hand.

Jimmie returned the gesture and peered to the horizon. In the distance was the Étain-Rouvres Air Base, distinguishable by the long earthen runways carved into a lush, green field. It was located adjacent to the village of Rouvres-en-Woëvre, near Verdun and the borders with Belgium, Luxembourg, and Germany. He imagined Luftwaffe squadrons, patrolling German air space, less than sixty miles away. *We'll be in the thick of it if a real battle erupts.* He buried his thoughts and patted his flight jacket pocket, which contained Piglet.

For the past month, Jimmie and the pilots of No. 73 Squadron performed patrols to cover ships that disembarked BEF troops at Cherbourg. During that time, the squadron had no encounters with enemy aircraft and, due to horrid weather conditions, the pilots were grounded for nearly two weeks. Jimmie had hoped for more flight time in his new Hurricane, but the downtime had given him a chance to get to know his fellow pilots and ground crew.

During the torrential downpours, most of the pilots hunkered in their bunks to read books or write letters to their families, while others went to the mess hall to play cards. But three days into the squadron's grounding, Cobber—who'd grown increasingly restless—approached Jimmie and asked, "Want to be on my team for a game of sevens?" Jimmie, not wanting to disappoint his section leader, accepted the offer. He'd assumed that Cobber was referring to a card game. It turned out to be seven-a-side rugby.

Cobber, despite the inclement weather, had recruited enough pilots and ground crewmen to form two teams. For nearly three hours, the men played like schoolboys on a showery holiday break. Jimmie didn't mind getting muddied and bruised. Nor did it bother him that Gord—who'd stood under an umbrella as a spectator on the sideline—jeered Jimmie about his Piglet getting wet. He'd failed to score points for his team, but he'd taken blow after blow to his body, and he'd insisted on remaining in the match, even after receiving a swollen eye and bloody nose. *I have much to prove in the sky*, Jimmie had thought, his boots squelching through the muck. *But for now, I can show my mettle on the ground.* His grit on the rugby field had earned his squadron's respect, Jimmie believed, given that Cobber and Fanny—as well as Horace, who'd chipped a tooth in the match—bought him pints of ale to celebrate their victory. For the first time since his arrival in France, he felt like a member of the 73.

At the end of September, his squadron moved to an airfield near Saint-Omer. But soon after arriving at the new base, the No. 73 Squadron was given orders to deploy to Rouvres, where they would be attached to the Advanced Air Striking Force (AASF), which consisted of several squadrons of Fairey Battles, single-engine light bombers. The Fairey Battle was considered by most pilots to be inferior to a German Messerschmitt Bf 109. Although it had the same high-performance Rolls-Royce Merlin engine that powered Jimmie's Hawker Hurricane, the Fairey Battle was nearly one hundred miles per hour slower than the Messerschmitt due to the weight of its three-men crew and bomb load. *They're assigning us to be bodyguards for the Battles,* Jimmie had thought after hearing the news of his squadron's deployment. *Without the protection of Hurricanes, the Battles could be decimated by Luftwaffe fighters.*

The radio speaker crackled inside Jimmie's helmet.

"Green Two, Green Three," Cobber's voice said, "we'll circle the perimeter. After the other sections land, we'll begin our drill."

"Wilco," Jimmie said. He checked his control panel and tightened his grip on the stick.

The Hurricane squadron was comprised of four sections—Red, Yellow, Blue, and Green. Cobber—call sign Green One—was the leader of Green Section and responsible for two wingmen—Benny, Green Two; and Jimmie, Green Three. Prior to their departure, Cobber was granted permission by the squadron leader to conduct a dogfight exercise to allow Jimmie an opportunity to practice his aerial combat skills. Despite being singled out amongst his peers, who would no doubt be observing the exercise from the ground, Jimmie was glad to have more flight drills.

Green Section circled the airfield at seven thousand feet while the rest of the No. 73 Squadron took turns landing at Étain-Rouvres Air Base. Most of the ground crew, including Horace, had left a day before the pilots to establish the squadron's base, and they were watching the planes land on the runway. In addition to French aircraft and a few hangars, the mostly grass-covered airfield was lined with parked Fairey Battles and a pole with a British flag.

The last Hurricane landed, leaving the three pilots of Green Section alone in the air.

"Tally-ho!" Cobber's voice boomed through the radio in Jimmie's helmet.

Jimmie's heart rate quickened. "Wilco—tally-ho!"

Cobber's Hurricane slewed to the right and accelerated.

Jimmie pushed the throttle. The plane's engine roared. He banked hard right and pulled back on the stick, fighting to get Cobber's plane within his ring sight. A massive G-force pressed his body into his seat, yet he pulled back harder on the stick. As he began to black out from the blood rushing from his head, he eased off on the throttle.

Cobber's aircraft continued the sharp turn. He leveled off and rolled his aircraft into a nosedive.

Damn it! Jimmie sucked in air, clearing the fog from his brain.

Benny's aircraft shot by Jimmie.

Jimmie straightened his Hurricane. He accelerated and followed Benny in pursuit of their section leader.

Cobber flew an Immelmann combat maneuver—making a 180-degree change in direction by performing a half loop and, when completely inverted, rolling to the upright position. His aircraft banked hard to the left and pitched upward.

Benny struggled to follow Cobber's maneuver, and his plane lost speed.

Cobber's Hurricane gained distance from his pursuers and disappeared into a cloud.

Jimmie caught up with Benny and, in tandem, they turned over the top of the cloud bank. Seconds passed as they waited for Cobber's plane to appear.

Jimmie turned his head from side to side, scanning the area. The cloud began to dissipate, revealing glimpses of the rolling French landscape, fifteen thousand feet below his Hurricane. He strained his neck to look behind him and discovered the nose of Cobber's aircraft rising from the mist. His adrenaline surged.

"Six o'clock low!" Jimmie shouted into his microphone. He dived to the left, and Benny dived to the right.

Cobber chased after Jimmie. He rolled and banked his plane to close the distance between them, as if he could anticipate each of Jimmie's maneuvers. In less than a minute, he narrowed in on his target, while Benny struggled to get his Hurricane within range.

"I'm on your tail, Green Three," Cobber said. "Make your move."

Jimmie shot his plane into a high-g barrel roll—a combination of a loop and a snap roll. It was a last-ditch defensive maneuver to shake Cobber from his tail, or at least disrupt his aim. But as he came out of the snap roll, Cobber's voice boomed inside Jimmie's helmet.

"You bought it, Green Three!"

Damn it. He strained his neck to find Cobber close behind him, as if the nose of his plane was magnetic and Jimmie's Hurricane was made of iron.

"Land your aircraft," Cobber said. "We'll go over what you did wrong when I'm on the ground."

"Wilco," Jimmie said, feeling defeated.

"All right, Green Two," Cobber said. "Let me see what you got."

"Roger that," Benny said.

Jimmie landed his plane and taxied to a grass clearing with a line of parked Hurricanes and a group of pilots, all of whom were observing the mock fight in the sky. He unbuckled his harness, removed his helmet, and climbed out of his Hurricane.

"How did it go up there?" Horace asked, approaching him.

"It could have gone better. I only lasted a few minutes longer than my last dogfight with Cobber."

"If I'm not mistaken," Horace said, "none of the pilots have gotten the best of Cobber."

He nodded, hiding his disappointment. "How is the new base?"

"Splendid," Horace said. "It's much nicer than the other airfields; we have an indoor loo."

Jimmie chuckled. "You'll need to write to Daisy and tell her about your luxury accommodations."

"Already did." Horace pointed at Jimmie's Hurricane. "The aircraft appeared to drag a bit on your altitude climbs. I'll work on tuning the exhaust system to see if we can increase the engine power."

"Thanks," Jimmie said. "It's comforting to know that the best fitter in France is working on this kite." He glanced at the pilots. "Time for me to go and receive my medicine."

"Good luck," Horace said.

Jimmie joined his fellow pilots, congregated on the grass, watching the aerial combat between Cobber and Benny.

"That was a ropey maneuver," Gord said.

Tension spread through Jimmie's chest. "I was running out of options, and I thought it might work to shake him from me."

"It didn't," Gord said. "Your choice to pull a high-g barrel roll was a cock-up."

Anger flared inside Jimmie but he held his composure. Through the corner of his eye, he saw the squadron leader—ten meters away—and wondered if he would tell him the same.

Fanny approached Jimmie and patted his shoulder. "Don't beat yourself up too badly. You were up against one of the best."

"And the most dangerous." Gord slipped a pipe from his pocket. "Cobber takes far too much risk. He sets a bad example for inexperienced recruits, like Jimmie."

"Cobber's willingness to take a chance is what makes him a superb pilot," Fanny said.

Gord packed tobacco into his pipe and lit it.

"The more daring we are, the more likely we are to outmaneuver the enemy," Jimmie said.

"Precisely," Fanny said.

Gord inhaled on his pipe and blew smoke through his nose. "There's a fine line between daring and reckless, and Cobber often crosses it."

"Go, Benny!" a pilot shouted.

The men turned their attention to the dogfight in the sky.

"I'm rather surprised that Benny has lasted this long," Gord said.

"Cobber's toying with him," Fanny said, "like a cat, playing with a mouse between its paws."

For several minutes they watched Benny continue to come within range of Cobber, and Cobber easily maneuvered away. After a series of loops and dives, Cobber slipped behind Benny's aircraft and never lost the position. Defeated, Benny descended to the airfield and landed his plane.

Cobber lowered his Hurricane toward the runway but leveled off and accelerated. Thirty feet above the ground, he did a series of snap rolls.

Jimmie's eyes widened. The jaws of some of the pilots dropped open, while a few of the men cheered.

"Bloody hell!" Squadron Leader Hank More shouted. He left the group and walked toward the runway.

The cheering evaporated.

"See what I mean," Gord said, crossing his arms. "Stunts like that will get our pilots killed."

"It wasn't the best decision to perform snap rolls while low to the ground," Fanny said, "but aerobatics are what will keep us alive if we encounter Luftwaffe fighters."

Gord shook his head and walked away.

Jimmie turned to Fanny. "What do you think Hank is going to do?"

"He'll likely give Cobber a verbal reprimand, like all the other times he performed low-altitude stunts to entertain the pilots. I doubt that he will ground his best pilot while we're at war."

"I suppose Cobber is thinking the same thing," Jimmie said.

"Indeed."

Cobber landed his plane and parked it in the field next to Jimmie's Hurricane. As he exited his cockpit, he was met by the squadron leader.

"What the hell do you think you're doing?" Hank shouted. "You're in the RAF, not the bloody circus!"

Cobber unzipped his flight jacket. "I thought the men could use something to lift their spirit."

As the squadron leader continued barking reprimands at Cobber, the other pilots cleared the area to give them privacy.

Jimmie went with Fanny to their new barracks, where some of the pilots were picking out their cots. Jimmie selected a bunk, its mattress less lumpy than some of the other beds. He leaned back to relax, and his mind drifted to Gord's and Fanny's comments. He pondered their views on whether bold aerobatics would keep them alive, or get them killed. And he wondered, *What if they both were right?*

CHAPTER 7

ROUVRES-EN-WOËVRE, FRANCE—
NOVEMBER 8, 1939

Jimmie sat alone at a long, communal table in the mess hall. Most of the pilots had finished their breakfast and left to begin their duties, except for Cobber and Fanny who were eating bowls of oatmeal at a table in the far corner of the room. With a bit of privacy, Jimmie removed a letter from his jacket pocket. He glanced at the address with his sixteen-year-old sister's handwriting, gently opened the envelope, and removed the stationery.

> *Dear Jimmie,*
> *I hope this letter finds you well. I pray that you are safe and that the war will be over soon. When is your next leave? It will be lovely to have you home, but I should tell you now that I moved into your room. Crumpet has grown quite fond of sunbathing in the window, which provides better light than my old room. It would be a pity to deprive an old cat from warming itself. Crumpet and I hope you will agree.*

Jimmie smiled. An image of his sister cuddling with Crumpet—a fluffy gray cat with orange eyes—flashed in his head. *The room is yours to keep.*

Mum has been working to transform her flower garden into a vegetable patch. It's nothing fancy, mostly beetroot, leeks, cabbage, peas, and broad beans. She says that she's digging for victory. With rationing, I understand the reason we need the extra veg, but I miss the vibrant colors and sweet scents of her roses and peonies. Our childhood garden has become a monochromatic green plot that reeks of compost and manure.

Mum and I don't see much of Dad. He's working nonstop at the shipyard due to new orders for navy vessels. In case you're wondering, Dad isn't disappointed that you joined the Royal Air Force. He merely wanted you to follow in his footsteps as a shipyard engineer because it was safer. It's sometimes hard for him to share his feelings, even in letters, so I thought I would pass them along for him. I'm proud of you for following your heart. You've always dreamed of flying, ever since that day you flew that homemade kite for me at the park. You attached it to a roll of Dad's fishing line. Do you remember?

His sister's sweet voice, encouraging him to fly a kite higher and higher, echoed in his brain. It had been the first day that Nora, who contracted polio many months earlier, was strong enough to stand with the support of crutches and leg calipers. He'd made the kite from newspaper and wooden dowels, and Nora had watched him fly it to celebrate her first steps of walking on her own.

I've grown a bit taller since you've left. I'm nearly the same height as Mum, and I surpass her by a hair when I wear my thick-heeled shoes. The doctor needed to adjust my leg braces, due to my sprouting limbs. He told me that I likely won't grow anymore because of my age. What do doctors know? Loads of them told me that I'd always be confined to a wheelchair.

School is going splendidly, except for maths. I wish all my courses consisted of literature and composition. I've been dropping hints to Mum and Dad about going off to study at King's College London to become a librarian. I know it's a few years away, but they worry about my mobility, and I don't want them to be gobsmacked when I leave the nest.

I'm proud of you, Jimmie thought. *You're the bravest person I know, and you're going to accomplish grand things in your life.*

Are you taking good care of Piglet? I suppose you might be teased by the other pilots for having him. Piglet isn't the manliest of good luck charms, but I have no doubt that he will keep you safe. Please remember to keep him with you when you fly. Selfishly, I take great solace in knowing that something so dear to me is with you while you're at war.

I miss you terribly. Please write when you can.

Love,

Nora

A wave of melancholy washed over him. He drew a deep breath and placed the letter back into the envelope.

Cobber and Fanny finished their breakfast. While Fanny left the mess hall, Cobber retrieved two metal cups of tea from a serving table. He approached Jimmie and said, "You look like you could use a cuppa."

"Thanks." Jimmie slipped the envelope into his jacket pocket.

Cobber sat across from Jimmie and slid him a cup. "Is the letter from Nora or your mum?"

"Nora."

Cobber took a gulp of tea. "How is she?"

"Plucky and full of guts," Jimmie said. "She's sixteen going on twenty-six, and she's not about to let her difficulty with walking get in the way of going off to university."

Cobber grinned. "I'd like to meet her."

"You will, after we win this Phony War that all the papers are writing about."

"I'll drink to that." Cobber clinked Jimmie's cup with his.

Jimmie sipped tea, rich with canned milk and sugar. "Nora said that my mum turned her flower garden into a vegetable plot. It feels unfair that we're getting the best provisions while the nation is rationing."

"It does," Cobber said. "I suppose the fine food is a consolation for placing our lives at risk, but if everyone back home knew how little action we've seen, they'd demand that the butter and choice chops be shipped back to Britain."

"You might be right." Jimmie said, "but try telling that to Ayerst."

"Good point."

Despite No. 73 Squadron's proximity to the German border, there had been few sightings of enemy aircraft and no successful interceptions. But two days earlier, Pilot Officer Peter Ayerst—an affable, nineteen-year-old Essex lad who spoke with a wide, toothy smile—accidentally flew off in the wrong direction while on patrol. Eventually, he found his way back to what he thought was the rest of No. 73 Squadron and flew in behind a grouping of nine planes, which turned out to be Messerschmitt 109s. Ayerst gave a burst of machine gun fire and dived away. Remarkably, he made it back to base with five bullet holes in his Hurricane's fuselage as a memento of his mishap.

Cobber took a drink of tea. "I would have loved to have seen the look on Ayerst's face when he recognized the black cross of the Luftwaffe on the planes."

"He's lucky to be alive," Jimmie said, feeling sorry for Ayerst.

Cobber nodded. "I wish it was me who'd flown off course and stumbled upon them while they were at a low altitude. The Messerschmitt pilots are cowards—they refuse to fight by flying where we can't reach them."

Jimmie had witnessed, on two occasions, Messerschmitt squadrons flying above his unit at twenty-seven thousand feet—two thousand feet above the Hurricane's maximum ceiling. The German pilots had refused to engage them, and Cobber's voice had boomed through the radio in Jimmie's helmet, "Come on down and fight!"

"They can't evade us forever," Cobber said. "The RAF is working to provide us with upgraded Hurricanes that can rival the service ceiling of the Messerschmitt."

"I hope the new planes arrive soon," Jimmie said. "I doubt that the Messerschmitt pilots will avoid us much longer."

"Why do you say that?"

"Poland has fallen to Germany, and Hitler is likely redeploying some of his military to the west. The way I see it, the Luftwaffe's appetite for air battle will likely grow with the buildup of German troops at their border with France."

"You're quite clever for an English bloke," Cobber said with his thick, New Zealand accent.

Jimmie chuckled.

"I also happen to agree with you," Cobber said. "It's best that we fight them now, before they outnumber us."

Jimmie's levity faded. He took a sip of tea and nodded.

"Me and the other section leaders were briefed by Hank this morning. He assigned our section to a defensive patrol this afternoon." A smile formed on Cobber's face. "It'll give us a chance to do a bit of sightseeing."

Jimmie shifted in his seat. "Are you sure that's a good idea? Hank was miffed with us for venturing into German territory."

"Don't worry about Hank," Cobber said. "I'm on his good side for curtailing my airfield aerobatics."

Since their first day at Étain-Rouvres Air Base, Cobber hadn't performed low-altitude stunts. Cobber did, however, disregard the squadron leader's commands to refrain from flying defensive patrols into German airspace.

"It was Gord who'd spotted us and told Hank about our roundabout route over the Saarland," Cobber said. "His section won't be with us on this afternoon's patrol, so there's no chance of Gord snitching on us. It will only be you, me, and Benny. I've spoken to Benny, and he's on board."

"And now you're seeking my support," Jimmie said.

"I am."

Jimmie knew that Cobber, if left alone to lead his section on patrol, would not be able to resist the thrill of flying over the Saarland, even though much of it was uninhabited and covered in dense forest. But he did appreciate that Cobber was candid about his intentions, and that he always worked to gain buy-in from his wingmen.

Two pilots entered the mess hall and sat at a nearby table.

Cobber leaned forward and lowered his voice. "You have nothing to worry about, mate. Even if we sight a Messerschmitt squadron, their Nazi rat pilots won't pick a dogfight with us."

Jimmie's mind raced, weighing the risk. "I'm not fond of breaking protocol, but I'll always have the backs of my wingmen." He looked at Cobber. "I'm in."

At noon, the Green Section pilots—Jimmie, Cobber, and Benny—climbed into the cockpits of their Hurricanes. The men went over their preflight checklist while armorers finished loading ammunition.

Horace, standing next to Jimmie's plane, wiped grease from his hands with a handkerchief and stuffed it into a pocket of his coverall. He peered up at Jimmie, who was checking his instrument gauges. "The electric starter was showing signs of wear, so I installed a new one."

"Thanks," Jimmie said. "You're keeping this kite in brilliant shape."

Horace smiled. "It's my duty."

Jimmie raised a gloved finger to the sky. "I'll do my best not to break anything while I'm up there."

"There's nothing on this plane that I can't fix."

"True." Jimmie fastened his safety harness and slipped on his helmet. "Farewell, Horace."

"Godspeed." Horace walked away and joined several members of the ground crew near a small hangar.

Jimmie closed the cockpit canopy and started the engine. The buzz of the propeller filled his ears. He patted his flight jacket, which contained Piglet. *He's safe and sound with me, Nora.*

Green Section was cleared to depart, and the pilots—one by one—accelerated their planes down the earthen runway and soared into the air. Once they were out of range of the airfield, Cobber guided his two wingmen through combat maneuvers on their journey to the border. With the passing of weeks under Cobber's instruction, Jimmie's aerial skills greatly improved. He'd gradually learned to mimic Cobber, who tossed his plane around in the air as if it were a toy. Although Cobber always bested him in a mock dogfight, Jimmie gave a valiant effort and held him off his tail for long periods of time.

At twelve thousand feet, Cobber banked his plane to the right and dived sharply toward the ground.

Benny and Jimmie followed his lead.

If I can get close to Cobber's skill level, Jimmie thought, pushing hard on the control stick, *I'll have a fighting chance against a Messerschmitt.*

For twenty minutes, the men performed combat maneuvers. Upon reaching France's Maginot Line, identifiable from the air by the vast string of concrete fortifications, they leveled off at fifteen thousand feet. In a Vic formation, they flew along the border for several miles.

Cobber, without communicating over the radio that was being monitored by their airbase, veered his plane to the northeast and led his section into German territory.

Jimmie's pulse quickened. He peered down at the thick pine forest of the Saarland. His anxiety grew as they zigzagged in and out of German airspace, all the while scanning the area. After an hour and a half of flying, they didn't encounter Luftwaffe aircraft, nor did they discover any evidence of German ground troops.

"All right, Green Section," Cobber's voice said over the radio, "let's head to base."

"Wilco," Jimmie said.

"Roger that, Green One," Benny said.

Jimmie and Benny followed their section leader, who banked his plane to the southwest and leveled off at fifteen thousand feet. Minutes later, they crossed into France and Jimmie's shoulder muscles relaxed. He peered through his cockpit glass as they approached the French town of Mertz, thirty miles from their airfield.

French antiaircraft guns flashed on the horizon.

Jimmie's eyes widened.

"Bloody hell," Benny said over the radio.

"Let's check it out." Cobber accelerated his plane.

Jimmie, his adrenaline surging, pushed the throttle and flew toward the area of gun bursts. Ahead and above him, a dual-engine

light bomber was racing eastward at approximately twenty thousand feet. As the Green Section narrowed in on the target, the
black cross on the plane's fuselage came into view. And Jimmie
recognized the aircraft, which looked like a flying pencil, to be a
Dornier Do 17 by its unmistakable twin tails and shoulder wing.
Reconnaissance mission. His heart thudded against his rib cage.

"Tally-ho!" Cobber shouted through his radio, his plane veering toward the German bomber.

Machine-gun fire erupted from the enemy aircraft.

Bullets whizzed by Jimmie's plane. His pulse pounded in his
ears.

The bomber climbed, attempting to flee the Hurricanes.

Cobber fired his machine guns.

Jimmie pushed the accelerator full throttle. He struggled to get
the bomber within his gunsight. Once he was clear of his fellow
pilots, he pressed the gun-firing button. Bullets exploded from his
Hurricane's eight machine guns but missed the target.

The bomber climbed higher. As it neared the maximum ceiling
of the Hurricanes, Cobber turned his plane upward and opened
fire.

Sparks came from the port engine of the German aircraft.

French antiaircraft guns exploded from the ground, and bullets
pierced Jimmie's fuselage. Fear flooded his veins.

"Bloody hell!" Benny shouted. "We're on your side!" He
banked his plane away from the friendly fire.

 . The German aircraft lost altitude and rolled into a steep dive.

Cobber chased after the bomber.

Jimmie, his plane functioning despite several holes, maneuvered into a dive. His engine roared as he gained speed. He
peered through his gunsight as he fought to close in on the target.

Cobber gave a long burst of machine gun fire. Smoke spewed
from the bomber and it pitched sharply toward the ground.

Jimmie's Hurricane shuddered violently from the strain of the
plummet. Bits of fabric began to peel from the plane's wings. He
pulled back on the control stick and leveled off, but Cobber continued his pursuit. A feeling of dread surged through him. "Pull
up, Cobber!"

Cobber, diving toward the earth, continued to fire his guns. Bullets riddled the Dornier Do 17's tail. It fell into a spiral and crashed into a small French village with no sign of its crew bailing out. Seconds later, Cobber leveled off, less than five hundred feet above the ground.

Jimmie lowered his oxygen mask and wiped sweat from his face.

"Are you boys all right?" Cobber called over the radio.

"Green Two—all good," Benny said.

Jimmie reattached his mask. "Green Three—my Hurricane's fuselage took a hit from ground fire. Except for wind whistling through holes, the aircraft is handling properly."

"Well done, lads," Cobber said. "Our work is done for today. Let's go home."

Jimmie placed a gloved hand over his pocket that contained Piglet. *You were right, Nora. He's quite a lucky fellow.* Feeling fortunate to be alive, he banked his plane and joined his wingmen on their flight back to base.

Green Section landed and parked their Hurricanes in a grass-covered field, where the entire squadron, both pilots and ground crew, were waiting to greet them. They climbed out of their planes to cheers, handshakes, and congratulatory pats on their backs. A few of the pilots hoisted Cobber onto their shoulders to celebrate him as the pilot with first aerial victory of the war for No. 73 Squadron.

Horace, his coverall stained with oil, approached Jimmie. "Splendid job, sir."

"I appreciate it, but Cobber deserves all the credit. He's the best pilot I've ever met." Jimmie stuck his hand through one of three punctures in the linen covering of his Hurricane's fuselage. "Sorry about the holes."

"Like I said—there's nothing I can't fix." Horace slipped his cap from his head. "I'm glad you made it back."

"Me too," Jimmie said. "How about you and some of the ground crew join me for a pint tonight? I'm buying."

"With pleasure."

Jimmie joined the pilots in the mess hall where Cobber was

encouraged by the men to describe the fight with the German bomber. The pilots had heard the news from either Hank, Fanny, or Gord, who'd listened to the dogfight over the radio in the command tent, but they wanted to hear Cobber's firsthand account of the victory. For several minutes, Cobber relayed what took place on the mission—leaving out the detour over the Saarland—and how he, Benny, and Jimmie intercepted the German bomber that was on a reconnaissance mission over France. The pilots listened intently to Cobber's story, except for Gord, who sat alone at a far table puffing his pipe.

Jimmie was relieved to learn from Hank that no French citizens were injured in the small village of Lubey, where the enemy aircraft crashed. While he was glad to have won in battle, mixed emotions swirled inside him. He was proud to defend Europe from Hitler's forces that had ravaged eastern Europe, but he also felt pity for the German crew who were killed. *They might be forced to fight for the Luftwaffe. Their loved ones will surely be heartbroken— like our families would be if we were killed.* Despite his resolve to fight for freedom, he hoped that he would never forget that aerial victories would entail the loss of human life.

CHAPTER 8

PARIS, FRANCE—NOVEMBER 10, 1939

Ruth's anticipation grew as she and Lucette approached a palatial stone building that held the French Army's recruiting office. According to newspaper and radio reports, the army was seeking hundreds of women to serve as civilian volunteers in auxiliary ambulance sections, which would be attached to the army in the field. Adjacent to the complex was a parking lot that contained a fleet of parked military vehicles, including a dozen olive-colored ambulance trucks with a large, red cross emblem on their sides.

Lucette stopped near that entrance and turned to Ruth. "*Merci.*"

She wrinkled her forehead. "For what?"

"For teaching me how to drive, and for not giving up on me when I failed my first driver's examination."

"We are in this together," Ruth said. "Remember?"

Lucette nodded.

It had been over a month since Ruth and Lucette had quit their jobs at Bal Tabarin. During this time, Ruth obtained her French driver's license and taught her friend how to operate an old bakery truck that was owned by a close friend of Uncle Julian. Ruth had expected that Lucette—a long-legged, physically coordinated dancer—would easily learn to drive a vehicle, but she struggled with using the clutch and often stalled the engine when shifting gears. Also, Lucette had difficulty using the side mirrors to judge the distance from objects to the rear and passenger side of the truck. It had taken weeks of practice for Lucette to become comfortable with driving the large vehicle in the narrow streets of Le Marais.

During Lucette's initial driver's examination, she backed into a yellow-painted garbage can that was used as a marker for parallel parking. She failed the test and was not permitted to retake the exam for a minimum of two weeks. Lucette felt defeated, but Ruth encouraged her that, with a bit more practice, she could pass the test. Lucette continued to work on her driving skills with Ruth providing instruction from the passenger seat. After more time behind the wheel, Lucette's confidence grew and she eventually passed her driver's examination.

Lucette clasped her arms. "I've only had my license for a few days. Do you think they might reject me?"

"*Non*," Ruth said. "You have nothing to worry about. The army is in dire need of women volunteers for their ambulance units. You have a valid driver's license, you're eager to serve France—" She glanced at the street. "And I don't see any rubbish bins that you could back into if they decide to test you."

Lucette chuckled. "That's good to know."

Ruth placed a hand on her friend's arm. "Ready?"

"*Oui.*"

They entered the building and traveled to a large meeting hall on the third floor where a few dozen women were seated on long wooden benches as they waited their turn to be called to the front of the room to be interviewed by a man and woman who were wearing military uniforms. They signed in with a bespectacled female receptionist by placing their names on a piece of paper, and they were given a pencil and two-page application that was affixed to a clipboard. As Ruth and Lucette scribbled answers on their questionnaires, the names of women were intermittently called. After a brief interview by the two-person panel, each candidate either went to a staging area at the far end of the room, or left the building.

"They're not taking everyone," Lucette said as a young, teary-eyed woman walked toward the stairs.

"They'll take us," Ruth said.

After forty minutes of waiting, the receptionist ran her finger down her list and said, "Lucette Soulier!"

Lucette straightened her spine.

"*Merde*," Ruth whispered.

Lucette smiled, appearing grateful to hear the customary expletive to wish a dancer good luck. She rose from her seat and went to the interview table.

Ruth fidgeted with her pencil. As she waited for Lucette to finish her interview, her mind drifted to her family. After resigning from her nightclub job, she spent most evenings and weekends with Aunt Colette and Uncle Julian. They went for long walks along the river Seine, and she cooked dinner for them, usually onion or vegetable soup with baguettes. During their meals they took turns telling fond stories of Marceau. Their togetherness had helped deaden their grief, although Ruth believed there would always remain a small void in each of their hearts. Also, the time away from work had given her a chance to communicate with her parents, through telegrams and letters, to explain why she'd placed her dream of singing on hold to support the fight for France.

Ruth removed a recent telegram from her purse and read it for the second time.

```
Dear Ruth,
We respect your decision to join the
war, like we once did when we were young.
We pray that you will remain safe in the
pursuit of Europe's freedom. We are proud
of you.
Love,
Maman and Dad
```

Ruth, feeling encouraged, squeezed the paper—extremely thin and almost transparent—between her fingers. She'd expected her parents, especially her father who incessantly worried about her, to continue their pleas for her to come home. She was surprised by their latest communication and believed that they'd finally come to terms with her not leaving France. Although she would join the fight, with or without the approval of her parents, she was grateful for their blessing. She slipped the telegram back into her purse and reviewed her answers on the application.

Wooden chair legs scraped over the floor. Women's eyes turned to Lucette as she left the interview table and approached Ruth.

"Did it go all right?" Ruth asked.

Lucette smiled. "*Oui*. I'll see you in the staging area; they're going to give us a driving test when the interviews are finished. Break a leg."

She nodded.

"Ruth Lacroix!" the receptionist called.

Ruth straightened her back. She stood and walked to the front of the room, where a thin, middle-aged man wearing a khaki-colored uniform was seated behind a table with an engraved nameplate that read: *Chief Corporal Faucher*. Seated to his side was a woman in her mid-thirties with a round face, pale complexion, and bags under her brown eyes. She wore a beret and olive-colored military style uniform with a white armband emblazoned with a red cross.

"I'm Chief Corporal Faucher," the man said. "Madame Bain, a civilian member of the ambulance corps, will be sitting in on the interview."

She extended her hand. "It's a pleasure to meet you. I'm Ruth Lacroix."

"Give me your application and driver's license, then sit," the man said, making no effort to shake hands.

Ruth, feeling foolish, gave him the documents and sat in a chair across the table from them.

"What makes you think that you're suited to be an ambulance driver?" the man asked.

"I grew up on a farm," Ruth said. "I learned to drive tractors and trucks before I turned sixteen. Also, I'm mechanically adept. My father and I performed the repairs on our vehicles. I have experience—"

"Where are you from?" the corporal interrupted.

"Maine, United States."

He frowned and scanned her application. "Are you a French citizen?"

"*Non*, but I'm a legal French resident." She reached for her purse. "I brought my passport and a foreigner's identity card."

"That will not be necessary." The corporal folded his arms. "We're only accepting French civilians."

Ruth's eyes widened.

Madame Bain wrinkled her forehead.

"Please," Ruth said. "There must be some exceptions. I have a French driver's license. I've been living and working in France for two years."

"It makes no difference," he said. "You're an American, and your country has declared its neutrality in the war."

Ruth felt sick to her stomach.

Madame Bain tentatively turned to the man. "*Excusez-moi*, Chief Corporal. I think we might have a woman in the corps who is from a neutral country—Switzerland, I believe. Would you like me to check the records?"

The corporal glared at her. "*Non.* You're mistaken."

The woman lowered her chin.

The corporal pushed Ruth's documents across the table. "*Au revoir, mademoiselle.*"

No! This can't be happening! She reluctantly rose from her chair but her feet remained planted. "The decision whether to accept me is yours, Chief Corporal, but I need to speak my piece."

The corporal, appearing startled, shifted in his seat.

"In the Great War, my father fought as an American soldier alongside Frenchmen on the western front, and my *maman*—a Parisian—served as a nurse in a field hospital." Ruth looked into the corporal's eyes. "Two months ago, my cousin was killed in Germany's Saarland while fighting for the French Army."

Madame Bain's jaw slacked open. "I'm deeply sorry."

"*Merci.*"

"You have my condolences," the corporal said. "But this doesn't change the fact that you're not a French citizen. That will be all, *mademoiselle.*"

Ruth clenched her hands, her fingernails digging into her palms. "Please, let me finish."

"Leave or I'll have you removed," the corporal said, raising his voice.

Women candidates put down clipboards and stared at Ruth. Lucette, standing in the staging area, cupped a hand to her mouth.

Ruth fought back her fear and held her ground. "My French roots run deep, regardless of the country on my passport. Nazi Germany is ravaging Europe, and I'm not about to abandon the people and country I love. You can reject me from serving in the corps, but I promise you this, Chief Corporal—I *will* join the fight, even if I need to drive my own truck to the Maginot Line."

The corporal's face turned red. "Out! Now!"

A wave of defeat washed over her. She collected her things and turned to the sound of boots clacking over the floor.

A tall man, wearing a French military officer's tunic, approached the table. "Is there a problem?"

The corporal got to his feet and saluted. "*Non*, Captain Joubert. I have everything under control, sir."

Ruth turned to the officer. "Captain, Chief Corporal Faucher has declined my request to join the ambulance corps on the basis that I'm an American, despite that I legally reside in France and meet the driving requirements."

The captain looked at the corporal. "Is this true?"

"*Oui, monsieur.*"

"Regulations do not exclude foreigners," the captain said.

The corporal shifted his weight. "I'm aware, sir. I thought that neutral Americans should be excluded from serving since this is a European conflict."

The officer rubbed his chin.

Ruth fought away the urge to speak and held her tongue.

"Does she meet our criteria?" the officer asked.

"She does," Madame Bain blurted. "She claims to have mechanical skills, which would be beneficial to the corps. Most of our women do not have experience with vehicle repairs."

The corporal clenched his jaw.

"See that she's moved on to be tested," the captain said.

"*Oui, monsieur*," the corporal said.

The captain stepped closer to the corporal. "To be clear, we have more ambulances than drivers. I expect that all qualified women—unless they're from an enemy nation—be accepted into corps."

"*Oui, monsieur.*"

The captain walked away.

"Give me your application," the corporal said, his voice bitter.

Ruth gave it to him, which he signed and handed back to her. She turned to Madame Bain. "*Merci.*"

The woman nodded.

Ruth left feeling sorry for Madame Bain, who would likely be the target of the corporal's resentment. The eyes of candidates fell upon her as she walked toward the staging area. Some of the candidates smiled or nodded their heads in approval. Ruth, her shoulder muscles tense, took in deep breaths to calm her nerves.

Lucette approached her. "I can't believe you stood up to them."

"Nor I," she said, feeling like she'd come within inches of being struck by a speeding train.

"I overheard pieces of your conversation. What happened?"

"I'll tell you everything after we pass their driving test," Ruth said. "The army needs women to drive their ambulances, and nothing is going to stop us from joining the corps."

CHAPTER 9

SAINT-QUENTIN, FRANCE—
JANUARY 7, 1940

Ruth gripped the steering wheel as she drove the ambulance over a rutted dirt road near the French border with Belgium. Despite wearing long underwear beneath her military-issued uniform and wool coat, her teeth chattered from the damp, frigid weather. Northern France was experiencing record cold temperatures, and the vehicle was not equipped with a heater. She and Lucette, who was following her in another ambulance, had been dispatched from a hospital in Saint-Quentin. Their orders were to transport ill soldiers from a section of the Maginot Line, near Maubeuge, to Saint-Quentin to receive medical care.

Ruth and Lucette had passed their military driving tests. They'd received a week of training, which was focused on dispatch procedures, reading road maps, the proper method to load injured soldiers into the ambulance's four cots—two bunks on each side of the compartment—and how to change a flat tire. Their preparation contained no medical instruction, with the exception of a brief lesson on repairing loose bandages and administering sulfanilamide and morphine.

"Your ambulance's medical kit is only for emergencies," an elderly instructor had said, holding a tin of sulfa powder. "Army medics will provide first aid. Your job is to transport injured soldiers to a hospital as fast as possible."

Time is of the essence, Ruth had thought. *Minutes could be the difference between life and death for a maimed soldier*. For the week of training, Ruth asked questions and listened intently, all the while determined to acquire the skills to evacuate people to safety.

After their indoctrination into the corps, Ruth and Lucette were assigned to the same post—an auxiliary ambulance section in Saint-Quentin that was attached to the French Army. The military didn't have a dedicated barracks for women, so they were provided living quarters at a dilapidated boardinghouse next to a hospital. Ruth didn't mind the faucets that dispensed water the color of rust, the mice infestation, or that the only means of heat was a woodstove in a communal kitchen. After all, she'd expected to be working around the clock and rarely in her sleeping quarters. But her days were filled with much idle time. The front was calm, except for occasional aerial skirmishes between Allied aircraft and the Luftwaffe, and most of her infrequent dispatches were to retrieve sick soldiers from the front. Ruth, a hardworking woman by nature, disliked having nothing to do. But she also knew that a busy ambulance driver meant that people were suffering. At night, under the scratching of rodents in the walls, she prayed that the Phony War would remain in a phase of purgatory until a peace treaty was signed.

A large rut bounced Ruth from her seat. She downshifted to the lowest gear, pressed the accelerator, and propelled her ambulance up a steep incline. As she crested the hill, a concrete blockhouse came into view. It was the only fortification in sight, and it was clear to Ruth that this area of the front was not as strongly defended as other sections of the Maginot Line.

A bearded army officer emerged from the blockhouse and waved his arms.

Ruth and Lucette parked their ambulances near the fortification.

"Lieutenant Legrand?" Ruth asked, getting out of her vehicle.

"*Oui*," the soldier said.

"We're here to transport some of your men to the hospital in Saint-Quentin."

"I'm glad you arrived," the lieutenant said, his breath misting in the cold air. "We have four men who've fallen ill with fever, diarrhea, and vomiting."

Dysentery, Ruth thought.

"We also have another man with frostbite on his feet."

"Are any of them able to walk?" Lucette asked.

The soldier blew air on his gloveless hands. "Everyone but the one with frostbite."

Ruth retrieved a stretcher from her ambulance, and the lieutenant led them around the blockhouse to a windowless steel door. Ruth entered the fortification and was met by a sour stench of sweat. Her eyes gradually adjusted to the space, lit by the dull glow of lanterns. Over a dozen soldiers—their faces unshaven and their eyes dark and sunken—were either hunkered on bunks or huddled around a small camp stove with a coffeepot. A string of dried sausage, covered in a layer of white mold, hung from the ceiling. There was no toilet and the only source of water appeared to be from canteens. The space was damp and plagued with pill bugs, and it reminded Ruth of her parents' root cellar back on the farm. Coughs and wheezes emanated from the far corner of the blockhouse, where five men were curled on cots with layers of blankets.

No wonder they're falling ill, Ruth thought.

She and Lucette, with the help of a few other soldiers to carry the frostbitten soldier on a stretcher, loaded the infirm men into their ambulances. They closed the rear doors, took their places behind the wheel, and pulled away.

"Wait!" a voice shouted.

Ruth glanced at her side mirror to see the lieutenant running after them. She and Lucette stopped the vehicles and got out.

"We received a radio message from a squad in a nearby bunker," the lieutenant said, catching up to them. He took gulps of air to catch his breath. "They saw your ambulances enter the area. One of their soldiers severely injured his hand. They sent a wireless transmission to request medical help, but the closest medic is forty minutes away."

Ruth swallowed. "Where are they located?"

The lieutenant pointed. "Two kilometers. The bunker is near

a railroad line. You'll reach it before you turn onto the main road that leads away from the front."

"Let them know that we're on our way," Ruth said.

The lieutenant nodded and fled toward the blockhouse.

Ruth turned to Lucette. "I have room in my ambulance. Go on ahead, and I'll meet you at the hospital."

"I'm not leaving you," Lucette said. "Besides, it's on our route."

"All right. I'll see you there."

Ruth and Lucette climbed into their ambulances and sped away. Within minutes, they reached a concrete bunker that protruded from an earthen mound. Two soldiers were tending to a man who was lying on the ground near a rail line, which appeared to be used by the military to transport heavy equipment, given the idle flatcars that were loaded with artillery guns and howitzers. They exited their vehicles to the sound of a man wailing with pain.

A cold chill ran down Ruth's spine. She grabbed her medical kit and ran with Lucette to the group. The injured soldier—his right hand wrapped in a handkerchief that was drenched with blood—cried out as his comrades tightened a belt around his forearm and applied pressure to his wound.

"We're here to help," Ruth said. "What's the injury?"

"We were preparing to transport artillery," a young soldier said, his voice quavering. "He got his hand caught between railcar couplers."

Ruth kneeled beside the injured soldier. "Can you tell me your name?"

He grimaced and sucked in air. "Claude."

"You're going to be all right, Claude," Ruth said. "I'm going to take a peek at your hand. Will that be all right with you?"

"*Oui*," he groaned.

The soldiers carefully unwrapped the handkerchief to reveal their comrade's hand, crushed and partially severed at the wrist. Blood spurted from the wound.

Oh God. Fear flooded Ruth's veins.

Lucette's eyes widened. "The belt is too loose—he needs a smaller tourniquet."

Ruth's mind raced. She thought of rummaging through her medical kit, but decided that bandages and gauze would do little good. She removed the necktie from her uniform. "Get me a stick or something to tighten it."

One of the soldiers darted to the bunker and returned with a screwdriver.

Ruth wrapped her necktie around the man's forearm, knotted the ends together, and twisted the makeshift tourniquet tight with the screwdriver.

Claude howled.

Lucette opened the medical kit, prepared a morphine injection, and kneeled to the injured soldier. "I'm going to give you something for the pain."

The man's body spasmed. His comrades struggled to hold him still.

Lucette trembled as she raised the syringe. She steadied her hand and injected the morphine into Claude's arm. As seconds passed, his breathing slowed and his muscles relaxed.

"He's lost a lot of blood," Ruth said, applying pressure to the tourniquet. "We can't wait for the medic to arrive. Could one of you come with me on the transport to the hospital? We need to keep pressure on his arm."

"I wish one of us could," a soldier said. "We have strict orders to remain at our post."

"Then you'll need to care for some ill men in one of our ambulances until we return."

"Of course," the soldier said.

Ruth looked at Lucette. "You drive and I'll sit in the back with Claude."

Lucette nodded. She sprinted away and retrieved a stretcher.

"Our ambulances aren't equipped with wireless radios," Ruth said, looking at one of the soldiers, his hands covered with blood. "Relay a communication to the medic and the hospital in Saint-Quentin to let them know what we are doing."

"I will," he said.

The soldiers carried Claude, while Ruth continued applying pressure to the tourniquet and placed him into the ambulance.

The rear doors of the ambulance closed, and the eyes of three infirm soldiers, hunkered on their cots, fell upon Ruth and Claude.

Lucette got into the driver's seat, started the engine, and pulled away.

"What happened?" the soldier with frostbite said, peering down from a top bunk.

"Railroad accident," Ruth said, seated next to Claude on a cot. She carefully leaned over him. "We're on our way to the hospital."

Claude's eyelids lowered. Blood dripped from the handkerchief onto the floor.

She tightened the tourniquet. "Talk to me, Claude. Can you tell me where you're from?"

"Lyon," he mumbled.

Her eyes gravitated to a gold band on the man's left hand. "Do you have a family back in Lyon?"

"My wife." He drew a raspy breath, and his head tilted to the side.

"Claude—stay with me. Can you tell me your wife's name?"

He swallowed. "Sabine."

"That's a beautiful name. What's she like?"

Tears pooled in his eyes. "She's sweet to me. I miss her."

"Tell me about her."

His body shivered. "I—I'm so cold. Am I dying?"

"*Non*." Ruth held him tight. "I got you."

The ambulance rumbled over the unpaved road. His face turned pale and his breath grew shallow.

"Lucette," Ruth called.

Lucette glanced at the rear compartment. "Is everything all right?"

"Drive faster."

Lucette pressed hard on the accelerator. The engine roared as the ambulance turned onto a paved road.

Minutes passed and Ruth, her hand aching from fatigue, fought to keep the tourniquet tight. Claude let out a frail whimper, like a fevered child too ill to wake. She pressed a hand on his handkerchief-covered wound, warm and sticky, and fought to control the bleeding. But the crushing injury, delivered by massive iron clamps that were used to connect rail cars, was far too severe. Blood dripped from the handkerchief to form a puddle. His face turned white. The floor turned red. As the ambulance rumbled en route to the hospital, Claude gave a gasp and his lungs deflated, like partially filled balloons snipped with scissors.

She pressed an ear to his chest. Her vision blurred with tears. With shaking hands, Ruth brushed over Claude's face to close his eyes.

CHAPTER 10

LONDON, ENGLAND—APRIL 9, 1940

Winston Churchill awoke hours before dawn and went to his study in the Admiralty House, a four-story building of yellow brick that had become his home when he was appointed First Lord of the Admiralty. A mix of anticipation and fervor stirred inside him. After months of lobbying to mine neutral Norwegian waters, to prevent the transport of Swedish iron ore to the German war effort, his controversial plan—Operation Wilfred—was finally coming to fruition. At this moment, a large force of British ships was on its way to lay two minefields, one at the mouth of the channel leading directly to the port of Narvik, and another adjacent to the peninsula of Stadlandet.

He sat at his desk and puffed on a cigar, flaring its ember. A sweet scent of burnt tobacco filled the air. He looked at a large map of the world on the wall. Colored pins, punched into the map, depicted locations of Allied and enemy forces. Determination flowed through his veins. *Nazi tyranny must be expunged from Europe at all costs,* he thought, clamping his cigar between his molars. Churchill, like a chess master, scoured the map, playing out Hitler's potential moves in his head.

Since the outbreak of war, Churchill had been a staunch proponent of creating a naval blockade against Germany by mining Norwegian waters. But Prime Minister Chamberlain had rejected

Churchill's proposal on the basis that it would result in political backlash from neutral countries, including the United States. Churchill, undeterred by Chamberlain's rejection, continued to lobby for Allied support of a blockade, and he took his prowess for public speaking to the airways. He believed that radio had the power to reach the hearts and minds of the British people, and he began to conduct broadcasts to galvanize support for the war. Additionally, he took every opportunity to engage Hitler's *Kriegsmarine* while many politicians favored diplomacy to pacify the conflict.

Several weeks earlier, Churchill ordered the commander of a destroyer flotilla to disregard Norway's jurisdiction and seize the German tanker *Altmark* to free nearly three hundred Allied prisoners, whose ships had been sunk by the German battleship *Graf Spee*. Norwegians, who feared being brought into the war, had protested that the action was a violation of its national sovereignty. But the success of the operation turned Churchill into a darling of the newspapers, and the British people began to view him as the sole leader in London who had the guts to take swift action in a dull and dismal Phony War.

Churchill had expected that Chamberlain would grow tired of his bold action and vigor to fight, and that he'd be relieved of his post. But as months passed, it became clear that Chamberlain's appeasement strategy with Hitler was doomed to fail, and the prime minister gave Churchill more responsibility, rather than less. Chamberlain invited Churchill to join him at the Anglo-French Supreme War Council (SWC) meetings, held in both Paris and London, that included Paul Reynaud, the new French prime minister, and his military leaders, including General Maurice Gamelin. Churchill felt like he had a voice in war strategy, even though the French did not agree with many of his plans, especially Operation Royal Marine, which called for floating fluvial mines down rivers which flowed into Germany from France. *They fear Hitler's retaliation*, Churchill had thought, as the French leaders shook their heads in disagreement.

With much debate behind closed doors, Churchill gradually persuaded Prime Minister Chamberlain that some combative

measures should be taken against Germany. Chamberlain reshuf-
fled his war ministry to make Churchill the chairman of the Military Coordinating Committee. With his increased authority and
the French refusing to participate in mining, Churchill decided
that Britain alone would undertake Operation Wilfred.

Churchill placed the stub of his cigar in an ashtray. He poured
a glass of whisky, added water, and swirled it, releasing peaty va-
pors. He took a drink, feeling the warmth of the alcohol settle into
his stomach.

The telephone on his desk rang.

He set aside his drink and picked up the receiver. "Churchill."

"Winston," Prime Minister Chamberlain's voice said. "You're
awake."

"Indeed, sir," Churchill said. "I'm expecting an update soon
on Operation Wilfred. I was planning to ring you with the news."

"No need," Chamberlain said. "I was contacted by French
Prime Minister Reynaud. Germany has commenced an invasion
of Denmark and Norway."

Churchill gripped the receiver. "When?"

"An hour ago. We've called an emergency meeting of the SWC.
Reynaud and his military cabinet are flying to London."

Churchill imagined German troops landing on the shores of
Denmark and Norway. Anger flooded his chest yet his demeanor
remained unflappable.

"I expect that you'll be briefed by British intelligence and prepared for the meeting," Chamberlain said.

"Of course."

"And Winston—"

"Yes, sir."

"I should have listened to you."

Churchill picked up his cigar stub and rolled it between his
fingers. Ashes fell to the floor.

"My appeasement of Nazi Germany to avoid war has been futile," Chamberlain said, his voice filled with regret. "Due to my
obstinance, we've wasted time and resources that could have gone
to preparing the country for war. It was foolish of me to insist that
most of the RAF's operations consisted of airborne leaflet drop-

ping over German towns. The propaganda did little, or nothing, to educate the German people about their tyrant dictator."

"Your intentions were admirable, sir."

"Perhaps," Chamberlain said. "But you were right, Winston. There is no reasoning with Hitler."

The prime minister ended the call. Churchill rose from his desk and went to his map. He inserted pins, marking the location of German troops in Norway and Denmark, and silently vowed to find the means to replace them with Allied forces.

PART 2

THE INVASION

CHAPTER 11

SAINT-QUENTIN, FRANCE—MAY 10, 1940

Ruth put on her uniform, left her room, and descended the stairs to the boardinghouse's communal kitchen. She found Lucette, who was seated at a table and having a breakfast of toasted baguette with butter. A smell of burnt oak emanated from the woodstove.

"I made coffee," Lucette said, pointing to a pot on the stove.

"*Merci.*" Ruth poured a cup and took a sip, lukewarm with an astringent sour taste. She winced.

"I should have warned you," Lucette said. "It tastes like turpentine."

Ruth swirled her coffee. "It's not that bad."

Lucette smiled. "Liar."

"Where is everyone?" Ruth asked, referring to the eight other women in their ambulance corps unit who resided at the boardinghouse.

"They left a few minutes ago."

Ruth glanced at her wristwatch. "We should get to work."

"We have some time, and you need to eat."

"I'm not hungry."

"Sit." Lucette patted a chair beside her.

Ruth sat.

Lucette slid a plate with a baguette to her. "Try some butter. It softens the dryness of the bread, and it cuts the bitterness of the coffee."

Ruth picked up a knife and scooped butter from a dish. As she spread it over her baguette, the knife slipped from her fingers and clanged onto the table. Using a napkin, she wiped the buttery mess from the table.

"You look a bit tired this morning," Lucette said.

"I didn't sleep well."

Lucette took a drink of coffee. "Another bad dream?"

Ruth nodded.

"I'm sorry."

After the death of Claude, Ruth was plagued with night terrors. In predawn hours, she'd awakened—gasping for air with the sensation of being suffocated. With visions of a bloody necktie-tourniquet still reeling in her head, she'd hunkered at a writing desk to study road maps for shortcuts to and from the Maginot Line. The only remedy to keep the nightmares at bay, it seemed, was to bury herself in work.

Lucette set aside her cup. "It's not your fault that he died," she said, as if she could read her friend's thoughts.

Ruth nodded, despite an ache of guilt that gnawed at her conscience. An army medic, as well as two nurses, had told her that there was nothing more she could have done for a man with a severed radial artery, but she still felt horrible.

"Last night, I saw a letter to you from Paul on the foyer table," Ruth said, eager to change the subject. "How is he?"

Lucette's eyes brightened. "He receives his leave next month, and he's coming here to see me."

Ruth smiled. "That's grand news. I'm happy for you."

"*Merci*." Lucette ran a finger over the rim of her cup. "Paul says that France has one of the largest tank forces in the world, which will deter the German military from attempting to cross the Maginot Line. He assures me that our country's military strength is much greater than that of Denmark or Norway, and that it will preempt an escalation of war between Germany and France." She lowered her eyes. "His spirit is cheerful, even though it's a hardship to be a tank commander. I hate the thought of him being confined inside a cramped chamber of armored steel, and I can't help brooding about his safety."

"He'll be all right," Ruth said.

She nodded. "I needed to hear that."

Ruth's mind drifted to the people of Denmark and Norway. Denmark surrendered within a day of their German invasion, while Norway was gradually losing its fight for freedom. She felt awful for their citizens who succumbed to Nazi aggression. *With the buildup of Allied forces in France, things will be different for us.*

She shook away her thought and nudged Lucette's arm. "After the war, you and Paul will get married. You'll have a stellar dancing career, and someday you'll have loads of children, all of whom will become stars of the Paris Opera Ballet."

Lucette chuckled. "That would be a beautiful future. How about you?"

Ruth ate a bit of her baguette. "I'll go back to singing, hopefully somewhere in Paris, but it might be difficult to land a gig considering how I left Bal Tabarin."

"I was referring to your private life."

"Oh, that." Ruth tucked her skirt around her legs. "I haven't given it much thought. I'll have plenty of time for personal affairs after the war."

It had been ages since Ruth had felt the comfort of a man. She'd had a few boyfriends in high school and while living in Paris, but none of the relationships were serious and she'd never been in love. Her focus on her career had hindered her dating life, she believed, and at times she wondered if she would ever experience true intimacy.

"Why wait to meet someone?" Lucette asked.

Ruth picked at a crumb on her plate. "I have my duties."

"Of course, but you have some free evenings." Lucette clasped her hands with elbows on the table. "I see the way that young army doctor looks at you."

"Which one?"

"Doctor Morin."

"Is he the one who wears two stethoscopes?"

"*Oui.*"

"I agree," Ruth said. "He does have his eyes on me—and nearly every woman who works at the hospital."

Lucette laughed. "True."

"I appreciate you looking out for me, but I—"

A siren sounded.

Ruth's skin prickled.

Lucette's eyes widened. "Is it a drill?"

"I don't know. We're usually informed about training exercises."

They got up from the table and darted outside. Several military trucks, loaded with soldiers, roared past them. As they ran down the sidewalk, a siren wailed from a nearby government building that was being used by the French military. Ruth's adrenaline surged, and she willed her legs to run faster.

A soldier with a duffel bag darted from a building and bumped into Ruth, nearly knocking her to the ground.

Pain shot through her shoulder.

The soldier extended his hand. "Are you all right?"

"*Oui.*" Ruth sucked in air, attempting to catch her breath. "What's happening?"

"The Germans have invaded the Low Countries," he said.

Oh, God. A knot tightened in the pit of Ruth's stomach.

"When?" Lucette asked.

"Early this morning." The soldier turned and sprinted away.

"What about France?" Ruth called after him, but received no reply.

Ruth and Lucette ran to their post in the rear parking lot of the hospital, a large four-story brick building in the center of town. The women of the ambulance corps, their eyes filled with concern, lined up in two rows of five in front of the parked ambulances. Ruth and Lucette took their places, standing at attention in the second row. As the women awaited their orders, they whispered to each other, desperately attempting to gain insight on what was happening.

Army Lieutenant Ravier, a silver-haired man with a lantern jaw and a bow-legged gait, emerged from a rear door of the hospital. His boots clacked over the pavement as he approached the women.

Whispers faded away.

Ruth's eyes widened at the sight of the lieutenant, who rarely addressed the women. Although the ambulance unit fell under his command, he almost always communicated his orders through a sergeant.

The lieutenant stopped in front of the women and raised a clipboard. "This is not a drill. Germany has invaded Luxembourg, the Netherlands, and Belgium."

A fusion of dread and anger surged inside Ruth.

He puffed his chest. "They have not entered French soil. I repeat—the Maginot Line has not been breached. As a precaution, I am deploying you to sectors of France's border."

The German military is on our doorstep! She drew a deep breath, attempting to quell her nerves.

The lieutenant looked at his clipboard. "Battier and Thibaut, you're assigned to Maubeuge. Toutain and Dubos, your post will be in Fourmies."

A sickening lump grew in the back of Ruth's throat. She raised her eyes to the sky, smeared with gray clouds, and waited for her name to be called.

CHAPTER 12

SEDAN, FRANCE—MAY 13, 1940

On the day German forces emerged from the Ardennes Forest and crossed the river Meuse into France, Ruth was racing toward the battlefront to evacuate injured soldiers to a hospital, twelve kilometers away from France's border with Belgium. Trailing behind her was an ambulance driven by Lucette. They navigated through a narrow, rural road that was clogged with fleeing French villagers. Many of the civilians scurried away on foot, while others fled by way of bicycles, trucks, or horse-drawn wagons that were loaded with luggage and family heirlooms.

A young woman, who was pushing a wheelbarrow that held a swaddled baby, passed within inches of Ruth's vehicle, making her heart sink. She honked the ambulance's horn and weaved through the throng, like a spawning salmon fighting a current.

As Ruth and Lucette neared the border, the crowd dwindled away and the air was filled with blasts, gunfire, and an acrid smell of expelled explosive. German Stuka dive bombers, accompanied by Messerschmitt fighters, darkened the afternoon sky like a swarm of black flies. French antiaircraft fire boomed. Black bursts exploded below the aerial armada.

Ruth, her pulse pounding in her eardrums, gripped the steering wheel and peered through the windshield at the battle unfolding on the horizon. High above, a squadron of Stuka dive bombers narrowed in on their target, the Meuse Line that contained over a hundred pillboxes—small concrete blockhouses with holes to fire machine guns—that were guarded by France's 147th Fortress Infantry Regiment. Several hundred meters behind this line was a reserve group of the 55th Infantry Division, and far to the north were troops of the British Expeditionary Force. Despite the heavy barrage by French antiaircraft fire, as well as combat from Allied planes, the Luftwaffe continued their assault on the Meuse Line. Sirens, mounted to the Stukas, screamed as the German squadron released their bombs on a group of antiaircraft gunners that exploded in a mountainous fountain of earth, steel, and bodies.

Shock and anger surged through Ruth. *God help us.* She set aside her trepidation and pushed the accelerator, propelling her ambulance into the conflict.

Ruth and Lucette had initially been sent to a post in Hirson, France, but things changed when the German military rampaged through Belgium and cut through the dense Ardennes Forest, which was thought to be impassable for Germany's Panzer tank divisions. They were reassigned to a sector outside of Sedan with the understanding that it would take at least four days for the Germans to cross the river Meuse. But German engineers completed bridgeheads at Monthermé, Dinant, and Sedan in under twenty-four hours.

Ruth's eyes locked on an army medic, who darted from a clearing and waved his arms. She veered from the road and cut across a grass field, scarred with shell craters. Within seconds, she reached a makeshift triage site near a group of pine trees. Five medics, who were outnumbered tenfold by wounded soldiers, were struggling to administer first aid. She and Lucette jumped out of their ambulances and threw open the rear doors.

Two hundred meters away, French artillery guns and howitzers unleashed their fury on the advancing German troops.

Concussive blasts pierced Ruth's ears, and the ground quaked beneath her feet. She fought back the fear rippling through her body and retrieved a stretcher. She ran to the medics, who were bandaging wounds and injecting morphine into wailing men.

"This one first!" a medic shouted, wrapping gauze around a man's head wound.

Ruth and Lucette helped the medic, his hands covered in blood, lift the moaning soldier onto the stretcher. The trio carried the injured man and loaded him into Ruth's ambulance. For several minutes, they transported maimed men, one by one, into the ambulances.

Lucette shut the rear doors of her vehicle, packed with soldiers. "Let's go!"

"Wait!" Ruth shouted, sliding the legs of an injured man under a cot. "I can make room for one more!"

She and Lucette ran to the closest soldier, who was unconscious with gauze stuffed into a hole, the size of a plum, in his abdomen.

A bark of machine guns pierced the air. Bullets whizzed over their heads.

The medic crouched low to the ground. "Let's get another man. That one has a severe stomach wound and likely won't make it."

Ruth kneeled to the injured man. His lungs wheezed as his chest rose and fell. "We're taking him."

Lucette placed the stretcher next to the man's body.

The medic scanned the rows of injured soldiers, as if he was searching for someone more likely to survive the trip to the hospital.

A German artillery shell detonated, no more than thirty meters away.

Bits of earth rained onto Ruth's head. "Help us—now!"

The medic joined Ruth and Lucette. They slid the soldier onto the cot and transferred him to Ruth's ambulance. The women got into their vehicles and sped away, leaving the small corps of medics to tend to the growing number of wounded being carried to the tree line. Kilometers down the road, the rumble of bombs faded and was replaced by the groans of pain-filled men. Ruth, determined to get them to safety, shifted gears and pushed hard on the accelerator.

What should have been a twenty-minute trip to the hospital took over forty minutes because the main road was congested with villagers who were running away to the south. Ruth, remembering the map routes that she'd studied, led them through several detours on back roads, otherwise it would have taken over an hour. With the help of orderlies, they transported the injured men inside the hospital, its corridors lined with wounded soldiers. Anesthetic, sweat, and a metallic smell of blood filled the air. Nurses, overwhelmed by the influx of patients, struggled to sort through the men to determine who would get treated first.

Ruth approached the soldier with the stomach wound, who'd been placed on a gurney. His chest rose and fell in a shallow cadence. "Over here!"

An elderly nurse with crooked, arthritic fingers examined the man's wound. "Can you hear me?" she asked, leaning to his left ear.

His eyelids twitched.

The nurse called for an orderly, who grabbed the gurney and wheeled the soldier toward an operating room.

Lucette turned to Ruth. "You may have saved his life."

"I hope so," she said.

They dashed to their vehicles and sped over rutted back roads to the front. Ruth, her hands gripping the steering wheel, prayed that Allied troops and aircraft had repelled the German forces. But, as the battleground came into view, she discovered that the Luftwaffe bombing raids had obliterated a narrow sector of the French line. *Oh, dear God—they've broken through!*

A Stuka siren drew Ruth's eyes to the sky. Her breath stalled in her lungs at the sight of the German aircraft, diving toward their ambulances. She jammed on the accelerator and her foot slipped from the pedal. She shifted gears, grinding the clutch, and her vehicle picked up speed. The Stuka's siren roared. She swerved onto a field, hoping that the enemy pilot would veer away at the sight of the large red cross emblem on the side of her vehicle. But the Stuka, flying at a high speed, closed in and fired its machine guns. Bullets blasted the ground in front of her vehicle, and a bomb fell from the belly of the aircraft.

Ruth turned sharply, nearly rolling the ambulance. An explosion jolted the vehicle, and her head struck the side window, sending a sharp pain through her neck. She steadied the wheel, regaining control of her ambulance, and glanced at her side mirror to see the Stuka pull up and Lucette's ambulance crash into a smoldering crater.

"No!" Ruth slammed her foot on the brake and her vehicle skidded to a stop. She jumped out and sprinted toward the crater. "Lucette!"

The Stuka veered to the north. French antiaircraft guns fired but missed their target.

Ruth, her leg muscles burning, reached the crater and peered down at the wreckage. The front of the ambulance was smashed with the wheels twisted outward, and the cab was partially crumpled over the engine compartment, like a fold of an accordion. Both doors were wedged against the sides of the hole, and steam from a ruptured radiator spewed over the decimation. Fear flooded Ruth's veins.

She lowered herself into the crater and peered through a hole in the broken windshield at her friend, slumped on the floor. "Lucette!"

Lucette lifted her head.

"Are you hurt?"

Lucette, using the steering wheel, pulled herself onto her knees and ran her hands over her limbs. "My ears are ringing and I have a cut on my forehead." She looked up and pushed hair out of her eyes. "Nothing broken."

"Thank goodness. Let's get you—"

The grinding of an aircraft engine swelled.

Ruth looked up and froze.

The Stuka, high above the field, descended toward them. Its siren screamed.

"It's come back!" Ruth tugged at the driver's side door, but it—as well as the passenger door—was wedged shut by mounds of dirt.

"Go!" Lucette shouted.

"I'm not leaving you!" Ruth crawled onto the hood. "Cover your head!" She sat and kicked the windshield with the heel of her shoe, sending broken glass over the cab.

Lucette reached her hand through the opening.

Machine guns fired.

"Get down!" Ruth curled into a fetal position. She expected her body to be riddled with bullets. Instead, the sound of plane engines, deeper in pitch than the Stuka, shot overhead. She peered to the sky and discovered that the enemy aircraft had veered away and was being chased by three French fighter planes.

Lucette brushed shards of glass from the dashboard with the sleeve of her uniform and looked up through the open windshield. "They're ours!"

Ruth clasped Lucette's hands and pulled her from the wreckage. They climbed out of the crater and scurried to Ruth's ambulance.

Ruth helped Lucette into the passenger seat, and then took her place behind the wheel. She removed a handkerchief from her pocket and gave it to Lucette. "Your forehead is bleeding, above your right eye."

Lucette pressed the cloth to her laceration.

French cannonade erupted. Shock waves rolled like thunder over the field and through Ruth's body. "Are you able to work?"

"*Oui*—let's go."

Ruth started the engine and drove toward the soldiers. For the remainder of the day, the two worked as a team to evacuate injured soldiers away from the battlefront. Hundreds, if not thousands, of German air assaults were conducted on the Meuse Line, and at dusk the bombing raids were replaced by attacks from the German infantry. The French Army casualty count soared, overwhelming medics and the ambulance corps. Rumors soon spread through the field that German tanks had gotten behind them, and some of the soldiers fled their posts, leaving a wide void in the French defenses. By midnight, the German infantry penetrated eight kilometers into French territory and the hospital announced plans for evacuation. But Ruth and Lucette were committed to saving as many lives as possible, and they returned to the front again and again.

CHAPTER 13

SEDAN, FRANCE—MAY 14, 1940

It was their second sortie of the terrible morning. Jimmie, flying at fifteen thousand feet, adjusted the control stick of his Hurricane to maintain his position in the Green Section that included Benny and section leader Cobber. The trio were in new, upgraded Hurricanes that had been delivered to their squadron. For the first time since the war began, their fighter planes were nearly on par with the performance of a Messerschmitt 109.

Their mission, which was the same as the other sections of No. 73 Squadron, was to escort separate groups of Fairey Battles, single-engine light bombers, to a narrow section of the front, where German Panzer tanks had broken through the Meuse Line. Ahead and below his plane, ten Battles flew in a Vic formation. There were twelve bombers in the last sortie; two failed to return.

Jimmie peered through his canopy. Explosions flashed, and streams of smoke rose from the horizon, as if the Allied and German bombardments had cracked open the earth, creating a gateway to hell. Hundreds of Panzers, exchanging gunfire with divisions of French tanks, were advancing through a gap in the inferno.

"We should have bloody been here yesterday," Benny said over the radio.

"Roger," Cobber said. "There's nothing we can do about it now. Stay alert and keep an eye out for bandits."

"Wilco," Benny said.

Jimmie's pulse rate quickened, and he tightened his grip on the control stick. "Wilco."

The day before, Air Chief Marshal Barratt, the officer in charge of the British air force in France, ordered a day of rest for the pilots after heavy losses incurred by the RAF in the Netherlands and Belgium. The pilots of No. 73 Squadron were infuriated with having to stand idle while their French allies flew alone to defend against the German invasion. And it sickened Jimmie to watch the French squadrons depart from the airfield and, two hours later, return with fewer planes.

Jimmie scanned the sky, and his adrenaline surged at the sight of six oncoming aircraft. "Messerschmitts—two o'clock high!"

"Roger," Cobber said. "Tally-ho, Green Section!"

Jimmie pushed the throttle and the engine roared. "Tally-ho!"

The Green Section Hurricanes ascended, narrowing in on their target. Jimmie placed his thumb on the gun-firing button and peered through his gunsight. He maneuvered his plane, bringing a Messerschmitt into his sight, and fired his machine guns. Bullets streamed through the sky.

Gunfire erupted from his fellow wingmen.

The Messerschmitt fighters, veering in separate directions, fired their guns and shot past them.

Turbulence jolted Jimmie's Hurricane. He banked hard right. G-force pressed him into his seat, and he dived toward a Messerschmitt that was closing in on a Fairey Battle.

The bomber's air gunner, his head and torso protruding from the rear cockpit like a passenger in the dicky-seat of a roadster, swiveled his Vickers machine gun toward the Messerschmitt. He opened fire but missed.

Jimmie swooped in, jostled the control stick, and pressed the gun-firing button.

Bullets pierced the Messerschmitt, producing sparks, and it retreated with smoke pouring from its engine.

For several minutes, the Green Section fought to defend the bombers from the Messerschmitts. Cobber shot down an enemy plane, which spiraled into the ground near a French tank division. And, as suddenly as the dogfight occurred, the Messerschmitts disengaged and flew away.

"Flak!" Cobber shouted over the radio.

Within seconds, German antiaircraft flak guns boomed from the ground. A barrage of projectiles exploded near the planes, sending jagged metal fragments through the air, and producing black clouds that hung in the sky. Shock waves blasted Jimmie's Hurricane. The control stick juddered in his hands.

The bombers descended, leaving their fighter escorts, and they dropped their payload on a line of Panzers, destroying three of the tanks. As the bombers fled from the front, one of them took a flak hit to a wing and struggled to climb to the safety of the clouds.

The German antiaircraft bombardment ceased, and the German fighters, like wolves smelling blood, came in for the kill. Jimmie, Cobber, and Benny attempted to fend them off, but they were outnumbered. Two Messerschmitts zeroed in and unloaded rounds of bullets into the faltering bomber. Its engine exploded, severing the left wing. Jimmie and his fellow pilots listened to the airmen's screams over the radio as the bomber tumbled from the sky.

A chill ran through Jimmie's body. *God help them.* He regained his focus and shot his Hurricane behind a Messerschmitt. He pressed the gun-firing button, but missed as the German plane slewed to the right. He struggled to keep up with the enemy aircraft as it rolled and dived. He fired bursts from his machine guns, over and over, until his ammunition was exhausted.

Two Messerschmitts swooped in behind him. Jimmie pulled back hard on his stick, shooting his plane upward and twisting through the atmosphere. He expected that he'd have to rely on his maneuvering to survive, but the Luftwaffe aircraft retreated to German-controlled territory, as if their pilots had been given orders to guard the Panzers and their assault path into France.

Jimmie eased his grip on the control stick and sucked in air from his oxygen mask. His neck and shoulder muscles relaxed.

He scanned the perimeter, tipped his wings, and flew his Hurricane to join Green Section in formation, above and behind the bombers.

"Green Section," Cobber said. "Is everyone all right?"

"Green Two—affirmative," Benny said.

Jimmie ran a gloved hand over his flight jacket pocket that contained his good luck charm. "Green Three—affirmative."

"Roger," Cobber said. "Well done, gents. Let's escort these kites safely back to base."

Jimmie's eyes gravitated to the vacant spot in the rear of the Fairey Battle squadron's formation, and he wondered if there was anything he could have done to save the aircrew. Despite feeling grateful to be alive, a mix of sadness and regret pricked at his conscience.

Thirty minutes later, they landed at an airfield in Reims, where the No. 73 Squadron and several Fairey Battle squadrons had been relocated days earlier because of its proximity to the breach at Sedan. Jimmie landed and parked his Hurricane. He cut the engine, removed his flying helmet, and climbed out of his cockpit to a frenzy of ground crew who were preparing aircraft for sorties. Fitters, riggers, and armorers buzzed over the area as the men loaded ammunition, fueled aircraft, and made repairs to flak-damaged engines and airframes.

Horace, his faced covered with sweat, approached Jimmie and gave him a canteen.

Jimmie's hand trembled as he gulped water. He returned the canteen. "Thanks."

"I'm glad to see that you and your section made it back safely."

An image of the Fairey Battle's severed wing flashed in his head. He felt sick to his stomach. "One of the bombers failed to make it back."

"I'm sorry, sir."

"Me too."

Horace shifted his weight. "We're hearing that there's a major tank battle at the front, and that the Germans have hundreds, maybe thousands, of Panzers."

"It's true," Jimmie said.

Lines formed on Horace's forehead. He rubbed stubble on his face and he lowered his voice. "Do you think we're capable of stopping them?"

"To be honest, I don't know," Jimmie said. "But we're going to use all of our power to try to fend them off."

Horace slipped his cap from his head and glanced to the sky. "Thank you for what you're doing up there."

"You too," Jimmie said. "You and the ground crew are keeping us in the fight."

"Merely doing our duty, sir." Horace looked at Jimmie's plane. "Any damage or mechanical issues?"

"No."

"I'll check it over. It'll be armed, fueled, and in tip-top shape for you for your next sortie."

Jimmie patted Horace's shoulder and walked to the front of an aircraft hangar where Cobber and Fanny were sitting on wooden folding chairs that overlooked the runway. Several meters away, Benny was resting on a cot with an arm over his eyes.

"Have a seat," Cobber said, gesturing to an empty chair. "We've got an hour until our next sortie."

Jimmie sat. He exhaled and wiped sweat from his brow.

Fanny puffed on a cigarette. "Did you score any victories?"

"One," Cobber said. "A Messerschmitt 109."

"I damaged a 109," Jimmie said, "but it got away."

Fanny flicked ash from his cigarette. "I shot down two of them on my last sortie. That puts me at thirteen destroyed enemy aircraft. Cobber, what's your total?"

Cobber, his eyes surrounded with dark circles from little sleep, peered over the runway. "I've lost count."

For several minutes the men recounted their dogfights with the German pilots, and Jimmie listened intently to learn about the tactics used by Cobber and Fanny to outwit and outmaneuver their adversaries. While Jimmie had become a formidable fighter pilot, given that he had two victories, a Messerschmitt and a Dornier Do 215, he had far to go to reach the skill level of Cobber and Fanny, both of whom were flying aces.

Two months earlier, Cobber had become the RAF's first flying ace of the war. Soon after, Fanny had become the second.
Together, they were credited for nearly two dozen destroyed enemy aircraft, and their fellow pilots believed the tally to be much
higher. The accounts of their victories were covered in the British
newspapers, and Cobber had been interviewed on BBC Radio,
which gave the New Zealander a bit of notoriety and much teas-
ing from the men of the 73. Neither man liked the attention, especially Cobber who was rather shy when not strapped inside the
cockpit of his Hurricane. Their motivation was to be good fellow
pilots and to fight for Britain. To the men of the squadron, Cobber
and Fanny appeared to be invincible. But things changed with
the German invasion of France. The full force of Hitler's Luftwaffe and Wehrmacht had breached the border and, in the past
few days, Jimmie had witnessed British and French airmen perish
in battle.

A drone of propellers drew Jimmie's attention to the sky. Six
Fairey Battles, one with a sputtering engine, approached the runway with a sole Hurricane as their escort. *There should be three Hurricanes, and at least ten Battles.* He rose from his chair and placed a
hand above his eyes to shield the sun.

Benny sat up in his cot, and the remaining men stood.

"Which section is it?" Fanny asked.

Cobber squinted. "Blue."

Gord's section, Jimmie thought.

"Bloody hell," Benny said.

"Which Seventy-Three pilot is it?" Fanny asked.

Jimmie strained to get a look at the Hurricane's markings. "I
can't tell."

The men ran toward the runway as the planes landed. The Battles traveled to the opposite side of the airfield, and the Hurricane
taxied to a clearing near the No. 73 Squadron ground crew. As the
Hurricane turned, its markings on the fuselage—covered in holes
from flak—came into view.

"It's Ayerst," Jimmie said.

Ayerst, a nineteen-year-old pilot, parked his Hurricane and

climbed down from his cockpit to be met by a growing number of pilots and ground crew, all of whom were anxious to learn what happened to their comrades.

Squadron Leader Hank More weaved his way through the group and was the first to approach Ayerst. "What happened to Gord and Jones?"

Ayerst slipped his flight helmet from his head. "They bought it."

Oh, God. Jimmie slumped his shoulders.

"The Germans have brought in more antiaircraft guns," Ayerst said. "There's a hellish amount of flak."

"Were they able to bail out?" the squadron leader asked.

Ayerst shook his head.

Cobber slipped his hands into his pockets and walked away from the crowd.

Jimmie followed Cobber and caught up with him outside a latrine. "Are you all right?"

"A little shaken by the news." Cobber, his face pale, retrieved a canteen from a hook on a wall and splashed water over his face.

"I feel the same way," Jimmie said.

Cobber turned to him. "Jones was a good man and easy to like. But Gord and I didn't get along—he blamed me for Taylor's death, and we rarely saw eye to eye as section leaders." His jaw quivered and he sucked in a deep breath. "I never expected to be so bloody upset over the death of Gord."

Jimmie paused, processing Cobber's words. "The Seventy-Three is a brotherhood. Much like a family, we don't always get along. But we always care for each other."

Cobber ran a hand over his hair and nodded.

"We're going to get through this," Jimmie said.

"We will," Cobber said, regaining his composure. He rubbed his eyes and glanced at his wristwatch. "I'm going to take a walk to clear my head before our next sortie. You're welcome to join me, if you like."

"Sure."

For thirty minutes, Jimmie and Cobber walked around the airfield. They spoke no further of the death of Gord and Jones, nor did they discuss tactics for their upcoming raids. They spoke only of fond family memories, sporting matches, and growing old and fat in their homelands after the war. They took solace in their brief intermission of the battle and, for the first time since joining the No. 73 Squadron, Jimmie felt like a mentor rather than a mentee.

For the remainder of the day, they flew three more sorties, each time returning with fewer Fairey Battles than when they had departed. By nightfall, the RAF had lost forty-one of their seventy-one bombers, and a decimated French air force was reduced to flying obsolete Amiot 143 bombers. Despite the catastrophic losses of aircraft, the Green Section pilots returned to their airbase unscathed. But Jimmie knew that it was only a matter of time before another member of No. 73 Squadron met the same fate as Jones and Gord. A looming sense of dread, knowing that he could be shot down on any mission, haunted him like a shadow. Surrounded by a barrage of flak fire, it was luck—not valor or skill—that determined which pilot would live or die.

CHAPTER 14

REIMS, FRANCE—MAY 15, 1940

Jimmie was unable to sleep, despite his exhaustion. His mind was plagued with horrid echoes of flak fire, burning planes, and shouts of airmen through the radio receiver in his flying helmet. He rolled out of his cot, wearing his flight suit and combat boots. He rubbed sand from his eyes and crept out of the barracks, trying not to disturb pilots who were getting an hour of rest before their next mission. Outside, the predawn sky was strewn with blue, violet, and red clouds. The ground crewmen, who'd worked through the night, were moving metal barrels of aviation fuel, and loading ammunition into aircraft. The sounds of fitters, their tools clinking against engines, drifted from a nearby hangar.

He walked to a solitary oak tree, perched on a hill that overlooked the airfield and an abandoned farm. He removed a piece of paper and pencil from his flight jacket. An image of his sister, her legs in calipers and holding her cat, Crumpet, flashed in his head. He placed the paper against his upper leg and, as his eyes adjusted to the semidarkness, he began to scribble.

> *Dear Nora,*
> *I suppose that you're following the news reports about the German invasion. Please know that I'm healthy, and my spirit is good. The men of 73 Squadron are putting up a valiant fight*

to keep the invaders at bay. We are giving it our all to stop them in France and prevent them from ever setting foot on British soil.

Piglet is always with me when I fly. He's in my jacket pocket as I write this letter. Most of the pilots have good luck charms, and I think Piglet is the best of them. He reminds me of you and your triumph of regaining your ability to walk. You're the strongest, most determined person I know. And having your Piglet with me is a constant reminder that the most splendid things in life come through toil, diligence, and faith.

Jimmie stretched his legs, his muscles tight from being con- fined to his cockpit. He rolled the pencil between his fingers, then continued writing.

It brings me joy to know that you're excited to go away to uni- versity. You're going to experience wondrous things and befriend students who make you feel good about yourself. Someday, you'll be a cracking librarian, enriching people's lives with loads of books. I am proud of you.

I'll write more in my next letter. Please excuse the handwriting. I'm sitting outside under a glorious twilight sky, quite unfitting for a world at war. Give Mum and Dad a hug for me—and a cuddle for Crumpet.

Love,
Jimmie

He placed the letter in an addressed envelope and slipped it into his jacket. He walked to his barracks, where pilots were rising from their cots and making their way to the mess hall. At breakfast, the men—who were physically and mentally knack- ered—spoke little as they chewed oats and sipped tea. After they ate their brief meal, Squadron Leader Hank More stood beside a chalkboard and addressed the men.

"I will be taking over for the Blue Section," Hank said.

Jimmie glanced at the empty chairs that Gord and Jones had occupied the previous morning, and he wondered how many vacant seats there would be tomorrow. His chest felt tight, as if it were being compressed in a vise.

"For today's sorties, I'll lead one group with Blue and Yellow Sections," Hank said. "Cobber will lead the other group with his Green Section and Fanny's Red Section."

Hank drew on the chalkboard to show the path of the advancing German Panzer divisions, and where the Hurricanes were to escort Fairey Battles on their bombing raid. Men shifted in their seats.

Jimmie's eyes widened as he viewed Hank's illustration. *How could the German tanks advance that far in a matter of hours? Could our intelligence be mistaken?* He shook away his thoughts and focused on memorizing the location of their target.

"I'm waiting for word of when more airmen, bombers, and Hurricanes will be deployed to France," Hank said. "Until then, we need to give them hell with what we've got." He dusted chalk from his hands and looked at his wristwatch. "We depart in eighteen minutes. Dismissed."

The pilots exited the mess hall, put on their flight gear, and made their way to their Hurricanes. On the opposite side of the runway, airmen of British and French bomber squadrons were getting into their aircrafts.

Fanny quickened his pace and wedged his way between Cobber and Jimmie. "It's about time I get to fly with you blokes," he said, as if he was trying to brighten their mood.

"You too, mate," Cobber said.

Jimmie nodded. He glanced at Cobber, his chin up and walking with a confident gait. The vulnerability that he'd displayed over the death of Gord was no longer visible. It was unnerving for Jimmie to go to battle, but he took comfort in knowing that he'd have Cobber and Fanny—two of the RAF's best fighter pilots—in his group. He gathered his nerve and lengthened his stride en route to their Hurricanes.

Jimmie joined Horace to complete a safety check on his plane. Together, they walked around the aircraft to examine the structure.

"How does she look?" Horace asked, wiping his hands with a rag.

"Perfect." Jimmie ran a hand over the smooth fuselage where there had been a four-inch-in-diameter hole from a hunk of German flak. He turned to Horace, whose face was covered in two days of beard stubble. "You've been up all night. Maybe you could get some rest while we're gone."

"I've got more repairs to do," Horace said. "Besides, I could never sleep during a sortie."

"Then take a few minutes to write a letter to Daisy; it'll take your mind off things. How is she and your baby, Olive, getting along?"

"Splendid," Horace said. "I got a letter from my wife yesterday. Olive took her first steps."

"Brilliant." Jimmie patted his shoulder. "I bet you feel like a proud dad."

"I do." Horace lowered his eyes. "I'd give anything to have been there to see it."

Jimmie nodded. "When's your next leave?"

"Not for four months."

"After we win this war, you'll never need to miss another momentous event with Daisy and Olive."

"I'm counting on it."

Jimmie placed his hands into his flight jacket pockets. "Speaking of letters—" He removed an envelope. "I didn't get a chance to put this in the post to my sister. Would you mind taking care of this for me?"

"Not at all." Horace took the letter. "How is Nora?"

"She's well, and feisty as ever."

Horace smiled.

Jimmie climbed into the cockpit of his Hurricane.

Horace peered up at him. "Godspeed."

"Thank you."

Jimmie strapped himself into his safety harness and started the engine, sending a vibration through his body. He checked the controls, put on his flying helmet, and closed the canopy, cutting off the acrid smell of exhaust fumes. The squadron was given permission to depart and, one by one, the pilots accelerated their planes down the runway and flew into the morning sky. They divided into two groups and escorted the bombers toward their target.

Nearing the bombing zone at twelve thousand feet, Jimmie was sickened by the sight of the ground devastation. The remains of hundreds of obliterated French tanks—far more than destroyed Panzers—littered the terrain. Thousands of German tanks had broken through the front line, outmaneuvered Allied armor divisions, and were traveling through open country, far ahead of the German ground troops. Prior to the invasion, France had three thousand tanks on its northeastern border, but most of them were not at the Ardennes Forest, which was deemed by the French military to be impassable for Panzers. French tank divisions were redeployed to the breach at the border but the Germans had already acquired superior ground position. Now, much of the French tank forces were in ruin while the Panzer divisions appeared to be at near full strength. Even more horrifying, to Jimmie, was that the Panzers had managed to acquire at least fifty kilometers of French territory in less than a day.

Jimmie's mouth turned dry as he peered at the landscape ahead of the Panzers. *Good Lord! There's nothing in the way to stop them!*

Cobber's voice boomed over the radio, "Bandits—three o'clock! Green and Red Sections—tally-ho!"

"Tally-ho!" Jimmie accelerated his Hurricane into a swarm of Messerschmitt Bf 110s—twin-engined fighter-bombers—that was far bigger than any enemy squadron he'd encountered before. He engaged an enemy aircraft that was veering toward a Fairey Battle. He moved the control stick to bring the Messerschmitt into his sight and fired his machine guns. Bullets struck its tail, sending the German aircraft into an uncontrolled steep dive. He banked to the right and targeted another Messerschmitt.

For minutes, the battle raged in the sky. Cobber and Fanny each shot down two 110s, but a Fairey Battle was destroyed and another fled away with a damaged wing. The remaining bombers dropped their payloads, much of which missed the Panzers that were traveling at a high rate of speed over the French fields.

As the bombers turned to fly back to the base, a Messerschmitt closed in on the tail of Fanny's Hurricane. Jimmie, determined to aid his friend, veered to the right and dived toward the dogfight. But before he could get within range, the German pilot unloaded a round of machine gun fire that punctured the engine of Fanny's Hurricane. Smoke poured over the aircraft.

"Fanny!" Jimmie swooped in and fired. Bullets sprayed near the Messerschmitt and it turned away. He peered down at his friend's plane as it lost altitude. A feeling of helplessness filled his chest.

The nose of the plane tipped toward the ground and Fanny bailed out. Seconds later, his parachute opened and he drifted toward the ground.

Thank God. Jimmie sucked in deep breaths of air through his oxygen mask.

"Behind you, Jimmie!" Cobber shouted.

Bullets shot over the left wing of Jimmie's aircraft. His adrenaline surged. He slewed to the right and glanced behind him, revealing a Messerschmitt locked in on his tail. His pulse pounded in his eardrums as he pulled up sharply, pinning his body to his seat. He veered to the northwest and accelerated, attempting to outrun his pursuer. He rolled to the left, and then to the right, but the German pilot remained on his tail. Bullets shattered his cockpit glass and pierced the engine compartment. Flames erupted and spewed over the exterior of his cockpit, and thick smoke blocked his view. With no hope of landing, he pulled the handle to the canopy. It slid a few inches and became lodged in its bullet-riddled frame.

"Get out!" Cobber shouted.

Jimmie, his heart pounding his rib cage, tugged harder on the enclosure of his cockpit but it remained frozen. His plane lost altitude, and he felt the loss of gravity as his stomach rose into his chest. With no other choice, he released the control stick and clasped the canopy handle with both hands. Heat from the flames scorched his gloves as he fought to pry it open. His plane rolled into an inverted dive and smoke engulfed the cockpit. Refusing to give up, he gave a final heave and the canopy slid several inches. He released his safety harness and tried to bail out, but his torso attached to the seat parachute wouldn't fit through the opening.

CHAPTER 15

HIRSON, FRANCE—MAY 15, 1940

Ruth opened the rear doors of her ambulance and climbed inside to a malodor of sweat and infected wounds. Four injured soldiers, three French and one British, were curled on bunks. She and Lucette had transported the men from a Catholic convent near Liart, where nuns were caring for maimed soldiers until they could be evacuated to a hospital.

Ruth kneeled to a shirtless British Expeditionary Force soldier with bandages covering his right shoulder. "Are you able to walk?"

"A little," he said, his voice hoarse.

She placed an arm around his back, got him to his feet, and helped him shuffle to the rear of the ambulance. Lucette and a hospital orderly, who were standing at the back of the ambulance, assisted him to the ground. The soldier, rather than being ushered inside the infirmary, was placed in a large military truck to be transferred to a base hospital in Arras.

The hospital in Hirson, like her two previous army medical facilities, had been ordered to evacuate. Due to lack of ambulances, Ruth and Lucette had been operating as a team by co-driving Ruth's vehicle. The German military, after they'd broken through the Meuse Line at Sedan, did not advance toward Paris. Instead, their Panzers stormed northward toward the English Channel. The German tanks, supported by thousands of Luftwaffe aircraft, were destroying everything in their path. And, for the past few days, Ruth and Lucette had been racing to evacuate injured Allied soldiers while fighting to stay one step ahead of Hitler's forces.

Ruth, her back muscles aching from fatigue, lifted the end of a stretcher. She helped Lucette and the orderly to place the last soldier into the transport vehicle, and then returned to her ambulance.

"How are you holding up?" Lucette asked.

"I'm all right." Ruth leaned against the driver's door of the ambulance. She'd consumed little food over the past few days, and her once form-fitting uniform sagged on her frame.

"You should eat something," Lucette said.

"I will after we transport the remaining soldiers from the convent." She stood up straight, attempting to shake off her fatigue. "Ready to go?"

Lucette nodded.

"Hold up!" A gray-haired French Army sergeant with sweat stains on the armpits of his tunic jogged to them. "We've received orders to redeploy six ambulance units—yours is one of them."

"Are we being sent to Arras?" Lucette asked.

"*Non*," the sergeant said. "To the English Channel."

Ruth's eyes widened. "What's happening?"

He handed Ruth a slip of paper. "I was informed that there's a need to station ambulance units near the coast. Your orders are to report to a field hospital in Dunkirk."

Ruth glanced at the paper that contained their names, the unit number of their ambulance, and the location of their new post. "When do we leave?"

"Immediately," he said.

Ruth swallowed. "But we need to evacuate three wounded men from Liart."

"We have our orders," the sergeant said. "Hopefully, another unit will get them on their way in from the field."

"We have no radios to communicate their position. We're the only unit that has been going to the convent—the others will have no reason to go there." Ruth placed her hands on her hips. "We can't leave them out there."

"I have my orders," he said.

"It won't take us long," Lucette pleaded. "We'll be back before the hospital is evacuated."

He lowered his eyes and rubbed the back of his neck.

"If you had an injured family member in Liart," Ruth said, "would you allow us to go?"

"That has nothing to do with it," he said.

"It has everything to do with it," Ruth said, holding her ground. "There are three wounded soldiers who are risking their lives to protect their families and France. They're in the path of the German Army, and they're counting on us to save them."

The lines on the sergeant's face softened. "All right, but if I'm questioned by an officer about this, I'll have no choice but to tell them that I gave you the order and you disobeyed it."

"Fair enough," Ruth said. "*Merci.*"

The sergeant turned and left.

Ruth got behind the wheel while Lucette jumped into the passenger seat. She started the engine, threw the vehicle in gear, and sped away.

They left Hirson and maneuvered over roads, clogged with fleeing French citizens. The Luftwaffe, in addition to dropping bombs on military targets, had raided small towns and villages to force people to flee their homes, which congested the roads and stalled the French military's ability to deploy troops and weaponry. Ruth veered around an elderly man and woman, each laboring to push a bicycle weighted down with travel bags hanging from the handlebars.

"What kind of person would order planes to bomb innocent civilians?" Lucette asked.

"A monster." Anger surged through Ruth. She honked the vehicle's horn and weaved her way through the throngs of people.

Forty minutes later, they approached the village of Liart. To the southeast, clouds of smoke filled the horizon and explosions echoed like thunder over the rolling, rural terrain.

Ruth tightened her grip on the steering wheel. "They're much closer than before."

Lucette rolled down the passenger window and leaned her head to listen.

"How far away do you think they are?" Ruth asked.

"Six kilometers. Maybe less."

Tank cannons boomed in the distance. Lucette rolled up the window and clenched the hem of her wool skirt.

"Are you okay?"

"It's the tank guns," Lucette said, her voice quavering. "I'm worried about Paul."

Ruth's heart ached. For the past several days, they'd inquired often about the whereabouts of the 503rd Combat Tank Regiment, in which Paul served as a commander. His battalion would likely have been deployed to the Ardennes to defend against the German Panzers, but none of the medics, soldiers, or army hospital staff could provide them with any news.

"We must have hope that he's safe." Ruth clasped Lucette's hand. "He's going to be all right."

She squeezed her fingers and blinked away tears. "*Oui*, he will."

The village of Liart was deserted, save for a woman who was loading three young children into a horse-drawn wagon that was lined with a mattress and blankets. Ruth turned onto a cobblestone street and parked the ambulance in front of a large stone convent that was partially covered in thick, green ivy. They jumped out of their vehicle to the sound of tank gunfire, louder and closer than before. Hairs rose on the back of Ruth's neck as she and Lucette ran to the entrance and rapped on the door.

A lock clicked and the door opened to reveal Sister Odette, a hazel-eyed nun of no more than eighteen or nineteen years of age.

"I'm sorry it took us so long," Ruth said. "How are the soldiers?"

Sister Odette cupped her hands. "The soldiers are in stable condition, but we moved them. The sound of explosions has gotten much closer. We were worried that you might not get here in time."

"Where are they?" Lucette asked.

"Sister Céline enlisted the help of a farmer with a truck. It was the last remaining fueled vehicle in the area. They left thirty minutes ago to take the soldiers to the hospital in Hirson. I pray we did the right thing."

"You did," Ruth said. "They'll get there before us, and before the hospital is evacuated."

"Thank you for caring for them," Lucette said.

Sister Odette nodded.

Cannon fire boomed a few kilometers away.

Odette raised her head toward an arched ceiling of the entrance hall.

"The sisters of the convent need to evacuate," Ruth said.

"We're servants of God," she said. "No harm will come to us."

"We've seen firsthand what the Germans are doing," Ruth said. "They're bombing villages. Civilians are being injured and killed."

"We must stay," Sister Odette said. "There will likely be others who will seek sanctuary with the church."

Ruth and Lucette attempted to persuade Odette to flee, but she held firm with her decision to remain at the convent.

Odette clasped a wooden cross, worn on a string around her neck. "May God support you in danger."

"*Merci*," Ruth said.

Ruth and Lucette exited the convent, got into their ambulance, and drove away. Leaving Liart, Ruth turned onto an unmarked, narrow back road that bordered an open field.

"Is this a faster route?"

"I don't know," Ruth said. "But, according to our map, it travels in the right direction."

"At least, for now, there are no crowds on the road," Lucette said. "We might make better time."

"I hope so."

"How is our fuel?"

Ruth glanced at the gauge. "It's getting low. We'll need to refuel before we get to Hirson."

They had two fuel cans, one of which was empty, in the rear of the ambulance. The mass exodus of civilians generated a hoarding of petrol. Now, most of the service stations were abandoned or out of fuel, and the only means of getting more petrol was through the French military.

The roar of airplane engines grew.

Ruth leaned forward and peered up through the windshield. To the east, a swarm of fighter planes were battling in the sky. Machine guns barked as the aircraft rolled and twisted through the air.

"French?" Lucette asked.

Ruth strained her eyes and recognized the roundels of the Royal Air Force. "British."

An RAF fighter veered away from the pack, and it was pursued by a German aircraft. The British pilot ascended, turned, and dived his plane in an attempt to shake the enemy fighter from his tail. But as seconds passed, the German pilot closed the space between their planes.

"Please get away," Ruth breathed.

A burst of machine gun fire erupted from the German fighter, and smoke poured from the RAF plane. The damaged aircraft lost altitude and, within a few seconds, it rolled into an inverted dive.

"*Non!*" Lucette shouted.

Ruth squeezed the steering wheel and prayed to see a parachute open. But the plane continued its plummet with no sign of the pilot bailing out.

"Jump!" Lucette shouted.

Ruth's breath stalled in her lungs. The front wheels of the ambulance rumbled over the berm. As she turned the wheel, getting the vehicle back on the road, they passed a dense area of towering pines that obstructed their view. She slammed the accelerator and raced ahead. As they arrived at a clearing, a solitary plume of smoke rose from behind a hill. The German pilot circled his aircraft once over the area, as if to confirm his kill, and headed toward the massive dogfight that raged on the horizon.

"Did he get out?" Ruth asked.

"I couldn't tell."

A tank gun exploded, less than a few kilometers away. Startled starlings flew from trees and blackened the sky above a field.

Ruth pressed the brake and slowed the ambulance to a stop.

She peered in the direction where the plane went down. "What do you want to do?"

"We need to see if he survived."

"I agree."

Lucette pulled a well-worn map from under her seat. She scanned it, and ran a finger over a route. "Up ahead, there looks to be an unpaved road. It should take us near the accident site."

Ruth sped ahead. Reaching what turned out to be a dirt lane that ran between two sprawling farms, she turned right. Ruts and potholes jostled them in their seats. Soon, they passed an old farmhouse with the front door wide open, as if the owner had hastily fled. At the end of the lane, a wooden gate blocked the entrance to a large, upward-sloping grass field.

Lucette pointed. "The gate has a chain and padlock."

"Hold on." She pressed the accelerator.

Lucette placed her hands on the dashboard.

The front bumper of the ambulance smashed through the wooden gate, shattering one of the vehicle's headlamps and sending broken boards over the ground.

Ruth downshifted and drove the ambulance up the hill.

"That way!" Lucette said, pointing.

She adjusted the wheel and continued the climb. At the summit of the hill, she stopped the vehicle under the branches of two thick beech trees for camouflage, and gazed over the landscape. From her high vantage point, she spotted the smoldering wreckage of the RAF aircraft, two hundred meters away. To the east and a kilometer away, two divisions of Panzer tanks—separated by a series of hills—were headed in their direction. She clenched the wheel to keep her hands from trembling.

"My God," Lucette said. "There are hundreds of them."

Ruth fought away her fear and turned her attention to the wreckage. "Do you see the pilot?"

Lucette looked at the smoke, drifting from the plane debris. "*Non*. I hope he got out. No one could survive that."

Ruth scanned a forest beyond the aircraft ruins, and her eyes locked on a piece of white material that protruded from a pine. "There!"

Lucette placed a hand above her eyes and squinted. "I see a parachute."

"Can you spot him?"

"*Non.*" Lucette glanced at the tanks, rolling over the hills and closing in on their location. "Can we make it there in time?"

"We'll have to."

Before either of them could change their mind, Ruth threw the vehicle into gear and sped down the meadow, placing them into the path of the advancing Panzers.

CHAPTER 16

LIART, FRANCE—MAY 15, 1940

Ruth barreled the ambulance down the sloping, grass-covered field, all the while praying that they wouldn't be spotted. The steering wheel juddered in her hands as the vehicle rumbled over the rough terrain. Within seconds, the ambulance neared the base of the hill, placing them out of view from the Panzers.

"Do you think they saw us?" Lucette asked.

"I don't know, but we'll soon find out if they did."

The terrain leveled off and Ruth veered the vehicle past the smoldering remains of the fighter plane, filling her nose with an acrid stench of burning aviation fuel. As she accelerated through an area of high grass, her hope of finding the airman faded at the sight of a large crevice.

"Brake!" Lucette shouted.

Ruth slammed the pedal and the ambulance skidded to a stop a few feet from a narrow but steep earthen incline. Beneath the hum of the idling engine, a sound of rippling water filled the air. With their focus on avoiding the Panzers and finding the pilot, they failed to notice a thin but deep runoff that cut through the base of the meadow.

Leaving the engine running, they got out of the vehicle and peered along the embankment of the stream, searching for a section that might be passable for their vehicle's ground clearance.

"It's too steep—we'll get stuck if we try to cross." Ruth glanced at the forest. "I'm going to wade over and search for him."

"I'm coming with you," Lucette said, making her way to the ledge.

They climbed down the slope and sloshed across knee-high deep water, soaking their shoes and hems of their skirts. Dirt and slivers of limestone dug into their palms as they ascended the opposite bank. They clambered to the high ground and darted into the forest where they'd sighted the parachute.

Lucette sucked in air, attempting to catch her breath, and scanned the trees.

Ruth pushed away prickly briars with the sleeves of her uniform and trekked deeper into the woodland.

A branch creaked.

Ruth peered up. Her eyes widened at the sight of a pilot—dangling from the cords of a deflated parachute and pointing a revolver. "Don't shoot!" she shouted in English. "We're French."

The airman lowered his revolver. "Sorry. I heard an engine. I needed to make sure you weren't Wehrmacht."

Lucette ran to Ruth's side and looked up at the pilot. "We haven't much time—the Panzers are coming this way. Can you get down?"

He winced as he slipped the revolver into his flight jacket. "My left arm is broken—I'm having trouble getting out of the harness." Using his good hand, he struggled to release a round, four-point safety buckle.

Ruth looked at the airman, three to four meters above her head. "I'll come up and help you." She turned to Lucette. "Give me a boost."

Lucette kneeled at the base of the pine and clasped her fingers.

Ruth placed a foot into her hands.

Lucette stood, lifting her friend.

Ruth raised her hands, grabbed a thick limb, and hoisted her right leg over it. She sat upright and climbed several limbs to the pilot, who appeared to be in his mid-twenties. Beads of sweat covered his upper lip, and a tuft of brown hair protruded from underneath his flight helmet.

He tried to adjust his limp left arm and grimaced. "You're a brilliant climber," he said, his voice filled with pain.

"I grew up on an apple orchard." Ruth clasped the man's harness. "Tell me what to do."

"Turn the disc clockwise to unlock it—then press to release the buckles."

She twisted the metal disc, producing a click. "Ready?"

He gripped the harness in his right hand. "Yes."

She pressed the disc, simultaneously releasing four buckles, and the airman slipped from the harness.

He dangled, gripping a harness strap with his good arm, and then dropped to the ground and rolled. Ruth climbed down from the tree while Lucette helped the pilot to his feet.

Explosions and gunfire echoed through the forest.

"They are getting much closer." Ruth looked at the pilot, clasping his left arm. "Can you run?"

"Yes." He removed his flight helmet and tossed it into the underbrush. "Lead the way."

They fled the forest to the stream. Lucette and Ruth aided the airman down and up the steep slopes, put him in the back of the idling ambulance, and then got into their seats.

Ruth put the vehicle in reverse and backed it away from the ledge. She shifted gears and pressed the pedal to the floor, surging the ambulance up the hill. Her anxiety grew as she peered at her side mirror. Halfway through the ascent, a group of Panzers—crossing the summit of the hill behind them—came into view. Her arms trembled. "They're behind—"

A tank gun fired and a shell exploded in front of their ambulance, spraying the windshield with a rain of dirt.

Lucette shielded her face with her arm.

"Hold on!" Ruth veered right, taking a diagonal route up the hill.

Two shells exploded near the ambulance. The driver's-side window shattered, sending bits of glass over the compartment.

Ruth, her ears ringing, fought to keep her foot on the accelerator and plowed the ambulance up the meadow.

Lucette pointed. "That way!"

Ruth drove the vehicle over the crest of the hill, turned sharply onto the dirt lane, and sped away. The tank fire ceased, and she hoped that they'd got away. But when they reached the main road, they spotted more Panzers that were flanking their position. With no other alternative, they fled in the opposite direction, a route that would place them deeper into the path of the German invasion.

CHAPTER 17

SIGNY-L'ABBAYE, FRANCE—MAY 15, 1940

Jimmie—clutching his arm, throbbing with pain—peered through the windshield from his seat in the back of the ambulance. A setting sun gave rise to a volcanic-like glow between masses of black clouds, and echoing explosions filtered through the cab's broken window. He helplessly watched the driver maneuver through rural back roads, following instructions of the woman in the passenger seat who was reading a map.

The driver veered the ambulance off the road. Tires crunched over dry leaves and fallen limbs. The vehicle slowed to a stop, the driver turned off the engine, and the women got out and opened the rear doors.

"Hurry," Ruth said, plucking a medical kit from the rear of the ambulance.

A pang pierced through his wrist and forearm as he climbed out of the ambulance. He clasped his arm to his stomach and scanned the surroundings. The vehicle was parked in a lush thicket, concealing the front and sides. Beyond the rear of the ambulance was a dirt road that led to a small river and a stone building, which appeared to be an abandoned water mill. "Where are we?"

"Signy-l'Abbaye," Lucette said, placing a map and an electric torch on the ground.

An explosion reverberated over the rural landscape.

"Why did we stop?" Jimmie asked.

"The French Army is nowhere in sight," Ruth said. "There are German tanks ahead of us, and the ones behind us are gaining ground. I think we're surrounded."

"Are there any routes we can take to avoid them?" he asked.

"*Non*," Ruth said. "We're going to hide and let them pass us by." She darted from the roadside and joined Lucette by pulling branches and ferns from the undergrowth and placing them against the back of the ambulance.

Ruddy hell—we have no choice but to dig in. Using his good arm, he helped rip away foliage and placed it over the ambulance until it was completely concealed.

He followed them to a two-story stone mill that had not been used in decades, given the broken windowpanes and the motionless waterwheel that was clogged with logs and mounds of driftwood. Despite the mill not being in use, the entrance was locked. Jimmie kicked the door—stinging the nerves in his arm—but it didn't budge. It took several more blows, all more painful than the first, for the lock to break.

Inside the place was empty, save a wooden crate, a large stone grain wheel covered in dust and cobwebs, and stacks of musty burlap sacks.

Jimmie, his faced drenched with sweat, turned and faced them. "Thank you for saving me. My name is Jimmie."

"I'm Ruth." She gestured with her hand. "This is Lucette. We're drivers with the ambulance corps of the French Army."

"My French isn't the best," Jimmie said. "But I can speak it if you wish."

"No need," Lucette said. "I'm fluent in English."

"You're lucky to be alive," Ruth said. "We saw your plane being shot down and weren't sure if you got out."

"I almost didn't." A memory of using his arm as a pry bar flashed in his brain. He placed a hand over the opposite sleeve of his flight jacket. "I fractured a bone while dislodging my cockpit canopy to bail out."

Ruth placed the medical kit on the floor and approached him. "Let's see your arm."

Jimmie unzipped his flight jacket and, with her help, carefully removed it. He unbuttoned his sleeve and slid it over his elbow to reveal an acorn-size bulge—below the wrist—on the thumb side of his forearm.

Ruth gently examined his arm and ran a finger over the protuberance. "It's definitely a fracture."

Lucette leaned in. "It's fortunate that the skin isn't broken. It looks like it could possibly be fixed without surgery."

"*Oui.*" Ruth looked at Jimmie. "We're out of morphine, so it's going to hurt when we set it."

Jimmie shifted his weight. "Perhaps we should make sure that we are safe before treating my arm."

Ruth shook her head. "It's best that we stabilize your injury while we have the chance."

"She's right," Lucette said. "And with German tanks storming over the countryside, it might take days to escape from the area and reach a doctor."

He stared at the bulge on his arm, from where a gnawing pain spread through his wrist and fingers. *I can't very well leave it like this.* "All right."

Jimmie, following Ruth's instruction, sat on the ground and leaned his back against the wall. The cold stone penetrated through his flight suit, sending a chill through his body.

"You're taller than me," Ruth said to Lucette. "It might be best that you apply the tension to his arm while I try to set it."

"I agree." Lucette sat on the floor facing him.

"Have you set many broken bones?" Jimmie asked.

"*Non*," Ruth said, kneeling beside him. "You're our first."

He swallowed. "Are you sure that you're up to this?"

Ruth nodded.

"We've seen medics do it," Lucette said.

His pulse quickened. "Very well—let's do this."

"Lucette is going to apply traction to your arm," Ruth said, "and I'm going to work the bone back into place."

Lucette removed her shoes, gently clasped the hand of Jimmie's injured arm, and then placed a foot to his armpit.

Ruth looked into his eyes. "Ready?"

He took a deep breath. "Ready."

Lucette pushed his armpit with her leg while pulling his hand toward her stomach.

Pain pierced his wrist. His muscles spasmed.

"Keep your arm relaxed," Ruth said, holding his forearm.

Jimmie closed his eyes and fought to keep his muscles from contracting.

Lucette tugged harder.

Ruth, using her thumbs, pressed on the bulge.

Pain surged through his arm. His stomach felt nauseous, producing the urge to vomit.

Ruth grimaced as she applied more pressure. "A little more."

Lucette stretched her leg and leaned back.

A muffled crack, like a stick being snapped inside a towel, pierced the air.

"Got it," Ruth said.

Lucette eased off and lowered her foot from his armpit. "Don't move."

Jimmie nodded and sucked in air. He glanced at his arm, filled with ache. His wrist and forearm were swollen but the lump was no longer visible.

Ruth and Lucette constructed a splint with bandages and broken pieces of wood from an old crate. They tied the splint securely to his arm and made a sling from a long strip of bandage with the ends tied together.

"How does it feel?" Ruth asked, adjusting the sling around his neck.

"Much better." He looked at them. "Thank you."

"You're welcome," Ruth said. "Rest a little. Lucette and I are going to have a look around."

He slowly got to his feet. "I'll join you."

"All right," Ruth said. "But be careful not to jostle your arm."

The trio explored the mill. The upper floor was empty and had a solitary window with a view that was blocked by an overgrown willow tree. A cellar, accessed by a ladder that was missing two rungs, had a damp earthen floor and no windows. They reached a consensus that the main level was the safest option, given that it provided escape routes through the door and windows. But they remained in the cellar to read a map with the aid of an electric torch, so the light could not be spotted by the Germans.

"Can you show me where we are?" Jimmie asked.

Lucette placed her finger on the map. "Here—north of Signy-l'Abbaye."

Ruth looked at Jimmie. "Tell us what you saw before you were shot down."

Jimmie eyed the map and ran a finger from Sedan to Signy-l'Abbaye. "There are at least three Panzer divisions that broke through the line at Sedan. They are south of us and traveling toward the Channel."

Lucette clasped her arms.

He ran his finger from Nouzonville to Liart. "Several kilometers to the north, there are two more Panzer divisions traveling in the same direction. And further north, more German tanks broke through at Houx."

"My God," Ruth said. "How could this have happened so fast?"

Jimmie stared at the map. "The German Army invaded in the most unlikely place—the Ardennes Forest—which was viewed to be impassible for Panzers, so it was the least defended area of the line. The Wehrmacht was supported by an armada of Luftwaffe aircraft, and their aerial bombardments overwhelmed French infantry." Anger surged through him. "The French and British lost many planes and airmen."

Ruth drew a deep breath and clasped her hands.

"Tell me what you know about the French tanks," Lucette said, her voice fragile.

"Some of their divisions were destroyed," he said, "and the Panzers are moving past them at lightning speed."

Tears formed in Lucette's eyes.

Ruth placed an arm around her shoulder. "We must have faith that Paul's unit isn't one of them. He's going to be all right."

Jimmie's heart sank. He looked at Lucette, her face filled with angst. "Is Paul your husband?"

"Fiancé."

"There are many French tanks that remain intact," Jimmie

said, trying to restore her hope. "They're fighting to get back into position to halt the invasion."

Lucette nodded and wiped away tears.

Ruth rubbed a hand over her friend's back, as if to comfort her, and then looked at Jimmie. "Assuming we can get out of here, which direction do you think we should go?"

"If the French Army can slow the progress of the Panzers, we might be able to head west. If not, the only route to safety will be to the south." He pointed to the map. "My airfield is in Reims, about sixty kilometers south of our location. If we can get there, we'll have protection from Allied forces."

"But we have orders to go to the Channel," Ruth said. "Our new post is in Dunkirk. There are soldiers counting on us."

She's brave and committed to her duties, he thought, *but a journey from here to the Channel will likely be impossible.*

A crack of gunfire resounded through the countryside.

Jimmie tried to straighten his swollen fingers, sending a twinge through his arm. "How about we see how things go tonight and decide what to do at dawn?"

Lucette nodded.

"Okay," Ruth said, folding the map. "There's nothing more that we can do for now. Let's get some rest. We can take turns with one of us remaining awake. I'll take the first shift on lookout."

"I don't mind staying on watch," Jimmie said.

Ruth shook her head. "You need to sit back and prop up your arm, otherwise the swelling will get worse and we don't want to risk having to reset your fracture."

"Very well," he said, reluctantly. "But I insist on taking a shift."

Ruth nodded.

Lucette turned off the electric torch, and they climbed the ladder to the first floor. Moonlight, coming through a shattered window, cast inky shadows over the mill. Once their eyes grew acclimated to the darkness, they placed burlap sacks on the floor to create sleeping mats. Ruth sat on the ground and peered through the front door, which was slightly open, while Jimmie and Lucette settled onto individual mats.

Jimmie lay on his back and elevated his splinted arm by propping it on his chest with the padding of his folded flight jacket. The throbbing in his wrist and hand gradually softened. He took a deep inhale, bringing in a dank odor of mildewed burlap. Soon, his mind drifted to the members of No. 73 Squadron, and he prayed that Fanny had safely bailed out of his downed Hurricane and made it back to the airfield. He thought of Lucette and hoped that her fiancé was among the French tank battalions that were not destroyed. Most of all, he worried about the innocent French civilians who were under siege, and the British people whose country would likely be the next target in Hitler's quest to conquer Europe.

Jimmie glanced at Ruth, standing watch by the entrance. *Canadian? American?* He was grateful for her decisiveness to set his arm, and he wondered, although briefly, about her motivation to join the ambulance corps. He closed his eyes and vowed to recover from his injury and return to the battles in the sky. Instead of sleeping, he listened to explosions, trying to estimate the distance from the enemy.

CHAPTER 18

SIGNY-L'ABBAYE, FRANCE—MAY 15, 1940

Jimmie, his arm aching, slowly sat up and looked to a window that faced the river. The sound of bombs and gunfire had stopped, and the night air was silent, except for babbles of water against the mill's broken waterwheel. He glanced at his watch, worn on his good wrist. *Ruth has been on lookout for over two hours.* He placed his flight jacket over his shoulder and stood, being careful not to move his splinted arm or to disturb Lucette, who was sleeping on an adjacent bed of burlap. He crept to Ruth and sat on the ground beside her.

"I thought you were going to wake us," he said, his voice soft.

"Lucette needs some shut-eye," she said. "She hasn't slept for nearly two days. And you need to take it easy."

"I'll prop up my arm while I keep watch," he said. "You must be knackered. Go and get some rest, and I'll take over for a while."

She shook her head, then peered outside through the slightly opened door. "I can't sleep knowing that they're out there—somewhere."

"Do you mind if I join you?"

"No."

He touched his sling. "You did a good job with setting my arm. The splint feels sturdy."

"I'm glad," she said. "Most of the credit should go to Lucette.

Without her height and strength to apply traction to your arm, I wouldn't have been able to set the broken bone."

A memory of Lucette, pulling his wrist while pushing his underarm with her heel, flashed in his mind. "I'm grateful to both of you."

She nodded. "How's the pain?"

"It's manageable," Jimmie said, downplaying the ache in his wrist. He adjusted his sling, rubbing the skin on the back of his neck. "Based on your English dialect, I'm thinking that you might be Canadian."

"Close," she said. "I'm American—born and raised in Lewiston, Maine, not far from the border with Canada. How about you?"

"Portsmouth, England." He looked at her. "I thought the United States Neutrality Act restricted its citizens from serving in the war."

"It does," she said, "but I came to France before the war started."

"To join the French Army?"

"No, and don't let my uniform fool you. I'm not an enlisted member of the army, I'm a civilian volunteer."

"I see."

"Actually," she said, turning to him, "I moved to Paris to pursue a singing career."

He straightened his back. "What type of music?"

"Mostly cabaret—but my passion is jazz, swing, and big band music."

"Sounds brilliant." He raised his eyes to the dark ceiling. "My sister, Nora, is quite fond of American jazz. She has a Duke Ellington record—its grooves are worn out from being overplayed. American recordings are expensive to replace, so she taped a coin to her gramophone's stylus to keep the needle from skipping."

"Nora sounds like a clever girl—and she has good taste in music."

"Indeed."

"Do you know the name of the song?"

He rubbed his chin, covered with stubble. "Something with St. Louis in the title."

"It's called 'East St. Louis Toodle-Oo.' I have that record, too. It's at my parents' home in Maine."

For several minutes, she told him about leaving her family's apple orchard to live with her aunt and uncle in Paris to chase a dream to perform at the Casino de Paris. For the first time in weeks, Jimmie's thoughts drifted from the war, and he became less aware of the gnawing pain in his arm.

"My dad was reluctant for me to go to France," she said, "until I convinced him that the Casino de Paris was a music hall—not a gambling house."

He felt a tug at the corners of his mouth and realized he was smiling.

"It was tough landing gigs, and I eventually worked my way to a singing role at a cabaret called Bal Tabarin. That's where I met Lucette."

"Is she also a singer?"

"No, she's a dancer." She rubbed her arms and shivered.

He slipped his flight jacket from his shoulder and removed the revolver, which he placed inside his tunic. "Put this on," he said, handing her the jacket. "The temperature has dropped."

"But you'll be cold."

"I'm fine, really. Besides, I have my sling to keep me warm."

"All right." She slipped on his jacket. "Thank you."

He glanced outside to the empty dirt road, illuminated by moonlight. "So, how did you and Lucette come to join the ambulance corps?"

"It's a long story."

"It's quite all right," he said. "I'd like to hear it, assuming you are willing to tell me."

"Okay." She paused, raising the zipper on the jacket. "My cousin, Marceau, joined the French Army before the conflict. While we were growing up, he spent several summers working on my family's orchard in Maine. We were close—more like siblings than cousins."

A dreadful feeling settled into his gut.

Ruth lowered her head. "Marceau was stationed at the Maginot

Line. He was killed in the Saar Offensive, near Saarbrücken, Germany. His body was never recovered."

"I'm so sorry."

"Thanks." She drew a deep breath and exhaled, as if she were trying to bury the memory. "After the news about Marceau, I lost my desire for music, and I wanted to honor his death by serving France. So, when I heard that women were being recruited by the French Army to drive ambulances, I worked my way into the corps."

"And Lucette came with you."

"Yes. Her fiancé, Paul, is serving as a tank commander. Like him, she wanted to support France and make a difference in the war."

"You both are." He looked at Ruth. "Marceau would be proud of you."

"You really think so?"

"I do."

She rubbed her eyes, then slipped her hands into the pockets of the flight jacket. She paused, peeking through the ajar door. "May I ask you something?"

"Of course."

"What's in the right pocket of your jacket?"

"A good luck charm," he said. "Pilots are a superstitious bunch. Most of us carry a charm, trinket, or medallion. Mine is a bit unique. You're welcome to have a look."

Ruth slipped it from the pocket and held it under a beam of pale moonlight that was cast over the floor. "It looks like a tiny stuffed pig."

"Piglet," he said. "It's a gift from Nora. She was—and still is—quite a fan of the children's book *Winnie-the-Pooh*."

"It's a splendid story." She ran a thumb over Piglet's head. "He brought you good fortune today."

"I suppose he did, if you believe in that sort of thing."

"I do. While growing up, I had a horseshoe mounted over the doorway to my room, and my parents kept a barnstar on the front of the cider house." She tilted her head. "Do you believe objects can bring people good luck?"

Jimmie ran a hand over his hair. "I think that a charm can represent different things to different people—good luck, safe travel, protection, and to ward against evil. But to me, this toy represents hope."

She looked at him. "What kind of hope?"

"A dream of a better future, and a belief that anything can be accomplished through perseverance and optimism." He patted Piglet. "That little guy got my sister through the worst of times, and with me going off to war, she thought that he could do the same for me."

Her eyes softened. She slipped the stuffed toy back inside the jacket pocket. "Do you mind telling me about Nora?"

"Not at all. She—"

The ground vibrated.

Ruth's eyes widened, and she got to her feet.

Lucette woke and sat up on her mat of burlap. "What's happening?"

Jimmie, his adrenaline surging, peeked through the doorway. A clacking of steel plates emanated from the road. "Tanks."

Ruth stashed the map and electric torch into the medical bag. "Are they French?"

Jimmie squinted, and his eyes locked on the silhouette of a Panzer—identifiable by its short-barreled, howitzer-like main gun. Within seconds, another tank emerged from the darkness and rumbled over the dirt road.

Jimmie turned. "German."

Ruth and Lucette darted to a window that faced the river.

Jimmie, remaining at the door, hoped that the enemy tanks would pass them by and continue their route. But as the lead tank neared the mill, it came to a stop and its steel hatch opened. A commander, wearing a radio headset over his cap, stood and waved his arms at the approaching tank.

Damn it. Jimmie shuffled to them and whispered, "They're stopping."

Lucette unlocked the window that faced the river. She tried lifting the sash, but it didn't move. "It's stuck," she breathed.

Jimmie and Ruth joined Lucette in trying to open the window, but its wood was severely warped from years of water damage and the sash remained frozen.

Guttural voices came from outside.

Hairs rose on the back of Jimmie's neck. He slipped his weapon from his tunic and motioned for them to break the glass and flee to the river.

Ruth shook her head and pointed to a hinged wood panel—the size of a hay bale—near the axle to the waterwheel. She undid a hook latch and opened the board, revealing a service opening to the waterwheel.

Jimmie faced the front door and raised his weapon.

Lucette scurried through the hole, feet first, and climbed onto the waterwheel.

Men's laughter grew.

Jimmie looked at Ruth and motioned to the opening.

Ruth, carrying the bag with their things, crawled through the hole and onto the waterwheel. She handed the bag to Lucette, who climbed down the paddles and lowered herself into the water.

Jimmie stashed his weapon into his tunic and sat. He scooched on his bottom and placed his feet on a wooden paddle of the waterwheel. Using his good arm and both legs, he clambered down the structure. On the next to last paddle, his boots slipped on a thick film of algae, and he grabbed the metal rail to keep from falling. As he dangled with one hand, he fought to regain his footing and banged his shoulder against the wheel. A piercing pang shot through his arm.

Ruth and Lucette, each submerged to their neck, reached up and clasped his ankles.

Jimmie, with their help, regained his foothold. He descended the last paddle and slipped into the frigid water as the mill's front door screeched open.

Jackboots clacked over the wood floor of the mill. Light flashed from the window above them.

They floated to a large mound of logs, branches, and driftwood that was lodged against the waterwheel and prevented it from spinning. They dropped under the water, worked their way inside the interior of the debris, and poked up their faces to breathe.

Jimmie's sling tangled on a branch. He pulled it free and peered upward through their hiding nest.

A German soldier stuck his head out of the service opening and scanned the waterwheel with an electric torch.

They submerged their bodies.

Light flickered over the surface of the river. Jimmie, his open eyes burning from the silt-filled water, watched a beam flash directly above them. As his oxygen dwindled, his lungs began to heave, and he fought to stay submerged. His pulse pounded inside his eardrums. A minute later, the light vanished.

They rose to the surface and silently drew in air. Voices of men, speaking German, filtered through the mill.

Jimmie, his body temperature plummeting, worked his way out of the debris. His soaked flight suit and boots weighted his body like a lead blanket. He huddled together with Ruth and Lucette, and they allowed the river to sweep them away. But as they floated downstream, three more Panzers rumbled past them and stopped eighty meters away near a bend in the river. They labored to get to shore, but the current was too strong. With no other choice, they treaded water to stay afloat and relented to the river's flow.

Jimmie, his strength depleted, strained to keep his mouth and nose above the surface.

Ruth clasped his tunic and tried to lift his head.

Using his good arm, he pulled her close and prayed that they'd pass the Panzers without being detected.

CHAPTER 19

PARIS, FRANCE—MAY 16, 1940

Newly elected prime minister Winston Churchill exited a British military plane and walked toward one of two black Peugeot limousines that were parked near a hangar. He flew to Paris to attend an emergency meeting of the Anglo-French Supreme War Council and was accompanied by General Hastings "Pug" Ismay, Air Marshal Joubert de la Ferté, and Sir John Dill, vice-chief of the Imperial General Staff.

Churchill and Ismay—a whip-smart, brutally honest general whom Churchill selected as his chief military assistant—got into the back seat of the closest limousine while the rest of the delegation climbed into the other vehicle. As the chauffeurs drove them away from the airfield, Churchill slipped a cigar from his pocket and lit it. He puffed, filling the limousine with the smell of burnt tobacco, and listened to Ismay—a tall, broad-chested military man with meaty jowls and a neatly trimmed salt-and-pepper mustache—provide his recommendations for the meeting.

Six days earlier, when Germany launched their invasion of France, Neville Chamberlain was replaced as prime minister by Churchill. Chamberlain had lost the confidence of respected members of the Conservative Party, who criticized his overall conduct of the war and, more specifically, his handling of Norway, which was on the verge of capitulating to the German invasion.

Chamberlain was also unsuccessful with forming a coalition with the Labour Party, which declared that they would not serve under his leadership, although they did agree to accept another Conservative leader. The candidate pool for Chamberlain's successor was minuscule—Winston Churchill and Lord Halifax, the Foreign Secretary. Chamberlain preferred Lord Halifax but the man was reluctant to serve as prime minister. Therefore, Chamberlain went to Buckingham Palace where he resigned and requested the king to summon Churchill.

Despite being Chamberlain's second choice as a successor, Churchill held no resentment. He was grateful that Chamberlain took full responsibility for naval failures in Scandinavia rather than assign blame to him, given the fact that the operation was under his leadership as First Lord of the Admiralty. In the end, Chamberlain's selfless act paved a path for Churchill to fulfill his destiny of becoming prime minister.

I was born to be a warrior, Churchill had thought, standing before the House of Commons for his inaugural speech. *I've spent my entire life preparing for this moment—to lead the British people to victory in its war against tyranny.*

Churchill had no time to get acclimated to the role of prime minister. He assembled his military staff and declared that he would direct the fight from the Cabinet War Rooms, an underground bunker located deep beneath the Treasury building in the Whitehall area of Westminster. He expected Britain's battles in France and Belgium to be long and arduous, like the Great War. But his view began to change when—on his fifth day in office—he was awoken by a call from French Prime Minister Paul Reynaud.

"France is defeated," Reynaud said in English.

Churchill, assuming he'd misheard the words, pressed the receiver tight to his ear.

"The front is breached at Sedan," Reynaud said, his voice filled with distress. "We have lost the fight."

Churchill listened to the French prime minister provide an account of the battle in France, which was followed by a plea for more British fighter squadrons. He reminded Reynaud that there were many bleak moments during the Great War that seemed every bit as hopeless, but the French prime minister remained fearful that all would be lost. Churchill promised to provide additional air support and told him that he would fly to Paris the next day to meet with him. And, within hours of ending his call with Reynaud, Churchill received more grave news—the Netherlands surrendered to Germany.

Churchill rolled down a rear window of the limousine and peered at the Paris skyline and its emblematic Eiffel Tower. A burning resolve flowed through his veins. *I must find a way to bolster the French leadership. Surely their great army can't be on the brink of collapse so soon.* He flicked ash and clamped his cigar between his molars.

Minutes later, Churchill and his envoy arrived at Quai d'Orsay, the French Foreign Ministry, located in the 7th arrondissement. He exited the limousine and was escorted into a majestic, four-story limestone building by two armed French soldiers. Inside a gallery with floor-to-ceiling windows that overlooked a garden, Churchill was greeted by Reynaud, a Frenchman in his early sixties who was wearing a three-piece charcoal suit, a burgundy-colored tie, and a white handkerchief that flared from a breast pocket. The tonic in his slicked-back hair emitted a scent of eucalyptus, and his short neck gave him the appearance that his shirt collar was glued to his jaw.

"I wish we were meeting under different circumstances," Reynaud said.

"Indeed." Churchill removed his hat and shook his hand.

The British greeted their French counterparts, all of whom looked dejected. The meeting got underway with the men choosing to stand rather than sit at a large oak table.

An elderly, white-mustached general named Maurice Gamelin, who was the commander-in-chief of the French Armed Forces, walked to the front of the room where there was an easel that held a map of the Allied front. Gamelin's military tunic was decorated with rows of colorful medals, and his hand slightly trembled as he pointed to a bulge on the front line—drawn in red—at Sedan.

"The Germans broke through here," Gamelin said.

Churchill eyed the map, taking in the location of the breach, as well as the marked positions of Allied and Axis troops.

The French general spoke uninterrupted for several minutes. He described the collapse at Sedan, the catastrophic losses of French armored units, and the locations of German Panzer divisions that were moving toward the English Channel—250 kilometers away.

The British military men, their eyes wide, stared at the map.

Gamelin finished his debriefing and lowered his hands to his side.

The room fell silent.

"Where are your reserve troops?" Churchill asked in French.

Gamelin looked at Churchill. He shook his head and shrugged. "There are none."

Anger boiled inside Churchill, yet his outward appearance remained calm.

The British officers glanced at each other.

Movement outside drew Churchill's eyes to a gallery window. In the garden, smoke rose from several bonfires, where French officials were tossing wheelbarrows of papers onto the flames. *They're already planning to evacuate.* Maintaining his composure, he looked at Gamelin and asked, "When and where do you plan to attack the flanks of the German line?"

Gamelin shifted his weight. "Inadequate quantities—inadequate armament—inadequate means."

Churchill shook his head. *Inadequate French military chiefs.*

While the British military men asked questions of Gamelin, Churchill stepped aside with Prime Minister Reynaud.

"We need six more Hurricane fighter squadrons," Reynaud said.

"After we spoke yesterday, I authorized four additional squadrons to be sent to France."

"It's not enough."

Churchill's mind raced as he weighed the risk. He glanced at the map. *If the Panzers are ordered to turn south, they'll take Paris. But if they continue their current path—and the French Army is unable to slow them down—the BEF in northwest France and Belgium could be placed in peril.*

Churchill clasped the lapels of his suit jacket. "Very well. But nothing more. I need a minimum of thirty-nine fighter squadrons to defend British war industries."

"Merci," Reynaud said.

An hour later, the meeting was adjourned and Churchill and his envoy left Quai d'Orsay. He stopped at the British Embassy, where he sent a wire to London to deploy the fighter squadrons that he promised Reynaud. While he was there, he was given an envelope that contained messages. Eager to return to London, he slipped the envelope in his jacket and traveled to the airfield.

Thousands of feet above France, he opened the envelope and read his messages, one of which was a response to a request he'd made to US President Roosevelt for naval ships. He drew a deep breath and turned to General Ismay, sitting across the aisle from him. "Roosevelt says that a loan of destroyers will require an act of Congress."

"As you suspected, sir." Ismay shifted in his seat and turned to the prime minister. "I've given more thought about the decision to deploy more fighter squadrons."

Churchill set aside his messages. "You don't approve, I presume."

"That is correct, sir," Ismay said, candidly. "Given the failing state of French defenses, I think it would be prudent to keep them to protect Britain."

"If we don't provide them with more air support," Churchill said, "France could crumble as swiftly as Poland."

Ismay rubbed his chin. "With all due respect, sir, France may fall with or without more Hurricanes."

"Perhaps, but if the French Army is unable to slow the progress of the Panzers, the vast majority of our BEF troops will be at risk of being cut off and pushed into the sea. It took months to deploy three-hundred-and-ninety-thousand soldiers. If we should need to evacuate them, the air support might grant us time to get them home."

Ismay gripped a leather belt on his tunic and nodded. "Your point is well taken, sir."

While the military staff discussed operational plans, Churchill looked out an aircraft window to the dark water of the English Channel. The severity of the situation weighed heavy on him as he pondered the day's events. He toiled over options that might create a way out of the plight, which seemed to grow worse by the hour. Determined to exhaust every possible course of action, he retrieved a piece of stationery and a fountain pen from a case under his seat and began to draft a letter.

Dear Benito Mussolini,

Churchill paused, the tip of the pen seeping ink through the stationery. As a drone of propellers thrummed in his ears, he conjured words that he hoped would dissuade the Italian dictator from joining the war in support of Hitler.

CHAPTER 20

SIGNY-L'ABBAYE, FRANCE—MAY 16, 1940

Ruth's damp clothes clung to her body as she crawled on her hands and knees through a dense thicket. Thorns pricked her scalp and cheeks. She pushed on for several meters to a clearing, where she peeked around a bush and scanned the countryside. It was long after daybreak and the sun was hidden by gray clouds. A boom of tank guns came from a few kilometers west of their location, and echoes of machine gun and artillery fire came from the north, east, and south. There was no sign of French troops and, beyond the hills in all directions, smoke plumes rose to the sky.

"The Panzers are gone," she said, glancing over her shoulder. "But we remain surrounded."

Lucette and Jimmie labored their way out of the underbrush and joined her.

The night before, they had floated past the Panzer tanks without being detected, but the strong river current pushed them at least a kilometer away from where they'd stashed the ambulance. Exhausted, cold, and fearing they would be spotted, they spent the night huddled together in the undergrowth as they fought off hypothermia and waited for the Panzers to leave the area. At dawn, they heard the engines of the German tanks rumble to life and resume their assault over the French countryside, but they remained hidden until they were certain the area was safe.

"Where now?" Lucette asked, clutching the medical bag.

"We try to make it to the ambulance," Ruth said.

"I agree." Jimmie brushed briars from his sling. "From there, we can determine if the roads are passable."

Lucette nodded.

Ruth, who had experience with hiking in rugged areas of Maine, led them through the forest that bordered the river. They did not speak and were careful with their path, avoiding areas of fallen branches that could snap under their feet. Instead, they chose routes near conifers so the sounds of their footsteps would be softened by fallen pine needles. Twenty minutes into their trek, the forest opened to a small, solitary farm that bordered the river. They hid behind a cluster of oak trees and surveilled a slate-roofed cottage, absent of vehicles or livestock. Minutes passed and they observed no movement.

"What do you think?" Jimmie whispered.

"I say we check it out," Ruth said.

"Me too," Lucette said. "There might be some fuel. We won't get far on what we have in the ambulance."

"Stay here." Jimmie slipped his weapon from his jacket. "I'll signal if it's safe."

"I'll go," Ruth said, placing a hand on his shoulder.

"I got this," he said. "I have a bad wing but my legs are good. I won't be long."

"Be careful," Ruth said.

"I will." He crept down a wooded slope, crouched down, and scurried to the house.

Ruth's heart rate quickened.

Jimmie skulked around the cottage and peeked through each of the first-floor windows. He paused, placing an ear to the front door, and entered.

Ruth pressed her hands together.

"He's going to be all right," Lucette whispered.

She nodded.

A moment later, Jimmie emerged from the cottage and waved an arm.

Thank goodness. Ruth's tension eased.

She and Lucette darted down the hill to the cottage and went inside. The place was sparsely decorated with antique furniture and the air smelled faintly of vinegar, as if the cottage had been recently cleaned. They found Jimmie in the dining room, standing beside a large oak table with four place settings, a basket of bread, a dish of butter, two jars of jam, a metal coffee pot, and a ceramic pitcher of milk. On a wall was a framed photograph of a young couple and three curly-haired children—two girls and one boy.

Ruth looked at a plate that contained a jam-covered piece of bread with a small bite mark, which she presumed to be from a child. A wave of sadness washed over her.

"They left in a hurry." Lucette lifted the coffeepot. "It's full."

"We should eat something," Jimmie said.

"It doesn't feel right," Ruth said. "It's not our food."

"I doubt that they will return soon." Lucette plucked a piece of bread and lathered it with butter. "We shouldn't let it go to waste, and we need our strength."

Ruth took a bite of bread, and a smidge of guilt gnawed at her conscience, despite knowing that they had little choice but to consume the nourishment. She silently gave thanks for the food and hoped that the family was safe and far away from German tanks.

They devoured the bread and drank the coffee, cold and bitter, but left the milk due to its sour smell. In the kitchen, they collected a baguette, handfuls of potatoes and beetroot, tins of meat, and tossed the items into a pillowcase that they took from a bed. They scoured the cottage and barn for weapons and fuel but found none. With their bellies full and their energy renewed, they fled the farm.

A half hour later, they found the ambulance as they had left it. They removed the camouflage of foliage and poured in the last of the fuel from a can in the back of the vehicle.

Lucette unfolded the map, soggy and warped from the river. "Let's decide which route to take."

"We have orders to go west to Dunkirk," Ruth said.

"And I'm required to return to my airfield," Jimmie said, "which is south of our location."

Lucette looked at them. "For a moment, let's set aside our duties and focus on the location of the German troops. Regardless of which direction we choose, we'll need to find a way to avoid them. Agreed?"

They nodded.

"Jimmie," Lucette said, "remind us again of what you saw from the air before you were shot down."

He grabbed a stick and drew lines in a section of dirt. "There are several divisions of German tanks storming toward the Channel. They are far outpacing the German infantry and supply units that are following behind them. So, there is a small window for us to escape to the south. If we try to go west toward the Channel, we'll likely be fighting our way—for three hundred kilometers— between Panzer divisions and Wehrmacht troops. It will be nearly impossible to make it."

Ruth chewed on her bottom lip.

"It's roughly sixty kilometers to Reims," Jimmie said. "We'll need to cross a line of the German invasion to get there. But if we can get through before the German infantry closes the gap, we'll have a chance of reaching the protection of Allied forces."

Ruth raised a finger. "You saw all that from up there?"

"I did," Jimmie said.

"What happens if the tanks change direction and head south for Paris?" Ruth asked.

"Then we made a mistake," Jimmie said, "and we might be in a worse predicament than we are now."

Ruth, her mind racing, glanced over the area.

Jimmie placed the tip of the stick in the dirt. "My hunch is that the tanks will continue west to head off divisions of the British Expeditionary Force. If the German military's intent was to capture Paris, I think their forces would not have turned toward the Channel."

Ruth looked at Lucette. "What do you think?"

"Like you, I feel a sense of duty to report to our post," Lucette said. "But I don't know how we could make it to the Channel with hundreds of Panzers in front of us and the German Army on our heels. I think we should go to Reims."

Ruth drew a deep breath and exhaled. "All right. Let's go to Reims."

She and Lucette mapped out a route and got into the ambulance.

Jimmie squeezed into the passenger seat with Lucette. Sitting next to the door, he rolled down the window and slipped his revolver from his jacket.

Ruth started the engine, backed out onto the dirt road, and then headed south. She worried that the German infantry would appear at any moment, and she listened through the open window for sounds of enemy fire. They traveled over ten kilometers without seeing a soul. The roads were empty, except for a few abandoned wagons, and they passed through two small villages, Mesmont and Sery, that were completely deserted. To Ruth, it looked as if France's rural residents had vanished.

"Take the next left," Lucette said, holding the map.

Ruth approached a narrow, unpaved road and made the turn. The vehicle bounced over ruts. "This road is barely wide enough for one vehicle. Are you sure this will take us where we need to go?"

Lucette ran a finger over a dotted line on the map. "*Oui.*"

Ruth shifted gears and turned the wheel to avoid a large hole. As she drove the vehicle up a slope, she noticed movement that looked like gray turtles cresting the hill. First, one turtle. Then another turtle. Within seconds, two Wehrmacht soldiers wearing shell-like helmets came into view. One man was looking through field binoculars, and his comrade was raising the antennae to a wireless radio. Several meters away, and parked in the middle of the road, was a motorcycle with a sidecar-mounted machine gun.

Fear flooded Ruth, and her foot slipped from the accelerator.

Lucette's jaw slacked and the map fell from her hands.

"Turn around," Jimmie said.

The German soldier lowered his field glasses, and his companion turned toward them and plucked a pistol from a holster attached to his belt.

Ruth, her heart racing, looked for a spot to spin the vehicle around but deep ruts covered both sides of the narrow road. A choice burned inside her. Before she changed her mind, she shifted gears and stomped on the accelerator.

CHAPTER 21

SIGNY-L'ABBAYE, FRANCE—MAY 16, 1940

Ruth's heart pounded against her chest as the ambulance, its engine roaring, barreled toward the German scout unit.

"Reverse!" Lucette shouted.

Jimmie, his eyes wide, aimed his revolver through his open side window.

A German soldier fired his pistol, and a bullet struck the vehicle's right fender.

Ruth flinched but didn't veer away.

Jimmie returned fire. Bullets pierced the ground near the soldiers, sending them sprinting for their motorcycle.

Ruth's eyes locked on the machine gun, mounted to the motorcycle's sidecar. She pushed hard on the accelerator, but the pedal was already to the floor. "Hold on!"

Lucette pressed her hands to the dash and lowered her head.

The soldiers reached the motorcycle and swiveled the machine gun, but its sidecar—positioned at over a ninety-degree angle from the oncoming ambulance—would not allow the gun's nozzle to point to the target. The Germans pushed on the gun's swivel but it wouldn't turn any farther. One of the soldiers fired the weapon, spraying bullets past the side of the ambulance.

Ruth, unwavering, squeezed hard on the wheel as she closed in on them.

The eyes of the Germans widened, and they dived to the side of the road as the ambulance smashed into their motorcycle.

The impact jolted Ruth from her seat, but she held firm to the wheel and kept the ambulance on the road. She plowed ahead and looked through her side mirror to find the motorcycle, smashed and flipped upside down in a ditch, and the soldiers on their knees aiming their pistols.

Bullets pelted the rear of the ambulance.

Ruth sped away and veered around a bend in the road, placing them out of sight from the German soldiers.

"Is everyone okay?" Ruth asked.

"Yes," Jimmie said.

Lucette nodded and placed her hands to her cheeks. "*Mon Dieu.* I can't believe you did that."

Ruth's arms trembled. "Me either."

Jimmie set his revolver on his lap and ran a hand through his hair. "How did you know that their machine gun wouldn't turn far enough to reach us?"

"I didn't," Ruth said. "There wasn't a place to turn around, and they'd surely catch us if I tried to run away in reverse."

"You're a cracking good driver and full of guts." He wiped sweat from his forehead. "Well done."

"*Merci.*" Ruth peered through the windshield at the ambulance's damaged right fender. "How does the front tire look on your side?"

Jimmie leaned his head out of the window. "Good for now."

"Do you think they'll radio ahead for soldiers to chase us down?" Lucette asked.

"It's possible," Jimmie said. "But they looked like a scout unit, given that they had a motorcycle and radio transmitter. They were likely scoping out the path ahead of the German Army." He adjusted his slinged arm and grimaced. "We could encounter more scout units, but I think we might have crossed the line between the Panzers and the oncoming Wehrmacht troops."

"I pray that we did," Lucette said.

"Me too," Ruth said. "But until we know for sure, let's keep an eye out for more soldiers."

Lucette plucked her map from the floor and peered through the windshield.

Ruth, her nerves surging like electrified wire, maneuvered the vehicle along the narrow dirt road. Minutes passed and they encountered no other scout units; however, they did spot two Luftwaffe bomber squadrons flying westward with no sign of either French or British planes. The German aircraft disappeared and, soon after, explosions rumbled over the countryside.

"I should be up there," Jimmie said, peering upward through the windshield.

"You'll fly again, when your arm is healed," Ruth said.

He nodded and scanned the sky, as if he were searching for his RAF squadron.

They traveled south for ten kilometers on arteries of back roads, each more rutted and overgrown with weeds than the one before. The area remained desolate until they took a shortcut across a farm field to the village of Balham, where a small group of refugees in a horse-drawn wagon were crossing a bridge over the Aisne River.

Ruth steered to the side of the wagon and decelerated. A gray-mustached man, his wrinkled face etched with sorrow, held the reins to a brown, swayback horse with protruding ribs. In the bed of the wagon were three women, one of whom was holding a baby.

"Is anyone injured?" Lucette called through the open passenger window.

The driver, his eyes void of spirit, shook his head.

Ruth pressed the accelerator and passed the wagon. A kilometer down the road, they came across another group of fleeing citizens on bicycles with cloth sacks tied to the handlebars. Soon after, they reached a junction of three roads, and the sole route heading south was congested—as far as they could see—with a mass of refugees.

Three women were pushing an automobile, which appeared to have run out of fuel, and sitting in the driver's seat was an adolescent boy who could barely see above the wheel. Beside them, a silver-haired man was driving a farm tractor with a flatbed wagon loaded with grammar-school-age children, two goats, and an antique treadle sewing machine. While some of the refugees had wheeled transportation, the vast majority were pedestrians. They either carried luggage, held the hands of young children, or pushed strollers—some of which held an elderly person who was too feeble to walk.

"There must be thousands on this road," Jimmie said.

Ruth's shoulders drooped. "It's gut-wrenching to see all these people who've abandoned their homes."

"*Oui*," Lucette said. "If all of northern France's routes that lead away from the invasion look like this one, there could be millions trying to escape to the south."

As Ruth maneuvered through the throng, she told Jimmie that she and Lucette witnessed Luftwaffe raids on villages to drive citizens from their homes, which clogged the roads and hampered the ability of the French Army to move troops and equipment to Sedan. But the crowd on this road was far greater than what she'd witnessed near the front, and it was clear, to Ruth, that the driving force of the massive flight of citizens was the rampage of German tanks over the countryside.

The large number of pedestrians forced Ruth to slow the vehicle to little more than a walking pace. She honked the horn, but it did little good, considering most of the refugees appeared far too exhausted and scared to pay heed to an ambulance. Eventually, she resorted to passing only in areas where there was a wide berm. She glanced at the fuel gauge, its needle pointed to slightly below half a tank, and she hoped that they had enough petrol to make it to Reims.

Ruth veered to the side of the road and passed a middle-aged woman, who was wearing an apron over a housedress and holding a leash to a well-groomed black poodle. As she looked for a spot to squeeze back onto the road, her eyes gravitated to movement near a sprawling linden tree, fifteen meters ahead.

An elderly man, wearing a charcoal-colored suit and walking beside a young girl, dropped his suitcase and stumbled.

"Oh, no," Ruth said.

Lucette perked her head. "What?"

Ruth pointed. "I think he might need help." She parked the vehicle and jumped out.

Jimmie and Lucette exited the vehicle and followed her.

The old man placed a hand to his chest and slumped to the ground. The young girl kneeled to him.

"Can I help?" Ruth asked, approaching them.

The old man drew a labored breath. "I'll be fine in a moment."

The girl glanced at Ruth. "Grandpapa needs his medicine." She reached into the man's jacket and removed a brown bottle.

The old man's hand trembled as he reached for the bottle.

"I'll do it." The girl unscrewed the cap and placed a small tablet into his mouth.

Ruth, Jimmie, and Lucette gathered around them.

The man's breathing gradually slowed, and he placed a hand to his granddaughter's cheek. "*Merci*, my little cabbage," he said in a deep yet sweet baritone voice.

The girl nodded and slipped the medicine bottle into the man's jacket.

"Do you need to find a doctor?" Ruth asked.

"*Non*," the man said. "There is nothing a doctor can do for my angina. I have my nitroglycerin pills, and I'll be better after a few minutes of rest."

"I'm Ruth." She gestured with her hand. "This is Lucette and Jimmie."

"Pierre." The man slipped a navy beret from his head, revealing mussed, gray hair. He patted the girl's arm. "My granddaughter, Aline."

"*Bonjour*," Aline said. The girl was approximately nine years of age, give or take a year, with curly, sandy blond hair and eyes the color of burnt caramel. She wore a gray wool cardigan over a blue plaid dress, scuffed black shoes with ankle-length white socks, and a brown leather book bag that was strapped to her back.

Tank fire erupted from several kilometers away, sending thunder-like echoes over the landscape. Refugees turned their heads but continued their migration.

"We must keep moving." Pierre took a deep breath. "Ready, Aline?"

"*Oui*," the girl said.

Jimmie stepped to the man and extended his good arm.

Pierre clasped Jimmie's hand and rose to his feet.

"Where are you headed to?" Jimmie asked.

"Any place that is free of cannonade." Pierre picked up his suit-case.

He's not well and needs to get off his feet, Ruth thought. *He'll struggle to stay ahead of the German Army, and I can't leave him here.* A decision stirred inside her. "How about coming with us? We have room for you and Aline in our ambulance. We're going to an Allied military airfield in Reims, assuming we have enough fuel to get there."

Pierre's eyes brightened.

"*Oui*," Lucette said. "You should come with us."

Pierre smiled. "*Merci beaucoup.* Our vehicle broke down last night, and we've been walking since dawn." He looked at his granddaughter. "How does a ride sound to you?"

"*Bien*, Grandpapa," Aline said. "You need to rest."

Pierre patted Aline's head. "You too, my little cabbage."

Together, they walked to the ambulance. Lucette took over as driver with Jimmie in the passenger seat, and Ruth sat with Pierre and Aline on the cots in the back of the vehicle.

"Where are you from?" Ruth asked as the ambulance pulled away.

"Lille," Pierre said.

"Do you have family elsewhere?"

"*Non.*"

"Any friends you can stay with in the south of France?"

Pierre shook his head. "It's only the two of us. Aline's father—my son, Leopold—is a soldier in the army." He placed his arm around his granddaughter. "Her mother was killed in a German air raid."

Ruth felt sick to her stomach. "I'm so sorry."

Aline's bottom lip quivered.

Pierre told Ruth that his wife, Zelia, died six years earlier from cancer, and that their only child was Leopold, the father of Aline. He also explained that Aline had no other living blood relatives.

Her mother was raised in an orphanage, and Aline's only living family members were him and her papa.

"It's Aline and I, until Leopold returns from the war," Pierre said.

A wave of sadness washed over Ruth.

Aline rubbed her eyes, as if fending off tears. "Would you like to see a picture of our family?"

"*Oui*," Ruth said.

Aline slipped off her backpack, undid a buckle, and removed a weathered photograph. "This is us when I was a baby."

Ruth looked at the image of an attractive woman, holding a swaddled baby while sitting on a piano bench next to a young man. Pierre and his late wife stood on opposite sides of the couple. "You have a beautiful family. What is the name of your *maman*?"

"Blanche," Aline said.

"That's a lovely name," Ruth said. "Your *maman* would be so proud of you for being such a brave girl."

"And for helping your grandpapa," Pierre added.

Aline nodded. She leaned over to put away the photograph, and a delicate silver chain dangled from her neck.

Ruth's eyes locked on a Star of David pendant. "I like your necklace."

She closed her backpack and sat upright. "It's a gift from Grand-papa."

"I'm Jewish, too," Ruth said, "on my mom's side of the family."

Aline's lips formed a faint smile.

The vehicle's engine hummed as they slowly traveled toward Reims. Ruth gave them a hunk of the baguette they'd looted from the farm, and water from a canteen. Soon after the two had eaten, Pierre grew tired and lay down to sleep.

Aline sat next to Ruth and looked at her uniform. "Do you take hurt soldiers to hospitals?"

"I do."

"Are you on your way to help them?"

"*Non*. The German tanks got between us and the French Army. But once we get you and your grandpapa to Reims, Lucette and

I will find a way to reach our soldiers." Ruth patted Aline's knee. "Jimmie's airfield is in Reims. You'll be safe there."

Aline picked at a hole in her cardigan. "Do you think we can stop them?"

She swallowed. "*Oui.*"

Ruth, hoping to divert Aline's attention away from the war, told her about her family and the move to Paris to pursue a singing career. And Aline reciprocated by describing her parents. Her *maman* had loved to play the piano and create watercolor paintings of a duck pond near their home. Her papa, before going off to war, had worked as an editor for a newspaper and gifted Aline lots of books, which she abandoned when fleeing Lille.

Aline yawned. Her head tilted and her eyelids began to close.

Ruth tucked her into a cot with a wool blanket. She quietly made her way to the front of the vehicle and squeezed into the passenger seat, next to Jimmie.

"I've been coasting down the hills to save fuel," Lucette said, veering around a wagon. "We might have enough to get us to the airfield."

Ruth nodded.

"How are they?" Jimmie asked.

Ruth frowned. She told them about Aline's mother and family. "It's only the two of them."

"I feel sorry for them." Lucette shifted gears. "Perhaps they might have some friends in the south of France that could take them in."

"I'm afraid not," Ruth said.

"Aline must be devastated," Jimmie said.

"She is," Ruth said. "But she's resilient and wants to be strong for her grandpapa, who is not well."

Jimmie rubbed the swollen fingers of his broken arm. "I wish I could do something for them."

"Me too," Ruth said.

They spoke little for the rest of the journey. At sunset, they reached the outskirts of Reims with little more than fumes left in the ambulance's fuel tank. The sound of tank guns dwindled, and there were no more sightings of Luftwaffe or Allied aircraft.

Lucette, following Jimmie's direction, turned onto a road that led away from the mass migration of people, many of whom were hunkered to the side of the road for the night. Minutes later, she drove through the open front gate of the Reims-Champagne Air Base and stopped.

A hangar was in ruin, and several burned planes lined an abandoned runway that was marred with bomb craters. An acrid smell of expelled explosives and charred wood filled the air.

"Oh, no," Jimmie said.

Ruth's hope sank. *My God, our air forces have fled, too.*

CHAPTER 22

REIMS, FRANCE—MAY 16, 1940

Jimmie exited the ambulance and stared over the deserted airfield. A handful of charred aircraft remained on a runway that was ravaged by bombs. The barracks and mess hall were destroyed, and a large hangar that had been filled with equipment and RAF ground crew was now a smoldering mound of steel and charred timber. A wave of shock and anger surged through him.

Ruth got out of the vehicle and clasped her arms. "They're gone."

Jimmie turned to her. "It looks like the pilots got most of the planes into the air before the Luftwaffe's raid."

Lucette, Aline, and Pierre got out of the ambulance. Their faces turned pale at the sight of the devastation.

"Will the Allied air forces return?" Ruth asked.

Jimmie looked at the runway, covered in holes the size of automobiles. "Not anytime soon."

"*Mon Dieu*," Lucette said, stepping forward. "Where have they gone?"

"To another base, most likely to the south. Perhaps the Villeneuve-les-Vertus Aerodrome, or the airfield in Gaye."

"How far?" Ruth asked.

"Vertus is fifty kilometers away. Gaye is about seventy-five."

Ruth folded her arms. "But you don't know for certain if they are there."

Jimmie shook his head. He approached the group, their eyes filled with uncertainty. "I'm sorry. You came here because of me."

"It's not your fault," Ruth said. "We all agreed to come here."

Aline leaned to her grandpapa.

Pierre placed a hand on Aline's shoulder and looked at Jimmie. "We're farther away from the German tanks than when we started—and for that, I am grateful."

Jimmie nodded, even though he felt like he'd failed them. He glanced at a dull red glow on the horizon. "There's barely any light left. We should stay here until morning. I'm going to look around the area to see if I can find any abandoned supplies or fuel."

"I'll join you." Ruth went to the ambulance and returned with the electric torch.

While Lucette, Pierre, and Aline remained at the ambulance, Jimmie and Ruth explored the airfield. First, Jimmie led Ruth to the burned remains of a Hawker Hurricane.

"It might be best if I take a look first," Jimmie said.

"Okay." She handed him the electric torch.

Jimmie flipped the switch and was surprised that it still worked after being soaked in river water. As he approached the remains of the Hurricane, a stench of burnt wood and aviation fuel penetrated his nostrils. He peeked into what was left of the cockpit and was relieved to find no remains of a pilot. At the tail, which was partially scorched, he shined a beam over the RAF markings. A chill drifted down his spine. "It's Benny's."

"Who?"

"A fellow wingman—and a friend." An image of the Yorkshireman's boyish, freckled face flashed in Jimmie's head.

"Is he—" Ruth swallowed.

"No. He's not here."

"Thank goodness."

"It looks like Benny's Hurricane was destroyed before he could get it into the air."

Jimmie dreaded checking the planes, but he was compelled by

his sense of duty to search for fallen airmen. For several minutes, he checked the cockpits and fuselages of the remaining destroyed aircraft, all of which were either French bombers or British Fairey Battles, and he was comforted to find no corpses. Afterward, he and Ruth scoured the area of the hangar for anything of use, but it had taken a direct hit from a bomb and everything was destroyed, either by the explosion or the ensuing fire. Refusing to give up their search for supplies, they made their way to a shed near the entrance to the airfield. Inside, they discovered old tires, an assortment of old propellers, a toolbox, and a rusty metal fuel canister.

Jimmie picked up the canister by its handle and felt its weight. "It's half full." He unscrewed the cap and took a whiff. "It's petrol, but it smells a bit sour and might be old."

"Our fuel gauge reads empty," Ruth said, "so it won't make much difference if the petrol is bad. Let's try it."

Jimmie carried the canister out of the shed and walked with Ruth toward the ambulance. His injured arm jostled in the sling, sending a sharp pang through his wrist. He grimaced.

"Are you okay?" she asked.

"Yes," he said, fighting back the pain.

"May I carry it?"

"There's no need."

Ruth stepped in front of him and stopped.

Jimmie's eyebrows rose and he halted, the fuel sloshing inside the canister.

"I know that you're capable of lugging that gas can," she said, "but you're in pain and there's no reason to refuse my help when you're at risk of reinjuring a broken bone." She extended her arm. "Give it to me."

He gave her the canister and paused, looking into her eyes. "I didn't mean to offend you. My insistence with carrying the load was my way of trying to fix things. Contrary to my stubbornness, I am quite obliged to you for your help."

The lines on Ruth's face softened. "You're welcome, and no apology needed."

At the ambulance, they poured the petrol into the tank, slightly raising the needle on the fuel gauge. They test started the engine and it idled normally, except for a few, intermittent sputters. Afterward, they prepared a sparse meal of raw potatoes and beetroot, and one of the tins of meat that was looted from a farm. Pierre recited a blessing and they ate in dark silence.

While everyone hunkered onto bunks in the ambulance for the night, Jimmie sat guard under an oak tree, perched on a hill that overlooked the airfield. As he leaned his back against the tree, his mind flashed to the letter he'd written to Nora. He wondered when the RAF would inform his family that he'd been shot down and was missing in action, and he hoped that he would find the No. 73 Squadron before the news was dispatched.

An hour into his watch, he heard approaching footsteps and reached for his revolver.

"Where are you?" Ruth's voice asked from the darkness.

He relaxed. "Over here—under a tree."

Ruth approached Jimmie. She adjusted a blanket, wrapped around her shoulders, and sat down beside him.

"Is something wrong?" he asked.

"No. I wanted to talk to you about some things."

"By all means," he said.

"Lucette and I were discussing which direction we should go in the morning." She tightened the blanket around her shoulders. "We think the best choice is Paris."

Jimmie straightened his spine. "That's a lengthy journey from here—much farther than the other air bases. Finding enough fuel will be a challenge."

"Getting petrol will be difficult no matter which direction we go."

He nodded. "Why Paris?"

"Two reasons. First, Lucette and I were reviewing the map. From Paris, we'll have more route options to get us to our post in Dunkirk. And if there is no viable road to the Channel, the French Army's ambulance corps headquarters in Paris can redeploy us to where we are most needed."

Jimmie rubbed his chin. "I see."

"Second, I have family in Paris. My uncle is a doctor and my aunt is a nurse. Pierre and Aline will have a place to stay and will be well cared for."

"I'm glad. It is very kind of you and your family to take them in." He plucked a blade of grass and rubbed it between his fingers. "Have you considered the risk of the German tanks changing their direction to Paris?"

"We have—it's a chance that Lucette and I are willing to take. We've spoken to Pierre and he's agreeable to going with us." She raised her head and peered at the night sky. "Hitler's military appears invincible, but I'm counting on the French Army to muster enough troops to stop them from reaching the city."

"It's a long way to Paris," he said, "but I think it's a safer bet for you and the others to go there. The city will also provide numerous routes to flee, should the Germans change their course."

She fiddled with the end of her blanket. "There's one more thing I want to talk about."

"What's that?"

"We think you should come with us."

He dropped the blade of grass. "I appreciate your invitation, but I'm required to report back to the RAF. I need to go to the airfield in Vertus to see if my squadron is there."

"What happens if the RAF is not in Vertus?"

"Then I'll continue on to the airfield in Gaye."

"And what if that base has been evacuated, like this one?"

His neck muscles tensed.

"Even if you do find your squadron, you're in no condition to fly." She gently placed a hand on his arm. "It's best for us to stick together."

"I don't want to split from the group," he said. "But, like you, I have a duty to return to my post."

"There's no need to make the decision tonight," she said, her voice soft. "All I ask is that you give it some thought."

"I will."

She slipped her hand away.

They quietly remained sitting, and Jimmie was surprised yet glad that she decided to stay a little longer. Despite their opposing views on what he should do, he felt relaxed and comforted by her presence.

"It must have been difficult to see Benny's plane," she said, breaking the silence. "Are you worried about the pilots in your squadron?"

"I am. They are like brothers to me." He drew a deep breath. "My friend Fanny was shot down minutes before me. I saw his parachute open after he bailed out, and I'm hoping he made it back to the squadron."

"I'm sorry. I'll keep him in my thoughts."

"Thanks." For several minutes, he told her about his fellow pilots Cobber, Fanny, Benny, and his fitter, Horace.

"They sound like grand friends."

An image of playing rugby with Cobber in the rain flashed in his mind. "The best."

She turned to him. "Back at the water mill, you didn't get a chance to finish telling me about your sister, Nora. You mentioned that she endured a rough time in her life. I'd like to know more about her."

"Of course." He leaned his back to the tree. "Nora and I are quite close. She's sixteen years old, clever, plucky, and a voracious reader. She's planning to leave home to go to university to become a librarian." He looked up through the silhouette of branches against the night sky. "When she was a child, she was stricken with polio."

"Oh, my."

"She nearly died. Her diaphragm was paralyzed and she spent two weeks in an iron lung."

Ruth placed a hand to her mouth.

"When I first saw her at the hospital, I was fearful that she might not survive. She was sealed—except for her head—in a large, horizontal cylinder that helped her to breathe." He rubbed his swollen fingers. "I remember Nora, looking at me through a mirror on the top of the machine, and telling me not to worry and that she'd be all right. Then she asked if I brought her Piglet and her favorite book."

Ruth lowered her hand to her lap. "*Winnie-the-Pooh*."

He nodded. "For two weeks during visitation hours, I read and reread the story aloud to her. Once she was able to breathe on her own, she was released from the machine. The polio had left her unable to walk, and doctors told her that she'd likely live her life in a wheelchair. But Nora proved them wrong. Through grit, determination, and months of rehabilitation, she learned to walk with the use of leg braces and calipers."

"I'm so glad. Nora sounds like an incredible young woman."

"She is."

She nudged his leg with her shoe. "You're a good brother."

He smiled, feeling grateful for her kind words.

For an hour, they talked about their families, Ruth's passion for music, and his ardor for aviation. For the first time since the war erupted, he felt at peace. Eventually, they grew tired and Ruth rested her head on his shoulder. His body relaxed as he took in her warmth. *It feels wrong to leave you, but I'm required to return to my squadron.* He lowered his cheek to her hair and tried to forget about their divergent paths. He gradually drifted to sleep, but at dawn he was jolted awake by the sound of German aircraft engines.

CHAPTER 23

REIMS, FRANCE—MAY 17, 1940

The distinctive drone of German dive bombers roused Jimmie from his slumber. He shot open his eyes and nudged Ruth, asleep on his shoulder. "Stukas."

Ruth awoke and gasped.

They scuttled to the edge of the tree's canopy and scanned the twilight sky, strewn with pinkish-gray clouds. A swarm of planes, flying at several thousand feet above the ground, approached the airfield.

Jimmie's adrenaline surged. He looked down the hill at the ambulance, fifty meters away, and cupped his hands around his mouth. "Lucette!"

Ruth raced down the slope.

Jimmie sprinted behind her as the buzz of propellers grew. His arm jostled in his sling, sending sharp pangs through his wrist. He fought back the pain and forced his legs to run faster.

"Lucette!" Ruth shouted.

The rear doors of the ambulance flung open, and Lucette jumped to the ground.

High above, the Stukas pitched their noses and dived toward the earth. Their sirens screamed as they narrowed in on the airfield.

Jimmie stumbled and nearly fell, but continued his sprint. "Take cover!"

Lucette helped Pierre and Aline to climb out of the vehicle. Ruth and Jimmie reached them, and the group ran toward the side of the airfield. Pierre struggled to run, so Jimmie wrapped his good arm around the old man's torso to quicken his pace. At the edge of the airfield, they clambered down a steep slope to a drainage ditch, filled with ankle-deep rainwater. They gulped air to catch their breath and Pierre, his face pale, leaned his back against the grass-covered slant.

"Grandpapa!" Aline darted to Pierre's side.

The Stukas leveled off, forty meters above the ground, and soared over the airfield without dropping a bomb. At the end of the runway, they ascended and flew southward.

"They're leaving," Ruth said, peeking her head up from their hole.

"Maybe they're satisfied that the airfield is destroyed," Lucette said.

The Stuka squadron continued to fly away, but seconds later one of their aircraft broke from the pack and veered around.

A wave of dread washed over Jimmie. "We've been spotted."

The sole Stuka dived toward the airfield. Its siren howled, and its engine grew to an ear-piercing roar.

The group crouched in the ditch, soaking their shoes and clothing in mucky water. Jimmie, as if by reflex, shielded Aline with his body.

The Stuka fired its machine guns. Bullets sprayed over the ambulance, puncturing holes in its roof and hood. It pulled up and swooped around for another attack, but instead of targeting the ambulance, it narrowed its sights on them.

Lucette's eyes widened. *Mon Dieu.* It's heading toward us."

"We need to split up," Jimmie said, his eyes locked on the approaching Stuka. "When I say go—Ruth and Lucette run to the right. Pierre, Aline, and I will run to the left."

"Okay," Ruth said.

The Stuka, its engine blaring, barreled down on the airfield.

"Get ready." Jimmie clasped the girl's hand. "I got you."

Aline gripped his fingers.

Jimmie fought the urge to run and waited patiently until the German pilot committed his plane's trajectory.

The Stuka's machine guns barked. Streams of bullets exploded over the ground ahead of them.

"Go!" Jimmie darted away with Aline and Pierre, while Ruth and Lucette dived to the right.

Bullets blasted the ditch, spraying mud and bits of rock over their clothing, and the Stuka roared past them.

"Is everyone all right?" Jimmie asked.

"*Oui*," Aline said.

Pierre nodded. He bent over and sucked in air.

Jimmie turned and was relieved to see Ruth and Lucette—their uniforms wet and muddy—rising from the ditch. As he prepared for the Stuka to make another pass, the German pilot veered his aircraft away and flew out of sight.

"Thank goodness," Ruth said.

Jimmie, his wrist throbbing, leaned his back against the slope and exhaled.

Aline released his hand and brushed a clump of mud from his sling.

Pierre raised his head. "I'm thankful for what you did for her, and me."

Jimmie nodded.

The group climbed out of the ditch and walked, their soaked feet squelching in their shoes, to the ambulance. The hood, roof, and the rear doors were covered with holes the size of walnuts. The windshield was shattered and beneath the vehicle was a large puddle of fluid.

Ruth opened the hood and frowned. "The radiator looks like Swiss cheese."

"Can it be fixed?" Lucette asked.

"*Non*." Ruth examined the engine block, battery, and fuel line, all of which were intact. "It might run, but we won't get far."

"It's worth a try." Lucette brushed mud from her uniform. "Each kilometer we ride is one less that we have to walk."

Ruth nodded. "Let's get on the road before more enemy planes show up."

Pierre and Aline climbed into the back of the ambulance, and

Lucette began to clear away broken glass from the driver and passenger seats.

Ruth approached Jimmie, whose sling was spattered with mud. "Is your arm okay?"

"Yes, thanks to your splint." He glanced at a bullet hole in the red cross emblem of the ambulance. Anger grew inside him. "What kind of pilot would open machine gun fire on an ambulance and innocent people?"

"The Luftwaffe kind—it's not the first time our ambulance has been a target." Ruth squeezed water from her wool skirt. "Have you made your decision on whether to join us?"

A choice roiled inside him. His brain told him that he should search for his squadron, but his heart told him otherwise. He looked into her eyes and said, "You're right. We should stick together."

"I'm glad to hear that," she said. "Sit up front with me and Lucette. We might need your weapon."

He nodded.

The vehicle successfully started and they drove away from the airfield. But within five minutes, the needle on the engine's temperature gauge pointed to the red, and the smell of burning oil filled the cabin. Ruth turned off the engine for twenty minutes to allow the engine to cool down, and then continued their journey for a few more kilometers, until they reached a main route toward Paris. The road was jam-packed with thousands of French citizens, forcing the vehicle to move at a slow rate of speed.

Soon, smoke began to spew from under the hood. The vehicle shuddered and the engine seized. They gathered their things, abandoned the ambulance, and joined the growing exodus of refugees heading south in search of freedom.

Part 3

The Exodus

CHAPTER 24

LONDON, ENGLAND—MAY 20, 1940

On the day that German tanks reached the English Channel, Prime Minister Winston Churchill entered the Cabinet War Rooms, deep below the streets of Westminster. His polished black shoes clacked over the concrete floor as he traveled down a dimly lighted, claustrophobic corridor to where two armed sentries stood guard by an open steel door.

The sentries snapped to attention and saluted.

Churchill, without breaking his stride, touched the brim of his hat and entered the Cabinet Room to find his chief military advisor, General Ismay, looking at a map on the far wall.

A sentry closed the door, clinking against its metal frame.

Ismay turned. "Hello, Prime Minister."

"Good day, General." Churchill put down his hat on a table and approached him. "You've received the intelligence briefing, I presume."

"I have, sir." Ismay clasped his hands behind his back, tightening his military tunic over his broad chest. "Shall we begin, or do you wish to wait for the remaining Chiefs of Staff to join us?"

"We will begin." Churchill removed a cigar from his suit jacket. "I did not summon the others. I would like to discuss recent developments and our course of action with you before calling a meeting."

"Of course, sir."

Churchill lit his cigar and puffed on the tip, filling his mouth with the taste of tobacco smoke. He stood beside Ismay and peered at the map, marked with colored pins to depict Axis and Allied troops. His eyes locked on a cluster of black pins, representing German tanks, at the coast of France. Ire swelled inside him yet his composed demeanor remained unwavering.

"Three days ago, when Antwerp and Brussels fell," Ismay said, "the Allies retreated to the coastline of France." He pointed to the map. "Most are in Dunkirk—six miles from the Belgium border."

Churchill rolled his cigar between his fingers, and ash fell to the floor.

"The Germans captured Abbeville," Ismay said, "and their tanks have reached the Somme River where it meets the Channel. The British and French armies have their backs to the sea, and they're trapped on three sides by the Germans."

Churchill lowered his brow. "How many Allied troops are surrounded?"

"Over three hundred thousand, sir," Ismay said. "Two-thirds are British and one-third are French."

Churchill's mind raced, searching for tactical methods that might enable the troops to fight their way out. *There is no chance of victory when outnumbered, outgunned, and surrounded by the enemy. If they remain on the shore of France, they'll most surely be killed or captured.* He took a deep inhale on his cigar, filling his lungs with smoke. "Make preparations to evacuate forces from Dunkirk."

"Yes, sir." Ismay adjusted the bottom of his tunic. "It might take several weeks, given the current positions of our naval vessels, to evacuate three hundred thousand troops. The men will need to dig in and fight until we can get them to safety."

"That is far too long, Pug," Churchill said, using Ismay's lifelong nickname, given because of his meaty, bulldog-like jawline.

Ismay straightened his back.

"If our men are left trapped on the beaches for weeks under German fire," Churchill said, "they'll be annihilated."

Ismay ran a hand over his thin hair. "We could request vessels from Canada, or make a plea to President Roosevelt for American hospital ships. But even if we are successful with acquiring them, they'd arrive too late. The best course is to redeploy Royal Navy vessels that are in defensive positions in the North Sea." He drew a deep breath. "Even if we utilize most of our naval vessels, it will take time to conduct an evacuation of this magnitude."

Churchill flicked ash from his cigar. "Then we will expand our navy."

Ismay wrinkled his forehead.

"We must call on the British Admiralty to muster all available vessels—and to assemble the aid of civilian seamen near the Strait of Dover. To save our men, we'll need the use of every ship, sailing craft, and fishing boat in the South of England."

"Civilian craft?"

"Indeed," Churchill said.

For several minutes, Churchill debated with his chief military advisor on whether an evacuation plan to include hundreds of civilian boats would work. He trusted Ismay's keen military logic and, most of all, he valued the man's willingness to challenge his impulsiveness.

"If we call on ordinary citizens to rescue our soldiers," Ismay said, "it may be viewed as an act of desperation. We could lose the confidence of our people, and our allies."

Churchill puffed on his cigar. "Dark times call for daring measures."

Ismay looked at the map, as if pondering the prime minister's plan. "Are you confident that this will work?"

"No," Churchill said, candidly, "but we must fight to save our armies at all costs. If they are wiped out on the beaches of France, we'll have no means of defending our island against a German invasion."

Ismay nodded. "You have my full support. Shall we notify the French?"

"In due time," Churchill said. "First, we prepare our evacuation plans."

"Yes, sir." Ismay pointed to the lines of Panzer tanks on the map. "Eventually, the Germans will make an advance toward Paris and the remaining coast of France. In addition to Dunkirk, we should prepare to evacuate those who are south of the German line. I recommend that we develop similar operations to take place in Le Havre and the Loire estuary."

Churchill nodded. "Do you have an estimate of how many will need to be rescued in the south?"

Ismay thumbed through a report on a nearby table. "Another two hundred thousand. Maybe more, considering that most of the RAF ground crews will need to be evacuated by sea."

An acidic burn rose from Churchill's stomach. He tamped out his cigar in an ashtray and looked at Ismay. "For now, our priority will be Dunkirk. But initiate plans to evacuate those who are left behind."

"Yes, sir."

Churchill eyed the map. "A thin sea separates our island nation from the forces of Nazi brutality. Belgium and France will inevitably fall, and Britain will stand alone against that madman and his quest to conquer Europe."

"In addition to evacuation plans," Ismay said, "we should prepare the Home Guard."

An image of old men with tarnished helmets and hunting rifles flashed in Churchill's head. "Very well." He looked at his pocket watch. "I will call an emergency meeting in an hour. It should provide you with ample time to inform the heads of the military before we convene."

"Indeed, sir," Ismay said.

Churchill retrieved his hat and left.

The prime minister traveled a short distance down the corridor and entered his private bedroom in the underground bunker. He poured a glass of whisky with a splash of water and sat at his desk. *It will require more than the navy to save our troops. We'll need fearless fishermen, sailboats, and a miracle.*

Churchill took a gulp of his whisky, the warmth of the alcohol doing little to soothe his vexation. He retrieved a piece of paper and a fountain pen and began to draft another plan, one with an aim to galvanize the hearts of the British people and instill the will to fight.

CHAPTER 25

BRUMETZ, FRANCE—MAY 28, 1940

Ruth—her feet and her legs aching—slogged alongside Aline, Jimmie, Lucette, and Pierre on a gravel road. Despite that it was late in the day and had started to drizzle, scores of refugees continued their trek through the countryside.

"Are you doing okay, Aline?" Ruth asked, walking beside her.

"*Oui.*" Aline wiped rain droplets from her face. "*Merci* for carrying my backpack."

"*Je t'en prie,*" Ruth said.

"When it starts to feel heavy," Aline said, "you can give it back to me."

Ruth patted the backpack's strap on her shoulder. "I'm good for now."

Jimmie, walking with his good arm wrapped over his sling, looked at Aline. "There should be a village a little farther ahead. We'll get out of the wet weather and find a dry place to rest."

Aline nodded. She turned to Pierre, who was holding Lucette's elbow as he shuffled along the edge of the road. "Grandpapa, we're going to stop in a little while."

Pierre, his shoulders slumped, raised a hand as he continued his walk.

Soon, dark clouds covered the sky. Wind gusts grew, and heavy rain marched through the trees, the drops striking the leaves sounding like a rolling crescendo on a snare drum. Refugees dispersed and made their way toward a forest for shelter.

As Ruth stepped from the road, she spotted a small bridge that crossed a creek, approximately fifty meters away. "Let's keep going," she called to her friends. "There's a bridge ahead."

The group, raindrops pelting their faces, scurried over the gravel roadway. At the bridge—which spanned a stream and was made of thick wood beams and planks—they climbed down an embankment and hunkered underneath the structure. Although the bridge provided some protection from the storm, rain poured from gaps between boards.

Pierre slumped onto the ground and took in shallow breaths.

Aline kneeled to her grandpapa. "*Médecine?*"

"*Oui.*" Pierre slid his drenched beret from his head. He reached for his jacket pocket but had trouble finding the opening.

"I'll get it." Aline, her eyes filled with worry, removed a bottle of nitroglycerin pills from his jacket. She unscrewed the top, fished out a pill, and gave it to him.

Pierre, his hand shaking, placed the pill in his mouth. Within minutes, his breathing slowed and he regained a bit of energy. He placed a palm to his granddaughter's wet cheek and smiled. "*Merci*, my little cabbage."

Tension faded from Aline's face.

Lucette approached Ruth and Jimmie and lowered her voice. "I don't think Pierre should walk any more today."

Ruth nodded.

"I'll explore the road ahead of us for a place to settle for the night," Jimmie said.

Ruth glanced over the stream, covered in rain ripples. "Maybe you should wait to see if the weather improves."

Jimmie shook his head. "The sooner we find an indoor shelter, the sooner Pierre will get some rest."

Ruth looked at Jimmie, his jaw covered in stubble and hair soaked with rain. *He's kind and refuses to allow a broken arm to hinder his desire to help us.* "Please be careful."

"I will."

She watched him scale the embankment and disappear into the downpour.

Over the past week, the group covered a little more than half of their journey to Paris. They'd walked most of the way, except when Ruth had convinced a woman to allow Aline and Pierre to hitch a ride in the back of her horse-drawn wagon. But after two days, the woman left them behind when she took a different route toward Sézanne to search for her sister. Pierre and Aline's stint of riding in the wagon, while Ruth and the others walked behind them, had not improved the pace of the journey. The roads were packed with an increasing number of asylum seekers, due to Luftwaffe air raids on villages, and the once scenic terrain of the Champagne wine region had been transformed into a befouled landscape of abandoned automobiles, trucks, and buses that had run out of fuel.

The slow pace of pedestrian traffic wasn't their only challenge. Pierre needed frequent breaks to rest and, at times, he needed to take his angina medicine to ease pain in his chest. Despite his physical limitations, his optimistic attitude never waned. In the evenings, he performed sleight of hand tricks using a coin or a weathered deck of playing cards to amuse the group, as if he were determined to distract them from their worries of war. He told stories to Aline about how her parents met, the day she was born, her first steps, and when she learned to ride a bicycle. But most of all, he reassured his granddaughter that they would be safe in Paris and would eventually reunite with her father after the war.

In addition to the frequent pauses in their journey for Pierre to rest, a great deal of time and effort was dedicated to searching for food. The village markets along the route had been looted, and much of their nourishment—mostly canned goods, root vegetables, and stale biscuits—was either found in abandoned farmhouses or gifted to them by fellow refugees. The week before, Ruth was deeply moved by the selfless act of an elderly man who gave their group one of his last two cans of peas. As days passed, and as food grew more scarce, most of the refugees began to hoard their rations. But Ruth held no ill feelings, considering she'd stashed away carrot tops to ensure that Aline would have something to eat when they were low on food.

At night, they slept in barns or vacant farmhouses, except for an evening when they'd rested in the basement of a church, packed with French and Belgium refugees whose towns were in the path of the German Panzers. During the day, they traveled on the road, all the while keeping alert for Luftwaffe air raids. They often sighted German squadrons flying overhead, which sent them and masses of refugees scrambling to trees for cover. The spotting of Allied planes was far less frequent, nearly five times less than enemy aircraft, and there was no sign of the French Army or British Expeditionary Force. Ruth hoped that the absence of Allied infantry and armored units meant that they were occupied with fighting back the German military, but deep down her gut told her otherwise.

Pierre, holding his beret above his head to fend off dripping rainwater, approached Ruth and Lucette.

"Feeling better?" Ruth asked.

"Much," Pierre said, his voice hoarse. "I'm sorry for slowing down the group. If it wasn't for me, you would almost be in Paris."

"Nonsense," Lucette said. "You're doing well with keeping pace."

Ruth looked at Pierre, his clothes wet and disheveled. Her mind drifted to an image of Aline smiling as Pierre magically plucked a coin from behind his granddaughter's ear. "We're lucky to have you with us, and so is Aline."

"You're too kind." Pierre glanced at Aline, sitting several meters away with her head on her knees. "I would like for both of you to promise me something."

"Of course," Ruth said.

He looked at them and intertwined his fingers. "If the German Army draws near, I want you to take Aline and leave me behind."

Ruth swallowed. "We are not leaving you."

Lucette placed a hand on Pierre's shoulder. "You're going to make it to Paris—with us."

"*S'il te plaît*," he said. "I need to make sure that Aline is taken care of."

"I promise," Ruth said. "I'll do everything in my power to make sure that she's safe."

"Me too," Lucette said.

The man's eyes filled with gratitude. *"Merci."*

While Pierre and Lucette sat down to rest, Ruth joined Aline, who was seated on a small, dry section of dirt under the bridge.

"Where is Jimmie?" Aline brushed away damp hair that clung to her forehead.

"He's looking for a place for us to sleep tonight." Ruth removed the girl's backpack from her shoulder and placed it on her lap.

"Will he be gone long?" Aline asked.

"Non. He's not going far."

Aline stared into the rain and shivered.

Ruth placed an arm around her. "Did you eat the carrot top I gave you?"

"Not yet," Aline said.

"You should eat some of it."

"I can wait a little longer."

Ruth patted the girl's shoulder, small and bony. "My stomach is grumbling. Will you have a little of it with me?"

"All right. It's in my backpack."

Ruth unbuckled the backpack, reached inside, and felt something soft. She peeked into the pack and discovered Jimmie's good luck charm.

Aline plucked the toy from the backpack and handed it to Ruth. "His name is Piglet. Jimmie gave it to me to carry for good luck. It was a gift from his sister."

Ruth ran a finger over the pig's oversize pointed ears, and a feeling of comfort swelled inside her.

"Jimmie told me that he's a character in a book," Aline said. "He's small and shy, but he tries hard to be brave and beats his fears."

Ruth looked at Aline, her caramel-colored eyes surrounded by dark circles. "You're brave, like Piglet."

A smile formed on Aline's face. "That's what Jimmie said."

"Because it's true." Rain dripped from the bridge and fell onto Ruth's skirt. "How about we put Piglet away to keep him dry."

The girl nodded.

Ruth tucked the toy away and retrieved the carrot top. She broke a piece of the wilted, green stem and gave it to Aline.

The girl took a bite and chewed. "I thought you were going to eat."

"I will in a minute," Ruth lied. *You are skin and bones and will need every morsel to keep up your strength.*

Aline ate two more hunks of the greens and leaned back, propping herself upright with her arms. Her eyes grew glossy as she looked out over the rain.

"What are you thinking about?" Ruth asked.

"Maman."

"Would you like to tell me about Blanche?"

Aline looked at Ruth and nodded, as if grateful to hear her mother's name spoken. "She was smart, pretty, and artistic. Most evenings, she played songs on the piano for me." She glanced upward to the bridge. "At bedtime, we took turns reading storybooks. Then she'd tuck me in, kiss me good night, and tell me that tomorrow would be a beautiful day."

Ruth smiled. "She sounds lovely."

Aline nodded. "She took me and my papa on lots of picnics at a duck pond, where she liked to paint. She usually brought a basket of cheeses, baguettes, and pears and plums, which are my and my papa's favorite fruits. After we ate, we played a game of throwing small, flat rocks across the pond."

Ruth tilted her head. "Skipping stones?"

"*Oui*," Aline said. "It was a contest to see who could jump them across the surface of the water the most."

Ruth folded her arms over her knees and listened to Aline describe the proper size and shape of a good skipping stone, and the method to toss them over water.

Aline drew a deep breath and exhaled. Her bottom lip quivered. "I miss them."

Ruth wrapped an arm around her.

"My papa doesn't know that Maman is dead," Aline said. "He wrote to her every day while he was away in the army. It makes me sad to think that he might still be sending her letters."

Tears welled in Ruth's eyes.

"I pray that Papa is safe, and that I'll see him again," Aline said, her voice faint.

"You will. After this war is over, you and your papa will be together."

Aline hugged her.

For quite some time, they sat quietly under the bridge and looked out over the stream. The rain gradually eased, and birds began to chirp from the trees.

"Someday," Ruth said, breaking the silence, "I'd like for you to teach me how to skip a rock."

Aline slipped away and stood. She gathered a handful of small, flat stones from the edge of the stream and handed one to her.

Ruth stood.

"Like this." Aline, using a sidearm motion, threw a stone low over the water. The stone skipped two times across the surface and submerged into the stream.

"Good one," Ruth said. She stepped forward and tossed her stone, which sank upon hitting the water.

"It takes practice," Aline said, giving her another stone. "Try again."

They took turns skipping rocks. Ruth improved by bouncing a stone twice over the water, but Aline surpassed her by jumping a rock four times before sinking into the stream.

"Bravo!" Ruth said, clapping her hands.

Aline grinned.

Soon, Lucette and Pierre joined in. They skipped stone after stone across the water, and for the first time in weeks they were joyful.

Jimmie—his boots muddy and uniform soaked with rain—returned to the bridge shortly before nightfall. He led them to a horse stall in a barn of an abandoned farm, which was being used by dozens of refugees as shelter. Fortunately for their group, a woman with two adolescent boys, approximately thirteen and fourteen years of age, saved them a spot in a stall while Jimmie left to bring his group to the farm. As a token of gratitude, Ruth insisted that the woman and her boys join them to eat their group's last jar of pickled beets.

The refugees, most of whom were wet and exhausted, spoke little as they settled down on either the barn floor, stalls, or a hayloft for the night. A dull light, coming from a lantern that hung on a post near the door, flickered over the crowded space. Coughs and hushed voices drifted through the air, which contained an odor of manure despite the absence of farm animals.

Pierre, Aline, and Lucette settled onto a mound of straw to sleep, while Ruth and Jimmie remained awake while seated in a corner of the stall.

"Your jacket is soaked," Ruth said, her voice soft.

Jimmie ran a hand over the front of his leather flight jacket. "It should dry by morning."

"There's a quicker way." Ruth helped him to remove his sling and jacket while being careful not to jostle his splinted arm. She then stuffed the sleeves of the jacket, heavy and wet, with handfuls of straw.

Jimmie rubbed the stubble on his chin. "Are you sure about this?"

"Yes, straw is absorbent. It's used to keep the hooves of horses dry." She zipped up the stuffed jacket, which resembled the torso of a mannequin, and placed it under a pile of straw.

"Did you have horses on your family's apple orchard?"

"I wish," she said. "We used a tractor and a truck to haul our produce. But many people in the rural areas of Lewiston had livestock. As a child, I played gobs of hide-and-seek in a neighbor's horse barn. The hayloft was the best place to hide."

"Maine sounds like a brilliant place to grow up."

She nodded. "In addition to farmland, there is lots of water—the Androscoggin River runs through Lewiston and empties into the ocean at the Gulf of Maine. It's a beautiful area to go sailing, although I've only watched the boats from shore."

"Someday, I would like to go there," he said.

"I think you'd enjoy it, especially with your father being a ship builder. There are scads of small islands dotting the coast. It's a well-known, scenic place to explore by boat."

He fiddled with a strap on his splint. "I've never been much of a sailor. I think I'd feel more at home in your family's apple orchard."

Ruth smiled. Although her muscles ached and her brain craved sleep, she longed to speak with him. She scooched next to him, her side inches from his. "Maine feels like a million miles away."

"Do you plan to go back home?" he asked.

She drew a deep breath. "Eventually, but I feel like I have two homes."

"How so?"

"Lewiston will always be special to me, and I dearly miss my parents and our dog, Moxie. But I feel like I've grown roots in Paris."

"Because of your singing career?"

"Yes, but it's more than that. I adore my aunt and uncle, and I made good friends, especially with Lucette. There's something about Paris—its sights, sounds, and smells—that makes me feel alive, and that dreams are possible." She crossed her ankles. "Does that sound silly?"

"Far from it," he said. "Someday, when Europe is at peace, I'll come to Paris to see you perform."

"I'd like that."

"So," Jimmie said, picking up a piece of straw, "what does your boyfriend think about you putting your singing career on hold to join an ambulance corps?"

She smoothed wrinkles on her skirt. "I don't have a boyfriend."

"Fiancé?"

Ruth smiled. "There is no one like that. I've dated a little, but nothing serious." She looked at him. "Do you have anyone special back home?"

"No," he said. "I was seeing a woman named Vera during my last year at King's College London, but it didn't work out."

"What happened?"

"She ended our relationship when I told her that I wanted to join the RAF. She thought it was a waste of my degree in general engineering, and that it was foolish of me to risk my life as a fighter pilot." He ran a hand through his hair. "Four months later, Vera was engaged to a barrister in Sussex."

"Gosh. Were you upset?"

"At first," he said. "But as time went on, I realized that we were quite different people. I've always dreamed of flying, but I joined the RAF to fight the rise of fascism. Someday, I want to be with a woman who is willing to chase their aspirations, as well as place the needs of a nation ahead of their own."

Her eyes met his. "It was a good thing that it didn't work out."

"Indeed."

Ruth glanced at Pierre sleeping beside Aline. "I'm glad they have a dry place to rest."

"Me too." Jimmie leaned his back against the wall.

She nudged his boot, the heel clumped with mud. "I saw that you gave Aline your good luck charm."

"She's been through a lot," he said. "I thought it might provide her with a bit of comfort and hope, and I think Nora would be glad that her Piglet is keeping her company."

You're sweet and kind. Ruth, as if by reflex, gently touched his hand. "I'm sorry that your plane was shot down and you injured your arm, but we're fortunate to have you with us."

He clasped her fingers. "I'm the one who feels lucky."

Her skin tingled, and she squeezed his hand.

A distant rumble of bombs rolled over the countryside. Several refugees lifted their heads and peered toward the ceiling.

Aline stirred, got to her feet, and approached them.

Ruth eased her hand away. "Is everything okay?"

Aline rubbed her eyes. "*Toilette.*"

"I'll take you." Ruth looked at Jimmie. "You should get some rest."

"I will, after you return."

She nodded and stood.

Ruth and Aline left the stall and crossed the floor of the barn, all the while being careful not to disturb people who were sleeping on the ground. Outside, the rain had stopped and the cool, damp air was decorated with the sound of chirping crickets. Moonlight shimmered over the landscape as they walked past the farmhouse, its front porch lined with slumbering people wrapped in blankets, to an outhouse near the edge of a forest.

"It looks empty," Ruth said, "but knock before going inside."

Aline nodded. She scurried ahead, tapped on the door, and entered.

Voices drifted from inside the farmhouse, packed with people. Far to the north, artillery fire flashed on the horizon. Seconds later, a rumble of explosions echoed over the farm.

Ruth's shoulder muscles tensed. She crossed her arms and scanned the area.

The outhouse door creaked open and Aline stepped out.

"I should go, too," Ruth said. "Wait here."

"All right," Aline said.

Ruth entered the outhouse and was met by a strong smell of ammonia and excrement. She held her breath, hiked up her skirt, and lowered her underwear.

The sound of footsteps grew outside.

Hairs rose on the back of Ruth's neck. She peered at a half-moon-shaped hole in the door.

Aline gasped.

Ruth, her heart racing, yanked up her underwear and sprang from the outhouse to find Aline, facing a young man in a French Army trench coat. She froze.

"Are you a soldier?" Aline asked.

"*Oui*." The man, holding a small bundle of clothes, glanced at the farmhouse.

Ruth, feeling confused, placed an arm around Aline. "What are you doing here?"

The man lowered his eyes and shifted his weight.

Ruth's heart rate quickened. "What's happened?"

"I—" The man swallowed. He tucked the clothing, which included a worn pair of leather shoes, inside his trench coat.

Oh, God. She pulled Aline close. "Why are you deserting?"

His shoulders drooped. "We can't stop them. Much of our army is defeated, and the British are being evacuated to England."

Ruth's legs turned weak. "*Non.* It can't be."

"I heard the orders over the radio," he said. "I'm a wireless operator. The BEF and French troops are surrounded by Panzer divisions at the Channel. They're being evacuated from Dunkirk as we speak. The German forces are unstoppable. France will be lost."

"We must try," Ruth said. "You need to return to your post."

He shook his head. "It's over. I have a wife and baby boy in Creil—I must get there before the Germans."

Aline slipped from Ruth and approached him. "My papa, he's a soldier stationed at the Maginot Line. His name is Leopold Cadieux. Do you know him?"

"*Non*," he said.

A rustling came from the farmhouse porch and an old man's voice shouted, "Thief!"

The soldier jerked.

"Someone stole a bag of my clothes! Thief!"

The soldier, his face filled with shame, looked at Ruth. "I'm sorry." He turned and ran into the woods.

Ruth, her nerves shaken, kneeled to Aline and clasped her hands.

Aline's jaw quivered. "Have we lost the war?"

"*Non*," Ruth said, struggling to maintain her composure. "That man is scared and he made a mistake."

"Are you sure?"

"*Oui*." Ruth squeezed Aline's hands. "You'll be safe in Paris. The Allied armies will never surrender." *And neither will I.*

CHAPTER 26

PARIS, FRANCE—JUNE 3, 1940

Ruth, her anticipation growing, gazed at the horizon from the bed of a horse-drawn wagon. The clopping of hooves filled the morning air as an elderly man steered the wagon—that contained Ruth's group and six refugees—over a dirt road. At the crest of a hill, the skyline of Paris appeared.

Tears of happiness welled in Ruth's eyes. She nudged her friends, who were resting on a bed of straw.

Lucette sat up and clasped her hands. *"Dieu merci."*

Pierre placed an arm around his granddaughter and pointed. "That's Paris, my little cabbage."

Aline smiled.

Jimmie leaned to Ruth. "We couldn't have made it without you."

She blinked away tears. "It took all of us."

Over the past few days, Ruth and her group hitched a ride in a wagon, owned by an elderly couple who'd fled their farm in Rethel and were on their way to live with relatives in Chartres, a town southwest of Paris. Along the journey, rumors of Belgium's surrender to Germany and a British evacuation of soldiers in Dunkirk grew rampant. Although their rural route did not provide them access to newspapers, radio broadcasts, or working telephone lines, they'd heard hearsay reports from refugees about the demise of

Belgium and BEF troops. The speculations by the masses were overwhelming, and Ruth believed them to be true, considering her encounter with the French Army wireless operator who deserted his post.

Ruth had no more encounters with soldiers who abandoned their duty, but she did witness two military-service-age men, dressed in civilian clothing, walking alone through a field. She wondered why the men, who were staying far away from other refugees, had chosen a southeasterly path that, if continued for three hundred kilometers, would take them to the Swiss border. It saddened her to think that France's military might be on the brink of collapse, but her hopes gradually improved when the rumble of artillery explosions disappeared. She wondered if the absence of gunfire meant that the French Army had somehow pushed back the Germans, or if Hitler's forces were concentrating their firepower at the Channel. She'd decided it was the latter when Jimmie, days earlier, spotted an RAF squadron of Fairey Battle bombers, accompanied by three Hurricane fighters, flying in the direction of the coast.

Over the past days, the Luftwaffe raids on villages diminished, but the masses of refugees continued their exodus to the south. Also, the sightings of French and British aircraft grew infrequent. Although Jimmie had observed several Hurricane fighters, none of them had the markings of his squadron. And Ruth could tell, by the discontent on Jimmie's face while looking up at the planes, that he was eager for his arm to heal and to return to the war in the sky.

Each night during their travel, Ruth and her group slept either in barns or the back of the wagon. Long after the others fell asleep, she and Jimmie—regardless of their exhaustion—remained awake to talk. Through whispers, they discussed their families and memories of happier times, but Ruth was reluctant to lower her guard and fully open her heart. *It's reckless to believe we might have a future*, she'd thought, lying beside him under a starlit sky. *There's a war, and we'll be going in separate ways when we get to Paris.* She resolved to keep her emotions at bay and hoped that, after the conflict ended, their destinies would cross again.

Jimmie leaned his back against the side of the wagon and looked at Ruth. "What will you do when we arrive?"

"I'll take Pierre and Aline to my aunt and uncle's apartment in Le Marais," she said. "After I get them something to eat, Lucette and I will report to the ambulance corps headquarters for our assignment."

Lucette turned to Ruth. "While you're getting them settled in, I'm going to stop by my apartment to see if there's any news from Paul."

Ruth placed a hand on her friend's shoulder. "Of course."

"If the telephones are working," Lucette said, "I'll ring my parents in Toulouse to let them know I'm all right. I won't be long."

Ruth lowered her hand. "Take as much time as you need."

Lucette nodded, then looked at Jimmie. "Are you going with Ruth?"

Jimmie shook his head. "I prolonged my reporting for service long enough. When we arrive in the city, I'll go to the British Embassy to see if I can get word to my family and the RAF to let them know where I am. Then I'll try to determine where the RAF wants me to go until I'm well enough to resume my duty."

He'll be gone by this afternoon, Ruth thought. A wave of melancholy washed over her. She looked at him, a bright summer sun shining on his mussed brown hair, and she yearned to extend their time together, even if it was only a few more hours. "Do you know the location of the embassy?"

"No," he said. "I'll inquire with people on the street until I find it."

"I know where it is," Ruth said. "It's located within walking distance of my aunt and uncle's apartment. Come with me and I'll show you the way there."

"It might be easier if you gave me directions," he said.

"The streets of Paris can be confusing, especially in the eighth arrondissement where the embassy is located. Besides, you need something to eat. We've been subsisting on handouts of canned peas and pickled preserves, and my aunt's pantry will likely have better rations."

"Are you sure it's not too much trouble?"

Her eyes met his. "No trouble at all. I'll take you there while I'm waiting for Lucette."

He smiled. "Very well. Thank you."

At noon, they reached a north suburb of Paris and the roads were clogged with refugees who were entering the city. Ruth and her group, deciding it was faster to walk, thanked the old man and woman for the ride and exited the wagon.

"I might not see you again," Lucette said to Jimmie. She gave him alternating kisses on the cheeks. "Take care of yourself."

"You too," he said. "I can't thank you and Ruth enough for what you've done for me. You and Paul will remain in my thoughts."

"*Merci.*" Lucette turned and walked down the street.

Ruth watched her disappear into a crowd and hoped that her friend would receive good news about her fiancé.

Ruth led them to the nearby Riquet station of the Paris Métro and discovered that the trains were not running. They were an hour or so walk from the apartment, and Ruth desperately wanted to notify her aunt and uncle that she was safe. She entered a telephone booth with dingy white tiles and a smell of stale cigarette smoke. She placed the receiver to her ear and inserted a coin, given to her by Pierre. Her adrenaline surged at the sound of ringing and, eventually, the voice of a female operator. Ruth, assuming her aunt and uncle would be at work, asked the woman to connect her to Saint-Antoine Hospital.

"Please hold," the operator said.

Seconds later a female receptionist answered. "*Bonjour*, Saint-Antoine *hôpital.*"

"May I speak with Colette Bloch," Ruth said, her voice shaky. "She's a surgery nurse on the second floor."

"Medical staff are not permitted to accept calls while on duty," the woman said. "I can take a message."

"*S'il vous plaît*, the matter is urgent."

"I'm sorry. Message only, or you can speak with her when she's off duty."

Ruth slumped her shoulders. "All right. Please give a note to Colette that her niece, Ruth, called. If she's unavailable, deliver the message to her husband, Julian Bloch, a surgeon at the hospital. The message should read that I have returned to Paris from the battlefront with two people who need a place to stay."

"Oh, my," the receptionist said. "Were you near the combat?"

"*Oui*, I'm an ambulance driver for the army."

The woman paused, as if she were scribbling on a piece of paper.

"Would you like me to repeat the message?"

"*Non*," the receptionist said. "I think I can make an exception in this case. May I place you on hold?"

"Of course, *merci*."

Minutes later, Colette's voice came through the receiver. "Ruth?"

Tears blurred Ruth's vision. "*Oui*. It's me."

"*Dieu merci*," Colette cried. "Are you safe?"

"I am. I arrived in Paris late this morning. I'll be at the apartment in an hour or two. I have much to tell you, but Lucette and I will be reporting back for duty later today, and I wanted to let you know that we're all right." Ruth drew a deep breath and glanced through the glass window of the telephone booth. "I brought two people who fled their home that was in the path of the German invasion. A man named Pierre and his nine-year-old granddaughter, Aline, need shelter. Aline's mother was killed in a German air raid."

"I'm so sorry," Colette said. "Please put them in Marceau's room, and tell them that they're welcome to stay as long as they need."

"I will. That's what I thought you would say. *Merci*." Ruth tightened her grip on the receiver. "Are you and Uncle Julian safe in Paris?"

"For now," Colette said, the happiness gone from her voice. "Most of the troops, who were guarding the city, have been sent north or to the coast."

"Are the rumors about the BEF evacuation at Dunkirk true?"

"I don't know," she said. "There's little information on the war available. Most of the newspapers have ceased publishing, and the government is controlling the amount of information that is released by radio."

Oh, God.

"I'll try to send a telegram to inform your parents, but it might not get through. We'll talk more later. I need to report to surgery; the hospital received an inflow of injured soldiers from the field. I don't know when your uncle and I will be able to come home."

"Lucette and I are going to the ambulance corps headquarters. There's a chance I might miss you if they decide to immediately redeploy us."

"I'm grateful to hear your voice," Colette said, her voice quavering. "I'm proud of you."

Ruth rubbed her eyes. "I love you."

"I love you, too."

Ruth hung up the receiver. A blend of sadness and dread swirled inside her. She exited the telephone booth and rejoined the others.

"Everything all right?" Jimmie asked.

"*Oui.*" She put on a smile and looked at Aline and Pierre. "It's all arranged. My aunt and uncle are expecting you, and you can stay in their apartment for as long as you need."

Aline's eyes brightened.

"Bless you," Pierre said.

They exited the station and walked for an hour over streets noticeably absent of motorized vehicles. Like the Paris Métro, the buses were not running. Other than a few military vehicles and fancy automobiles—no doubt owned by wealthy Parisians—the roads were being used by horse-drawn wagons, pedestrians, and bicyclists, most of whom appeared to be traveling through the city on their way south. Also, Ruth was surprised to see that many of the stores, coffee shops, and patisseries were open, even though most of the displays in the windows were bare. To Ruth, it appeared as if Parisians were either doing their best to maintain a sense of normalcy, or they were in a deep state of denial of the looming threat of Hitler's armies.

Ruth looked at Jimmie, carrying Aline's backpack over his good shoulder. "How's your wrist?"

He raised his arm in the sling. "Getting better each day. No pain this morning."

"I'm glad." She pointed. "It's not much farther. The neighborhood ahead is Le Marais, where my—"

A siren sounded.

Ruth froze.

Another sired wailed, then another.

Aline's eyes widened. "What's happening?"

"Air raid," she said, struggling to remain calm. "Follow me. I
know the location of a shelter."

Ruth led them around a corner and down a street, but their
route became clogged with hundreds of residents who were leaving apartment buildings in search of underground bunkers. She
clasped Aline's hand and weaved through the throng as the sirens
grew to an ear-piercing roar. Antiaircraft guns, stationed in parks
and green spaces around the city, began to fire. White puffs of
smoke dotted the sky. Her heart pounded inside her chest.

"Hurry!" Ruth shouted.

Pierre labored to keep up. "Go without me!"

"Grandpapa!" Aline tried to pull away.

Ruth held tight to the girl's hand and weaved her through the
crowd.

Jimmie ran to Pierre, wrapped an arm around him, and helped
him to quicken his pace.

The mass of people jostled their way over the sidewalk, nearly
knocking Ruth from her feet. She struggled her way forward, all
the while determined to get Aline to safety. A block away from the
shelter, screams erupted from the crowd, compelling Ruth to turn
her eyes to the sky. Over a hundred German bombers flew high
above Paris, contested only by a squadron of French fighter planes
and inaccurate antiaircraft fire. Seeds of destruction dropped from
the bellies of the bombers and whistled to the ground.

Fear flooded Ruth's veins. She pulled Aline through the multitude of people, and she prayed that there would be enough bunkers in Paris for everyone.

CHAPTER 27

PARIS, FRANCE—JUNE 3, 1940

Jimmie's adrenaline surged from the sound of bombs detonating over the city. He helped Pierre, who was struggling to keep pace with the fast-moving crowd, to the entrance of an underground metro station that served the neighborhood of Le Marais. They followed Ruth and Aline down a narrow set of concrete stairs that was swarmed with people who were desperate to get underground. Once inside, they squeezed their way through the throng and hunkered together on the landing.

The ground trembled, and a piece of ceiling tile fell onto the train track. Beneath the rumble of bombs, whimpers and recital of prayers filtered through the subterranean passage. The lights, mounted to the tunnel walls, flickered and everything went black. A woman screamed, and a baby began to cry. Several people ignited cigarette lighters, and a few others turned on electric torches that they'd brought with them to the shelter.

Aline hugged her grandpapa.

Pierre drew a raspy inhale and held her tight. "It'll be all right. The bombs can't hurt us here."

Jimmie looked at Ruth. A dull torch light shimmered on her face, filled with apprehension. He reached out his hand and felt her clasp his fingers.

More bombs rumbled from above. Heads rose to the arched, tile-covered ceiling.

Pierre kissed his granddaughter on her head. He stood straight with his chin raised high, placed his beret over his heart, and began to sing the French national anthem.

Ruth squeezed Jimmie's hand. She closed her eyes, drew a breath, and sang along with Pierre. Her enchanting voice, like the timbre of a rare violin, resonated through the tunnel.

Wails and whimpers faded away, and Parisians steadily joined in, drowning out the muted rumble of explosions.

Jimmie, who didn't know the words, hummed the chorus. He admired Ruth's and Pierre's determination to inspire people with hope and unity. A deep resolve burned within him, and he vowed to return to his squadron and do his part to rid the Luftwaffe from the sky.

The singing ended, but the raids continued. In total, five waves of German bombers dropped their payloads on Paris before the all-clear siren sounded. People, many of whom were fearful to leave the protection of the underground, cautiously made their way out of the station.

On the street, Jimmie was met by an acrid smell of expelled explosives. A fire burned in a nearby neighborhood, but—in the west of the city—countless thick plumes of smoke rose high into the atmosphere. Horns of fire trucks blared.

Bloody hell. How could pilots knowingly drop bombs on civilians? Anger flared inside him.

"Come on," Ruth said, touching his shoulder. "We need to go."

Jimmie turned away from the fire plumes. He followed her and the others down a congested sidewalk, packed with people—their mouths agape in a state of shock and dismay.

The four traveled several blocks to a Lutetian limestone building next to a closed Jewish bakery. They entered, climbed the stairs to a third-floor landing, and Ruth removed a key from a pocket of her uniform and opened the door. Inside, Ruth showed Aline and Pierre their room straightaway, and she told them to help themselves to food in the kitchen.

"My aunt and uncle will be working late at the hospital," Ruth said. "I wish I could stay, but I need to report to the ambulance corps."

"I understand," Pierre said.

Aline approached Ruth and wrapped her arms around her waist. "Please don't go."

She stroked the girl's hair. "I need to leave. There are people that need my help. My aunt and uncle will help care for you and your grandpapa." She gave her a hug and looked at Pierre. "Do you remember the route to the air raid shelter?"

"I do," Pierre said. "*Merci*, for everything."

"You're welcome."

"I need to go, too," Jimmie said, looking at Pierre, "but I'll stop back here after I check in at the embassy."

Pierre nodded.

He and Ruth left the apartment and descended the stairs. They exited the building and faced each other.

"I'm sorry that I will not be walking you to the embassy," she said, "and that you didn't get something to eat."

"It's all right." He gently touched her shoulder.

She leaned into him.

He wrapped his arms around her and lowered his cheek to her hair. "I was hoping for a long goodbye."

"Me too." She squeezed him tight.

"Please—be careful."

She nodded. "Promise me you'll be safe."

"I will."

"*Adieu.*" She relaxed her embrace and slipped away.

Jimmie felt torn as he watched her disappear into a crowd. His heart urged him to run after her and never let her go. But his mind told him otherwise. *We're at war. Our people and countries come first, and we each have our duties to uphold.* He fought back his emotions and made his way toward the central area of the city, all the while hoping to reach the embassy before another wave of German bombing.

*   *   *

An hour after leaving Le Marais and asking several residents for directions, Jimmie arrived at the British Embassy. The entrance was absent of sentries, and he walked into a towering foyer— covered in black-and-white tiles that created a checkerboard pattern—where several men in black suits were lugging away stacks of cardboard boxes. A huge pile of papers and government documents covered an unattended receptionist desk.

Oh, no, Jimmie thought. *They're evacuating.* He approached a stout, middle-aged man who was carrying a box. "Excuse me, sir. I'm an RAF pilot, and I'm looking for someone who might be able to help me to reconnect with my squadron."

The man stopped, and his eyes narrowed in on Jimmie's sling. "Were you shot down?"

"Yes, sir."

"Do you need medical attention?"

"No, sir. I'd like to get word to the Seventy-Three Squadron on my position, and receive instruction on where to report."

The man put down his box and wiped sweat from his forehead. "At the moment, things are quite chaotic and there's little the embassy can do for you. Due to the bombing, much of the staff has yet to return to work, and others are in emergency meetings. I recommend that you report to a French military base in Paris to seek direction, or you could come back to the embassy tomorrow."

Jimmie furrowed his brow. "With all due respect, sir, there might not be a tomorrow."

The man stepped back, as if he were poked in the chest. "I'm sorry. I regret that I have nothing more to offer. Good luck to you, young man." He picked up his box and walked down a corridor.

Jimmie, feeling frustrated, glanced at a British flag that was displayed at the entrance, and he wondered how many days the embassy would remain in operation. He exited the building and walked along the sidewalk.

A clacking of shoes on the pavement came from behind him. He paused and turned.

A young, bespectacled man, wearing a gray suit, ran to him.

"Pardon me," he said with an English accent. "I was inside the embassy and overheard your conversation."

Jimmie nodded. "Any chance you could point me in the direction of the nearest air base?"

The man glanced over his shoulder, as if to make sure he was out of earshot. "There is little chance of reaching your squadron. The RAF is in the process of relocating their forces to airfields, farther south of the enemy."

"I'm aware," Jimmie said. "After I was shot down, I returned to my airfield and found it abandoned."

The man removed his wire-rimmed glasses and wiped the lenses with a handkerchief. "The BEF troops at Dunkirk are being evacuated across the Channel. There weren't enough military vessels, so Churchill requisitioned every available civilian boat in England." He slipped his glasses on his face and looked at Jimmie. "They are trying to save our bloody army with a flotilla of fishing boats and leisure yachts."

Jimmie's eyes widened.

"Dunkirk will soon be captured by the Germans, and they'll turn their Panzers to the south. The French don't have the troops to stop them. In a week, perhaps two, Paris will fall."

Hairs rose on the back of Jimmie's neck. "How do you know this?"

"I'm an interpreter," the man said. "I sit in on the Anglo-French Supreme War Council meetings that are held in Paris. I'm privy to Allied military strategy and intelligence."

Jimmie swallowed. "Surely, you're sworn to secrecy. Why are you telling me this?"

"Because you might get killed by trying to search for an RAF squadron that will, in short order, be flown back to Britain. I can't, in good conscience, sit idle and allow that to happen." He ran a hand over his hair. "In the coming months, we'll need pilots, like you, to defend British airspace and to keep the Germans from storming our shores."

A deep foreboding swelled within Jimmie. "If you were me, what would you do?"

"I'd leave Paris and travel south to the coast," he said. "The

British Admiralty is working on plans for more evacuation of British and French troops—as well as ground crews of the RAF—that are unable to reach Dunkirk."

"Where?"

"I don't know for certain," the man said. "But I heard senior British military leaders of the council discuss several potential evacuation points in Brittany, including Brest and the Loire estuary. They also mentioned other locations, as far south as Saint-Jean-de-Luz on the Basque coast."

Good God. We're giving up the fight for France. He felt sick to his stomach. "What will you do?"

"I will remain here to destroy any material that could be of value to the Germans. Eventually, the embassy will close and I'll get to one of the evacuation ports—hopefully before Hitler's Panzers do."

Jimmie's mind raced as he tried to absorb the man's story. He didn't want to believe the claims, but—deep in his gut—he believed the man's words to be true. He extended his arm. "Thank you. I'm Flying Officer Jimmie Quill."

"Nigel," he said, as if reluctant to reveal his full name. He shook Jimmie's hand. "Godspeed."

"And you."

Nigel turned, jogged down the sidewalk, and entered the embassy.

Jimmie, shaken by the man's revelation, made his way out of the 8th arrondissement. He walked along the River Seine with a view of the Eiffel Tower, its wrought-iron lattice structure pointed to a sky marred with smoke. He imagined Wehrmacht troops, their jackboots clacking as they marched over the Avenue des Champs-Élysées, and a Nazi swastika flag on the Arc de Triomphe. Ire grew inside him. Despite Nigel's warning and the grim outcome for Paris, he had no plan to leave the city until he informed Pierre and Ruth's family.

The sun gradually set as he walked on his route toward Le Marais. Most of the citizens had gone to their apartments or an underground shelter for the night, and fire trucks raced over barren streets to the west side of the city, where fires continued to rage. A light wind, drifting through the streets, reeked of charred wood and expelled explosive.

At a small park, a group of old men—wearing tarnished tin helmets from the Great War—were stacking sandbags around an antiaircraft gun that had been placed next to a children's swing set. A frail, bow-legged man struggled to lift a bag of sand, and Jimmie came to his aid. Using one arm, he helped the man to load sandbag after sandbag, even though a barricade would be futile in slowing the German Army.

CHAPTER 28

PARIS, FRANCE—JUNE 4, 1940

Jimmie woke to the smell of brewed coffee and fried egg. He rose from a sofa in the living room of Ruth's aunt and uncle's apartment and peeked out the window. Below, the street was empty except for a group of women and children, who were carrying blankets and pillows as they walked on the sidewalk. *They slept in a bomb shelter.* He hoped that yesterday's German air raid missed their targets and there were no casualties, but he knew that would not be the case, given the roar of fire trucks and ambulances that had lasted through much of the night. *Hitler intends to break the will of the French by bombing communities and sending fear through the population.* He flexed the hand of his injured arm, and he pledged to himself that he would return to the fight.

Jimmie shook away his thoughts and entered the kitchen to find Pierre, standing in front of the stove. Eggs sizzled in an iron skillet.

Pierre, holding a spatula, turned to Jimmie. *"Bonjour.* I made us breakfast."

"Smells good."

"I'm not much of a cook," Pierre said, "but I can assure you that it'll taste better than the pickled onions and radishes we've been eating on the road."

"Indeed." He rubbed thick stubble on his face. "Did Ruth's aunt and uncle come home last night?"

Pierre shook his head. "Have a seat. We'll have coffee while we wait for Aline to wake."

Jimmie sat at a table. His mind drifted to Ruth, and he hoped that the ambulance corps deployed her someplace that would give her an escape route to the coast.

Late last evening, Jimmie arrived at the apartment. Pierre and Aline were asleep, and Ruth's aunt and uncle had yet to come home from the hospital. Hungry and exhausted, he ate a hunk of a stale baguette that he found in the kitchen and fell asleep on the sofa.

"Here," Pierre said, placing a cup of coffee in front of Jimmie.

He took a sip, acidic and bitter.

"What do you think?"

"It's splendid. Thank you."

Pierre grinned. He poured himself a cup and sat across from him.

Jimmie's mind flashed to his discussion with the interpreter. "I have news on the war from my visit to the embassy."

Pierre took a gulp of coffee. "Good, I hope."

"It's not, I'm afraid."

Pierre frowned.

For several minutes, Jimmie told him about what he'd learned from the interpreter—the BEF evacuation across the Channel, the lack of French troops to defend Paris, and a supposed operation to save military personnel who are left stranded in France after the evacuation at Dunkirk.

"*Mon Dieu*." Lines formed on Pierre's forehead. "Are you certain the man's information is accurate?"

"His words rang true. He claimed that his role as an embassy interpreter provided him with direct access to conversations between senior British and French leaders of the Anglo-French Supreme War Council."

Pierre clasped his hands with his elbows on the table. "What are you going to do?"

"Eventually, I'll head south to find a way across the Channel, but I won't leave until I've exhausted efforts to locate Ruth and

Lucette to inform them about what I know. Also, I want to speak with Ruth's aunt and uncle about the news."

Pierre nodded.

"In the meantime, I will make a visit to Orly Air Base, on the south side of Paris. There's no RAF there, as far as I know, but I have an obligation to try to get word to my squadron." Jimmie shifted in his seat and looked at Pierre. "Will you stay in Paris?"

"*Non*," he said. "When it becomes evident that Paris will fall to the Germans, I will leave with Aline."

A memory of Aline, helping her grandpapa take a nitroglycerin pill, flashed in Jimmie's brain. "Without motor transport, the journey to the coast will be arduous, and twice as long as the route we took to Paris. The bombings will cease if the city becomes occupied by the Germans. Perhaps it might be safer for you and Aline to remain here until the region is liberated."

"Never," Pierre said firmly.

"Why?"

"Because I have firsthand experience of how German conquerors treat their captives." Pierre, his eyes surrounded in dark circles, looked at Jimmie. "I was a prisoner in Lille during its German occupation in the Great War."

Jimmie clasped his cup.

"I was in my late forties and too old for service in the last war. My wife, Zelia, and I were in Lille with our son, Leopold—he was nine years old at the time—when the German Army seized our city. I was arrested and imprisoned in the Citadel of Lille. Each day, I was forced to march, with my hands and feet in shackles, through the town." Pierre rubbed his wrist, as if the memory had resurrected the pain he'd experienced. "Putting prisoners on display to the citizens of Lille was the German military's way of demoralizing us."

"I'm sorry."

Pierre nodded. "It was worse for Zelia and Leopold. Thousands of Lille women were rounded up by German soldiers and taken away to farm the French countryside—Zelia was one of them."

Oh, God, Jimmie thought.

"Leopold found refuge with an elderly woman, but she died soon after the German occupation. To survive, he worked as a stable boy for the German cavalry."

"I can't imagine what you and your family went through," Jimmie said.

"We were lucky to survive. Zelia never spoke about her experience in the labor camp, and I never wanted to know. I was grateful for us to be together to raise our son. After the Great War, we had many joyful years, and we never took our freedom and togetherness for granted." Tears welled up in his eyes and he wiped them away. "Forgive me. Even though it has been six years since Zelia died, my sorrow sometimes feels raw."

"It's quite all right," Jimmie said. "I can tell that you loved her a lot."

"More than anyone could care for another soul."

Jimmie thought of Ruth, curled next to him in a wagon, and the immense contentment that flowed through him. He set aside his memory and took a sip of coffee.

"In this war, a German occupation will be much worse for Jewish people, like me and Aline." Pierre tapped the side of his cup. "The Nazis persecute Jews."

Jimmie nodded.

"For years, the Germans have enforced laws which marginalize Jews. But the racism and hate has grown." He swirled his coffee. "Are you familiar with *Kristallnacht?*"

The Night of Broken Glass, Jimmie thought. "Yes, it was a riot by the Nazi Party against thousands of Jewish-owned businesses. I read about it in *The Times* of London."

"It was far worse than that. They destroyed hundreds of synagogues. Thousands of Jewish men were arrested and sent away to concentration camps, and many people were killed."

Muscles in Jimmie's shoulders tensed.

"In Lille, I had a close Jewish friend named Ernst who had family in Berlin. The night of the riots, Ernst's brother was dragged from his apartment above his clock store. While some of the members of the Nazi paramilitary set his home and business ablaze, others beat him to death with clubs while his wife and children were forced to watch."

"Oh, God." Jimmie felt sick to his stomach.

"I tell you this not to disturb you, but to reveal my reasoning for not remaining in Paris if it falls to Germany." He looked at Jimmie. "I need to protect Aline, and will stay one step ahead of Hitler's army no matter how far I need to walk."

Jimmie leaned forward. "Then you and Aline should come with me to the coast."

Pierre shook his head. "You are searching for an unknown port that is supposed to have a naval operation to remove the remaining military personnel from France. Even if we find it, I doubt that civilians would be permitted to board the boats."

"I will find a way to gain passage for you and Aline."

"That's kind of you to try to help us," Pierre said, "but I will need to choose our destination based on the direction of the German troops."

Door hinges squeaked, soft footsteps grew in the hallway, and Aline—holding Piglet—entered the kitchen. "*Bonjour.*"

"*Bonjour*, my little cabbage," Pierre said, putting on a smile. He stood and gave her a hug.

"Did you sleep well?" Jimmie asked.

"*Oui*," she said. "I'm glad you're back."

"Me too," Jimmie said.

"I made breakfast," Pierre said. "Fried eggs and bread."

"*Merci.*" Aline peeked into the skillet that contained three well-cooked eggs with bits of baguette. "It's been a long time since we had a real breakfast. We should do something special for Ruth's aunt and uncle for allowing us to eat their food."

"I agree," Pierre said. "Do you have any ideas for how we could earn our keep?"

"We should clean the apartment," she said, "and do all of the dishes."

"I'll wash and you'll dry," Pierre said.

She nodded.

Pierre slipped a hand into his jacket pocket and glanced over the room. "Perhaps you could draw a few pictures for them. You're a gifted artist, like your *maman*. I bet they would enjoy having a few drawings to brighten up their apartment. What do you think?"

"I could try to make a picture of the duck pond that Maman liked to paint."

"*Magnifique!*" Pierre reached behind Aline's ear and, using his sleight of hand, produced a coin.

Aline grinned. "You must perform your magic for them."

"I will." He helped her into a seat and served breakfast.

Jimmie chewed a bite of egg, rich and well salted, and washed it down with a gulp of coffee. His energy began to grow, and with it came a deep admiration for Pierre. He wished that someday he'd be fortunate enough to have his own family, and if he ever became a grandfather, he hoped he would be as good of one as Pierre.

They silently ate their meal and Jimmie's mind drifted to the looming threat of the Germans capturing Paris. He felt helpless with a broken arm that rendered him unable to fly, yet he was determined to do everything he could to combat the enemy. He glanced at Pierre and Aline, collecting bits of oily bread with their forks. *I may be powerless to fight the Luftwaffe, but I won't give up the battle to protect them.* He sipped coffee and resolved to persuade Pierre to go with him to the coast, and to find a way to get him and Aline on a ship to freedom.

CHAPTER 29

LONDON, ENGLAND—JUNE 4, 1940

On the morning that the German Army hoisted swastika flags on the docks at Dunkirk, Prime Minister Winston Churchill was working at his bedroom desk in the underground Cabinet War Rooms. Using a fountain pen and stationery, he toiled away at drafting a speech to give to the House of Commons of the Parliament. The purpose of his address was twofold—to allay the euphoric public response to the evacuation from Dunkirk, and to pledge to never surrender. He wrote, revised, and revised again, all the while carefully choosing words to inform and inspire the minds and hearts of the British people.

A knock came from the door.

"Come in," he said with his eyes focused on his draft.

General Ismay entered. "Good day, sir." He glanced at Churchill's paper, covered in cursive handwriting with a multitude of changes and deletions. "I see that you're preparing for your address. Shall I return later?"

"No," Churchill said, scrawling on his stationery. "I was about to summon you. Please sit."

Ismay removed his military cap and sat in a green upholstered chair next to the desk.

Churchill ceased writing, examined his work, and frowned. "A great number of our citizens are of the opinion that the evacuation at Dunkirk is a victory. Wars cannot be won by evacuations."

"I agree, sir," Ismay said. "Britons are desperate for good news. Since the start of the war, Europe has endured little more than fear and devastation from the Germany military. Over the past week, we achieved an unprecedented feat, using both military and civilian vessels, to save most of our army. It has given our people hope."

"Indeed," Churchill said. "However, they must know that we suffered an immense military disaster, and they need to be apprised of a possible invasion attempt by that barbaric dictator's military, without raising doubt that we will—in the end—be victorious."

"Point taken, sir," Ismay said. "I'm quite confident that you will find the proper words to do so."

Eventually. Churchill raised his eyes from his draft. "I assume that Vice Admiral Ramsay has briefed you on the results of the Dunkirk evacuation."

"He has, sir." Ismay shifted in his seat. "As we expected, Dunkirk has fallen."

"When?"

"An hour ago." Ismay folded his arms. "The Royal Navy estimates that over thirty thousand French troops didn't make it out and were captured."

Churchill rolled his pen between his fingers. "Do you have an analysis on the number of evacuees?"

Ismay removed a note from his pocket. "A rough count is three hundred and thirty-eight thousand troops—two hundred fifteen thousand are British, and one hundred twenty-three thousand are French. Included in the tally are several hundred unarmed mule handlers from the Royal Indian Army Service Corps."

Churchill nodded. "How many BEF casualties?"

"We're still working to confirm numbers of soldiers who were either killed, wounded, missing, or taken prisoner."

"An estimate will suffice," Churchill said.

Ismay adjusted his tunic, tightly fitted over his broad chest. "It will likely be over sixty thousand casualties, sir."

Churchill put down his pen and rubbed his forehead. "Tell me the tally on lost weaponry and supplies."

"Most of our equipment was destroyed or abandoned." Ismay flipped over his piece of paper and viewed a list. "We lost over two thousand antiaircraft guns and antitank guns, sixty thousand motorized vehicles, seventy thousand long tons of ammunition, four hundred thousand long tons of supplies, and one hundred sixty thousand long tons of petrol."

The Germans will use the undestroyed weapons and supplies against us. Anger burned inside Churchill yet his appearance remained composed.

"Also," Ismay said, "approximately two hundred British and Allied sea craft were sunk, including the six Royal Navy destroyers, which you already know about."

He retrieved a cigar from a box on his desk and lit it. He took a long drag, bringing smoke into his lungs and steadying his nerves. "What about the RAF?"

"We lost over one hundred and forty aircraft. No word on the number of pilots and crew who perished." Ismay put away his note. "The RAF indicates that we shot down an equal or slightly higher number of German planes."

Churchill flicked ash into a bronze cigar tray. "Our air victories will be meaningless if we fail to evacuate the remaining troops who are stranded in France. We need the full force of our military to defend our island."

Ismay nodded.

Churchill swiveled his chair and looked at a map of Europe that was posted on the wall behind his desk. "Do you have an update on the plans to evacuate the remaining Allied troops?"

"I do." Ismay gestured to the map. "If I may, sir."

"By all means."

Ismay stepped forward. "We have plans for two additional naval evacuations. The first one, called Operation Cycle, will be in Normandy." He placed a finger on the map. "Within a week, we will commence an evacuation at the port of Le Havre. Our aim is to remove twenty thousand Allied soldiers."

Churchill clamped his cigar between his molars.

"The port is currently one hundred fifty kilometers from the German line, and we expect Le Havre to fall within days of commencing the operation."

Churchill puffed smoke. "We must do better, Pug," he said, using the general's nickname. "We have far more souls to save."

"Yes, sir." Ismay ran his finger down the French coastline on the map. "We have a second evacuation—Operation Aerial—that will commence in Brittany at Saint-Nazaire, near the mouth of the Loire River. It will be a large-scale mission. Our goal is to remove two hundred thousand British, French, Polish, and Czech troops, as well as some civilians."

Operation Aerial, Churchill thought. "Given the name of the mission, I presume that the RAF will play a significant role."

"Correct. The Allied rescue ships will be covered by five RAF fighter squadrons located at French bases. There will also be assistance from aircraft in England."

Churchill took a drag on his cigar. "When will Operation Aerial commence?"

"The Admiralty is working on the precise date. Our best estimate is ten to fourteen days from now."

"Too long."

"With all due respect, sir, it will take time for the bulk of the troops to make their way to Saint-Nazaire."

"It will also provide the enemy with ample time to arrive there as well."

Ismay shifted his weight.

"I was contacted by French Prime Minister Reynaud this morning," Churchill said. "He provided no details on the Luftwaffe bombing raid on Paris, but he did inform me that they have begun the process to relocate the French government to Tours."

Ismay rubbed his jowl.

"Every effort should be exhausted to accelerate the timeline of Operation Aerial."

"Yes, sir."

Churchill gestured with his cigar to the map. "Italy is planning to enter the war on Germany's side, Norway will likely negotiate its surrender to Hitler within the week, the French line at the

Somme will soon succumb to Panzers, and France will inevitably fall."

General Ismay drew a deep breath and nodded.

"It will be Britain that stands alone in the fight." Churchill tamped out his cigar and looked into the eyes of his chief military assistant. "We shall not fail. We shall bring back our troops, rebuild our military might, and achieve nothing less than victory."

Ismay raised his chin. "Indeed, sir."

"I will call a war cabinet meeting after my speech at the House of Commons," Churchill said. "I trust that you will inform the Chiefs of Staff about our discussion."

"I will, sir. Have a good address at the House of Commons." Ismay put on his cap, exited the room, and closed the door behind him.

Alone, the burden of the war weighed heavy on Churchill. *The fight for Britain's survival has barely begun, and yet far too many souls have been lost.* He resumed his work on the draft of his speech. Unsatisfied with the words, he crumpled the paper and dropped it into a rubbish bin. He took out a fresh sheet of stationery and started over from scratch.

CHAPTER 30

PARIS, FRANCE—JUNE 4, 1940

Ruth's back muscles flared as she helped Lucette and two gray-haired medics to place a stretcher—holding a wheezing, unconscious man with his body and face covered in soot—into the back of a hospital ambulance. The medics slid the man, his limbs limp, onto a cot and handed the stretcher to Ruth, who stood outside the vehicle. As the ambulance raced away from the parking lot, she and Lucette returned to the vast, smoldering remains of the Citroën automobile factory.

The factory, which had been converted to military production for the war, was now a mountainous mound of melted steel, fallen brick, and burned-out armored vehicles. It had taken a direct hit from German bombs, and the only part of the complex that remained unscathed was an annex, where manufacturing materials were stored. Scores of firefighters searched through the rubble, while hundreds of people—hoping to find their loved ones alive—stood vigil near the parking lot.

A piercing whistle shrilled through the air.

Ruth's body stiffened.

"There," Lucette said, pointing to a group of firemen pulling away chunks of debris.

Ruth, along with Lucette, lifted the stretcher and clambered over thirty meters of rubble. The air reeked of burnt chemicals, and Ruth coughed from breathing in ash. She pushed on, struggling to maintain her footing on mounds of broken bricks, until they reached the firemen.

Ruth and Lucette placed down the stretcher.

A fireman—his soot-smeared face streaming with sweat—looked at Ruth and shook his head.

Her heart sank.

The firemen placed a lifeless body onto the stretcher. Ruth, Lucette, and two of the firemen carried the corpse to a makeshift morgue in the annex building, where over two hundred perished men covered the ground.

Ruth and Lucette, along with dozens of civilian volunteers, had labored through the night to aid firemen with recovering victims from the wreckage. At the time of the Luftwaffe bombing raid, a thousand or more employees were working on the day shift at the factory. Firemen, who'd come from stations across the city, searched and removed victims from the rubble, while medics and ambulance workers carried away the casualties. In addition to the two hundred dead that were dug out of the ruins, three times as many injured workers were rushed away to hospitals across Paris. But as hours passed and night turned to day, few people were found alive.

Ruth and Lucette had not gone directly to the Citroën automobile factory. They initially reported for duty at the headquarters of the French Army's ambulance corps, and Ruth found Lucette, waiting for her at the front of the building. The headquarters was sparse of military personnel and the parking lot—once lined with freshly painted ambulance trucks—was empty. They found Chief Corporal Faucher, the man who'd reluctantly admitted Ruth into the corps, seated at a desk in an office on the second floor. Faucher's face was pale and his eyes were lackluster, as if the air raid had put him into a mild state of shock. He had difficulty recognizing Ruth and Lucette, and he twice asked for their names, which he verified with a list of volunteers in his desk.

"I am unable to assign you an ambulance," the corporal had said, placing down his list. "The army has run out of vehicles."

My God, Ruth had thought. *How will the army transport their injured without ambulances?*

Ruth and Lucette had pressed the corporal on a location to report to, but he'd shrugged and told them that there was nothing more he could do. They exited the ambulance corps headquarters to the wail of fire engines, racing through the city toward plumes of smoke. Despite having no ambulance or post assignment, they were determined to help with the aftermath of the German raid. So, they waved down the driver of a local hospital ambulance, who allowed them to hitch a ride on his route to the west side of the city. Thirty minutes later, they arrived at the destroyed Citroën automobile factory. Firefighters put Ruth and Lucette to work, helping to place the injured in nonmilitary ambulances and vehicles to be rushed to hospitals, and to move the dead to a nearby annex building.

By late afternoon—over twenty-four hours after the German air raid—the search and rescue effort subsided. Haggard firemen gradually began to leave, but a long line of grieving family members stretched from the makeshift morgue, where a priest and medic were assisting people to identify the dead.

Ruth, her mind and body drained, sat down on a pile of bricks. For the past day, she'd fought to remain strong and resilient while seeing horrific things. But now that her work was finished, the floodgates that held back her emotions broke open. Her body trembled, and tears spilled from her eyes.

Lucette settled beside her.

"All those poor people," Ruth said, her voice raw.

Lucette's bottom lip quivered. "Unspeakable."

"It's not supposed to happen this way," Ruth said. "Wars are supposed to be fought on battlefields and in trenches." She wiped her eyes and glanced at a wailing woman who was being consoled by a priest. Her stomach felt nauseous. "Hitler's Luftwaffe has taken the war to cities, with no regard for the killing of civilians."

Lucette placed a hand on her friend's shoulder.

Ruth blinked tears from her eyes. "No matter how bad things get, I will never give up."

"Neither will I."

Ruth and Lucette silently remained on their pile of bricks until the sun began to set and their sorrow subsided. They hitched a ride on a firetruck to the center of Paris and climbed out to sidewalks bustling with people who were exiting their apartment buildings with bags and luggage. A woman, pushing a stroller packed with clothes and two wheels of cheese, brushed past them.

"The bombing has accelerated the exodus," Lucette said.

"It has, and it will only get worse in the coming days."

Lucette nodded. "What do you think we should do about trying to find a post with an ambulance?"

"I don't know," Ruth said. "We've been up for two days and I'm having trouble thinking clearly. Perhaps we could decide tomorrow, after we get some rest."

Lucette nodded.

"What are your plans?" Ruth asked.

"The telephone lines were down when I stopped by my place before the air raid. I'd like to check again to see if I can get a message through to my parents in Toulouse."

"Did you receive any news on Paul?"

"*Non*," Lucette said, lowering her eyes.

"You will," Ruth said. "He's going to be okay."

Lucette nodded.

"After you stop by your apartment," Ruth said, "come over and stay with us. Maybe my aunt and uncle's telephone will be working. I forgot to check it when I was there."

"But your place is full—Pierre and Aline are staying with you."

Ruth wondered, although briefly, where Jimmie had gone after reporting to the embassy. *He might have been ordered to go to an air base, or maybe he was directed to a port for passage to Britain. Either way, I may never see him again.* She shook away her thought and said, "It's safer if we stick together. You can sleep in my room. The bed is plenty big enough for two."

"I'm filthy," Lucette said, running a hand over her uniform. "I need to bathe and clean my clothes."

"Then wash, put on some old clothes, and bring your dirty uniform over to my apartment. We can clean them together."

"You're not giving up on this, are you?"

Ruth shook her head. "I'm not going to let you be alone after what we've been through. I'm sure you'd do the same for me if I was going off to an empty apartment."

"True." Lucette, her eyes filled with gratitude, looked at Ruth. "*Merci.* I'll be over late this evening."

They went their separate ways and Ruth began her walk toward Le Marais, all the while weaving through people who were on their way out of the city. Her body ached and her brain was foggy, but when she neared Saint-Antoine Hospital, she felt compelled to check in on her aunt and uncle, even if she would likely be turned away. *At least I'll know that they are okay.*

She entered the hospital to a frenzy of nurses and doctors who were caring for bomb victims. Moans and cries cut through the air, filled with a smell of antiseptic, and the lobby and a main corridor were lined with occupied gurney beds. She'd expected that most of the injured would be workers from the Citroën automobile factory, but many of the patients were children. Several meters away, a young boy—whimpering while being held by a nurse—was having his head laceration stitched by a doctor. The wheels of a gurney squeaked as a grammar-school-age girl, her hair matted with dirt and her legs wrapped in bandages, was rushed toward an operating room.

Oh, God. Her muscles turned weak.

"Ruth!"

She turned.

Aunt Colette, her nurse uniform smeared with blood on one of the sleeves, ran to Ruth and wrapped her arms around her.

Ruth hugged her.

"*Dieu merci!*" Colette released her and looked at Ruth's soot-covered clothing. "Are you all right?"

"I am," Ruth said. "I was helping to remove injured workers at an automobile factory." Ruth glanced at a child who was receiving stitches. "What happened?"

"A bomb struck a school," Colette said. "Eighteen of the wounded children were sent here."

A wave of anger surged through Ruth.

"The hospital has run out of rooms," Colette said. "We're putting patients on gurneys in the hallways."

"Is there anything I can do?"

Colette placed a hand to her cheek. "You've done your part. Go home and rest."

"What about you?"

"I have more to do," Colette said, slipping her hand away. "Julian is still in surgery. We should be home by morning, assuming there is not another attack."

"Maybe I could do something to help," Ruth said. "I know how to apply bandages and—"

"*Non*. You've done enough."

A child's cry grew from a hallway.

"I need to go." Colette touched a hand to her lips and darted away.

Ruth reluctantly left the hospital. Outside, the streets were dark due to the blackout rules. Some refugees continued their southward journey through the city, while others, mostly the elderly and young women with babies, camped in cemeteries and parks for the night. As she continued her walk, visions of injured children on gurneys echoed in her head. An image of a crushed man pulled from rubble flashed in her mind. A profound feeling of sadness twisted inside her, and she wished she had the means to save them all.

CHAPTER 31

PARIS, FRANCE—JUNE 4, 1940

Ruth reached the apartment building, its windows covered with heavy curtains to prevent the escape of light. She entered the front door to a silent foyer. No radios. No creaks of floorboards. No voices drifting from apartments. To Ruth, it was as if the residents were either asleep or had fled the city, or a combination of both. She climbed the stairs using the handrails to ease the weight on her leg muscles, tired and riddled with ache. At the landing, she reached into her uniform jacket and searched for the key. Before she could find it, a lock clicked and the door swung open. Ruth looked up, and her breath stalled in her chest at the sight of Jimmie. She shot forward and wrapped her arms around him.

"You're still here," she said.

"I couldn't leave." Jimmie, using his good arm, held her tight. "Are you all right?"

I am now. She released him and nodded. "Why didn't you go?"

"I needed to speak with you." He helped her inside and shut the door.

"What about?"

Jimmie looked at Ruth, her face smeared with soot and her clothes soiled. "It can wait. Let's take care of you first. How about some food and rest?"

"I don't think I can eat anything," she said, "but I need something to drink."

They went to the kitchen and Jimmie, using one hand, poured her a glass of water from a faucet and handed it to her.

She gulped water, soothing a dry burn in her throat. "Where are Pierre and Aline?" she asked, setting down her glass.

"They're asleep in their room."

"How are they?"

"Well," he said. "The rest has given Pierre renewed energy, and Aline's spirit is better. She's quite a resilient girl."

Ruth, feeling relieved, drained her water. She refilled the glass and gulped it down. "Sorry. I'm a little dehydrated."

"It's all right. I'm happy you're safe."

"You too." She turned to him. "How's the arm?"

He smoothed a hand over his sling. "Getting better each day."

"I'm glad." She set her glass on the counter. "I'm going to wash and change, and then I want you to tell me why you're still here."

He nodded.

Ruth went to the washroom and filled the bathtub. Using a greenish-hued chunk of Marseille soap, she washed her hair and scrubbed away the dirt embedded in her skin and under her nails. The water turned brown, so she refilled the tub and bathed a second time. She brushed tangles from her towel-dried hair, and she put on an old gray skirt and white blouse that she hadn't used since she joined the ambulance corps. She looked at her reflection in a mirror above the washbasin and saw a stranger. Dark circles surrounded her eyes. She'd lost a good deal of weight, and her cheeks were sunken and her clavicles protruded from the neckline of her blouse. *I look awful*, she thought, but her self-pity was soon erased by a wave of sorrow. *I'm alive, unlike so many Parisians who perished in the bombing raid.* She shook away her thoughts and left the washroom.

Ruth entered the kitchen to the aroma of brewed coffee. "Smells good."

"Have a seat," Jimmie said, placing a steaming cup on the table. "I must warn you, I guessed at the measurements. I'm more skilled at preparing tea."

"*Merci.*" She took a drink, savoring the coffee's warm bitterness. He sat next to her.

She turned her chair to face him. "Okay. Tell me why you're still here."

Jimmie paused, adjusting his sling. He leaned forward and, for several minutes, he told her about what he'd learned from the embassy interpreter—the troops that were evacuated across the Channel, the lack of Allied forces to protect Paris, and the speculation that naval operations were being planned to save military personnel who didn't make it out of Dunkirk.

The color drained from Ruth's face. "Are you sure about this?"

"Yes, I believe the man's story."

Ruth's shoulders tensed and she clasped her cup with both hands. "If it's true, it means that Paris will fall."

"And France, I'm afraid."

Her stomach ached. "The French armies were immense, and the battle at Sedan began less than a month ago." She pushed aside her cup. "The Great War lasted for four years. How can the country be lost so fast?"

"The same way as Poland, the Netherlands, Belgium, and others," he said. "Germany's Panzers and Luftwaffe are too strong to stop."

This can't be happening! "Maybe the French Army can hold them off until the BEF can return."

He shook his head. "It will take a long time before a counterattack can be made. I suspect that the forces will be placed in defensive positions to protect Britain from a German invasion."

Her mind raced, struggling to come to terms with what her gut already knew. She'd seen the devastation on the front, the speed of the German tanks, and the bombs and death bestowed on Paris, a place that the French believed would be immune from the ravages of war. But still, she clung to hope that France would somehow retain its sovereignty.

"The war is not lost," Jimmie said, as if he could read her thoughts. "The soldiers, who are evacuated to Britain, have survived to fight another day. Someday, France will be free."

She drew a deep breath and nodded. "What are you going to do?"

"Eventually, I will travel to the coast, likely somewhere in Brittany, perhaps the Loire estuary." He looked at her. "I wanted you, Lucette, and your aunt and uncle to know about the information that is not being reported in broadcasts. I've been searching for you since my visit to the embassy. I was worried that you might have gone away to the front, and I decided to wait here to inform your aunt and uncle, but they haven't come home."

Ruth placed her palms on the table. For several minutes she told him everything—the French Army having no reserve ambulances, her rescue work at the demolished Citroën automobile factory, and her aunt and uncle who were treating injured children whose school was struck by German bombs.

"Bloody hell." Jimmie ran a hand through his hair. "I'm so sorry."

Ruth nodded and picked at a scratch on the table. "My aunt and uncle will not be able to leave the hospital until morning, perhaps later."

"How are you holding up?"

Her chest felt tight. "Not so well. You?"

"Same." Jimmie shifted in his seat. "Will you leave Paris?"

"I don't know," she said. "I'm scared to stay, but I also feel that it is my duty to help injured soldiers and civilians."

"Even if there is no ambulance for you to drive?"

"I can volunteer at a hospital, or maybe I can find another post." *Until the German Army reaches Paris.*

Jimmie rubbed his forehead. "Pierre has decided that he and Aline will go south, before the Germans reach Paris. I plan to go with them, and I'll try to get them on board a ship to cross the Channel." He looked into her eyes. "I want you to come with me."

Ruth swallowed. "I don't think I can bring myself to give up, at least not yet, and I can't abandon Lucette and my aunt and uncle."

He touched her hand. "We'll bring them with us."

Ruth felt torn, like a string of paper dolls cut in half. "We need to inform them about your news so they can make their own decision, but I can't promise to go with you."

"You do not need to decide tonight." He squeezed her fingers. "Please give me your word that you'll consider it."

"I will," she said.

Jimmie, appearing satisfied, gently slipped his hand away. He rose from his seat and went to the pantry.

"What are you doing?" she asked.

"I'm making you something to eat." He retrieved a zucchini and an onion.

"I could simply have some bread or a piece of cheese, if there is any left."

"Nonsense. You need a warm meal."

I'm exhausted. It'd be best for me to eat something easy and go off to bed, Ruth thought. *But, even more than sleep, I need his closeness.* "Thank you. Will you have some with me?"

"Perhaps a bit." He turned to her. "I have an idea."

"What's that?"

"Tonight, let's forget about the war. Let's be two ordinary people who enjoy a meal together, then you'll get some sleep."

"That sounds lovely."

He sliced a zucchini and a peeled onion, placed them in an iron skillet with a splash of olive oil and salt, and put it on the stove to heat.

She sipped her coffee as he stood over the stove with a wooden spoon. Soon, the succulent aroma of sauteed vegetables filled the kitchen, awakening her hunger. Her mouth watered. "It smells wonderful. I didn't know that pilots could cook."

"Some can." Jimmie raised his spoon. "Even one-armed aviators."

She smiled and finished her coffee. "Do you like Armagnac?"

"What's that?"

"A type of brandy. My uncle, Julian, usually keeps a bottle in the cabinet near the sink."

"Splendid," he said, stirring vegetables.

She retrieved the Armagnac and two small snifter glasses.

He placed the sauteed zucchini and onion onto plates and put them on the table with silverware, napkins, and glasses of water.

"I feel doted on," she said.

"Good." He sat beside her, and poured the Armagnac. "To freedom," he said, raising his glass.

"Freedom." She clinked his glass with hers and took a sip, tasting notes of vanilla and candied plum. A warmth of alcohol drifted down her throat and into her stomach.

Jimmie took a drink. "It's quite good."

She chewed a bite of zucchini, rich with caramelized onion and olive oil. "Superb."

"I'm glad you like it." He swirled his brandy.

"We're lucky that my aunt and uncle had some fresh vegetables."

"They had a few, but Pierre, Aline, and I ate them."

She forked a slice of onion. "Most of the market shelves are empty. Where did you get the vegetables?"

He raised his arm, revealing a bare wrist. "I traded my Omega watch for some zucchini, three onions, and a bag of carrots."

"That was generous and sweet. Thank you."

"It's the least I can do. It's kind of your aunt and uncle to open their home to people in need. I'm looking forward to meeting them."

"Me too." She took a gulp of brandy and her body relaxed. *Jimmie is selfless and sincere. I feel true to myself when I'm with him, and he gives me hope that days ahead will be better.*

Jimmie took a sip of brandy. "When this war is over, what do you want your life to be like?"

"Lately, I haven't given it much thought."

"You must have dreams—they make life worth living."

She paused, picking at her food. "I want to return to my singing career, but someday I hope to have a life like my mom and dad. They behave like newlyweds—holding hands, laughing, and kissing—even after decades of marriage."

Jimmie grinned. "Brilliant."

"What do you want your life to be like?" she asked.

"I hope to pilot a plane, perhaps to carry airline passengers, but I'd gladly accept any job that will keep me in the sky."

She smiled.

"Someday," he said, "I'd like to be married and have a family of my own."

"Are you saying that you want children?"

"Indeed."

"How many?"

"Loads of kids."

She chuckled. "Like a dozen?"

"No," he said, smiling. "Two would be nice. How about you—do you want children?"

"I do. Someday, if I'm lucky, I'd like to have a couple of children. Being an only child, I always wished that I had a brother or sister to grow up with."

He nodded and gently touched her arm. "You've barely eaten."

Her skin tingled. "It's delicious. I was preoccupied by our conversation." She glanced at his full plate. "Aren't you hungry?"

He shook his head. "I ate earlier. I'll save it for someone else."

For an hour, they chatted while Ruth ate the rest of her food. They finished their glasses of Armagnac and set aside their plates.

"Thank you for the meal."

"My pleasure." He rose from his chair. "I'll take care of the dishes. You should get some rest."

Ruth stood. "I can help." She gently placed a hand on his injured arm.

"No need." He touched her hand, his fingers lingering against her palm.

Her heartbeat accelerated, and she intertwined her fingers with his. "It's no trouble at all," she said, her voice soft.

He moved close and looked into her eyes.

As if by reflex, she leaned into him and felt his arm wrap around her back. Butterflies fluttered in her stomach. She closed her eyes and raised her chin as his lips approached her own.

A knock came from the door.

Ruth eased back. She felt his arm drift down her spine and slip away.

"Are you expecting someone?" he asked.

Her eyes widened. "Oh, gosh. It's Lucette. I didn't want her to stay alone, so I told her to come here. I'm sorry I forgot to tell you."

Jimmie gently placed a hand to her cheek. "It's all right. It's good that you invited her." He stepped away to open the door and returned with Lucette.

Lucette, wearing casual clothing, put down a piece of luggage and a bag with her dirty uniform. Her eyes gravitated to the table with plates, snifters, and a bottle of Armagnac. Her lips formed a smile. "I hope I didn't interrupt."

Ruth's face flushed. "*Non*, we were—" She smoothed her blouse.

"We were having a bite to eat," Jimmie said. "Would you like some?"

"*Oui, merci*," Lucette said. "I'm famished, and I could use a drink." She went to a cabinet, retrieved a glass, and poured Armagnac.

"Give me a minute to reheat the food," Jimmie said.

"It's not necessary." Lucette sat at the table and took a gulp of brandy.

Ruth slid Jimmie's untouched plate of food to Lucette, and then gave her a clean fork and napkin.

Lucette devoured a slice of zucchini and washed it down with brandy. She looked at Ruth. "It tastes incredible."

"Jimmie bartered for the food," Ruth said, "and he cooked it."

Lucette turned to Jimmie. "*Merci*."

He nodded.

Ruth's eyes met Jimmie's and a wave of contentment washed over her. She regretted that their time together was cut short, but she was glad that Lucette was not alone in her apartment, where she would worry about Paul and brood over the casualties at the bombed factory. Most of all, she was grateful for Jimmie's kindness, for making her feel wanted, and helping her to forget about the war, if only for a little while. *Perhaps we'll have time for each other when all of this is over. Or maybe this is all there will ever be between us.* She set aside her thoughts and chatted with Lucette as she ate.

As Lucette finished her food, Ruth looked at Jimmie and said, "Do you want to tell her, or would you like me to?"

Lucette put down her fork and wiped her mouth with a napkin. "Tell me what?"

CHAPTER 32

PARIS, FRANCE—JUNE 10, 1940

Ruth, wearing her clean uniform, opened a living-room window in her aunt and uncle's apartment and leaned out her head. A faint odor of resin and burning trees penetrated her nose. On the street below, a dense throng of refugees was making its way out of Paris on a hot and cloudless summer day. Beyond a cacophony of crowd commotion and police whistles, a distant gunfire echoed over the city.

Ruth's skin prickled. She turned to Aunt Colette and Uncle Julian, who were dressed in their hospital clothing and standing in the center of the living room. "They're getting closer."

The lines on Colette's face deepened.

Julian placed his arm around his wife.

Ruth closed the window, shutting out the noise of the exodus and the advancing German Army.

Five days after Paris was bombed, the sound of German guns could be heard in the capital. Rumors grew rampant amongst Parisians that French Army battalions, fighting to hold the line in the north, had been overrun or captured. Soon after, French soldiers—unarmed and their uniforms tattered—began to arrive in the city, sending shock and fear through the masses.

In addition to French military deserters, the exodus of refugees continued to multiply. The streets of Paris were congested with people passing through the city, mostly on foot, bicycles, or in horse-drawn wagons. Huge numbers of people from Belgium and northern France had abandoned their homes in search of sanctuary. But today, the exodus had swelled to biblical proportions when it was announced that the French government had decided to leave the capital city of Paris. To Ruth—given the surge of people passing through Le Marais—it looked as if a million Parisians had fled their homes, joining the many millions already in turmoil.

For the past week, Ruth and Lucette volunteered at the hospital to help with victims of the bombing. The patients, who were not severely injured, were gradually released and she and Lucette were assigned less urgent duties of washing sheets, making beds, and cleaning bedpans. Jimmie had urged her, as well as Lucette, to join him, Pierre, and Aline on their journey to the coast, but she struggled to forsake the city and people she cherished, especially Colette and Julian, who were committed to remain at the hospital. Ruth had pleaded for Jimmie to leave without her, but he didn't flee the city. Instead, he'd made excuses for delaying his departure, as if he were holding out hope that she would change her mind.

Each day the rumble of explosions grew closer, and Ruth and Lucette gradually came to terms that the city would be breached by Hitler's army. The tipping point to leave occurred when the government announced its evacuation from the city. And soon after the radio broadcast, Julian and Colette rushed to the apartment, gave Ruth the keys to a truck, and implored her to save as many people as she could.

Ruth stepped away from the window and approached Colette and Julian. "I'll go, but I want you to come with us. It's not too late to change your mind."

"We're needed at the hospital," Colette said. "There are many Parisians who are unwilling or are physically unable to leave. Doctors and nurses are required to care for the ill and injured."

"It's not safe," Ruth said. "The German Army will be here within days, if not sooner."

Julian shook his head. "We must stay."

"*Non*," Ruth pleaded. "The Nazis persecute Jews."

"This is France, not Germany," Julian said. "We're medical staff and will be of no threat to them. They won't hurt us."

A feeling of dread twisted inside her. She stepped forward and hugged them. "*S'il te plaît*, you need to leave."

They wrapped their arms around her.

"We took an oath to care for the sick," Julian said, slipping away. "Our minds are made up—we will remain here."

Ruth's heart ached. "I hate leaving you."

"It's temporary, *ma chérie*." Colette released her and looked into her eyes. "You are not casting aside your duties by going away— you're aiding the fight. Without your help, it would be difficult for Aline and Pierre to reach safety. And by getting Jimmie out of France, the Allies will have one more airman to battle for Europe's liberation."

Tears welled in Ruth's eyes and rolled down her cheeks. "I promise to come back."

"You will—when France is free." Using her hand, Colette wiped away Ruth's tears.

The door to the apartment opened and Jimmie—his arm in a recently made plaster cast—entered the room. He glanced at Ruth and paused, placing a hand into his flight jacket pocket, as if he didn't want to interrupt her goodbyes.

Julian went to Jimmie. "Is the truck loaded?"

"It is," Jimmie said. "Everyone's outside and ready to go."

"Good luck to you," Julian said, extending his hand.

"And you." Jimmie shook his hand. "I'm grateful for the cast that you made me."

"You're welcome. Ruth and Lucette did a remarkable job with setting the bone and making a splint. It's healing straight and, in four weeks, you can have it removed."

Jimmie nodded.

Colette approached Jimmie. "We've only been together for a few days, but you feel like family. I wish you could have met my son, Marceau. Your spirit reminds me of him."

"I appreciate you telling me that," Jimmie said. "I feel honored to be compared to Marceau. Ruth has told me wonderful stories about him."

Colette kissed him on both cheeks. *"Leich l'shalom,"* she said, softly.

"What does that mean?" Jimmie asked.

"Go toward peace."

Jimmie nodded. *"Leich l'shalom* to you, too."

A calm smile spread over Colette's face, and she turned to Ruth. "Julian and I said our farewells to the others, but we can walk you outside."

"Non. It's chaotic on the street." Ruth embraced her aunt and uncle one last time, holding them long and tight. *"Je t'aime."*

"Je t'aime aussi," Colette said.

Ruth, gutted and heartbroken, left the apartment with Jimmie. They descended the stairwell, partially blocked by a man who was lugging an antique steamer trunk down the steps. Outside, they maneuvered through a river of people and approached a bakery truck that Colette and Julian had acquired from their friend. A strange sense of déjà vu washed over Ruth as she looked at the vehicle that she'd used to teach Lucette to drive.

Lucette, dressed in her ambulance corps uniform, emerged from the opposite side of the vehicle with Aline and Pierre.

Aline weaved past three women with bags of luggage and reached Ruth. She looked up at her and said in a sweet, confident voice, "I'm sorry you are sad. It's going to be okay."

Ruth kissed her on the top of the head. "It will."

Pierre gave Ruth a pat on the shoulder, and then climbed into the back of the truck with his granddaughter.

Lucette held out a key. "Do you want to drive first or second?"

Ruth wiped her eyes. "I could use a bit of distraction. How about I take the wheel first?"

Lucette gave her the key and turned to Jimmie. "Sit up front with Ruth. I'll join the others in the back."

"Are you sure?" he asked.

"I insist," Lucette said.

Ruth got behind the wheel and Jimmie sat in the passenger seat. She started the engine and looked at the fuel gauge. *Three quarters of a tank, and more petrol will be impossible to come by.* She blared the horn until the crowd began to move aside, and then she slipped the truck into gear, released the clutch, and carefully pulled away from the curb.

The shops were shuttered, and the streets of Paris were jammed with refugees. Despite police officers, who were laboring to direct pedestrian traffic at intersections, the stop-and-go pace was slow, and she was unable to accelerate the truck to little more than a walking speed. It took over an hour to exit the city center and, as Ruth made a left turn, a reflection of the Eiffel Tower appeared in her side mirror. A pang of sadness pierced through her. She gripped the wheel, peering at Paris's beautiful wrought-iron structure, and silently vowed to return.

As they traveled through the outskirts of Paris, the skyline of the city gradually disappeared. Densely placed apartment buildings turned to plots of individual houses and eventually rural farmland. But the open space did little to diminish the congestion of people. An endless crowd covered both sides of the roadway, its berms littered with abandoned vehicles that had run out of fuel. Masses of pedestrians roamed over pastures, like huge herds of sheep. Ruth honked the truck's horn, but weary people, shuffling along the roadway with their heads down, made little to no effort to move aside for her to pass.

"I'm sorry," Ruth said, glancing at Jimmie.

"For what?"

"We should have left days ago. The roads are worse than anything we experienced on the way to Paris from the front. We're making little progress at this speed—" She glanced at the fuel gauge. "And we won't get far on half a tank of petrol."

"It's all right. We'll walk like we did before." He turned to her and gently touched her hand on the gear shift. "It'll all work out."

Ruth squeezed his fingers and nodded, despite a deep regret that gnawed at her gut. She felt his touch slip away, and she turned the wheel to weave around a gaunt-faced man who'd stopped to fix the chain on a bicycle.

They drove for an hour through the rural countryside and, along the way, Ruth picked up three elderly women pedestrians, a man walking with a cane, a young mother pushing a toddler in a stroller, and a teenage boy who was carrying a small black bulldog with pointed, batlike ears. Kilometer by kilometer, Ruth maneuvered the vehicle southward, all the while stopping to pick up people whom she thought could use a break from walking. Soon, the back of the truck was at capacity, and she had to turn away people who tried to wave her down to hitch a ride. She felt horrible as she drove by, telling them through her open window that there was no more room in her truck.

Nearly seven hours later, the needle on the fuel gauge pointed to empty. A few kilometers farther, the engine began to sputter. She slowly veered through the dense crowd to the side of the road. The motor shuddered and stopped. One by one, the refugees whom Ruth had given a ride climbed out and disappeared into the exodus. The echoes of gunfire had faded, but could still be heard over the shuffling of feet and clopping of hooves.

Ruth approached her group, congregating at the back of the vehicle. "Do we want to walk or search for a place to rest for the night?"

"There is plenty of sunlight left," Pierre said, "and my legs are fresh." He placed a hand on his granddaughter's shoulder. "What do you think, my little cabbage?"

"Let's walk," Aline said. "Maybe someone will let us ride in their wagon."

Lucette and Jimmie nodded.

As the group removed luggage and supplies from the back of the vehicle, Ruth went to the driver's compartment and checked the odometer. She did the math in her head. *Nearly three hundred more kilometers to reach the coast of Brittany. We can do this.* She closed the door and joined the others.

For two hours, they slogged over the road, filled with refugees as far as they could see. The temperature was hot, and the late afternoon sun beat down on their heads.

Ruth glanced at Pierre, his head drooped and shoulders slumped, as he shuffled his feet over the road. "How about we stop for water?"

"A drink would be good," Lucette said.

Pierre nodded.

They made their way to the side of the road and sat at the edge

of an overgrown field, covered in tall grass, weeds, and wildflowers. Ruth removed a canteen from her bag and gave it to Aline.

The girl took two gulps and handed the canteen to her grandfather, who drank and passed it along.

While Lucette guzzled water, Pierre removed a medicine bottle from his pocket, unscrewed the cap, and plucked out a tiny
nitroglycerin pill with his finger.

An uneasiness stirred inside Ruth. *We need to slow the pace or find
a ride for him on a wagon.*

Pierre placed the pill under his tongue. As the medicine dissolved in his mouth, his breathing slowed and tension eased from
his face.

"Are you all right, Grandpapa?"

"*Oui,*" Pierre said.

Jimmie perked his head. He stood and peered up.

"What's wrong?" Ruth asked.

A thrum grew in the air.

"Stukas!" Jimmie shouted.

Ruth's heart rate soared. She scrambled to Aline and clasped
her hand.

High in the sky, a squadron of Stukas dived toward the ground.
The sirens, attached to the aircraft, began to wail.

Screams grew from the crowd. Pedestrians dropped their luggage and ran. People crawled underneath a nearby wagon, while
others frantically searched for a place to hide.

"Away from the road!" Jimmie shouted.

Ruth sprinted with Aline across the field. Weeds and high grass
lashed at their legs.

"Grandpapa!" Aline cried.

Pierre struggled to keep up. "Go!"

Lucette clasped the old man's arm and pulled him along, while
Jimmie closed in behind them.

The Stuka sirens grew to a horrid howl.

Ruth's leg muscles burned as she pushed through the overgrown vegetation. Her eyes locked on the tree line of a forest,
thirty meters away. *It's too far.* She fought back her fear and ran
faster.

A roar of engines grew from beyond the forest.

Oh, no! Ruth thought. *We're surrounded.*

Planes shot over the trees and machine gun fire erupted.

Ruth pulled Aline to the ground and shielded her with her body.

The Stuka sirens waned.

"They're ours!" Jimmie shouted.

Ruth sat up and sucked in air. She looked to the sky and her eyes were drawn to three RAF Hurricane fighters in pursuit of the Stukas, which had pulled out of their dive and veered away.

People cheered from the roadway.

Jimmie raised his good arm above his head and shouted, "Get them!"

A wave of relief rolled over Ruth. She stood and helped Aline to her feet. "Are you okay?"

"I am," Aline said.

Ruth turned to Jimmie. "Do you recognize them?"

Jimmie placed a hand over his eyes to shield the sun. "They might be with my squadron, the Seventy-Three, or perhaps with Number One Squadron. I can't tell for sure."

Lucette walked toward Jimmie and pressed her palms together. "*Dieu merci.*"

While Jimmie, Lucette, and Aline watched the planes disappear on the horizon, Ruth approached Pierre, who was standing alone in thigh-high weeds.

"Are you okay?" Ruth asked.

Pierre turned to her. His face was pale, and sweat clung to his forehead and wispy, gray hair. His beret was clutched like a rag in his left hand. In the other, he held an open medicine bottle.

She froze.

"I—I failed to put the cap on before we ran away," Pierre said, his voice frail. He looked out over the vast, overgrown field. "They're all gone."

CHAPTER 33

BELLÊME, FRANCE—JUNE 11, 1940

Jimmie and his group entered a small town of approximately a thousand residents, given the number and size of structures. Stores and businesses were shuttered and most of the town's people appeared to have fled. The population of the town, however, had grown five-fold with refugees who were making their way to southern areas of France. Jimmie's legs were tired, and his arm ached inside his plaster cast. He adjusted the sling, rubbing the skin on his neck raw, and slogged through a congested cobblestone street.

Ruth looked at Pierre, who was shuffling along while holding her elbow. "Do you want to stop?"

"*Non*," Pierre said, his voice hoarse.

"You should rest, Grandpapa," Aline said, following close behind with Lucette.

"A little further, my little cabbage," Pierre said.

Jimmie felt conflicted. He admired Pierre's determination, but he also worried that he was overexerting himself. He decided to walk a few more minutes, and then make an excuse that he needed to stop to drink water. But his plans changed when they neared a stone building with a sign that read *PHARMACIE*.

Jimmie's pulse rate quickened. "There," he said, pointing.

"Thank goodness," Ruth said.

Aline scurried to her grandpapa. "We can get you *médecine*."

Pierre raised his head to the sign and his eyes brightened.

The group made their way to the sidewalk and climbed three stone steps to the entrance of the building. But Jimmie's hope sank at the sight of a broken storefront window and an open front door. He entered the pharmacy, his boots crunching over shattered glass, to find it had been ransacked. Most of the shelves were empty, and behind a service counter was an apothecary cabinet, its drawers missing or ajar.

"Oh, no," Lucette said, staring at the mess.

Aline slumped her shoulders. "What happened?"

"Looters," Ruth said.

Pierre slowly stepped over shards of glass. "Forgive me," he whispered to himself, as if he were ashamed of trespassing. He walked behind the service counter and examined a shelf with large cork-top jars, some of which were toppled and broken on the floor. One by one, he went through the apothecary cabinet's remaining drawers and turned to the group.

"Any luck?" Ruth asked.

Pierre shook his head.

A knot formed in Jimmie's stomach.

Pierre approached his granddaughter.

Aline's bottom lip quivered. "Why would people steal?"

"They're afraid that there will be nothing left." Pierre placed a hand on his granddaughter's shoulder and smiled. "It's all right. There will be more towns and pharmacies on our journey."

Aline nodded.

Lucette hooked her arm around Pierre's elbow and walked him outside. Jimmie, Ruth, and Aline followed them and, together, they rejoined the stream of refugees flowing through the town.

After the near Stuka attack, Jimmie and the group had scoured the overgrown, weed-covered field in search of Pierre's nitroglycerin pills. They'd crawled on their hands and knees, exploring the bug-infested, thick undergrowth, until the sun set and it became too dark to see. But even in bright sunlight, the thigh-high, dense foliage made it nearly impossible to find Lilliputian-size tablets. In all, two pills were recovered—both by Aline, who found them near the original spot where they fled the enemy planes. And Pierre, who'd strained himself in the search, needed to take one of the salvaged pills to alleviate a pain running through his chest.

They, as well as countless refugees, had slept the night under a forest canopy that stretched along the roadside. They'd woken before sunrise, eaten a breakfast of sliced turnips and stale bread, and commenced their slog through the countryside. Within an hour of walking, Pierre began to wince and, minutes later, slipped the last pill under his tongue—out of sight of Aline, who was walking ahead of the pack. Jimmie insisted to Pierre that he needed to stop and rest, but Pierre declined, claiming that he was feeling well enough to walk. So, Jimmie bartered some of their food in exchange for Pierre to ride in a peddler's cart that held a kindergarten-age boy on a small mattress. Pierre was reluctant to accept the ride, but relented when Aline implored him to get in. For six kilometers, Jimmie—using his good arm—helped a man to push Pierre and the boy in the cart. The ride for Pierre ended at an intersection, where the owner of the peddler's cart took an inland route toward Le Mans.

Pierre's vigor had faded in comparison to his journey from Reims to Paris. The days on the road, as well as his struggles since the Germans invaded France, had taken a toll on him. He'd lost a significant amount of weight. His jacket sagged over his bony shoulders and, due to his slim waist, he'd cut an extra hole in his leather belt to hold up his trousers. His feet shuffled lower to the ground, and his hunched back was more pronounced. Although Pierre's condition was frail, his optimism did not wane. He was thoughtful and caring, he never complained, and he was reluctant to rest, as if he were fighting a duel against time to save his granddaughter.

Jimmie wished that he could find a vacant dwelling and convince Pierre to rest for a few days, even though it might risk that the advancing German Army would bear down upon them. *You can't keep this up*, he'd thought, helping Pierre to sit on the ground for a water break. Jimmie knew that his duty was to find a way to return to England, get healthy, and return to the air war. But for now, he felt that his purpose and responsibility was to protect

Pierre, Aline, Lucette, and Ruth—the woman who had stolen his heart.

He'd never met a woman like Ruth. *She's beautiful, brave, and kind*, he often thought walking beside her. They hadn't had time or the opportunity to develop their relationship, but he cared deeply about her, and he sensed that she felt the same way about him. For the first time in his life, his heart felt unguarded and fully capable of giving and receiving affection. He imagined—although cautiously, considering the casualty rate of fighter pilots—what it would be like to create a life with her. He visualized waking up each morning, nestled in each other's arms. More than ever, he was determined to fight for Europe's freedom, not solely for his country and people, but so that he and Ruth could have a chance of a future together.

Ruth, walking beside Jimmie, leaned in and lowered her voice. "Any thoughts on how to convince Pierre to take a break?"

"Perhaps." Jimmie thought for a moment. He turned and, while walking backward, said, "Pierre, how about we stop early for the night."

"*Non*," he said, shuffling along between Lucette and Aline. "If my angina acts up, I'll rest a bit, but for now I want to keep walking."

"A little break might be good," Lucette said.

Pierre shook his head. "I don't want to slow us down."

"I'm sorry, my words weren't clear," Jimmie said. "I was thinking that an early start to find a place to rest for the night might give us a chance to find shelter. It would be nice if Aline could sleep someplace indoors."

Pierre glanced at Aline, lugging her backpack. "*Oui*, it would."

"Got enough in you for another kilometer?" Jimmie asked.

"Two," Pierre said.

"Very well—two it is." He turned and quickened his pace to rejoin Ruth.

Ruth looked at him and mouthed, "Thank you."

He gave a subtle nod.

They exited the town, walked for what they estimated to be two kilometers, and left the mass of refugees by crossing a barren pasture. At the top of a hill, they spotted a remote building that looked to have a church steeple, so they slogged for twenty minutes to reach what turned out to be a small village. Although there were refugees passing through the area, it was less congested than the towns along the main road. They located the church and discovered several nuns who were providing bread, water, and shelter to refuge seekers. Although they were offered nourishment, they'd arrived too late to claim a place inside. The chapel's floor and pews were lined with people, many of whom suffered from exhaustion and dehydration.

"I'm sorry," said an elderly nun with dainty, age-spotted hands. "There's no more room in the chapel, but you're welcome to use the washroom and rest in the church cemetery."

Jimmie, feeling a mix of gratefulness and disappointment, led the group outside and into a cemetery behind the church. Amongst ancient, crooked headstones, dozens of refugees were resting on blankets and bundles of clothing.

"I'm worried that if we continue to walk," Ruth said, "we'll exhaust ourselves by trying to find someplace inside. I'm thinking that almost everywhere will be overcrowded. How about we stay here for the night?"

"I agree," Jimmie said.

Lucette and Aline nodded.

As they searched for a spot to hunker down, Pierre removed his beret, ran a hand over his thin hair, and walked around the side of the church.

"Where's he going?" Lucette asked.

"I'm not sure," Aline said, slipping off her backpack. "Maybe the washroom."

Lucette nodded and put down a bag with supplies.

A few minutes later, Pierre appeared at a rear door of the church with the elderly nun, who motioned for their group to come inside. They gathered their things, entered the church, and were led to a small room which appeared to be a sacristy, given a row of wall-mounted hooks with vestments, a bookcase, and shelves with sacred items and vessels. The air was hot and smelled faintly of old wood and beeswax.

"*Merci*," Pierre said to the nun.

The woman nodded and left, closing the door behind her.

Aline's eyes widened as she gazed over the tiny but private space.

Lucette put down her bag and looked at Pierre. "What did you do?"

"I begged her to allow my granddaughter to sleep inside." Pierre slipped his hands into his pockets. He approached Lucette, reached behind her left ear, and magically produced a shiny coin. "And I told her I'd gladly make an offering to the church."

Ruth raised her brow. "You're joking."

"*Non*," Pierre said, slipping his trick coin into his pocket. "It made her smile, and she told me she would make an exception by giving us this space until morning."

Jimmie chuckled, perhaps for the first time in many days.

"I think I impressed her with my magic," Pierre said.

Lucette smiled. "You do know—that I know—and that nun knows—that your magic is sleight of hand."

"*Non*," Pierre said, raising his chin. "It's magic."

Aline grinned.

"Well," Ruth said, "your trick certainly charmed her into finding a room for us. I would call that a magical feat."

Pierre beamed with pride.

As they unloaded their things and set out blankets, Jimmie felt a deep admiration for Pierre. Despite the man's fatigue, his will to protect his granddaughter burned bright. He made them feel good about themselves, he inspired laughter under dire circumstances and, perhaps most admirably, he made them feel human. And for that, Jimmie would be eternally grateful.

As night set in, Pierre told Aline a bedtime story about how her parents met. Aline had heard it many times, Jimmie believed, considering that she corrected her grandpapa in a few sections of the tale, and she added a couple descriptions of her own. And it struck Jimmie that Pierre was purposely creating variations of the story to entertain, as well as to encourage his granddaughter to tell the tale. Soon the room grew dark and everyone settled onto blankets on the floor, lined up tightly like tinned sardines. They gradually drifted to sleep, except for Ruth and Jimmie, lying side by side.

"Are you still awake?" Ruth whispered.

"Yes," Jimmie said.

"What are you thinking about?"

A memory of Hurricanes, chasing away Stukas, flashed in his head. "I was wondering how my fellow pilots and ground crew are doing. It feels like an eternity since I've seen my friends—Cobber, Fanny, Benny, and Horace. I hope they are alive and well."

"You'll see them again, soon after I get you on a ship."

"I hope so." Jimmie moved his injured arm, resting the cast on his stomach. "What are you thinking about?"

"My aunt and uncle, and if the Germans have reached Paris." She swallowed. "I pray that they'll be okay."

"They will," he said. "Doctors and nurses will be safe."

"I needed to hear that," she said softly. "*Merci.*"

Jimmie peered up into the darkness. "What will you do when we get to Brittany?"

"Hopefully, Lucette and I will see you, Pierre, and Aline board a ship bound for England."

"I was referring to you and Lucette. Have you thought about where you will go?"

She drew a deep breath. "I'll travel with her to Toulouse, where her parents live, until it's safe to return to Paris. Toulouse is not far from Andorra and Spain, so we can escape from France if needed. In the meantime, we'll find a way to support what remains of the French Army, or join resistance fighting. I must do something, other than run away."

He turned on his side to face her, the outline of her body illuminated by a bit of moonlight coming through a window. "Come with me to England—you and Lucette."

"*Non,*" she said. "Lucette needs to see that her parents are safe, and I don't want her to make the journey on her own."

"You're a good friend to Lucette," he said. "Selfishly, I want you to be far away from the conflict, but I understand and accept your decision. To be honest, I'd do the same thing if I were you."

Ruth rolled onto her side. "It doesn't mean that I don't want to be with you."

Jimmie reached out his good hand and found hers. He felt her fingers intertwine with his, and a deep yearning tore at his heart. "When this is all over, I will find you."

She nuzzled next to him. "I'll wait."

CHAPTER 34

VAIGES, FRANCE—JUNE 13, 1940

An intense morning sun beat down on Jimmie as he walked between Ruth and Lucette on a dusty, unpaved road filled with thousands of refugees. The clopping of hooves—coming from a mule that was pulling a wagon with Pierre, Aline, and two young boys—filled his ears. He rubbed the back of his neck, stinging from sunburn, and continued his trek through the countryside.

"How far do you think we've come today?" Lucette asked, adjusting the strap of a leather bag on her shoulder.

"Ten, maybe eleven kilometers," Jimmie said. He wiped sweat from his brow and wondered if he and the others had the stamina, given the heat and humidity, to walk until sundown.

Ruth slipped a folded map from her pack and, while continuing her pace, scanned their route. "Ten is about right. There's a village up ahead. We should stop for water and something to eat."

"Sounds good," Lucette said.

Jimmie approached the cart with Aline and Pierre. "In a little while, we'll be stopping at a village."

Aline nodded. She nudged Pierre, curled on a shallow layer of straw in the back of the cart. "Grandpapa, we're getting out soon."

Pierre cracked open his eyes and patted his granddaughter's hand.

The past two days had been grueling. The unseasonably warm weather and lack of cloud cover slowed the progress of the exodus. Scores of people, stricken with exhaustion, lined the sides of the road. Some people sought a reprieve from the heat by setting up camps under the shade of trees, but the masses—driven by the fear of Luftwaffe air raids—carried on with their pilgrimage toward freedom.

The sound of gunfire had dissipated, Jimmie believed, due to their increased distance from Paris, and he had little doubt that the German Army was closing in on, if not already breached, the country's capital. Although their immediate threat of Panzers had dwindled, the Luftwaffe continued their relentless air raids on towns, villages, and roadways. Several times, the grind of German aircraft engines sent Jimmie and his group scrambling for cover under trees. They'd avoided direct gunfire and bombs from the Luftwaffe, but other refugees were not as fortunate.

The day before, they'd walked upon a series of demolished wagons and a lone, burned-out automobile that was riddled with bullet holes. Near the roadside were six fresh mounds of dirt and makeshift crosses constructed from fallen tree limbs. The worst part, for Jimmie, was recognizing that two of the graves were half the size of the others. He'd attempted to block Aline's view of the atrocity by walking next to her, but she'd already spotted the burials.

"Some of them were children," Aline said, looking up at Jimmie.

"*Oui.*"

"I hope they didn't suffer."

"Me too," he'd said, his heart breaking. "Nothing is going to happen to you. You're going to be safe."

She nodded, removed Piglet from her backpack, and clutched him to her chest.

Encounters with the Luftwaffe weren't the only barrier to reaching the coast. They were nearly out of food and well water was hard to come by, so most of their drinking supply came from streams or ponds. The rations that Colette and Julian had given them, which was everything in their pantry, didn't last long.

They had to barter a good deal of food to convince people to allow Pierre to ride in the back of their wagon. While Pierre received a few lifts as a gesture of compassion and good will, many people were unable or reluctant to add another body to their wagon, overflowing with family members and possessions from their abandoned homes. Jimmie hoped that he'd never reach a point where he'd turned down someone in need, but he also understood that fear of starvation or the pain of having one's child go hungry could drive one to do unthinkable things.

"Hold up," Jimmie called, upon reaching a village.

A gray-bearded man tugged on reins and the mule slowed the wagon to a stop.

Jimmie thanked the man for the ride, and then he, Ruth, and Lucette helped Pierre out of the wagon.

Aline jumped out and put on her backpack.

They walked to a calm stream, which resembled a shallow canal, that ran through the center of the village. They put down their bags and took off their socks and shoes. While Pierre rested under the shade of a willow tree, the others filled canteens, drank water, and soaked their aching feet in the cool stream.

Jimmie and Ruth approached Pierre, who was resting on his back with an arm over his eyes.

"We brought you some water," Ruth said.

Pierre stirred and raised his head.

Jimmie helped him to sit up and Ruth handed him a canteen.

Pierre took a few gulps. Water dribbled down his gray-stubbled chin. "*Merci.*"

"How about something to eat?" Jimmie asked.

"I will in a little while," Pierre said.

Ruth wiggled her bare toes. "The stream feels good. Would you like to soak your feet?"

"*Oui*, after a short nap." Pierre settled on his back and peered upward at the drooping willow branches.

Ruth poured water from the canteen onto a handkerchief, squeezed out excess water, and placed it on Pierre's forehead.

"Bless you." A soft smile formed on his face and he closed his eyes.

Jimmie and Ruth returned to the edge of the stream, where
Lucette and Aline were drying their feet in the sun. As Ruth retrieved a bag with food, a clack of boots grew from the road.

Jimmie perked his head and turned.

A dozen men in weathered French Army uniforms stepped
from the road and shuffled down to the waterway, fifteen meters
upstream from Jimmie and the others. The soldiers, their faces
unshaven and dirty, crouched at the stream and guzzled handfuls
of water.

Lucette's eyes turned wide. "Oh, my."

"I'm going to talk with them," Jimmie said.

"I'll join you," Ruth said.

Lucette clasped her arms. "Me too."

Ruth glanced at Pierre, sleeping under the tree, and turned to
Aline. "How about joining your grandpapa?"

"*Non*," Aline said. "I'm coming with you."

"All right," Ruth said, reluctantly, "but stay behind me."

The group, cautious and barefooted, made their way upstream
to the soldiers.

"*Salut*," Jimmie said, approaching.

A young man, no more than twenty years old, splashed water
onto his face and turned. He paused, eyeing Jimmie's sling and
RAF tunic. "Shot down?"

Jimmie nodded.

The soldier looked at Ruth and Lucette. "Ambulance corps?"

"*Oui*," Ruth said. "But we no longer have an ambulance to
drive. We're on foot, like you."

The other soldiers, hollow-eyed with disheveled uniforms,
glanced their way but made no effort to join their comrade.

"Can you tell us what is happening?" Jimmie asked.

"Much of the defenses along the Seine have fallen," the soldier
said. "We were ordered to retreat to the coast for an evacuation
across the Channel."

"Where?" Ruth asked.

"Saint-Nazaire." The soldier wiped his sweat-covered forehead
with his sleeve. "Are you headed there, too?"

"We are now," Ruth said.

"Is that in Brittany, near the Loire estuary?" Jimmie asked.

"It is," the soldier said.

The interpreter at the embassy was right, Jimmie thought.

Lucette glanced at the soldier's rifle on the ground near his feet. "You're not giving up, are you?"

"Never," the soldier said. "My unit will continue to fight, after we regroup with Allied forces in England."

Lucette shifted her weight. "My fiancé is with the Five Hundred Third Combat Tank Regiment. Do you know anything about his tank group?"

"*Non*," he said. "I'm sorry."

Lucette lowered her eyes.

Ruth placed a hand on her friend's shoulder.

"If you're headed to Saint-Nazaire," the soldier said, "it's best that you keep moving. I was told by my superior officer that the evacuation at Saint-Nazaire won't last long. You will need to get there within six days, or risk not getting out."

"We will." Jimmie shook the man's hand. "*Merci*."

The soldier nodded, gathered his rifle, and left with his unit.

They returned to their spot at the stream's edge, and Ruth grabbed her bag and retrieved the map. She placed it on the ground and studied it while the others gathered around.

"This is where we are." Ruth placed her finger on the map and drew an imaginary line to Saint-Nazaire, a harbor town on the coast of Brittany. "This is where we need to be in less than six days. I think we can make it."

A smile spread over Lucette's face. "We're going to get you home, Jimmie."

But you and Ruth will remain in France with the enemy, and we still need to find a way to get Aline and Pierre on board a ship to England. Jimmie nodded, hiding his disquietude. *I'll figure things out when we get to the coast.*

"Let's get something to eat and get on the road." Ruth looked at Aline. "Get your grandpapa while I prepare the food."

Aline nodded and stepped away.

Ruth put away her map and unpacked three shriveled turnips and a minuscule piece of dry-cured ham, which she placed on a large flat rock.

"Time to eat," Aline said, approaching Pierre.

Jimmie retrieved a pocketknife and handed it to Ruth, who opened the blade and sank it into a turnip.

Aline kneeled to Pierre. "Wake up."

Ruth cut a slice of turnip and handed it to Lucette, who took a nibble.

"Grandpapa." Aline nudged his shoulder.

Ruth lowered her blade, looked up, and her face went pale.

Jimmie turned and his eyes widened.

Aline leaned over Pierre and pushed on his chest. "Grandpapa!"

Jimmie shot forward. River rock dug into his bare feet as he sprinted toward Aline and Pierre.

Ruth dropped her knife and ran with Lucette.

"Please wake up!" Aline cried.

Jimmie, his pulse pounding in his ears, fell to his knees and patted Pierre's cheek. "Pierre—can you hear me?"

Ruth kneeled, clasped Pierre's wrist, and lowered her cheek to his face. She looked at Lucette. "No heartbeat and he's not breathing."

"*Non!*" Aline sobbed.

"Holger Nielsen method," Lucette said.

Lucette and Ruth rolled Pierre onto his stomach with his head to the side. They took turns lifting Pierre's arms and pressing on his back.

Jimmie felt helpless as he watched them struggle to resuscitate Pierre. He wrapped his arms around Aline, whimpering and her body trembling.

Ruth and Lucette worked on Pierre for several minutes, then rolled him onto his back and checked for a pulse and respiration. They repeated the process two more times and eventually crossed Pierre's arms over his chest.

Tears flooded Ruth's eyes as she looked at Aline. "There's nothing more we can do—I'm so sorry."

"*Non!*" Aline cried. She pushed away from Jimmie and fell to her grandfather's side. "Please wake!"

Lucette lowered her head into her hands and sobbed.

"Wake!" Aline bawled.

Jimmie's vision blurred with tears as Aline lowered her head to Pierre's still chest and wept.

CHAPTER 35

TOURS, FRANCE—JUNE 13, 1940

On the day that Paris was declared an open city, Prime Minister Winston Churchill and his military delegation flew to Tours for what they thought might be their last Anglo-French Supreme War Council meeting. Churchill peered out the window of the plane as it safely landed on a badly bombed airfield. The aircraft rumbled to a stop, the engines turned off, and the pilot exited the cockpit and opened the door. Churchill left the plane and was met by a faint smell of burnt petrol and expelled explosive. The airfield—scarred with bomb craters—was silent and barren, except for five parked French fighters and the charred remains of Amiot bombers.

Nearly all is lost for France, Churchill thought. He gripped the lapels of his jacket and gazed over the destruction. *Britain alone shall carry on the fight.*

General Ismay exited the plane with the other members of the delegation and approached Churchill. He scanned the airfield and adjusted his military cap. "It appears that there is no one to meet us, sir. Would you like for us to search for transportation?"

"By all means." Churchill took out a cigar and lit it. He took a deep drag and blew smoke through his nostrils.

The members of Churchill's delegation explored the airfield's two undamaged hangars and eventually tracked down French military staff with automobiles. Twenty minutes later, they arrived at a large, Renaissance Revival–style hotel in the center of Tours, a town between the Cher and Loire rivers. They entered through an unguarded door and traveled down a hallway lined with stacks of crates and cardboard boxes. Churchill found French Prime Minister Reynaud and his military leaders in a dining room with several tables pushed together to form a meeting area.

Reynaud approached Churchill and shook his hand. "*Merci* for coming, and my apologies for the disarray."

"Understandable," Churchill said.

"The Luftwaffe is conducting frequent air raids on Tours," Reynaud said. "Tomorrow, we will move the government again."

"Where?" Churchill asked.

"Bordeaux."

You are running out of places to hide, Churchill thought. "Shall we begin?"

"*Oui*," Reynaud said.

The delegations sat at the grouping of tables—British on one side, French on the other.

Reynaud adjusted his burgundy tie, pulled tightly around the collar of his crisp white shirt, and looked at Churchill. "General Weygand has declared Paris an open city."

"When?" Churchill asked.

"This morning," Reynaud said. "We expect the Germans to enter Paris tomorrow."

A few of the British delegation shifted in their seats.

Churchill, calm and composed, looked at Supreme Commander Weygand—an elderly mustached man who'd replaced General Maurice Gamelin, who'd been dismissed because of his weak leadership and disastrous military errors. "France must defend Paris at all costs."

Weygand folded his arms. "We have no choice."

"You have the option to fight," Churchill said. "For France and for Europe's freedom."

Marshal Pétain, a white-haired deputy prime minister of France, placed his hands on the table and looked at Churchill. "I encourage you to listen to General Weygand. He has a complete understanding of all military matters taking place in France."

"Paris must be defended," Churchill said.

"We have no reserve troops," Pétain said. "Britain should be sending more soldiers to aid France."

We've given the support of our BEF and RAF. Your military strategy has failed, allowing the Germans to drive our Allied forces into the sea. Anger burned inside Churchill yet he maintained his diplomatic tone. "Thousands of French soldiers are being evacuated to England. Your remaining military should go to North Africa to carry on the war."

"It will be futile," Weygand said.

Churchill leaned forward in his chair. "The French should pursue the use of guerrilla warfare."

Pétain shook his head. "It will destroy the country. Turning Paris into a ruin will not change the result."

Churchill glanced at the French prime minister, who remained silent as his military leaders fought for their country's surrender. He imagined the German Army marching unopposed on the streets of Paris, and he hoped that Reynaud would replace his military leaders with the younger and more confident General de Gaulle. Churchill was impressed with de Gaulle, and he believed that the Frenchman exhibited the tenacity and courage needed to prevent France from conceding to Nazi rule.

For thirty minutes, members of Churchill's staff asked questions and made recommendations to their French counterparts. And it soon became clear, to Churchill, that French leadership was determined to accept defeat, rather than struggle to fight for the future of France and its people.

Prime Minister Reynaud looked at Churchill. "I'm waiting on a reply from US President Roosevelt on a request for American assistance."

"I've also requested his support," Churchill said.

"I believe you will agree," Reynaud said, smoothing his tie, "that we need the help of the Americans, as neither of us on our own can defeat Germany."

Churchill furrowed his brow. "Is there something more that you want to tell me?"

Reynaud put his elbows on the table and intertwined his fingers. "The condition of our army is desperate, and the pursuit of French resistance is hopeless." He glanced at his military leaders. "We believe that the best option is to seek an armistice with Germany."

Churchill rubbed his jowl.

"If we were to achieve an armistice," Reynaud continued, "we would never allow our naval vessels to go to Germany as part of the agreement."

The room went silent.

General Ismay leaned forward in his chair, its wood creaking under the man's weight.

"Britain has no intention of releasing France from our agreement," Churchill said. "When our countries declared war, we pledged that we would not seek separate peace agreements."

"But we are defeated," Reynaud said, his voice sounding desperate. "We can do no more. We've given everything—our soldiers—our people—our blood."

"I understand and sympathize with France's predicament," Churchill said. "We have no intention to pursue recriminations, however, Britain is not prepared to release France from its promise not to make a separate agreement with Germany." He looked into Reynaud's eyes, filled with defeat. "Britain will wage war until we are victorious."

Reynaud took out a cigarette but made no effort to light it. "Perhaps this is an appropriate time for us to take a brief recess to reflect on the matters we've discussed." He glanced at his wristwatch. "Let's reconvene in fifteen minutes."

The French and British delegations rose from their chairs, and Churchill and his military advisors adjourned to a garden. While their group walked the flower-covered grounds, a fervid argument between Reynaud and his military staff emanated from the building.

"It sounds like they are not unified in their position to surrender," General Ismay said, walking beside the prime minister.

Churchill glanced at a hotel window. "Perhaps the generals are displeased with Reynaud for failing to convince us to agree to their request for an armistice."

"Either way," Ismay said, "I think our work is done here for today. Regardless of what you say, they will remain intent on pursuing negotiations with Hitler. We must be prepared for France to seek an agreement with, or without, our mutual consent."

Churchill paused, contemplating his chief military advisor's recommendation. *In the last war, our soldiers fought valiantly—side by side in the muddy trenches—to defeat the enemy. Even in the darkest times of the conflict, our countries remained united while forging ahead toward victory.* A deep disappointment and regret festered in his heart. He turned to Ismay and nodded.

Churchill and his group meandered through a labyrinth of rosebushes, until the robust arguments amongst their French counterparts subsided. Upon returning to the dining room, Churchill briefly reiterated his position, promised to keep Reynaud informed on any response from US President Roosevelt, and bid them farewell.

They returned to the airfield and got into their plane. The engines grumbled to life and the buzz of propellers filled the cabin. An angst grew inside Churchill and he looked at Ismay, seated next to him.

"We must prepare for the fate of the French fleet," Churchill said. "We cannot allow a single vessel to fall into the hands of Germany, even if we must sink them ourselves."

Ismay's face turned somber, and he smoothed his neatly trimmed, salt-and-pepper mustache. "I concur."

The plane rumbled down a runway, passed within several meters of a bomb crater, and flew sharply into the air. Soon, the aircraft reached cruising altitude and leveled off. Churchill lit a cigar and puffed on the tip, taking smoke into his lungs. He peered through a window at the verdant terrain, thousands of feet below the plane. He analyzed the discussions of the meeting in his brain, unaware that it would be four years until he would again set foot on French soil.

CHAPTER 36

SAVENAY, FRANCE—JUNE 16, 1940

Shortly before sunrise, Ruth was awakened by the squeak of door hinges. She sat up, rubbed sleep from her eyes, and scanned the interior of a barn. Twilight, coming from gaps in the wood siding, dimly illuminated the space with dozens of refugees who were asleep on the ground. A few inches away, Jimmie was slumbering with his head on his bundled flight jacket. On the opposite side of Ruth was an empty space next to Lucette, whose diaphragm slowly rose and fell as she slept. *Where's Aline?*

Ruth drew a deep breath, bringing in recycled air that smelled of old manure, earth, and sweat. She carefully stood—her legs achy and stiff—and navigated her way through the barn by stepping over people who were curled on blankets and mounds of straw. Outside, a predawn chorus of chirping sparrows decorated a row of birch trees. She walked a short distance and spotted Aline at a stone well. A wrought-iron wheel grinded as she reeled in rope that was threaded through a pulley. Tension eased from Ruth's shoulders.

"You're up early," Ruth said, approaching her.

Aline turned. "I thought I would fill our canteens before the crowds set in."

"Mind if I join you?"

"*Non.*"

Ruth helped her to raise the rope, attached to a wooden bucket.

Aline submerged an open canteen into the water-filled bucket and paused, watching bubbles stream to the surface. She filled three canteens, screwed on the caps, and placed them next to the well.

Ruth glanced at the barn. "Everyone is still asleep. Rather than risk waking them, how about we rest here for a bit?"

Aline nodded. She sat, leaning her back against the well.

Ruth sat beside her and wrapped her arms around her skirt-covered knees. She looked at Aline, her hair tangled and her eyes surrounded in dark circles. "You could use a little more rest. How about taking a nap before we get on the road."

"I don't want to sleep."

"Did you have another bad dream?"

"*Oui.*"

"I'm sorry," Ruth said.

Aline plucked a blade of dry grass and held it between her fingers. "I miss him."

"Me too."

They'd buried Pierre in a cemetery in Vaiges. Several refugees, who were traveling through the village, had helped them with digging and filling the grave with the use of a shovel they'd found in a groundskeeper's shed. With no rabbi to perform a service, Ruth presided over an ad hoc ceremony where she, Aline, Lucette, and Jimmie took turns saying a few words about Pierre and what he meant to them. With tear-filled eyes, they placed handfuls of wildflowers over his plot and left the cemetery. For Aline, there was no sitting shiva to provide her with emotional healing. Her time to grieve was stolen by the Luftwaffe, whose air raids continued to drive them and millions of refugees across the French countryside.

For the past three days, they carried their sorrow while making their way toward the coast. Initially, Aline barely spoke and she refused to eat. At water breaks, Ruth and the others prodded her to consume the little amount of food that remained in their bags. As the days passed, Aline gradually began to talk about her grandpapa, as if the arduous trek had jolted open a door between her head and heart.

"I loved him so much," Aline had sobbed, standing at a roadside.

Hundreds of refugees had passed them by while Ruth, Jimmie, and Lucette consoled Aline. But the girl's tears were cut short by a drone of German aircraft, flying high over the area, which compelled the group to gather their bags and carry on their journey.

In addition to Aline's heartbreak, Ruth was saddened and tormented by Pierre's death. The time on the road allowed her to ponder if there was anything she could have done to change the course of events. *If I had convinced him to stay in Paris with my family, he might still be alive. I should have made him stop more often to rest. Why didn't I try to get an extra supply of medicine from Uncle Julian?* But most of all, she questioned her resuscitation technique, the Holger Nielsen method, which she and Lucette had learned by observing medics at the front. She wondered, most often at night when the others were asleep, if her timing of compressions had been off, or if she'd performed the arm lifts incorrectly. Ruth had administered first aid under the most horrible of circumstances, but it was different with Pierre. Unlike the injured soldiers whom she didn't know, Pierre had become a dear friend whom she considered to be like family.

"Your grandpapa adored you," Ruth said, leaning her back against the well. "He was so proud of you."

"*Merci.*" Aline fiddled with her blade of grass, then tied it into a knot and dropped it on the ground. "How long do people hurt when someone they love dies?"

Ruth smoothed her hands over her skirt. *Her mother and grandfather have perished, and the whereabouts of her father's army unit is unknown. It's far too much heartache for anyone, especially a child, to experience in a month's time.* "I wish I knew the answer, but I do believe that hearts heal with time. Someday, your bad dreams will fade away, and they'll be replaced by blissful memories of Pierre and your *maman*."

"Do you really think so?" Aline asked, her voice faint.

"I do."

Aline leaned back and rested her head against the well.

A recollection of discussing Aline's welfare with Lucette and Jimmie entered Ruth's brain. "I've told you this already, but I think that it's good for you to hear again—you need not worry about being alone. You're going to stay with me and Lucette until your father returns from the war."

Aline nodded.

"After we get Jimmie on a boat to England, you'll come with me and Lucette to her parents' home in Toulouse. The city is far to the south, near the border with Spain, where it will be hard for the German Army to reach us. You'll be safe there."

"*Oui*." Aline crossed her ankles. "I overheard you and Lucette talking last night. You both want to find a way to help the fight."

"We do." Ruth turned to her. "We feel that we need to do something to aid Allied forces, or support resistance fighters. We cannot accept Nazi occupation, and we won't give up until the country is free. I hope you understand."

"I do, but I'm worried you'll get hurt or—" Aline pursed her lips.

"I'll do everything I can to be safe." Ruth placed a hand on her shoulder. "If serving France should require me and Lucette to leave Toulouse, you'll stay with Lucette's family until we—and your father, Leopold—return home."

The anxiety on Aline's face softened, as if hearing her father's name had strengthened her spirit. She leaned in and hugged Ruth.

Ruth squeezed her tightly and kissed the top of her head. "The sun is nearly up. If we get an early start, we'll arrive in Saint-Nazaire by this afternoon. How about we wake Lucette and Jimmie and get on the road?"

Aline nodded and slipped away. They stood, picked up the canteens, and walked—water sloshing inside the containers—to the barn and crept inside.

By midmorning, Ruth and her group reached Donges, a village on the Loire River, approximately fifteen kilometers upriver from the sea. Ahead, their path merged onto a main road, filled with throngs of refugees and hundreds, if not thousands, of French soldiers and BEF troops.

"*Mon Dieu*," Lucette said, her eyes wide. "So many have given up."

Ruth fought back an angst, rising in her chest. "*Non*. If they intended to flee the war, they wouldn't be here. They're headed to the evacuation point, so they can reassemble and continue to fight."

"Let's find out," Jimmie said. "How about we split into two groups and mingle in to find out what they know?"

"Okay," Ruth said.

Jimmie looked at Aline. "Would you like to come with me?"

Aline nodded and scurried ahead with Jimmie.

Ruth and Lucette worked their way forward, weaving around slow-moving pedestrians and a disabled wagon with a broken wheel. They approached a group of seven haggard French soldiers, most of whom were unarmed and missing their helmets.

"Can you tell us what's happening?" Ruth asked of a soldier, his left eye covered with a bandage.

"We were ordered to go to Saint-Nazaire for evacuation," he said.

"Do you know if it has started, or how long it will last?"

"*Non*." The soldier lowered his head and continued his slog, his boots scraping over the pavement.

Ruth and Lucette maneuvered through the crowd and spoke with several more French soldiers. In addition to French and BEF troops, they encountered Polish, Czech, and Belgian soldiers making their way toward the sea. And word began to spread through the masses that a British evacuation was currently underway at the harbor.

A wave of hope surged through Ruth. "We're going to make it in time."

"We will," Lucette said.

Ruth adjusted the strap of a bag, digging into her shoulder. She looked at Jimmie, twenty meters ahead and keeping Aline close to him as he conversed with two BEF soldiers. *He'll be evacuated soon*, she thought. A strange mix of joy and sadness flowed through her.

"You miss him already," Lucette said, as if she could sense Ruth's feelings.

"Is it that obvious?"

"It is," Lucette said. "Have you told him how much you care about him?"

"A little."

"That is not enough," Lucette said.

"There's no time for us," Ruth said. "We're going in separate ways."

"It doesn't matter." Lucette gazed over the people on the road. "I can't stop searching the crowd for Paul, and any sign of a soldier wearing a tank battalion badge so I can ask if they know anything about his group. I pray that he's safe, but the longer we travel and the more devastation we see, the less sure I am that I'll see him again."

"He's going to come home—you must believe that."

Lucette swallowed. "What I'm trying to say is—I wish I would have said more to Paul before he left for the army. At the time, we both didn't think the war would happen. If I could go back in time and do it over again, I would have said so much more to him before he got on that train and left."

Ruth's chest ached. She looped her arm around Lucette's elbow.

"I don't want you to have any regrets," Lucette said. "Regardless of how things turn out, you shouldn't waste a chance to tell him what's on your mind—and in your heart."

Ruth glanced at Jimmie, walking like a father beside Aline. She wondered, although briefly, what it might be like to create a life with him, and have a family of their own. Her heart desired to be with him, but her brain prodded her with logic. *We're fighting a war and France is falling. It isn't in the cards for us.*

Lucette unhooked her arm and lengthened her stride.

"Where are you going?"

"To walk with Aline on the final leg of the trip," Lucette said. "I'll send Jimmie to join you."

"You don't need to—"

"I do." Lucette quickened her pace, weaved her way around a group of refugees walking with bicycles, and disappeared.

Minutes later, Jimmie worked his way through the crowd to Ruth. He settled in next to her and matched her walking pace. "Lucette filled me in on your conversations with French soldiers."

Ruth nodded. An odd feeling of nervousness, much like what she felt before performing onstage, grew in her stomach. "Did you learn anything from the BEF?"

"I did."

For several minutes, Jimmie told her about his conversation with BEF soldiers, whose unit avoided the lines of Panzer tanks that surrounded most of the British troops in northwest France. "They were told that the evacuations at Saint-Nazaire began yesterday."

"Do they know how long it will last?"

"They're not sure—they suppose it will continue until the Germans invade the area."

"We'll be there in a few hours—in time to get you aboard a ship."

He nodded.

"How does Aline seem to you?" she asked.

"She's hurting a lot, but she's talking, which I think is a good sign."

"I agree." She glanced at him. "She has grown fond of you."

"Same." He adjusted the sling, holding his cast-covered arm. "It feels wrong to leave you. I'm hoping that when we get to Saint-Nazaire, you, Lucette, and Aline will change your minds and get on a ship to England."

"I wish it were that easy," Ruth said.

"It can be," he said.

"In Toulouse, we'll have Lucette's family to help us care for Aline. Besides, what would happen to Aline if we went to England?"

"I don't know. But I do think that you'll be safer if you were out of France."

"I appreciate you looking out for us." She shifted her bag on her shoulder. "Our minds are made up—we're going to Toulouse."

"I don't like it," he said, "but I respect your decision."

"That's all I ask for," she said. "*Merci.*"

They traveled around a bend in the road and the dark, bluish-gray water of the Loire came into view. The silt-covered riverbank contained countless footprints, as if an army had traversed along the waterway during the night.

Ruth thought of her conversation with Lucette, and her anxiousness grew. "There's something that's been on my mind that I want to talk to you about."

"Of course," he said.

"Let's stop for a second." She led him away from the crowded road. At the riverbank, she put down her bag, faced him, and looked into his eyes. She drew a few short breaths, attempting to dispel butterflies in her stomach.

"It's all right," he said, touching her hand. "You can tell me anything."

She swallowed. "I wish I had been more open about—"

A grind of plane engines broke the air. On the road, soldiers and refugees raised their heads to the sky.

Ruth's breath stalled in her lungs.

A horrid crescendo of shouts and screams came from the crowd, which was followed by the piercing shriek of Stuka dive bombers.

CHAPTER 37

DONGES, FRANCE—JUNE 16, 1940

Several thousand feet above them, six German Stukas dived toward the ground. Their sirens blared, flooding Ruth's body with fear. *Oh, dear God!*

Jimmie grabbed her hand and pulled her along the riverbank. Soldiers and refugees scattered from the road in search of cover.

"Aline!" Ruth shouted. "Lucette!" Her heart pounded against her rib cage. She struggled to breathe as they sprinted to a dead, leafless oak tree and fell to the ground.

The wail of sirens grew.

"Hold on!" Jimmie covered her with his body.

A hundred meters away, a large cargo crane and empty docks lined the Loire River. Ruth dug her fingernails into the silty soil, all the while praying that the dockyard was the target of the Stukas. Her body trembled as the planes released their bombs and pulled up. Explosions erupted over the docks, spewing a giant fountain of wood, water, and hunks of steel into the air.

She took in gulps of air, and her body relaxed under his protective weight. But her seconds of solace were erased by a second wave of Stuka sirens. She strained her neck and peered upward. Her eyes traced the trajectory of the German planes—pointed at hundreds of soldiers and refugees scrambling to find cover. "No!"

She felt powerless as bombs dropped from the bellies of the

aircraft and detonated along the roadway and nearby trees. The ground shook beneath her body, sending shock and anger through her veins. Screams poured from the crowd. People scrambled down the riverbank, hurled themselves into the water, and struggled to swim away.

"We need to find them!" Ruth struggled to push away from Jimmie.

"Wait!" He held her tight.

A Stuka, flying solo and low to the ground, buzzed over the area. Machine gun bullets sprayed the riverbank and the road, nearly striking a woman and two children hiding under an abandoned wagon.

A roar of plane engines, deeper in tone, shot overhead. Within seconds, six Hurricane fighter planes narrowed in on the enemy aircraft. A dogfight erupted, and some of the soldiers crawled from their hiding places to watch. Soon, a squadron of British Spitfires—coming from the direction of the Channel—joined the fight. One of the Stukas was shot down, crashing near the village of Donges. A Hurricane with smoke pouring from its engine escaped by flying inland. As abruptly as the air battle began, it ended with the remaining German planes retreating to the north. The British planes circled the area, as if to survey the damage, and flew away.

Ruth and Jimmie, their feet sinking in silt and mud, clambered up the riverbank.

"Aline!" Ruth ran down the road, beginning to fill with people who'd come out from under bushes and canopy of trees. "Lucette!"

Jimmie, pressing a hand over his slinged arm, followed Ruth. "Aline—Lucette!"

"Ruth!" Aline screamed.

Ruth sprinted toward the girl's voice. She pushed through a crowd, a mix of soldiers and refugees, gathered in a circle on the side of the road.

"Jimmie!" Aline cried.

Ruth broke through the line of people, and her legs turned weak at the sight of Lucette on the ground. Aline was on her knees and holding Lucette's hand as a BEF soldier pressed a blood-soaked handkerchief to her right knee.

"Lucette!" Ruth dropped to her side.

"My leg," Lucette gasped.

"Are you hurt anywhere else?" Ruth asked.

"I don't think so."

Ruth stroked her forehead. "You're going to be okay."

Jimmie squeezed through the crowd and the color drained from his face. He kneeled beside her.

Lucette winced. "Ruth, check my leg and tell me how bad it is."

Ruth turned to a young British soldier applying pressure to the leg. "*Merci*. I'll take over from here."

He nodded and gently removed his hands, smeared with blood, from Lucette's leg.

Ruth lifted the handkerchief to reveal a deep, six-inch laceration above the right kneecap. She fought to contain her composure as she examined the wound. "You took some shrapnel. I don't think you damaged any arteries, so I'm going to use pressure to slow the bleeding."

Lucette swallowed. "All right."

"You're doing a good job, Aline," Ruth said. "Keep holding her hand."

Aline nodded.

"I need something bigger for a bandage," Ruth said, eyeing the wound.

Jimmie removed his sling, made of white cotton material. "How about this?"

"It'll work." She took the sling, untied the knot, and wrapped the material around the knee. Using both hands, she applied pressure to the bandaged wound.

Lucette flinched and grimaced.

"Try to breathe," Ruth said, pressing down on her knee.

Lucette drew a jagged breath and exhaled.

"We're going to get you medical help," Ruth said. "You're going to be okay."

Lucette closed her eyes and nodded.

"Where should we go?" Jimmie asked, turning to Ruth.

Her mind raced, searching for options. "Donges is too small of a village for a hospital, and we may not find a doctor there. I think our best bet is to get her on a wagon to Saint-Nazaire. The evacuation vessels might have nurses and doctors. On the way there, we'll search for army medics."

"All right—I'll find someone to help us transport her." He stood and disappeared into the crowd.

Ruth continued to apply pressure to the wound while Aline comforted Lucette by talking to her and holding her hand. Several BEF soldiers and refugees remained with them as they waited for Jimmie to return.

Ten minutes later, Jimmie approached with a bearded man and two French soldiers who were pulling a two-wheeled cart that was loaded with blankets and a few pieces of furniture. The horseless cart, powered by men, gave the wheeled contraption the appearance of a large rickshaw. They pulled the cart near Lucette and stopped.

The bearded man removed the furniture—two chairs and an antique side table—from the cart and rearranged the blankets.

The soldiers lifted Lucette, while Ruth continued to apply pressure to her leg, and placed her in the cart. Ruth scooched in beside her and adjusted her grip on the bandage, warm and saturated with blood.

Ruth looked at Lucette, her face pale. "You'll be okay."

She nodded and lowered her eyelids.

Aline scrambled to collect their bags and placed them next to Ruth.

The bearded man and the soldiers lifted the wood shafts on the front of the cart.

Ruth felt a tug and the wheels rolled forward.

"Is there anything you need?" Jimmie asked, walking alongside the cart.

A memory of failing to save a soldier named Claude—who'd been mortally wounded during the Phony War—flashed in her head. A chill ran through her body. "Give me your belt."

Jimmie, using one hand, unbuckled his belt and placed it on Ruth's lap.

"Please," Ruth said, looking at Jimmie, "see if they can pick up the pace."

"I will." Jimmie ran ahead, joined the men, and the cart gathered speed.

Ruth pressed on Lucette's wound. She prayed that the bleeding would stop, and that she wouldn't need to resort to using a tourniquet.

CHAPTER 38

SAINT-NAZAIRE, FRANCE—JUNE 16, 1940

The muscles in Ruth's hands and arms burned with fatigue as she fought to keep pressure on Lucette's wound. Soldiers, their faces covered in sweat, labored to pull the cart over the road that was congested with trudging refugees and troops. Ahead, the Loire River widened into a vast estuary.

Ruth strained her eyes, trying to catch a glimpse of Saint-Nazaire. "I think I can see open water." She looked at Lucette, her skin pale and eyes closed. "Can you hear me?"

Lucette stirred and tilted her head.

"You need to fight to stay awake."

Lucette cracked open her eyelids.

"Stay with me."

"I will," she said, her voice hoarse.

"We're about an hour from Saint-Nazaire—you're going to be all right."

Lucette placed a palm over Ruth's hands, pressing against her wound. She took in a shallow breath. "I'm sorry I got hurt."

"Nonsense," Ruth said. "You were protecting Aline. She told me that you pushed her away as the bomb was falling. She's safe because of you."

Tears welled up in Lucette's eyes and she blinked them away.

Ruth glanced at the belt beside her. "I'm going to take a look at your wound to check the bleeding."

Lucette nodded.

Ruth removed her hands from Lucette's knee, peeked under the bandage, and her heart sank. She covered the wound with the bandage and squeezed.

Lucette grimaced with pain.

"It bleeds when I release the pressure," Ruth said, trying to control the fear in her voice. "I'm going to keep up the compression with my hands. A tourniquet will cut off circulation to your foot—I'll use it only as a last resort."

"All right."

Ruth looked into her friend's eyes, filled with angst. "I'm with you. You're going to be okay."

The lines on her face softened.

A grind of airplane engines pierced the air, and a Luftwaffe bomber squadron soared overhead toward Saint-Nazaire. Although the planes were headed away from the crowd, scores of people fled the road in search of cover. Soon, sound waves of explosions rolled over the riverway.

Oh, no. They might be attacking ships in the harbor. Ruth's anxiousness grew.

The group traveled another kilometer and more German planes, as well as a British Hurricane squadron, were sighted on the horizon. Gunfire and bombs echoed over the Loire estuary. Waves of refugees, their faces etched with fear, fled in the opposite direction. But most of the soldiers, including the ones who were lugging the cart, continued their trek toward the sea.

Jimmie approached Ruth and Lucette, and he held his cast-covered arm to his chest as he traveled alongside them. "It appears that the Luftwaffe has set its sight on the British naval evacuation. It'll likely get worse as we get closer."

Ruth nodded.

A woman and two teenage girls pushed their way back through the crowd, like fish swimming against a tide.

Jimmie looked at Ruth. "It might be best if you and Aline backtrack to Donges, and then make your way to Toulouse. I'll carry on with taking Lucette to Saint-Nazaire for medical help."

"*Non*," Ruth said.

Lucette strained to lift her head. "Take Aline."

"I'm not leaving you," Ruth said. "We need to stick together, remember?"

"One of the soldiers can apply pressure to my wound," Lucette said.

Ruth glanced at Aline, lugging her backpack as she walked beside the soldiers at the front of the cart. Her heart felt torn. *I don't want to abandon Lucette, but I need to make sure that Aline is safe.*

"It's all right," Lucette said. "Go with Aline."

Ruth struggled to come to terms with leaving her friend, but deep down she knew that she—as well as Lucette and Jimmie—would each risk their life to save Aline. She felt sick to her stomach. "I hate leaving you, but—"

Bomb blasts echoed from behind them.

Lucette flinched.

Ruth turned, while continuing to press her hands tight to the bandage.

Smoke plumes rose from Donges, several kilometers behind them. High in the sky, three German bombers veered around and flew away.

Ruth's skin turned cold.

The soldiers pulling the cart glanced behind them and quickened their pace.

Aline scurried to Jimmie and walked beside him. "They're behind us, too."

"They are." He put an arm around her shoulder. "It's going to be okay."

Aline nodded, despite a fear in her eyes.

Lucette clasped Ruth's sleeve. "It's your call."

Her mind raced as she scanned the area. *We're surrounded on three sides—two by the Luftwaffe and one by the German Army to the north. The river is far too wide to cross, and even if Aline and I made it through Donges, we'll likely be plagued by air raids on the journey to Toulouse.* She considered the choices and, before she changed her mind, she looked at her friend and said, "The enemy has us fenced in. I say we go to Saint-Nazaire and try to board a ship."

Lucette swallowed.

"We're out of options, and we need to make sure that Aline is safe and you receive medical care." Ruth's chest tightened, and her mouth felt dry. "I'm sorry you won't see your parents. They'll understand. I'm sure they would want you—and all of us—to do everything possible to remain safe. You'll see them again."

Lucette drew a breath and squeezed Ruth's arm. "All right—let's get on a boat."

An hour later, they arrived at the harbor. The area was swarmed with tens of thousands of people, the majority Allied soldiers, who were lined up near a dockyard that was partially destroyed by bombs. Ruth had expected to see a large fleet of ships that were loading evacuees. Instead, the harbor contained a mere three vessels.

Two troopships—packed with soldiers standing on their decks—had already departed the docks and were making their way to the Atlantic Ocean. The last remaining vessel at the dockyard was a British hospital ship, covered in white paint and several huge, red cross emblems. While injured soldiers were loaded onto the vessel, three RAF Hurricanes patrolled the sky above the harbor.

"We're here," Ruth said, leaning to Lucette.

Lucette, her face pallid, lethargically tilted her head and peered toward the harbor.

She's getting weaker, Ruth thought. She buried her trepidation and said, "We're in luck. There's a hospital ship at the dock."

"We made it," Lucette said, her voice faint.

"We did. Try to stay awake."

Lucette gave a subtle nod.

The cart stopped, and Ruth scanned the masses of troops and refugees in search of a medic and found none.

Jimmie and a few of the soldiers who'd pulled the cart ran to the dock. Minutes later, they returned with a stretcher.

"Lucette," Ruth said. "I'm going to use a tourniquet to apply pressure over your leg while we transport you to the ship."

"All right," she breathed.

Ruth tightened a belt around Lucette's leg, and the soldiers helped them to place her on the stretcher.

"Thank you," Jimmie said to the soldiers. "Let's get her to the dock and loaded—"

An air raid siren sounded.

Ruth's adrenaline surged. "Hurry!"

The soldiers lifted the stretcher containing Lucette and maneuvered their way through the hordes of troops and refugees who were waiting to flee the harbor. Ruth walked alongside, holding tight to the belt around Lucette's leg, and Jimmie and Aline followed close behind. At the entrance to the dockyard, a BEF soldier stood guard with a rifle.

Luftwaffe planes appeared above the harbor, and machine gun fire erupted from the Hurricane fighters.

People ducked and searched for cover.

"Keep going!" Jimmie shouted to the soldiers carrying the stretcher.

The guard glanced at Lucette, waved for the group to go through, and peered upward at the aerial dogfight.

They made their way down the pier, maneuvering around scores of uninjured soldiers, who appeared to have refused to leave the area after failing to get on a vessel.

A Stuka siren howled, and a bomb detonated in the harbor, fifty meters from a troopship. Water sprayed high into the air. The Hurricanes veered toward the enemy planes and fired their guns.

Ruth's heart pounded in her chest. "Go!"

The group struggled to push through the crowd, growing denser as they traveled down the pier.

"She's full!" a young Royal Navy midshipman shouted, blocking the entrance to the gangway. "No more passengers!"

Oh, God. No! Ruth's legs turned weak.

The soldiers stopped and put down the stretcher. They wiped sweat from their brows and rubbed their arms.

Ruth gathered Jimmie and the soldiers. "We need to get Lucette on board. She's lost a lot of blood and we don't have time to wait for another ship."

"It's full," one of the soldiers said.

"I don't care," Ruth said. "She's getting on board, even if I have to carry her myself."

The soldiers nodded.

Jimmie glanced at the naval officer, arguing with soldiers who were trying to talk their way on board. "We likely have one shot at this. Let's try to get Aline on board with her."

"Okay." Ruth's mind raced, fighting to come up with a solution. She kneeled to Lucette and loosened the belt around her wound.

Lucette's eyes met hers.

"We are going to try to get Aline on board with you."

Lucette nodded and touched her knee, as if she understood what Ruth was thinking.

Ruth carefully ripped away a strip of bandage, saturated with blood. She approached Aline and said, "I'm going to wrap your hand."

"Why?" Aline asked.

"They're only taking injured people, and it's full. We're going to try to squeeze you and Lucette on board the ship."

Tears welled up in the girl's eyes. "What about you and Jimmie?"

"We'll take the next boat."

"*Non*," Aline cried. "Come with us."

Ruth shook her head. She clasped the girl's hand and wrapped the bandage around her left hand and wrist, and then hugged her tight. "Everything is going to work out—I'll see you in England in a day or two—I promise."

Aline released her and nodded.

Ruth wiped away the girl's tears. "I need you to get on the stretcher with Lucette and be still."

"Wait." Aline pulled away, and she darted to Jimmie and hugged him.

Jimmie, using one arm, squeezed her tight.

The ship's horn sounded. Hairs prickled on the back of Ruth's neck. "We're running out of time."

Aline slipped away from Jimmie, took off her backpack, and removed Piglet.

"Please keep him," he said.

"*Non*," Aline said, holding out her hand. "He's your good luck charm, and he'll keep you and Ruth safe. If you want, you can give him back to me when I see you again."

"We need to go," Ruth said.

Jimmie reluctantly took Piglet and stashed him in his flight jacket.

Aline got on the stretcher and curled next to Lucette with her bandaged hand exposed.

Ruth kissed Lucette on both cheeks. "I'll see you in England."

Tears fell from the corners of Lucette's eyes.

"All right," Jimmie said to the soldiers. "Let's move."

The men lifted the stretcher and followed Jimmie and Ruth, clearing a path through the crowd.

Ruth ducked under the arm of a French soldier and shot ahead to the midshipman who was blocking the entrance to the gangway with a rope tied between two posts. "We have a badly injured woman with a child."

"She's full," the officer said, looking at Ruth. "Step back. We're preparing to depart."

Gunfire blasted in the sky, and the Luftwaffe invaders veered away from the Hurricanes and retreated over the town.

Cheers boomed from soldiers along the harbor.

"Please," Ruth said. "The woman is losing blood. She can't wait for another boat."

The midshipman eyed Ruth's and Lucette's uniforms, as if he were trying to determine if they were with the French Army. "I'm sorry."

Jimmie pushed his way forward. "You must let her through— she needs immediate medical care."

The officer shifted his weight. "I have my orders."

"To hell with your orders!" Jimmie shouted. "Let her through!"

The midshipman held his ground.

A nurse caring for an injured soldier on the ship's deck perked her head.

"Prepare for departure!" a Royal Navy commander called, walking down the gangway.

Ruth locked eyes with the commander and extended her hand. "Sir, I beg you, please allow this woman and child to come aboard."

The commander glanced at Lucette and Aline, who were lying silently on the stretcher. Lines formed on the commander's face. "Please forgive me. There's no—"

"Commander!" a nurse shouted, running down the gangway. "I can make space for them."

The commander glanced at the nurse and turned to the midshipman. "Let them through."

Thank God. "She needs pressure to stop her blood loss," Ruth called to the nurse.

"I'll take care of her," the nurse said.

A wave of relief rolled over Ruth. "Thank you."

The nurse nodded.

The midshipman removed the rope, and the soldiers carried the stretcher with Lucette and Aline on board. The nurse guided them through throngs of injured soldiers and refugees on the deck, and Lucette and Aline were placed on the ground near a lifeboat. Afterward, the soldiers were escorted by a naval officer to leave the ship.

Ruth and Jimmie thanked the soldiers, and then labored their way through the crowd and exited the pier. They sat on a concrete seawall and looked out over the harbor. For Ruth, the hardest part was waiting for the hospital ship to sail away, knowing that the Luftwaffe could appear at any moment and rain down their bombs.

The ship's horn sounded, the gangway was removed, and the ship floated away from its dock.

She felt Jimmie's arm wrap around her. She leaned into him, and together they watched the ship sail through the harbor, enter the Atlantic, and gradually disappear out of sight.

CHAPTER 39

SAINT-NAZAIRE, FRANCE—JUNE 16, 1940

Ruth, sitting next to Jimmie on a seawall, looked out over the dark blue water of the shipless harbor. She silently prayed that Lucette would survive, and that she and Aline would safely arrive in England.

Jimmie rubbed her shoulder. "Are you ready to go?"

She nodded.

He stood and helped her to her feet.

They made their way past thousands of soldiers and refugees who were waiting in long lines that extended from piers. Instead of taking a place at the back of a column, they approached a Royal Navy officer, who was smoking a cigarette as he gazed over the shore.

"Excuse me, sir," Jimmie said. "Do you know when more transport ships will arrive?"

"Tomorrow morning." The officer, his hand slightly shaking, placed the cigarette to his lips and took a drag. He exhaled smoke through his nose and faced them. "The vessels are ocean liners, requisitioned by the government. They'll have greater capacity to carry both troops and refugees."

"Will the navy be spreading the word to the evacuees?" Ruth asked.

"We did." The officer flicked ash from his cigarette. "They refuse to lose their place in line."

Ruth's shoulders slumped. *They fear being left behind more than the chance of being killed in an air raid.*

Ruth and Jimmie left the shore and went to their abandoned cart, where they recovered Ruth's bag and a few pieces of clothing that were strewn over the ground. The canteens and the last of their food had been pilfered, but Ruth held no resentment. She felt only pity for the hungry people, struggling to keep their strength until they could be rescued.

"Your hands and arms must be tired," Jimmie said. "How about I carry your bag?"

An image of applying pressure to Lucette's wound flashed in her brain, resurrecting a sense of dread, deep in the pit of her stomach. She flexed her hands, filled with ache, and gave her bag to him.

He took off his jacket and stashed it, along with his revolver and items from the pockets of his tunic, in the bag.

"What now?" she asked.

"It'll be dark in an hour or so. We could get in line and wait until morning for the ships to arrive, but I think it will be safer to get away from the harbor. The Luftwaffe will likely continue raids on the evacuation point."

Ruth nodded. "Let's find a shelter away from the masses and return before daylight."

Jimmie lifted the bag. "Lead the way."

They left the harbor, made their way through the streets of Saint-Nazaire, and then walked along the shoreline, distancing themselves from the crowds. The sun began to set, and wind gusted in from the ocean, pushing their bodies as they slogged over a sandy dirt path. After twenty minutes of walking, they spotted an isolated fisherman's shack, absent a boat and any sign of being inhabited.

Ruth knocked on the door and jostled a secured padlock. "Let's see if there is another opening."

He nodded.

They walked around to the rear of the shack and discovered a small window. Ruth placed her hands above her eyes and peeked inside. "There's no one inside—only equipment," she said, stepping back.

Jimmie, using his elbow, broke a pane of glass. He cleared away shards, undid the lock, and—with Ruth's help—pried open the sash.

"Any chance you could give me a boost?" Ruth asked. "It's a bit high for me to get through."

Jimmie kneeled, and then lowered his back to prop himself on two knees and one hand.

Ruth carefully placed a foot between his shoulder blades, pushed upward, and crawled through the window. She got to her feet, her shoes crunching on broken glass, and faced him.

Jimmie handed her the bag and she helped him to climb inside.

The shack was dimly lit by one window, and the air smelled of old fish and wood. The space contained oars, tarps, a large mound of nets, a folded boat sail, and a pole with a steel hook that was hung above the door. In addition to fishing equipment, the place had a small table with three wood crates as stools, a cast-iron stove, and a weathered cabinet with drawers. On a side wall was a fish cleaning station with an assortment of fillet knives, shelves, and a sink with a corroded spigot.

Ruth approached the sink and turned the valve to the spigot, producing a rust-colored liquid. She waited for the sediment to clear, and then scrubbed away remnants of blood from her hands and fingernails until her skin felt raw. Afterward, she took in gulps of water, quenching her thirst and soothing a burn in her throat.

"The water tastes like iron," she said, wiping her hands on her skirt, "but it's drinkable."

Jimmie lowered his head to the spigot and drank. He cupped water in his hand and splashed it on his face and neck, and then went to the table that held an oil lamp and a box of matches. He checked the fuel and lit a wick, casting a dull glow over the room.

Ruth rummaged through the cabinet and discovered hooks, rolls of string, and tools to mend fishing nets. Upon opening the third drawer, her eyes widened at the sight of three tins of mackerel, a metal twist can opener key, and a half-eaten jar of hazel-nuts.

"Food," she said, holding up a tin.

"Splendid." Jimmie joined her to search the rest of the draw-ers and shelves. While inspecting the bottom of the cabinet, he discovered a dust-covered bottle of liquor. "What is Lambig?" he asked, reading the label.

"Bal Tabarin served it—I think it's brandy made from cider."

They placed the food and Lambig on the table and sat on crates. She opened the jar and poured nuts onto the table. She tossed one in her mouth and chewed, filling her mouth with a sweet, earthy flavor. "I never knew stale hazelnuts could taste so good."

Jimmie smiled. He ate a handful of nuts, clamped the bottle of Lambig under his arm, and removed the cork.

Using the metal key, Ruth opened the tins of mackerel and slid one to Jimmie.

He plucked a filet with his fingers and took a bite. "It's bril-liant."

Ruth chewed a piece of the mackerel, savoring the mild-flavored fish in rich olive oil. She finished off the tin and felt her energy begin to return.

Jimmie slid the bottle of Lambig to Ruth.

She sniffed the top. "Smells strong."

"Want me to try it first?"

She shook her head and sipped a bit of the brandy, which tasted more like whisky spiced with vanilla. A warmth drifted down her throat and settled into her stomach. She passed the bottle to Jim-mie, who took a swig.

For several minutes, they remained silent as they ate their food under the glow of lamplight. Night set in but the sound of guns, coming from many kilometers away, continued to echo over the coast.

"Do you think they're okay?" Ruth asked, breaking the silence.

"Yes," he said. "The hospital ship reached the Atlantic, and we didn't see any Luftwaffe squadrons flying overhead after their departure. I think they're safe."

She picked at a piece of hazelnut. "I'm worried about Lucette."

"Me too," he said. "I'm sure she's receiving good medical care."

She nodded. "I wish I could have done more."

"You did everything you could for Lucette, and you got her and Aline on board the ship. Soon, they'll be in England with a sea between them and the German Army."

Her muscles gradually relaxed. The lamp's flame dimmed and began to flicker.

He slid his hand next to hers. "You're going to see them again."

She touched his fingers.

"Leaving France doesn't mean that you're giving up your fight." He squeezed her hand. "I have no doubt that you'll find a way to serve the Allies while you're in Britain."

She nodded.

"When the war is won, you'll return to Paris and reunite with Colette and Julian, and you'll resume your dreams of a singing career." He looked into her eyes. "You're going to have a long and beautiful life."

Even in the worst of circumstances, you give me hope and make me feel good about myself. Butterflies fluttered in her stomach. "What if I want more?"

"Like what?"

She swallowed. "You."

He straightened his back.

"I've been reluctant to tell you how I feel, because I thought that I needed to choose serving the country over my personal desires." She drew a deep breath. "I was speaking with Lucette, shortly before she was injured, and she reminded me how important it is to open your heart to the people you care about when you have the chance."

He gently caressed her hand with his thumb.

Her skin tingled. "I've come to realize that there are no guarantees of tomorrow. With the war, I feel like our lives can be taken away in an instant. Even if there might not be a future for us, I don't want to let another day pass without telling you that you mean the world to me."

"I feel the same way," he said. "I can't imagine my life without you."

A surge of happiness enveloped her.

He stood and helped her up from her seat. He paused, resting his hand on her arm.

She stepped close and her heartbeat accelerated.

The lamp's minuscule flame flickered and extinguished, turning the room black.

"I'll search for more oil," he said.

"No need." She found his arm, and then led him toward the mound of fishing nets. She lowered her hand, her fingers lingering against his palm. "I think there's a sail to use as a blanket," she whispered.

Jimmie found the sail and slid it over the mound of nets to create a bed. He drew close and touched her hand. Their fingers entwined.

As if by reflex, she leaned into him and felt his cast-covered arm wrap around her back. Her breath quickened. She looked up, sensing—through the darkness—his lips approach her own.

Jimmie gently kissed her. His lips drifted from her parted mouth to her chin, and then rested against her neck.

Ruth's heart thudded beneath her sternum. "I want to be with you," she whispered.

He placed a hand to her cheek. "Are you sure?"

"Yes," she said, her body molding to his. She relished his kiss, deeper and longer. As their embrace faded, they undressed each other, gliding their fingers to find buttons. Buckles. Zippers. Delicately, she slid his tunic and shirt over his cast. With her lips, she caressed his shoulder, and then placed his hand against her bare chest.

"I will never do anything to hurt you," he said, his voice falling to a whisper.

"Nor I," she breathed. Her heart fluttered, like a bird attempting to free itself from a cage.

They slipped onto their makeshift bed, where they fell into an embrace, their hands and lips exploring each other. There were no guarantees for a future together, but she wanted nothing more than to be with him. As their bodies became one, Ruth's heartbeat soared, and she wished that their time together would never end.

CHAPTER 40

SAINT-NAZAIRE, FRANCE—JUNE 17, 1940

Jimmie, being careful not to wake Ruth, slipped out of the sail-covered bed of fishing nets. Moonlight glowed through the shack's window, casting shadows over the room. He paused with his eyes drawn to Ruth. Sailcloth, draping over her body, accentuated the curvature of her hip. Her chest rose and fell, synchronized with the tranquil cadence of her breath. An exposed leg extended from the bedding. *You're beautiful.*

Ruth stirred and opened her eyes. Appearing a bit shy, she covered her bare leg with the sailcloth. "Hi."

"Good morning," he said, stepping to her.

"Do we need to leave?"

"Yes," he said. "The sun will be rising soon."

She extended her hand. "I wish we had more time."

"Me too." He clasped her fingers, fighting his desire to slide in next to her. "Last night was wonderful."

"It was," she said. "Sometime, we'll spend the entire day in bed."

He smiled, feeling his body flood with warmth. He pulled her close. "I'll bring you breakfast in bed."

She nuzzled to him. "That would be lovely."

He lowered his cheek to her hair. He felt the softness of her skin next to his, spawning images of their night together.

She glided her fingers over his neck.

His skin tingled.

She looked up, and their eyes met.

Jimmie drew close, his breath stalling, and gently kissed her lips. He felt her arms wrap around his shoulders and pull him tight.

She eased back and glided her fingers over his stubbled face. "We should go."

He nodded, and she slipped away.

They put on their clothes and, not knowing when they would acquire more potable water, they drank heavily from the spigot. Jimmie gathered Ruth's bag and they climbed out of the window to a full moon that illuminated the coast of Brittany. The echoes of gunfire were gone, and the sound of crashing waves filled the cool, predawn air. They located the earthen path and headed toward town, leaving their interlude of bliss behind.

An intense yearning to be with Ruth grew inside him. Since the war began, he'd felt little more than anguish, but Ruth had awakened his heart. She'd given him warmth, affection, and—most of all—hope. But upon reaching England, he and Ruth would go their separate ways. He would report to the RAF and, once his arm was healed, he would return to the air war, most likely to defend the coast of Britain against the Luftwaffe. Ruth, he believed, would first make certain that Aline was cared for, and then she'd volunteer to serve in a branch of the armed forces, perhaps as an ambulance driver for Britain's Auxiliary Territorial Service. Regardless of which service Ruth pursued, he knew that she would continue to fight until the war was won.

France was nearing its defeat to Nazi Germany and Hitler would, in all probability, focus the full fury of his military upon Britain. Even if the country could muster the means to fend off a German invasion, it might take years, Jimmie believed, for the Allies to mount a counteroffensive to liberate France. During this time, he and Ruth would remain apart. And given the casualty rate of fighter pilots, the likelihood of surviving a long, drawn-out war was bleak. He prayed that he'd find a way to beat the odds and reunite with Ruth.

They reached Saint-Nazaire before dawn, and the town was

bustling with soldiers and refugees who were making their way to the waterfront. The streets were strewn with masses of discarded uniforms, and hundreds of rifles were propped against walls like abandoned walking sticks. Several burned-out military vehicles, including a dispatch motorcycle, blocked an intersection, which required them to take a detour on a side street. Jimmie had assumed that the ruined vehicles were a result of the previous day's Luftwaffe raids, until they encountered a BEF driver dousing his lorry with petrol.

Jimmie and Ruth stopped.

The soldier lit a match and tossed it into the driver's compartment of the lorry, engulfing it in flames. He turned, his eyes locked on Jimmie and Ruth, and he stuffed his hands into his pockets. "Orders to destroy what we can't remove."

Jimmie nodded. A smell of burnt petrol stung his nostrils.

The soldier darted down the street and disappeared around a corner.

Ruth clasped Jimmie's arm, and they continued their walk through the town.

At the harbor, countless soldiers and refugees were gathered in long lines at the piers. Thousands more were huddled in groups around the seawall.

"I don't see any ships," Ruth said.

Jimmie scanned the dark harbor, its water calm and empty of vessels. "They'll be here."

"The number of evacuees has grown," she said.

Muscles tensed in Jimmie's shoulders, and he wondered, although briefly, if there would be enough ships to save them all. He buried his angst and turned to her. "How about we get in line?"

"Okay."

They traveled to the last pier, which appeared to be slightly less crowded than the others, and stood behind a group of BEF soldiers, some of whom were hunkered on the ground with their heads in their hands. Several meters away, two chaplains—in khaki uniforms with clerical collars—sat on a stack of luggage and sobbed.

Ruth leaned to him.

He put down Ruth's bag and held her hand. "It's going to be all right."

She squeezed his fingers.

"Soon, we'll be in England."

"We will," she said, as if repeating an affirmation.

For an hour, they stood in line while new arrivals of soldiers and refugees flooded into the harbor. The lines grew to immense length, forcing people to wait in town.

Shortly before sunrise, a ship horn sounded in the distance.

Heads of evacuees turned toward the water.

A cacophony of horns sounded from off the coast and the opposite side of the estuary. Cheers boomed from the crowd, and hundreds of soldiers waved their arms.

"We're going home!" a man shouted.

Tears of happiness welled up in Ruth's eyes.

Thank God. Jimmie wrapped an arm around her shoulder.

Over the next forty minutes, scores of vessels—a mix of small destroyers, tugs, fishing boats, and leisure craft—entered the harbor and docked along the piers. Soldiers and refugees loaded onto the vessels, which took turns departing the harbor for the ocean.

"Are the tiny boats going to cross the Atlantic?" Ruth asked.

"I don't think so. The naval officer we spoke with yesterday mentioned that there would be cruise liners. The smaller vessels might be transporting everyone to ships that are too large to get into the harbor."

"I hope you're right," Ruth said. "We'll need huge boats to get everyone out of here."

An hour later, the same vessels—their decks empty—began to return to the piers. Evacuees were gradually loaded onto boats, and the line crept forward.

Jimmie's anticipation grew as he shuffled ahead with Ruth. "Given our location, I'm thinking that the evacuation ships might disembark in southwest England, perhaps in Falmouth, Plymouth, or Southampton. If we're lucky, it'll be Southampton."

"Why?"

"It's close to my family in Portsmouth, and it might give me a chance to see them before reporting to duty." He adjusted his grip on the bag. "How do you feel about meeting my parents and my sister, Nora?"

A smile spread over her face. "I'd love to."

It took two hours for Jimmie and Ruth to reach the end of the pier, where a tugboat with a French flag was docked. They climbed onto the craft, packed with a few hundred British and French soldiers, as well as a few dozen refugees. It was too crowded to sit, so they stood at a spot along the port-side rail. Soon, a rope was untied, the tug's engine growled, and the boat pulled away from the dock.

The tug chugged through the harbor, spraying a mist of salt water over the evacuees. As the boat reached the mouth of the Atlantic, the captain reduced the engine throttle and two crew members stood lookout over the bow.

"Why's the captain going so slow?" Ruth asked.

Jimmie leaned over the rail and peered ahead at the open ocean. "I don't know."

"The Luftwaffe dropped sea mines," a soldier said, standing next to them. "The captain is being careful to avoid them."

Jimmie rubbed his neck. He turned to the soldier and nodded.

The soldier removed a tin from his pocket and held it to Jimmie and Ruth. "Cigarette?"

They shook their heads, turned to the rail, and scanned the water for floating mines.

Twenty minutes into the journey, a huge ship appeared in the distance. People strained their necks and jostled to get a view as jubilant shouts erupted over the deck.

"I see it!" a British soldier called out. "It's bloody colossal!"

Jimmie's tension eased. He drew a deep breath, bringing salt air into his lungs, and loosened his grip on the railing.

The tug gradually made its way toward the cruise liner, which Jimmie estimated to be approximately six hundred feet in length. Its huge sides were painted battleship gray and the portholes were blacked out. Towering high above its seven decks was an enormous funnel that exhausted black smoke from its engine. To Jimmie, the vessel looked like a Mediterranean cruise ship that had been requisitioned and refitted for war.

The tug grew close, and Jimmie's eyes gravitated to the name on the starboard bow—*Lancastria*.

Ruth leaned into him. "She's the most beautiful thing I've ever seen."

He wrapped an arm around her. "She is, indeed."

CHAPTER 41

SAINT-NAZAIRE, FRANCE—JUNE 17, 1940

Jimmie's pulse rate quickened as the tugboat revved its engine and pulled alongside the *Lancastria*. Soldiers, some of whom were assisting refugees, began to disembark the tug and climb up a cargo net that hung down the hull of the massive ship. He looped the strap of Ruth's bag over his head and shoulder, and peered up at a large opening in the side of the vessel.

"Maybe we should ditch the bag," Ruth said.

"It's light," he said. "It won't get in the way."

"Do you need help climbing?"

"No." Jimmie patted the cast on his forearm. "I'll hook my elbow around the rungs as I climb. If I have any trouble, I'll get a soldier to help me."

"Are you sure?"

"Yes," he said, hoping to alleviate her concern. "I'll be fine. Go ahead and I'll follow."

Ruth kissed him on the cheek. "See you on board." She stepped to the edge of the tugboat, clasped the net, and climbed upward.

Jimmie watched her, along with several soldiers, safely scale the cargo net and enter the opening in the side of the ship. He drew a deep breath and exhaled, then focused his attention on the net, rising and falling as the tug bobbed in the sea. As the boat reached a crest of a wave, he grabbed a rung with his good hand and stepped onto the net. He steadied his legs, carefully inserted his cast-covered forearm through the webbing, and—using his elbow for leverage—reached upward. He clambered, rung by rung, up the cargo net. At the top, two BEF soldiers pulled him aboard.

Ruth wrapped her arms around him. "Well done."

"You too."

They made their way into the boarding compartment, where some of the evacuees were picking up life jackets from a small pile on the deck.

Jimmie plucked one and handed it to Ruth.

"What about you?"

"We'll share," he said. "There isn't enough for everyone."

She glanced at the paltry supply of life jackets and nodded.

They continued forward and were met by two stewards in white uniforms with shiny, brass buttons. To Jimmie, they looked like cruise line staff who remained on as crew after the government requisitioned the vessel.

"Keep moving!" one of the stewards shouted.

Troops, packed close together, shuffled ahead.

As Jimmie neared a steward, he glanced at the man's clipboard, which held papers with tally marks. "How many on board?"

"I'm not sure," the steward said. "We stopped counting at six thousand."

Ruth's eyes widened. "How many passengers does she normally hold?"

The steward rubbed the back of his neck. "Thirteen hundred."

Good Lord, Jimmie thought. *It's terribly over capacity, but what choice does the military have? Soldiers who are left behind will likely be killed or captured.* Jimmie set aside his concern and clasped Ruth's hand. Together, they shuffled to a stairway that led to the upper and lower decks.

"Down below!" a Royal Navy midshipman shouted, directing troops.

Angst pricked at Jimmie's gut. He held tight to Ruth's hand. "Follow me."

She nodded.

At the stairway, Jimmie bypassed the midshipman and traveled up the steps.

"Down below, sir!" the midshipman called. "There's no room above!"

Jimmie ignored the man's directive, made his way with Ruth to the next deck, and weaved into a crowd of soldiers.

"Why did you do that?" Ruth asked.

"It's safer on top."

He led Ruth upward, squeezing through stairways packed with troops, until they reached the main deck. They worked their way through the crowd, a mix of servicemen and refugees, and claimed a spot at the railing.

Ruth raised her nose and took in deep breaths.

"Better?"

"Much."

Jimmie smiled. He looked over the rail and inhaled sea air.

"Hello, mate!" a man's voice boomed.

Jimmie turned.

A young man in an RAF pilot uniform approached him. He wore a tied-together pair of boots—each holding a bottle of whisky—around his neck.

Jimmie grinned and shook the man's hand. "It's smashing to see another pilot. I'm Jimmie."

"Peter."

"This is Ruth," Jimmie said, gesturing.

"Pleasure," Peter said.

Ruth shook his hand.

Peter lifted a half-empty bottle of whisky from a boot. "Care for a drink?"

"No, thank you," Ruth said.

Jimmie shook his head. "Maybe later."

The pilot glanced at Jimmie's cast. "How did you injure the wing?"

"I broke a bone while bailing out of my Hurricane."

Peter nodded. "Two days ago, our Blenheim was shot down by a Messerschmitt 109. My copilot, Charlie, and I were able to bail out, but our gunner bought it."

"I'm sorry," Jimmie said.

"Thanks."

"What was his name?" Jimmie asked.

"Manny. Everyone liked him." Peter raised the whisky bottle and took a swig, as if to pay tribute to his fallen airman. "Did you come in with your ground crew?"

"No," Jimmie said. "I haven't seen my unit in weeks."

"What's your squadron number?"

"Seventy-Three."

The pilot turned and shouted, "Charlie!"

A man smoking a cigarette and wearing an RAF pilot uniform peeked around a group of soldiers and raised his eyebrows.

"Is the Seventy-Three Squadron's ground crew on board?" Peter asked.

Charlie nodded.

Jimmie's eyes turned wide. "Where?"

Charlie plucked the cigarette from his mouth. "Down in the hull."

"Are you sure?" Jimmie asked.

"Yes," Charlie said. "They were on the pier with us. All ground crews were ordered to go down into the holds." He took a drag and returned to chatting with soldiers.

Jimmie looked at Peter. "I'm surprised I didn't see them at the harbor."

"You wouldn't have seen them there," Peter said. "The ground crews embarked from a pier in the estuary—upriver from the harbor."

Jimmie nodded.

"We came in with our ground crew late last night," Peter said. "Most of the RAF pilots have flown their kites back home, and their ground crews were ordered to make their way to Saint-Nazaire for transport."

"How many ground crew are here?" Jimmie asked.

Peter scratched his head. "About eight hundred."

Jimmie imagined the men, crammed together in the hold of the ship, and tension spread through his body.

Ruth placed a hand on Jimmie's arm. "I'm glad the men in your squadron made it out."

"Me too," he said, his voice drab.

"Cheer up, mate," Peter said. "You'll see them when we get to England."

Jimmie nodded, despite a knot in the pit of his stomach.

Peter took a sip from his whisky bottle and left to join his co-pilot.

Jimmie leaned his head over the rail and peered down at the sea, lapping against the hull of the ship.

"What's wrong?" Ruth asked.

"Do you remember me telling you that my dad is a shipyard engineer?"

"Yes."

"Before I left for service, he told me that if I ever ended up on a transport ship, to never allow myself to be placed in the hull."

"Why?"

"He said that there would be no chance of getting out if the ship was struck by a torpedo."

Ruth swallowed. "They're going to be okay, and so will we."

Jimmie glanced at the troops, many of whom were celebrating as if they were already safe at home. "The soldier on the tug said that the Luftwaffe dropped floating mines. A mine can sink a ship as easily as a torpedo."

She clasped his fingers.

An image of Horace, whistling as he worked on a Hurricane engine, flashed in Jimmie's brain. "I have friends down there. I need to tell them to go to a deck above the waterline."

"I'll come with you."

He shook his head. "There's no reason for both of us to leave."

She squeezed his hand. "Please, we should stick together."

"I'll be all right," he said. "Troops are still boarding the ship. I'll be down and back before we set sail."

"Are you sure?"

"Yes." He kissed her on the lips and hugged her tight, all the while never wanting to let her go. Before he changed his mind, he slipped away and weaved through the crowd.

A disquietude churned inside Jimmie as he descended a stairway clogged with a multitude of men who were working their way topside. He exited the stairwell and maneuvered his way, squeezing through hordes of people, to a dining room with an Italianate ceiling and ivory-colored columns. The tables were filled and there were long queues with soldiers waiting to receive chocolate bars, cups of tea, and slices of bread with marmalade. He weaved through the dense crowd, traveled down a narrow interior corridor, and searched for a passable stairway to the bowel of the ship.

Every bit of space on the *Lancastria* was filled with weary soldiers and refugees. People slept on floors, played cards, or conversed with comrades or family members. The cabins—once used to accommodate posh travelers—were packed with dirty soldiers who were washing and shaving. Jimmie, while squeezing by an open cabin door, caught a glimpse of a man soaking in a tub with water the color of mud. He located a stairway and descended, but found the base of the stairs blocked with soldiers who were moving trunks of equipment. He backtracked, turned onto an adjacent corridor, and traveled to the opposite side of the ship. Eventually, he found a usable stairway that led to the lower decks.

Forty minutes after he'd left Ruth, he stepped down through an open, water-tight hatch in the floor, and descended stairs to the hull of the ship. The dimly lit space of the cargo hold, surrounded in steel, reminded Jimmie of a mortuary. It was packed with RAF ground crewmen, who were standing or sitting in tight groups. The temperature was hot, given its proximity to the engine room, and the air reeked of sweat and cigarette smoke.

"Seventy-Three!" Jimmie shouted, squeezing by a group of men. "Anyone here with the Seventy-Three!"

A ground crewman pointed. "Four compartments that way."

"Thanks!" Jimmie's hope rose as he pressed forward. *The ship hasn't moved. There's plenty of time.*

He crossed through two compartments, both of which he accessed by spinning a wheel to unlock a bulkhead door. As he maneuvered by a group of men hunkered on the ground and playing cards, a familiar voice shouted from across the cargo bay.

"Jimmie!" Horace darted past servicemen, nearly knocking a man over who was drinking from a canteen, and hugged him. "You're alive!"

Jimmie's spirit soared. He embraced his friend and patted him on the back. "Indeed, I am."

Horace slipped away, removed his glasses, and wiped his eyes. "I'm gobsmacked. We thought you bought it."

"Escaped with a broken arm," Jimmie said, showing him his cast. "An ambulance driver named Ruth saved me. She's on the ship's main deck, and I'm excited for you to meet her."

"Excellent," Horace said, grinning. He slipped on his glasses. "I'm so happy you're all right. The others will be chuffed to bits to see you."

"Me too," Jimmie said. "Where are they?"

"A few compartments ahead. I was on my way to find some food."

Jimmie nodded. "I saw Fanny bail out before I was shot down. How is he?"

"He suffered burns to his hands and was sent to a hospital in England to recover. I heard that he's doing well and should return to service in a few weeks."

"Brilliant," Jimmie said. "While I was trying to find the squadron, I came across the burned-out remains of Benny's Hurricane at the airfield in Reims. Is he all right?"

"He is," Horace said. "His parked Hurricane was destroyed in a raid. He was issued another one, and he's scheduled to fly out of France today with the other pilots of the squadron."

Thank goodness.

"We were constantly on the move," Horace said. "The advancing Panzers and Luftwaffe raids forced us to change airfields eight times—our last location was in Nantes."

Jimmie nodded. "How's Cobber?"

The color drained from Horace's face. "He's dead."

"Oh, God." Jimmie felt like he was punched in the gut. He leaned against a steel bulkhead and lowered his head.

"I'm sorry." Horace placed a hand on Jimmie's shoulder. "I know how much you looked up to him. Cobber thought of you as a brother. He was quite distressed after you were shot down."

An image of Cobber—laughing as he splashed through the mud

like a schoolboy while playing rugby in a downpour—flashed in Jimmie's brain. He clenched his hands, sending a pang through the wrist of his partially healed arm. "I can't believe it."

Horace nodded.

"He was the best fighter pilot of the lot. Everyone thought of him as invincible—that there wasn't a German aviator capable of getting the best of him in a dogfight."

Horace slipped his hand from Jimmie's shoulder. "Cobber wasn't shot down."

He furrowed his brow. "What happened?"

"It was an accident." Horace paused, shifting his weight, as if he was reluctant to relive the tragedy. "Cobber refused to rest, flying sortie after sortie. He shot down seventeen enemy aircraft, but the strain of battle took its toll on him. He was exhausted, both mentally and physically, and—about ten days ago—he was ordered to return to England to rest."

Jimmie felt sick to his stomach.

"The pilots and ground crew had gathered at the airfield in Échemines to say their farewells to Cobber. He departed in his Hurricane, but instead of flying straightaway, he performed low-level aerobatics to raise the spirit of the men."

Oh, no.

"On his third pass of performing flick rolls, he miscalculated his altitude and hit the ground." Horace swallowed. "Cobber was ejected from his cockpit and killed instantly."

"Bloody hell," Jimmie breathed. A mix of heartbreak and anger twisted inside him. "It's so damn senseless."

Horace rubbed his eyes and nodded.

"Did we lose any others?" Jimmie asked.

For several minutes, Horace filled him in on the welfare of the men in the squadron, including two fallen pilots who were shot down days before Cobber's death.

Jimmie drew a deep breath and ran a hand through his hair. "Time to go home, Horace."

"It is, indeed."

Jimmie buried his heartache, lowered his voice, and told him about his father's advice to avoid transport in the hull of a ship. "As a precaution, you and the ground crewmen should get to a higher deck."

"But we have orders to be here."

"Don't follow them," Jimmie said. "Pretend that you're sick. Go to the latrine and don't come back. Find any means possible to get up top."

Horace folded his arms. "I don't know, Jimmie. It's different for you—you're an officer. The members of the ground crew are lower rank and were ordered to the hull by the command of the RAF in France. I doubt that our men will want to risk getting reprimanded, especially for disobeying a directive from top brass."

"There's about forty ground crew in the Seventy-Three. They won't be missed in a hull with eight hundred others."

A nearby group of men glanced at them, then resumed playing their game of cards.

Jimmie stepped close and spoke in a low tone. "Take a look around. How will you get out of here if a torpedo blasts a hole in this hull?"

Horace glanced at a steel, watertight door, and lines formed on his face.

"Leaving here might get you a reprimand, but it could also ensure that you make it home to Daisy and your baby, Olive."

Horace rubbed his jowl.

"The choice is yours. What's it going to be?"

"All right," Horace said. "Let's talk with the others."

Jimmie relaxed his shoulders and nodded.

They made their way through the hull, stepping around scores of soldiers. As Jimmie passed through a bulkhead door into another compartment, the eyes of the Seventy-Three Squadron's ground crew fell upon him.

"Jimmie!" a man shouted.

Crewmen scrambled to their feet, surrounded him, and gave him pats on the back.

Jimmie, feeling elated, shook hands and hugged the ground crew members of his squadron. But his joy evaporated when the ship's engine rumbled to life, sending a vibration through the steel under their feet.

"Hurrah!" a man shouted. "We're going home!"

Another man kneeled and kissed the floor.

Cheers from hundreds of ground crewmen boomed through the hull compartments. And Jimmie worried that it might be impossible to convince the men of his squadron, who were overjoyed and feeling secure, to disobey orders and follow him topside.

CHAPTER 42

SAINT-NAZAIRE, FRANCE—JUNE 17, 1940

Anxiety flooded through Ruth as exhaust smoke thickened above the *Lancastria*'s funnel. *He's been gone too long and the ship is preparing to depart.* She turned away from soldiers, who were cheering and clapping, and looked out over the sea that led to the harbor, approximately eight kilometers away. Dozens of small craft—packed with evacuees—continued to make their way to large vessels anchored far from shore. High above the estuary, three French fighter planes patrolled the sky.

A tugboat, filled with French soldiers, pulled alongside the ship. But sailors of the *Lancastria* began to pull up the cargo nets that led to the boarding hold.

The Frenchmen on the tug cried out and waved their arms.

"We're overcapacity!" a naval officer called through a loud-hailer.

Ruth felt sick to her stomach.

"Turn back!" the naval officer shouted. "We're overfull!"

The side doors on the *Lancastria* closed, provoking an eruption of profanity and hand gestures from French soldiers on the deck of the tug.

Ruth's heart sank as the boat pulled away, and she hoped that the men would find another ship with room for them to board.

In the time that Jimmie had been gone, there were several

sightings of Luftwaffe aircraft flying overhead. Sporadic explosions and machine gun fire echoed over the coastline, and word soon spread through passengers on the main deck that another ocean liner, anchored near the estuary, had been attacked by a German dive bomber. The mood of the soldiers on the *Lancastria* remained ebullient, despite a looming threat of air raids. The immense ocean liner, Ruth believed, provided the evacuees with a sense of security, and some of the BEF soldiers behaved as if they'd already reached the British shore.

Minutes passed and the ship had yet to weigh anchor. Ruth scanned the crowded deck in search of Jimmie.

A soldier standing near Ruth approached a seaman who was peering through binoculars over the estuary. "Why aren't we leaving?"

"The captain wants to wait for a destroyer escort," the seaman said, holding the binoculars to his eyes.

Hairs rose on the back of Ruth's neck.

"How long?" the soldier asked.

"I don't know." The seaman lowered his binoculars and made his way toward the stern of the ship.

An ache grew in Ruth's stomach. With little to do but wait, she sat on her life jacket as a cushion, and hugged her bag to her chest. Unable to rest, her mind drifted to Lucette and Aline. *They should have reached a port in England by now.* She prayed that Lucette was recovering in a hospital, and that a British refugee agency was providing proper care for Aline. It sickened her to think that Aline, who was already heartbroken from the loss of her *maman* and grandpapa, might be alone and scared in an orphanage or asylum camp. She glanced at a group of haggard French soldiers, and she wished for Aline's papa as well as Lucette's fiancé to be two of the lucky ones who survived the battlefront.

Ruth pressed her bag to her chest, and she turned her thoughts to Jimmie and their night together. *I never met a man like him before. He's tender, sweet, and kind.* She yearned for when there would no longer be a war between them, and she imagined what it would be like to be married to Jimmie, have children with him, and grow old together. She supposed that it might be a bit foolish, or perhaps selfish, to plan her life with a man while Europe was at war, but deep down she knew that her passion for him would never fade.

Ruth, desiring to be close to him, opened her bag and slipped out his flight jacket. She pressed it to her cheek and drew a deep breath, taking in his scent. An image of their bare bodies, entwined in an embrace, appeared in her brain. A warmth spread through her, and her concern of an unknown future dissolved.

Ruth lowered the jacket and her eyes were drawn to his good luck charm, peeking from a pocket. She removed Piglet and ran a finger over his worn, floppy ears and smiled. "No wonder he refused to ditch the bag," she whispered to herself.

A roar of aircraft engines broke the still air.

Goose bumps cropped up on her arms.

Hundreds of evacuees raised their heads and scanned the sky, spattered with puffy cotton-like clouds.

A soldier pointed. "There!"

Ruth, her heartbeat quickening, got to her feet.

High in the sky, a twin-engine German bomber emerged from a cloud and dived toward the *Lancastria*.

Oh, God. Ruth, as if by reflex, stashed the toy into a jacket pocket of her uniform and threw on the life jacket.

CHAPTER 43

SAINT-NAZAIRE, FRANCE—JUNE 17, 1940

Jimmie worked his way through the crowded hull with six men, including Horace, who agreed with his recommendation to disobey their orders and follow him topside. Most of the Seventy-Three's forty ground crew members feared a reprimand and refused to leave, while others diplomatically declined Jimmie's advice by saying that they would think about coming up after they finished their card game. Considering that the men were playing a time-consuming RAF card game called Clag, an acronym for Clouds Low Aircraft Grounded, he doubted he'd see any of them for hours, or at all.

The group squeezed by several men who were smoking cigarettes, and Jimmie turned to members of his ground crew and lowered his voice. "If anyone questions you, say you're sick and need to go up to the ship's railing to vomit."

"All right," Horace said. "Lead the —"

The ship's siren sounded.

Hairs rose on the back of Jimmie's neck.

Horace's eyes widened.

Behind them, hundreds of men—stationed in compartments throughout the hull—got to their feet and looked up at the ceiling.

"Hurry," Jimmie said, darting forward.

They scurried through a bulkhead door and weaved their way

through the crowd to the stairwell, and discovered it to be blocked by ground crewmen who were waiting to ascend. Men piled in tightly behind them and pressed against their backs. The siren continued to blare, but the line leading upward did not move.

CHAPTER 44

SAINT-NAZAIRE, FRANCE—JUNE 17, 1940

The ship's alarm filled Ruth's ears as she helplessly watched the bomber—diving at a high rate of speed—narrow in on the *Lancastria*. The roar of the bomber's engines grew. A French fighter plane soared in behind the bomber and fired its machine guns, but the enemy aircraft continued its dive.

Ruth, her body shaking, crouched on the deck and covered her head with her hands.

Bombs fell from the belly of the German aircraft and shrilled through the air. The nose of the enemy plane pulled up, and the bombs exploded to the side of the ship, sending mountainous columns of water onto the deck.

Soldiers cheered.

"They bloody can't hit us!" a soldier shouted, shaking a fist in the air.

Ruth stood on unsteady legs and watched the French fighter continue its pursuit of the German bomber. She sucked in air, attempting to catch her breath, and struggled to see through the mass of people. "Jimmie!"

The enemy aircraft avoided the guns of the French fighter and gained altitude. Instead of disappearing into the clouds, it looped around and came in for another attack.

"It's coming in again!" a man shouted.

Passengers huddled together and covered their heads.

Ruth, feeling powerless, fell to her knees and watched the bomber bear down upon them.

Chapter 45

Saint-Nazaire, France—June 17, 1940

Jimmie weaved his way between men—their faces filled with alarm from the sound of an explosion that reverberated through the hull. He squeezed his way forward and climbed the stairwell, congested with men, until he reached the front of the line. At the open, watertight hatch, he was met by a young clean-shaven midshipman, who was standing on the deck above him and pointing a pistol.

"Get below!" the midshipman said. "We're under attack!"

"The men need to go topside," Jimmie said.

"They have orders to remain in the hull," the midshipman said. "It'll be safer there."

"No, it won't. There are no exits." Anger flared through Jimmie. He stepped upward, placing him close to the man's pistol. "Move aside."

The midshipman swallowed. "You're a pilot, so you may come up, but the ground crew remains below. I don't want to do it, but orders are orders."

"Let us through!" Horace called from behind Jimmie.

"They're coming with me," Jimmie said firmly.

Shouts and panic-stricken voices boomed from the upper decks. The midshipman's hand, brandishing the pistol, began to tremble.

"For God's sake, allow them to pass."

The midshipman's eyes rose to the ceiling. "To hell with it." He lowered his weapon and ran away.

Jimmie looked at Horace and the ground crewman on the stairwell below him. "All right. Follow me."

He ascended the final steps from the hull, and a clamor erupted from the upper decks. His adrenaline surged and he shot forward, hoping to lead the men topside before another attack.

CHAPTER 46

SAINT-NAZAIRE, FRANCE—JUNE 17, 1940

Ruth's breath stalled in her lungs as she watched the German aircraft release four bombs. The first fell down the *Lancastria*'s huge funnel, the next two struck the holds of the ship, and the last landed near the vessel's port side. Enormous explosions hammered the cruise liner, casting bodies and hunks of steel high into the air.

Ruth's back slammed against a steel railing. A sharp pang pierced through her neck and spine, and she tumbled to the ground. Her brain, shaken from the concussive blast, struggled to process the chaos and destruction that surrounded her.

Soldiers scrambled across the deck and looked over the railing to assess the damage. An elderly refugee couple hunkered on the ground and clutched each other. A sailor, holding a hand to a laceration on his face, stumbled through the crowd in a state of shock.

Dozens of people stepped over Ruth, curled in a fetal position as she fought to clear cobwebs from her head. The heel of a boot smashed her hand, sending pain through her fingers and stimulating her senses. She pushed herself into a sitting position and shakily got to her feet. Fires flared from the bow and stern of the ship, sending thick smoke into the air. An acrid smell of cordite burned her nostrils, and her ears throbbed with high-pitched ringing and shrieks of injured people.

Oh, my God! This can't be happening!

She scanned the deck and her eyes were drawn to a huge hole, surrounded by maimed soldiers, splintered wood, and billows of smoke. Her heart pounded inside her chest. She gathered her strength and made her way through the pandemonium to help the wounded.

CHAPTER 47

SAINT-NAZAIRE, FRANCE—JUNE 17, 1940

Jimmie was the first man to exit the hull through the watertight hatch. He stepped forward and a massive explosion hurled him over the passageway. His head slammed against the overhead, he tumbled over the ground, and the lights went out. Something heavy struck his shoulder, sending a twinge through his bad arm. The ship listed, and a hot gust of air shot up from the hull, as if doors of a blast furnace had swung open. Groans and yawps filled the stygian darkness.

A toxic-smelling vapor penetrated Jimmie's nose, giving rise to a flurry of coughs. *We need to get out of here.* He got to his feet, but the tilt of the ship forced him to lean against a wall to maintain his balance. "Horace!"

"Down here!" Horace shouted.

"Move!" Jimmie, his pulse pounding his eardrums, blindly clambered forward and located a stairwell leading upward. With each step, the howls of men in the hull continued to grow.

"Help!" a man yelled. "Water is coming in!"

Jimmie froze. "Come on!"

"We can't get through!" Horace shouted. "The hatch is blocked, and she's flooding fast!"

His blood went cold. Gushing water resounded from the hull. Jimmie, refusing to leave the ground crewmen behind, reversed his course and descended the pitch-black stairwell toward cries for help.

CHAPTER 48

SAINT-NAZAIRE, FRANCE—JUNE 17, 1940

Ruth, her heart racing, darted to a soldier who suffered scalds to his face and hands. Several meters away, a ruptured boiler pipe spewed steam over an entrance to the interior of the ship. She kneeled to the man, on his back and grimacing in pain.

"I'm here to help," Ruth said, trying to keep him from touching his face.

"I can't see," the man gasped.

"You're going to be all right," Ruth said. "I'll get you to a lifeboat. Do you think you can walk?"

"I think so."

Ruth got behind him, placed her hands under his arms, and helped him to his feet. She led him over the tilted deck and discovered that several of the lifeboats were destroyed in the raid. *Oh, no. We're sinking and there's not enough boats.* She gathered her nerve, worked through a crowd of panicked refugees, and placed him on the ground next to an undamaged lifeboat. She enlisted the help of a sailor to place the soldier into the boat, partially filled with women, children, and injured military men.

She navigated through people who were shrieking and shouting. Near the side of the ship, she aided a well-dressed, elderly woman who was pressing a handkerchief to a laceration on her scalp. She led the woman to a lifeboat, packed with people who were standing. A crewman took the woman's hand and helped her to squeeze into the boat.

"Clear away!" a naval officer called through a loud-hailer.

Two seamen released ropes and the lifeboat gradually lowered to the water.

Ruth glanced at a section of nearly full lifeboats and the dense crowd of people who were vying for a place on board. She shook away her dread and labored her way to the deck, all the while searching for Jimmie. She joined a group of soldiers to carry a man with a shattered leg and place him in one of the few remaining spaces in a lifeboat. Within seconds, the lifeboat began to lower but one of the ropes jammed in a davit and the boat tipped, tossing its occupants into the sea.

"No!" Ruth cried, feeling helpless.

Men shot to the ship's railing and tossed pieces of broken boards into the water. Passengers, who were struggling to swim, fought to cling to floating debris.

She returned to the deck to provide aid, but the *Lancastria* tilted, and its stern rose into the air.

"She's going down!" a naval officer shouted.

Fear flooded through her. She struggled to see through the masses of people, most of whom were racing to the sides of the ship.

Scores of soldiers climbed over the railing and jumped into the water.

"Take off your boots!" a seaman shouted. "You won't be able to swim!"

Soldiers began to untie their laces and remove their boots. A few others stripped off their shirts.

Ruth, holding on to the rail, made her way over the sloped deck. Her eyes locked on an entrance that led to a stairwell, from which a few soldiers were scrambling to exit. She pushed her way forward and, as she was about to enter, a midshipman grabbed her hand.

"You can't go in there!" the midshipman said.

"I need to find someone—he went to the hull to—"

"It's too late," the man said, pulling her away.

"No!" She fought to free herself but the man's grip held firm. The ship listed badly, and she and the man fell onto the deck. The man released her. "Get to the side!"

Ruth, her heart breaking, crawled over the steeply sloped deck to the rail. She pulled herself up and looked out over the water, covered with debris, bodies, and oil from the *Lancastria*'s ruptured fuel tanks. With no other choice, she removed her shoes, secured her life jacket, and leaped from the vessel.

Ruth plunged hard into the frigid sea, shooting salt water and oil up her nose. She broke the surface, choking on the water and fuel that she swallowed. Around her were men, a few with life jackets, who were treading water to stay afloat.

"Get away from the ship!" a man, his face covered in oil, shouted. "It'll suck us down when it sinks!"

Ruth paddled her arms and kicked her legs, but the current was strong and the oil was thick as tar. After a few minutes, her lungs and muscles burned with exhaustion. She stopped and floated, her life jacket bobbing her body like a cork in the water.

The *Lancastria* tilted higher, exposing its giant propeller. Three seamen cried out as they tumbled down the ship's deck. A few soldiers escaped by crawling out of portholes, while dozens more jumped from the rails and fell into the sea.

Ruth struggled to clear oil from her eyes. She gasped for air and scanned the ocean and ship for Jimmie.

"Here they come again!" a soldier in the water shouted.

Ruth looked up and her muscles turned weak at the sight of a German plane descending toward them. It swooped low and strafed the *Lancastria* with machine gun fire. Bullets pelted its deck and sent more men jumping into the sea.

"Bloody bastards!" a soldier shouted, clinging to a floating piece of wood.

More German planes appeared, like sharks smelling blood. They dropped flares and strafed the sinking ship, again and again. But the Luftwaffe pilots did not solely target the vessel. They rained down bullets upon the defenseless soldiers in the water.

This is not war, Ruth thought, watching a German plane fire its guns over floating soldiers, *it's murder.*

"Take off your life jacket!" a soldier called to Ruth. "Dive under when they come in!"

"I'm spent," Ruth said, her voice strained. "If my life jacket comes off, I'll drown."

The roar of aircraft grew. She rolled onto her side as a German plane swooped in. Bullets pierced the water, inches from her body, and she prayed for it all to end.

CHAPTER 49

SAINT-NAZAIRE, FRANCE—JUNE 17, 1940

With the absence of light, Jimmie followed the sound of screams and gushing water to locate the hatch in the floor that led to the hull. Although the hatch remained open, it was blocked by a large steel beam and a section of bulkhead that had been sheared away in the blast.

"Try to squeeze through!" Jimmie shouted, searching with his hands for a gap in the debris.

"There's no room!" Horace's voice cried out from below. "Hurry—it's flooding!"

Jimmie wrapped his arms around the beam and pulled, but it didn't budge.

Wails grew from inside the hull, its steel groaning from immense pressure.

He adjusted his grip and placement of his feet. Using both hands, he heaved with all his strength. A piercing pain shot through his bad arm, he lost his hold, and fell back.

"I'm unable to move it!" Jimmie yelled. "Can you get to another stairwell?"

"No! It's too late!"

"You must try!"

"Go!" Horace screamed. "Save yourself!"

"I'm not leaving you!"

Jimmie wrapped his arms around the beam. He desperately heaved—his muscles burning and pangs shooting through his wrist. Within seconds, the shrieks were silenced by water gushing through the steel debris above the hatch. *No!*

He fought to move the obstruction, but the force of water, like a powerful stream shooting from a breach in a dam, hurled him against a bulkhead. By the time he got to his feet, the water had reached his waist. The strength of the surge prevented him from returning to the hatch, and he blindly searched for the stairwell as the compartment flooded, now rising above his chest. His hand clasped a handrail and he pulled himself upward, but the water swelled over his head.

Holding his breath, he swam upward and his face struck an overhead, shooting pain through his skull. He kicked his legs and paddled arms, his cast feeling like it was made of lead. He twisted through what he thought was a doorway, rose upward, and located an air pocket the size of a shallow upside-down bucket. Pressing his mouth and nose to the overhead, he sucked in deep, rasping inhales. The water level continued to rise. As the air pocket was about to vanish, he took a final breath and went under. He kicked and pulled as he propelled himself through the submerged passageway, littered with wreckage.

His eyes, burning from seawater, scanned for an opening but found only darkness. With each stroke, his oxygen depleted. His heartbeat hammered his eardrums. As he was about to give up, a glimmer of light appeared in the distance. He kicked harder, working his way through the murk. But his chest heaved, recycling used air in his lungs, and his body weakened with each stroke.

An image of Ruth flashed in his brain as he extended his hand toward the faint glow, too far to reach. His legs and arms gradually went limp. Amid his pain and regret, one vision held steady. *Ruth.* He relented to the water, and everything fell silent.

CHAPTER 50

SAINT-NAZAIRE, FRANCE—JUNE 17, 1940

Ruth, floating in the sea with her life jacket, struggled to wipe and blink away oil from her eyes. A roar of aircraft engines and shouts of despair filled her ears. Her vision began to clear and she raised her head. High in the sky, German bombers veered to the north and disappeared into clouds. Cold and exhausted, she gripped the front of her life jacket and scanned the water.

The coastline—approximately eight kilometers away—was too far to swim to safety, and at least a thousand people were clinging to buoyant debris or treading water to remain afloat. Soldiers removed life jackets from people who'd been killed by strafing and released their bodies to the deep. The few lifeboats that were deployed were drifting away from the masses, as if their occupants feared that their boat would be capsized by people fighting to climb aboard.

The *Lancastria* rolled over, exposing its hull and giant propeller. The vessel sank low in the water, and dozens of soldiers—their eyes filled with fear and fatigue—crawled onto the hull. Clustered together, some of the men began to sing a patriotic song called "There'll Always Be an England." Ruth, in a state of shock and anguish, fought to paddle through the oil-covered water in search of Jimmie.

Twenty minutes after the German bombs struck the *Lancas-*

tria, it sank below the surface. The men, who'd rested on her hull, either swam away or were pulled under by the turbulence of the sinking ship. For nearly two hours, Ruth and the people in the water fought to survive. There were two more strafing attacks by German planes, which killed scores of soldiers and refugees. There were few life jackets and many drowned, and countless others perished from hypothermia or were choked by fuel oil.

Ruth's teeth chattered uncontrollably, and her frigid joints were like seized pistons. She strained to move her arms and legs, and to keep her head upright. She felt her chances of surviving dwindle with each labored breath, until a fleet of rescue vessels appeared.

A mix of fishing boats, military ships, and sailing craft circled the area and plucked survivors from the sea. Ruth was pulled aboard a British antisubmarine trawler, wrapped in a wool blanket, and placed on a crowded deck that contained hundreds of survivors, some naked and nearly all covered in oil.

A young sailor, who was carrying a metal container that resembled a garden watering can, approached Ruth. "Excuse me, miss."

Ruth, her body shivering, raised her head.

"Would you care for some tea?"

She nodded.

The sailor poured a steaming brew into a tin cup and gave it to her.

Her hands trembled, spilling tea. "Thank you," she said, her voice raw.

"My pleasure, miss," the sailor said. "You're all right, now. You're going home." He turned and squeezed through the crowd.

Ruth took a sip of tea, cleansing a foul taste of oil from her mouth. As she finished off her drink, her body temperature rose and the fog lifted from her brain. She gathered her strength and mingled through the hundreds of survivors, all the while praying to see Jimmie. After hours of scouring the ship, she didn't find him, nor did she encounter any RAF ground crew members who were confined to the hull of the *Lancastria*. Gutted and heartbroken, she collapsed onto the deck and wept.

CHAPTER 51

LONDON, ENGLAND—JUNE 17, 1940

Prime Minister Winston Churchill traveled down a corridor of the underground Cabinet War Rooms and entered his private bedroom. He sat at his desk, equipped with a radio receiver and a microphone that was linked to the BBC broadcasting room. Instead of preparing to give a speech, he lit a cigar and turned on the radio. Seconds of silence passed as the vacuum tubes warmed, and the voice of Marshal Pétain, the newly appointed French prime minister, filled the room.

An intense disappointment flowed through Churchill as he listened to Pétain's first radio address, calling for France's armistice with Germany. He took a drag, filling his lungs with smoke. *France has fallen, and Pétain will be a puppet ruler for that barbaric dictator.* It sickened him to think that Pétain, who'd been one of France's prominent military heroes of the Great War, was bowing to the Nazis.

The day before, French Prime Minister Reynaud resigned and he was replaced by Pétain, who was adamant that France should seek an armistice. Churchill anticipated that Pétain might attempt to reach an agreement with Germany without Britain's consent. Therefore, he sent a telegram informing him that Britain would agree to an armistice on the condition that the French naval fleet was moved to British ports. Pétain accepted. But if France did not comply with the provision, Churchill—who was resolute to prevent French vessels from falling into the hands of the enemy—would order the fleet to be sunk.

Churchill listened to Pétain's speech, which lasted less than two minutes. He turned off the radio and flicked ash from his cigar. He imagined French soldiers setting down their weapons and surrendering to German troops. Vexation surged through him. He poured a glass of whisky from a crystal decanter, added a splash of water, and took a gulp. The warmth of the alcohol flowed into his stomach but did nothing to allay his unrest.

A knock came from the door.

"Come in," Churchill said.

General Ismay entered, closed the door behind him, and removed his cap. "Good evening, sir."

Churchill swirled his whisky. "Take a seat."

Ismay sat in a green upholstered chair next to the desk.

"You listened to Pétain's broadcast, I presume," Churchill said.

"I did, sir—in the conference room with members of the Chiefs of Staff. Pétain's speech was precisely what you expected."

Churchill nodded and took a sip of his drink.

"As I was leaving the conference room," Ismay said, "I was given an intelligence message on Operation Aerial."

"Good news, I hope."

"It's not, sir." He clasped the belt around his tunic. "During the evacuation, the Luftwaffe sank a cruise liner called the *Lancastria* off the coast of Saint-Nazaire."

Churchill set aside his drink and looked at him. "How many casualties?"

"We expect a large loss of life—between five and seven thousand souls."

An ache spread through Churchill's chest.

"It's a rough estimate. The ship was overloaded with soldiers, as well as some civilians."

Churchill lowered his head. Throughout his military career, ships under his command had suffered huge losses, but nothing in comparison to this. "If the estimate is accurate, it will be the largest loss of life in British maritime history."

Ismay's eyes filled with sadness. "Indeed, sir."

Churchill suppressed his sorrow and fury. His mind toiled with potential ramifications that the news of the disaster would have on British morale, as well as German military strategy. He ground out his cigar in a bronze ashtray and turned his chair toward Ismay. "Has word about this gotten out?"

"Not yet, sir. Information coming out of France is collapsing, and the rescue ships—carrying the *Lancastria*'s survivors—will not reach England until tomorrow afternoon."

"I will order a D-notice," Churchill said, referring to an official request to newspapers and broadcasters to withhold information for purposes of national security.

Ismay shifted in his seat. "With all due respect, sir, the British people have a right to know. Are you sure about this?"

"I am," Churchill said, despite a growing sense of disquietude. "I will release the ban when the time is right, perhaps in a few weeks. We've had enough bad news for today."

Ismay nodded. "The news might spread once the rescue ships reach England."

I cannot allow the spirit of our people to falter when we are at the eve of the fight for our island's survival, Churchill thought. "Order the Royal Navy and the survivors not to speak about the *Lancastria*."

"Yes, sir." Ismay rubbed his jowl. "How do you wish to handle military death notifications to families?"

"Missing in action—nothing more."

"Very well, sir."

"Call a meeting with the Chiefs of Staff," Churchill said. "I will personally inform them of my decision."

"Of course, sir." Ismay stood and exited the room.

Alone, Churchill's decision chewed at his conscience. He poured whisky into his glass and gulped it down, all the while knowing that he would not repeal a ban to release news of the disaster. *After the war is won, the families of those who perished on the* Lancastria *will know the truth.* He rose from his chair, exited his bedroom, and made his way down the corridor to address his Chiefs of Staff.

CHAPTER 52

PLYMOUTH, ENGLAND—JUNE 18, 1940

Ruth clasped a deck rail and looked out over the coast as the British trawler approached port. Her hair was matted with oil and her uniform was filthy, but she was in a better state than many of the survivors of the *Lancastria*. Injured soldiers and refugees covered much of the main deck, and a slew of people, who'd shed their clothes to help them stay afloat in the sea, were wrapped in little more than newspapers.

She had nothing to eat on the voyage, except for cups of tea and a bit of warm milk with crushed aspirin. Her stomach ached with hunger and continuous dull pain ran through her muscles, but—most of all—her chest was filled with heartache. Despite her exhaustion, she didn't sleep during the eighteen-hour journey from Saint-Nazaire to Plymouth. Each time that she'd closed her eyes to rest, her mind was flooded with images of Jimmie descending into the bowels of the *Lancastria*, exploding bombs, and passengers fighting to keep their head above water. She'd prayed that Jimmie found a way to escape and was on another rescue vessel, even though she knew that the men in the ship's hull likely did not survive. Throughout the journey, her mind and heart remained on him, and their life together that might never be.

The trawler docked and passengers—a mix of *Lancastria* survivors, military evacuees, and refugees—began to disembark from a gangway. The injured were removed first, and the others followed. The line moved extraordinarily slow, and Ruth inched her way over the crowded deck that reeked of fuel oil and was covered in discarded clothes. At the end of the gangway, two Royal Navy officers spoke with passengers before allowing them to step foot on the dock. Initially, Ruth thought that they might be recording names, but as she moved close, she noticed that the officers did not have writing materials, and that one of them was speaking in French to civilian refugees.

A shirtless soldier, his skin and pants streaked with oil, stepped forward and saluted one of the officers.

"You are to never speak of the sinking of the *Lancastria*," the officer said.

Ruth's breath stalled in her chest.

"If you utter a word about what happened in Saint-Nazaire," the officer continued, "you will be violating King's Regulations and will face harsh discipline. Do you understand?"

"Yes, sir," the soldier said.

"Carry on."

The soldier stepped onto the dock and made his way into a crowd.

The officer eyed Ruth's uniform and pointed to his comrade. "*Français.*"

Ruth disregarded his directive and approached him. "I speak English, and I overheard what you said. Why are we not permitted to talk about what happened?"

He clasped his hands behind his back. "Orders."

"From whom?"

"The British government. You're on *our* soil. You must adhere to the mandate, like everyone else, or suffer the consequences."

She nodded reluctantly.

"Carry on."

Ruth, barefoot and dirty, shuffled by the officer and left the dock. She followed the crowd to a food line where women—of the Salvation Army, British Red Cross, and Women's Voluntary Service—were passing out sandwiches, canned bully beef, and tins of milk. Although Ruth desperately wanted to find Lucette and Aline, her body craved nourishment. So, she waited in line to receive a tin of milk and a fried egg sandwich on stale white bread with margarine. She sat on the ground near the dock, along with hundreds of ragged soldiers and refugees, and devoured her food.

A Red Cross woman, who was carrying a box of cards and pencils, approached Ruth. "Excuse me, miss. Would you like a postcard to write home to let your family know that you're all right?"

Ruth got to her feet and wiped crumbs from her mouth. "Yes, but I'm from America."

"It might take a long time to get there," the woman said, "but we'll put it in the post for you."

Ruth accepted a postcard and pencil, and then scribbled the address and a message.

> *Dear Maman and Dad,*
> *I fled France for England, and I am safe. Colette and Julian remained in Paris to care for patients at Saint-Antoine Hospital. I will write you a letter soon. I love and miss you, more than you will ever know.*
> *Ruth*

Ruth handed the pencil and postcard to the woman. "I was separated from my friends during the evacuation. Do you know how I would go about trying to locate them?"

The woman pointed to a gray-haired woman with a clipboard. "Talk to Ivy. She's in charge of the women who are working to track down civilians and military service members."

"Thank you," Ruth said.

She left her spot and met with the woman named Ivy, who took down information on Lucette and Aline.

"They came in on a hospital ship," Ruth said.

Ivy nodded and adjusted her glasses on the bridge of her nose. "Is there anyone else?"

"Yes," Ruth said, her heart breaking. "Flying Officer Jimmie

Quill of the Seventy-Three Squadron RAF." Ruth glanced at the navy officers on the gangway and folded her arms.

Ivy scribbled on her clipboard. She took out a piece of paper, wrote down information for the Red Cross, and gave it to Ruth. "We don't know where you will be, so you'll need to check in with us. The list of people who are trying to reunite with others is quite long. Inquire in a week or two. In the meantime, I suggest checking the hospitals and docks in Plymouth, Southampton, and Falmouth—where most of the evacuees came into port."

"Thank you."

"Take care," Ivy said.

Along the dock, military evacuees gave three cheers to the trawler's crew, and Ruth joined a group of female evacuees who were led by a Salvation Army woman to a nearby naval barracks. Inside, they were taken to a communal shower room with galvanized metal wash tubs. The women were instructed to undress, place their ruined clothing in a wheelbarrow, and bathe. Ruth unbuttoned her tunic and removed Piglet, stained with oil, from a pocket. It was her only possession that survived the sea, mainly due to the protection of her life jacket, which had covered the pocket and pressed securely around her torso. She blinked away tears, removed her clothing, and stood in a tub with calf-deep, lukewarm water.

She scrubbed, using laundry detergent flakes and a bath brush, until her skin turned raw. Even after washing her hair several times, it remained oily and smelled of petroleum. She replaced the water and bathed again, and again. Using a palmful of detergent, she carefully laundered Piglet but stopped short of removing all the black stains when a seam on his back began to tear. Rather than risk further damage, she rinsed him in a washbowl and squeezed out excess water.

The women dried with towels and were taken to a room with piles of old undergarments, clothing, and shoes. Ruth, her hair damp and tangled, picked out pieces and got dressed. The blue housedress with pockets was several sizes too big, and one of her shoes had a hole in the sole, but she was grateful to wear anything that didn't stink of oil. As the women exited the barracks, they were given a bit of money for a train ticket, and were told that they could sleep the night in a shelter, a ten-minute walk away.

Most of the women opted to go to the shelter or train station, but Ruth returned to the port. She sat near the harbor and watched a rescue vessel, packed with survivors of the *Lancastria*, pull into the dock. One by one, the evacuees disembarked through the naval officers who were giving orders of silence. Refusing to give up hope, she scanned the passengers for Jimmie until everyone had left the gangway.

When the sun began to set, and no more vessels could be seen approaching the port, Ruth left the dock. She spoke with a Red Cross volunteer, who gave her directions to Prince of Wales Hospital. Thirty minutes later, she arrived at a large stone building on Chapel Street and entered a waiting room that was packed with people. She waited in line and gradually worked her way forward to speak with a woman at a front desk.

"May I help you?" the woman asked.

"Yes," Ruth said. "I'm looking for two French evacuees—a woman ambulance driver and a nine-year-old girl."

"Names."

Ruth gave her the information.

The woman thumbed through an admissions list and shook her head.

Ruth slumped her shoulders. "Are you sure?"

"Yes. Are you certain they came to Plymouth?"

"No. They were on a hospital ship that should have arrived in England yesterday."

"Try Plymouth City Hospital."

"Where is it located?"

"Other side of town." The woman wrote down directions on a piece of paper and gave it to her. "If they're not there, try the hospitals in Southampton and Falmouth. I overheard an ambulance driver say that lots of civilian refugees disembarked in Falmouth."

"Thank you."

Ruth exited the building and walked through the dark streets of Plymouth, its citizens abiding by blackout rules, much like the people of Paris. An hour later, she entered Plymouth City Hospital, an old three-story Victorian brick building. Although the medical center was smaller and older than the last hospital, it was far more congested. The waiting area was filled, elbow to elbow, with people searching for loved ones, and the main corridor was lined with patients on gurneys.

They've run out of rooms, Ruth thought, getting in line to speak with an attendant.

After forty minutes of waiting in line, Ruth reached a window counter with a gray-haired woman wearing a nurse uniform and cap. She provided information on Lucette and Aline, and gripped the edge of the counter as the woman searched through a registry.

"Lucette is here," the woman said, looking at Ruth.

"Thank goodness," Ruth said, feeling relieved. "What about Aline?"

"There's no one here by that name."

"Could you check again. Her last name is Cadieux."

The woman sighed and thumbed through her records. "Like I said—she's not here."

Ruth folded her arms. "May I see Lucette."

"Visiting hours are over. You can come back at nine tomorrow morning."

"Could you tell me her room number?"

The woman pursed her lips.

Ruth glanced at the line of people behind her. "You're quite busy. It'll prevent me from taking up more of your time tomorrow."

The woman looked at her records. "Room two-eleven."

"Thank you," Ruth said.

"Next," the woman called.

Ruth turned and made her way to the exit, but she paused, pretending to adjust her shoelace. The attendant lowered her head, and Ruth casually changed direction and walked down the corridor. She tiptoed up the stairs to the second floor and peeked around the corner to find a nurse exiting a room. She pressed her back against the wall and listened to the woman's footsteps disappear, then crept down the hallway. A thick smell of antiseptic and floor cleaner filled the air. Her heartbeat quickened as she located the room, and she slipped inside and closed the door behind her.

The small room contained six female patients in beds with no partitions or curtains. On the far wall near a window was Lucette, who was sleeping with her leg bandaged and elevated on pillows. Ruth crept forward, and the eyes of the other patients fell upon her.

Ruth smiled at a woman, who had a bandage over one eye and was reading a book. "Hello."

The woman lowered her book. "Hi."

"I won't be long—I'm checking in on my friend."

The woman nodded.

Ruth went to the last bed, kneeled, and gently placed a hand on her friend's shoulder.

Lucette stirred and opened her eyelids. "Ruth!"

Ruth placed a finger to her lips.

Lucette leaned over and hugged her. "*Dieu merci*," she breathed.

Ruth squeezed her tight. "I'm so happy you're alive."

"You too." Lucette slipped away. "A refugee agency took Aline to an orphanage—I don't know the location. I didn't have a say in the matter. A doctor put me to sleep to perform surgery on my leg and, when I woke up, I was told that she was gone. I feel horrible—I'm so sorry."

"It's okay. I'm sure she's in good care. We'll find her after you get out of here."

Lucette nodded. She shifted her body and winced.

"How's the leg?"

"The doctor removed three pieces of shrapnel. I'll be walking soon, but the doctor told me my dancing days are over."

"He doesn't know you like I do," Ruth said, squeezing her hand. "You'll be doing the can-can until you're old and gray."

Lucette smiled. "I see that you got rid of your uniform."

Ruth nodded. An ache grew beneath her sternum.

"Where's Jimmie?"

Tears welled up in her eyes. She fought to find her words, and her bottom lip quivered.

Lucette's face went pale. "What happened?"

She drew a serrated breath. "Our ship was sunk by a German air raid. Jimmie was in the hull of the ship when the bombs struck—he didn't make it out."

"*Non!*" Lucette cried. "It can't be."

Ruth lowered her head and sobbed. She felt Lucette's arms wrap around her. Together, they wept until a nurse made her rounds and ordered Ruth to leave.

CHAPTER 53

PLYMOUTH, ENGLAND—JUNE 22, 1940

On the afternoon that a French delegation signed an armistice with Germany, Ruth was sitting at the docks in Plymouth. She looked out over the harbor that contained an array of fishing boats and military ships, yet none of them were evacuation vessels. A deep sense of loss and grief gnawed at her core. *The mission to evacuate Allied forces and civilians from ports in France is over. He's not coming back and I need to move on.* She got to her feet, brushed off the back of her dress, and made her way to the hospital to visit Lucette.

It had been days since an evacuation ship, carrying soldiers and refugees, arrived in Plymouth. However, Ruth continued to spend hours at the harbor, before and after visiting hours at the hospital. Even though she'd encountered no survivors from the hull of the *Lancastria*, her heart had struggled to let go of hope that he survived. But with each passing day, and with the end of evacuations from France, she'd gradually come to terms that her Jimmie was gone.

Since her arrival in Plymouth, she'd lived at a Salvation Army shelter for women that was overflowing with refugees. She'd slept twelve hours per day on an old army cot, not including naps, as if her mind and body craved hibernation. She and the other women had been fed well by selfless, volunteer aid workers. Fried cod and chips. Egg sandwiches. Slices of cottage pie. Tins of milk. She gradually gained weight and her strength improved and, for the first time in weeks, her belly didn't ache with hunger. She felt eternally indebted to the women of the Salvation Army and Red Cross, and she promised herself that, for as long as she lived, she would give generously to their charities.

She'd spent hours at the hospital. Lucette had contracted a post-surgery infection, which delayed her physiotherapy and release date. However, the setback in her health did not prevent her from diligently working to locate Aline. In addition to Ruth requesting the Red Cross to find Aline, Lucette enlisted the help of the nurses on her floor to track down the name and location of her orphanage. To date, they were still working to find Aline. And it was shocking, to Ruth, how a hospital could allow a nine-year-old girl to be taken away without any records—regardless of the chaos with tens of thousands of refugees pouring into England.

At the hospital, Ruth went to the second floor and entered Lucette's room. She froze at the sight of her friend's empty bed.

"Where's Lucette?"

"Down the hall with a nurse," a female patient said, scribbling on a crossword puzzle while propped up in bed. "She'll be back in a few minutes."

"Thanks."

Ruth's shoulders relaxed. She sat in a communal chair and chatted with a few of the women patients, French refugees who'd been admitted for exhaustion and open sores on their feet. Minutes later, Lucette entered in a wheelchair that was being pushed by a young nurse.

"*Bonjour*," Lucette said.

"It's good to see you up and around." Ruth stood and helped the nurse to place Lucette onto the bed and prop up her bandaged leg.

"You're going to be sore tomorrow," the nurse said, "but we'll do another round of physiotherapy."

"I look forward to it," Lucette said.

The nurse removed a pill from her pocket and placed it on the stand next to a glass of water. "Here's your sulfa tablet."

"I'll take it after I visit with Ruth."

The nurse nodded and left.

"How was your first treatment?" Ruth asked.

Lucette ran a hand over her bandaged leg. "Painful. The infection is better, but it hurts like hell to bend my knee with stitches."

Ruth nodded. "The therapy will get you out of here sooner."

"The doctor told me this morning that I might be released on crutches by the end of the week."

Ruth smiled. "That's wonderful."

"I've made some progress with locating Aline," Lucette said. "One of the nurses thinks that the refugee agency took Aline to a London orphanage, but she doesn't know for sure. We've made some telephone inquiries, but haven't tracked her down."

"We will," Ruth said.

"When I get out of here, let's go straight to London."

"I agree. After we find her, we need to obtain a government job to serve the war effort, and secure a place to live. Then, I'd like to try to get Aline out of the orphanage to live with us until France is free." Ruth slipped her hands into the pockets of her dress. "How do you feel about all that?"

Lucette smiled. "It's a beautiful plan."

"I'm glad you think so." Ruth glanced out the window. "I'm going to take a trip to Portsmouth to see Jimmie's family."

"When?"

"In a few days."

"If you wait a bit longer, I could go with you."

"I'd love your company," Ruth said, "but I feel that this is something I need to do on my own."

"All right. If you change your mind, I'm here for you." Lucette retrieved her pill and glass of water.

The anticipation of meeting with Jimmie's parents and sister, Nora, caused Ruth's diaphragm to tighten. She took a deep breath and exhaled. As Lucette placed the pill into her mouth and chased it down with water, Ruth wished for a miracle medicine—one that could erase dreadful memories and mend broken hearts.

CHAPTER 54

PORTSMOUTH, ENGLAND—JUNE 24, 1940

Ruth, her nose filled with a smell of diesel and creosote, traveled down a landing of the Portsmouth & Southsea railway station, and made her way to the street. She hailed a black-colored taxi, climbed into the back seat, and gave the address to a driver. As the taxi pulled away from the curb, her uneasiness grew. *How do I even begin to tell them what happened?*

The day before, Ruth had rung Jimmie's mum, Harriet, from a red telephone box on a street corner near the Plymouth City Hospital. She'd explained that she met Jimmie in France and was in possession of his good luck charm that she wished to return. Harriet, her sorrow raw from news about her son, eagerly invited Ruth to visit. "Last month the RAF sent us a telegram informing that Jimmie's plane was shot down and he's missing, believed to be killed," Harriet had said. "I'm hoping you might help us to understand what happened to him." Ruth expressed her condolences and, rather than discuss details on the telephone, arranged for a date and time to visit. She'd hung up the receiver feeling bitter that the government was imposing secrecy among the *Lancastria* survivors. *I don't care if I'm punished. Jimmie's family deserves to know the truth.*

The taxi stopped on a tree-lined street of terraced houses with ornate chimney pots.

"That's the address," the driver said, pointing to a white door with a transom window.

"Thanks." She paid the driver, using money given to her from the Salvation Army, and exited the taxi. She walked briskly, trying to shake the collywobbles in her tummy, to the front door. As she prepared to knock, the door swung open.

"Ruth?" a woman with wavy, gray-and-brown hair asked.

"Yes." Ruth squeezed the handle of her purse, a charity gift from an aid worker.

"I'm Harriet. Please come in."

Ruth entered and was greeted with a hug.

"This is my husband, Archibald," Harriet said, turning to a tall man in his fifties who was wearing dark trousers with a blue button-up shirt.

"Welcome, and thank you for coming," he said. "I wish we were meeting in better circumstances."

"Me too." Ruth hugged Archibald.

"Hello," a female voice said.

Ruth turned to a petite young woman, approximately sixteen years of age, who was on crutches. Leg calipers were visible below the hem of her plaid skirt, and her facial features were similar to those of Jimmie, especially her high cheekbones and hazel eyes.

Ruth smiled. "Hi. I'm Ruth."

"It's nice to meet you. I'm Nora." She propped a crutch against a wall and extended her arm. "I won't break. You're welcome to hug me, too."

Ruth's tension eased and she embraced her warmly.

They settled into a reception room that smelled faintly of soap and vinegar, which reminded Ruth of the scent of her childhood home after her *maman* had given it a good cleaning. Ruth sat on a sofa with Nora, while Harriet and Archibald settled in matching, dark blue upholstered chairs.

Harriet intertwined her fingers, as if she were about to pray. "You mentioned on the telephone that you met Jimmie in France."

"Yes," Ruth said. "I was a volunteer ambulance driver for the French Army, before I was evacuated to England." She shifted in her seat as she struggled to find the right words. "I will do my best to tell you everything I know about what happened to Jimmie."

"We'd be grateful for any insight you can provide us," Archibald said. "The telegram we received said that he was shot down and missing, believed killed. We've contacted the RAF, but they have provided us with nothing."

"I don't know how to say this," Ruth said, gathering her courage. "So, I'm just going to say it. Jimmie was killed during the mass evacuation of troops from a port in France, not from being shot down. I'm deeply sorry."

Harriet lowered her head into her hands and cried.

Nora's eyes filled with tears.

Archibald stood and placed an arm around his wife.

For the next hour, Ruth told them everything—how she and Lucette rescued Jimmie after he bailed out of his plane, their escape to Paris and journey to the coast at Saint-Nazaire, and the German raid on the *Lancastria*, which was carrying in excess of six thousand evacuees.

"Oh, dear God," Harriet said, her voice dropping to a whisper.

"There has been nothing in the newspapers about this," Archibald said.

Ruth looked at him, his face etched with sadness. "Officers of the Royal Navy ordered the survivors to never speak about the sinking of the *Lancastria*. They'd told us that if we said anything about what happened in Saint-Nazaire, we'd be in violation of King's Regulations and would be severely punished."

Nora drew a deep breath and smoothed her skirt. "Why are you taking such a risk to tell us?"

Ruth's chest tightened. "Jimmie gave his life for his country—and for France. His family deserves to know the truth."

Harriet wiped her eyes and sat forward in her chair. "Is there any chance he could have gotten out?"

Ruth shook her head. "He was in the hull, where none of the hundreds of RAF ground crew members escaped."

Archibald ran a hand through his thin hair. "I don't understand it. He knows better than to allow himself to be put in the hold of a ship."

Ruth felt sick to her stomach. "Jimmie knew the hull wasn't safe. He went there to try to get members of his ground crew to come topside. The bombing occurred while he was there."

Archibald's hands trembled. He plucked a handkerchief from a pocket and dabbed his eyes.

"Forgive me," Harriet whimpered. "I need a moment to get a bit of fresh air."

"I'll come with you." Archibald helped his wife from her seat, and they walked through a rear door to a garden.

Ruth looked at Nora. "I'm so sorry. Would you like me to leave?"

"No." Nora wiped her face. "I'm grateful that you came. We've been agonizing over the telegram for weeks. It's painful to hear what happened to my brother, but it'll help me and my mum and dad to gain a sense of peace and closure to his death."

Ruth placed her hands on her lap. She buried her horrid thoughts of the *Lancastria* and turned her mind to fond memories. "Jimmie spoke about you often."

"What did he say?"

"He told me you were the bravest person he knew."

"He did?"

Ruth nodded. "He told me how you proved all your doctors wrong and regained your ability to walk. He said you were incredibly clever, and that he was chuffed that you were planning to go away to college. And, on more than one occasion, he told me that you were going to make a brilliant librarian."

Nora smiled.

"He adored you, and he was hugely proud of you."

"Same. He was the best brother anyone could ask for." Nora rubbed her knees, strapped with calipers.

"I have something for you." Ruth reached inside her purse, removed Piglet, and gave him to her. "Jimmie left him in my bag for safekeeping. I think he would have wanted him to be returned to you."

Nora ran a thumb over the cuddly toy, stained gray from oil. Tears formed in her eyes and she blinked them away. "I thought it would keep him safe."

Ruth placed a hand on her arm. "He took great comfort in having something so dear to you with him. To Jimmie, this charm was a symbol of hope."

Nora squeezed Ruth's hand. "Thank you for saying that."

Ruth nodded.

A fluffy gray cat padded into the room. It peered up with its orange eyes, and jumped onto the sofa.

"This must be Crumpet," Ruth said.

"Indeed, he is," Nora said, releasing her hand.

Crumpet crept to Ruth and rubbed his cheek against her arm. "He likes you."

Ruth smiled and gently stroked the cat's head.

"It sounds like Jimmie told you all about me and my family."

"He did." Crumpet crawled onto her lap and purred.

Nora scooched next to Ruth. "You and Jimmie were quite fond of each other."

Ruth, her heart aching, gave a subtle nod.

"Were you in love with him?"

Her vision blurred with tears. "Yes."

PART 4

THE BATTLE OF BRITAIN

CHAPTER 55

LONDON, ENGLAND—JULY 16, 1940

At the same time that Hitler was issuing an order to begin plans for a land invasion of the United Kingdom called Operation Sea Lion, Winston Churchill and General Ismay were studying a wall map in a conference room of the underground Cabinet War Rooms. Colored pins, inserted into the map, depicted locations of Allied and enemy forces. A fiery resolve burned inside Churchill as he eyed German-occupied countries of Europe—Czechoslovakia, Poland, Denmark, Norway, Belgium, Luxembourg, the Netherlands, and France. *Britain stands alone against Nazi tyranny.* He clasped the lapels of his jacket and lowered his brow. *We shall fight and never surrender.*

Only the Channel separated Southern England from northern German-occupied France, and the Luftwaffe had begun bombing English ports and coastal shipping convoys. The war had come to Britain. It was only a matter of time, Churchill believed, before the Luftwaffe directed their bombs on factories, RAF airfields, and cities—a strategy to cower citizens into submission before the German military launched an amphibious assault on Britain.

"Our primary aim," Churchill said, turning to his chief military advisor, "is to inspire resistance at all costs. Our people must be hardened to war on our soil, and they must accept nothing less than complete victory."

"I concur, sir," Ismay said. "The spirit of our government and citizens is the backbone for survival. I recommend that you schedule frequent public broadcasts."

"Indeed. We must instill a sense of duty for our people to do their utmost—day and night—to defend our island nation."

Ismay nodded.

"Our second issue at hand is to plan for the defense of our island and, in due time, use Britain as a stronghold to liberate Nazi-occupied Europe." Churchill removed a cigar from his pocket and lit it. "Do you have the most recent tally on the number of troops evacuated in Operation Aerial?"

"I do." Ismay picked up a clipboard from a nearby table and ran his finger down a list. "One hundred ninety-one thousand soldiers. We also evacuated approximately forty thousand civilians."

Churchill puffed on his cigar. His mind drifted to the sinking of the *Lancastria*, and his order for a D-notice to withhold the information for purposes of national security. Despite his pity for the perished passengers and their grieving families, he had no intention of rescinding his directive. *I will not permit the release of disastrous news that might weaken the morale of our people.*

Ismay lowered his clipboard. "Including both the evacuations at Dunkirk and Operation Aerial, we saved over a half a million soldiers."

"We retained our army to defend the country." Churchill flicked ash from his cigar. "But in the process, we lost much of our military equipment in Belgium and France."

"I have confidence that your personal relationship with US President Roosevelt will expedite the rebuilding of our armament."

Churchill took a deep drag on his cigar and exhaled smoke. "Roosevelt is working to provide us with supplies, while promising the American public that their young men will not be sent into a European conflict. It will take months to replenish our arsenal. Until then, the weight of our defense will fall upon the RAF."

"Our airmen are up to the task, sir," Ismay said, confidently. "They'll give us the time we need."

For an hour, they discussed placement of troops, equipment,

and military strategy to defend Britain. They also speculated on the locations—most likely between Brighton and Dover—where the German military might attempt a land invasion.

A knock came from the door.

"Enter," Churchill said.

A female secretary opened the door and stuck her head inside the room. "Excuse me, Prime Minister, the Minister of Economic Warfare is here for your meeting."

Hugh Dalton, Churchill thought. "I will see him in a few minutes."

"Yes, sir," the secretary said. "I'll have him wait for you in the Cabinet Room." She left and closed the door.

Churchill looked at Ismay. "There is one matter that we haven't discussed—our guerrilla warfare."

Ismay clasped his hands behind his back.

"I will be requesting Dalton to establish the Special Operations Executive."

"Excellent choice," Ismay said. "He has the right temperament and skills to head our espionage and sabotage operations in German-occupied countries."

Churchill rolled his cigar between his fingers. "I expect the secret army to subvert the enemy."

"I'm quite certain it will."

An unwavering determination pumped through Churchill's veins. He tamped out his cigar and looked at Ismay. "We're at a crossroads, Pug," he said, using his nickname.

Ismay's faced turned solemn.

"We have chosen the path of resistance," Churchill said. "Along our arduous journey to freedom, the British people will endure immense suffering and sacrifice. Nevertheless, we shall carry on the fight and—in the end—we will achieve victory and liberate Europe from the menace of tyranny."

"Indeed, we will," Ismay said.

Churchill bid him farewell, left the conference room, and walked toward his destiny.

CHAPTER 56

LONDON, ENGLAND—SEPTEMBER 11, 1940

At dawn, the last wave of German air attacks stopped and Ruth, who was sitting on the ground next to Lucette, peered up at the masonry ceiling of the Liverpool Street Underground station. A siren gave the all-clear signal, a long deafening drone that stirred the occupants of the shelter. People stretched their arms and rubbed sleep from their eyes. A gradual crescendo of whispers turned to normal voices as citizens—who spent the night in the tube station—gathered their blankets, pillows, and bags.

Ruth stood, smoothed her blue skirt and tunic of her Women's Auxiliary Air Force (WAAF) uniform, and helped Lucette to her feet.

"*Merci*," Lucette said.

"Get any sleep?" Ruth asked.

"A little." Lucette adjusted the belt around the tunic of her WAAF uniform.

"How's the leg?"

"Stiff. It'll improve once I walk a bit."

Lucette's shrapnel wound had healed, but chronic stiffness and pain remained in her knee, and she sometimes limped after spending too much time on her feet. Ruth felt bad for her friend, but Lucette never complained or showed self-pity, despite that her career as a dancer was likely over.

Ruth glanced at her watch. "Go to the flat and get an hour of rest. I'll check on Aline and meet you at the airfield for our shift."

"I'd like to see her."

"She'd like to see you, too, but I got more sleep than you, and we are likely to spend the night again in the tube." Ruth placed a hand on her shoulder. "How about you stop by to see her after our shift?"

Lucette rubbed her eyes, surrounded in dark circles. "Are you sure?"

"Positive."

They left the underground station to a roar of fire brigades and an acrid smell of burning wood and petrol. Down the street, firemen—covered in sweat and soot—sprayed water onto a storefront that was engulfed in flames. Ruth, her heartbeat racing, parted ways from Lucette and made her way through the East End of London, marred with scores of smoke plumes rising into the morning sky.

For the past four nights, the Luftwaffe had raided London with tons of high-explosive bombs. An ashen haze would dissipate throughout the day as fire brigades valiantly battled raging fires. But night would bring another wave of bombing and more destruction, driving Londoners to burrow into underground shelters like moles, only to emerge each morning to learn what remained of their beloved city.

In early July, Ruth and Lucette arrived in London and reunited with Aline. But the director of the orphanage—an elderly woman with thick, wire-like gray hair named Mrs. Webb—declined Ruth's request to release Aline into her foster care on the basis that Ruth was neither a relative nor a British citizen. "Aline will be well taken care of at Dankworth Hall," the director had said, sitting behind a large wooden desk. "After the war, she'll be sent back to France and returned to her father, assuming he is alive." Ruth felt shattered, but she remained determined to protect Aline. After a lengthy discussion, Ruth convinced Mrs. Webb to permit her and Lucette to have visits with Aline under the supervision of the staff at Dankworth Hall.

They had left the orphanage and enlisted in the Women's Auxiliary Air Force. Their first choice would have been an ambulance corps, but Lucette was worried that the duties of an ambulance driver might be too strenuous for her leg. Rather than split up, they joined the WAAF together. After a week of training at RAF West Drayton, they were each assigned the role of a parachute packer at RAF Croydon and provided living arrangements at a requisitioned flat in Spitalfields.

At a huge hangar with low-hanging bright lights, they worked eight-hour shifts in teams around the clock, carefully packing parachutes on long tables that resembled elevated bowling lanes. On a wall was a large, hand-painted sign that read, *An Airman's Life Relies on Each Parachute You Pack.* It was tedious and skillful work, and Ruth took great pride in knowing that she was doing something to protect downed pilots and crewmen. But she felt strange to be distanced from the battlegrounds of France, and she continued to grieve from the death of Jimmie. Fueled by heartbreak and patriotism, she aspired to do more to make a difference in the fight.

Soon after Ruth began her duties, RAF Croydon was attacked in the first significant air raid on the area of London. Two hangars, an armory, and forty aircraft were destroyed, resulting in six deaths—five airmen and a female telephone operator. Fortunately, the hangar that contained Ruth and forty WAAF parachute packers was spared in the raid. She'd expected that the Luftwaffe would continue to target RAF airfields, but things changed when—four days ago—an armada of German aircraft bombarded London, killing hundreds of innocent civilians. And for the next three consecutive nights, waves of German bombs rained down on the city.

Twenty minutes after leaving the Liverpool Street Underground station, Ruth arrived at Dankworth Hall, a three-story Georgian-style house with a wrought-iron front gate. She drew a deep breath and exhaled, feeling relieved to find the building unscathed. Inside, she greeted an orphanage worker named Marjorie, who left and traveled up a staircase to retrieve Aline.

Ruth sat in the entrance hall on a wood bench that looked like a section of a pew that was salvaged from an old church. A moment later, the sound of footsteps grew from above.

Aline's eyes brightened as she came down the stairs. She ran to Ruth and wrapped her arms around her.

Ruth squeezed her tight. "How are you?"

"Better, now that you're here."

Ruth smiled and released her. "Did you spend the night in a shelter?"

"*Oui.* Tilbury Shelter."

An image of the colossal warehouse with railway viaducts flashed in Ruth's mind. It had been the Commercial Road Goods Depot, but it now served as the East End's largest bomb shelter. "What was it like?"

"It's crowded and smells bad. There are thousands of people, lying side by side, and no washrooms." Aline sat on the bench beside her. "Did you find a shelter?"

"A tube station with Lucette. She wanted to be here, but I insisted that she get some rest before going to work. She's going to stop by to see you after our shift."

Aline nodded.

A group of children between the ages of six and ten scurried down the steps and entered a hallway.

Tension spread through Ruth's shoulders. *Evacuation is voluntary and many children remain in the city, but if it were up to me, they'd all be given sanctuary in the countryside.*

Over the past month, Ruth had written two letters to the United States Committee for the Care of European Children (USCOM), a new organization chaired by Eleanor Roosevelt to bring Jewish refugee children to America. To date, she received no response.

"I spoke to Mrs. Webb about children moving out of the city."

Aline lowered her head.

"She told me that she's working to get some of the children into private homes, far away from London. I asked her to include you, if possible."

Aline sat up straight. "I don't want to go. It'll mean that I'll never see you and Lucette."

"I don't want to be away from you either, but it will be safer for you outside the city."

"Why can't I live with you?"

"I've tried, and will continue to try, but I have no authority in the matter."

Aline looked up at Ruth. "It's not fair. I wish we could run away—someplace with no bombs or guns—until the war is over and my papa comes home."

Ruth's chest ached. She placed an arm around Aline's shoulder. "Me too."

They sat silently for a moment while more children descended the stairs and made their way down the hallway.

"I've been thinking a lot about Grandpapa, Maman, and Jimmie," Aline said.

Ruth drew a deep breath. Upon her arrival to London, she'd told her that Jimmie was killed in a raid while evacuating from France, but did not provide the details. "Would you like to talk about it?"

"Sometimes I'm angry, and other times I'm sad."

Ruth swallowed. "I am, too."

"You are?"

"*Oui*. It's okay for you to have these feelings."

Aline picked at a loose thread on the sleeve of her shirt. "I miss them."

She leaned to Aline. "We're going to get through this."

The orphanage worker approached them. "Excuse me. Aline needs to join the others for breakfast before going to school."

Ruth nodded.

The woman turned and joined a group of children who were shuffling down the hallway.

"I'll see you after work," Ruth said.

Aline hugged her and left to join the others.

Alone, Ruth felt miserable. She left the orphanage, made her way through the East End, and boarded a train to RAF Croydon. Throughout her eight-hour shift of packing parachutes, her mind remained on Aline and the Luftwaffe air raids. *I need to do more to get her out of London*, she thought, carefully folding the silk fabric of a canopy.

After her shift, she and Lucette left the airfield for Dankworth Hall. Before they could get there, air raid sirens sounded, sending them and thousands of Londoners scrambling to nearby underground shelters. Within minutes, a rumble of antiaircraft fire and bombs resonated through the overcrowded tunnel. She hoped that Aline made it safely to Tilbury Shelter, and she was disappointed that Lucette would not get to see her.

Ruth, determined to not allow the Luftwaffe to hinder her endeavors, borrowed a pad of paper and a pencil from a businessman who was carrying a leather briefcase. She hunkered on the concrete floor and placed the pad of paper against her leg. First, she wrote a letter to her *maman* and dad. Then, she began to draft her third letter to USCOM.

Dear First Lady Eleanor Roosevelt,

A detonation shook the ground, and bits of mortar fell from the ceiling. Cries and whimpers echoed through the tunnel.

Ruth dusted bits of sand from her paper. Her mind raced, searching for the right words, and she continued to write.

CHAPTER 57

LONDON, ENGLAND—SEPTEMBER 17, 1940

Ruth, along with Lucette, reported to work at RAF Croydon and entered the hangar that contained the WAAF parachute packers. She went to her assigned table, where she labored to untangle a mass of parachute cords. Her hands and fingers ached, and she was exhausted from lack of sleep, due to spending ten consecutive nights in an underground station. For Ruth, the worst part was worrying about Aline's safety. Although the frequency and intensity of the bombardments had escalated, Dankworth Hall had yet to find countryside homes to evacuate its children.

For several hours, Ruth untangled, folded, and packed parachutes. Then, she carried the packed harnesses to a pile at the entrance to the hangar.

A WAAF supervisor named Enid entered the hangar, cupped her hands around her mouth, and called, "A driver has fallen ill—can anyone drive a lorry?"

"I can," Ruth said, standing near the woman.

"The lorry is outside. Load thirty chutes into the back and take them to number twelve hangar to be unloaded."

"May I bring another person with me to help?"

"No. It's a one-person job." Enid handed Ruth a key and left.

Ruth locked eyes with Lucette, several tables away. She held up the key and mouthed, "I tried."

Lucette smiled, then focused her attention to folding a parachute.

Ruth loaded the lorry with packed harnesses and got behind the wheel. She started the engine, released the clutch, and the vehicle moved forward. As she drove across the airfield, mixed emotions swirled inside her. It felt refreshing to be released from the confinement of the production line, but the sensation of the wheel in her hands reminded her of racing to hospitals in an ambulance filled with maimed men.

At the opposite end of the airfield, she parked in front of a hangar, where rows of British fighters and bombers were being outfitted with ammunition. She got out of the lorry and paused to watch a military passenger plane land on a runway, taxi to the hangar, and cut its engines. A smell of expelled aviation fuel penetrated her nose. As she opened the back of the lorry, several French aviators and a British Army officer exited the aircraft.

Ruth unloaded a harness and carried it to the hangar, where she placed it in a bin. Upon exiting the building, she approached two of the French aviators who were smoking cigarettes.

"*Bonjour. D'où venez-vous?*" Ruth asked.

"*Magnifique! Une française!*" one of the pilots said, his voice filled with delight.

The British officer, several yards away, leaned his back against the side of the hangar and lit a cigarette.

Ruth chatted with the French airmen, one from Lyon and the other from Rouen. They'd bailed out of their fighter planes in an air battle near Nantes, but by the time they reached the coast, the naval evacuations from France were over. So, they made their way to southern France, Spain, and eventually Portugal, where they boarded a ship for Britain. They arrived by plane in London to join the Free French Air Forces stationed in England.

Ruth wished them good luck and returned to the lorry. The French pilots, who appeared grateful for her interest in them, helped her finish unloading the packed parachutes and said farewell.

Ruth approached the driver's door.

"Pardon me," a deep voice said.

Ruth turned and faced the British military officer, holding a half-smoked cigarette. He was clean-shaven, in his early thirties, and athletically fit, like a rower for a crew team.

"My name is George. I overheard your conversation. Are you French?"

"American."

The officer raised his brow. "Your French is impeccable. I thought it was your native language."

"Thanks. My mother was born in France. We spoke French at home."

"What are you doing here?"

"I was living in Paris when the war started," she said, feeling an urgency to return to her duties. "I came to England on an evacuation ship."

He took a drag of his cigarette. "What were you doing in Paris?"

She crossed her arms. "If you're trying to get me to go on a date, I'm not interested. I need to get back to work."

He chuckled. "I'm not interested in a date. I'm happily married and have two lovely children. I'm simply curious, and if you should get in trouble for being tardy, I will gladly tell your supervisor that I was responsible for your delay."

Ruth shifted her weight. "All right."

For several minutes, she told him about leaving her job as a cabaret singer in Paris to volunteer as driver for the ambulance corps of the French Army. He asked questions, prompting her to tell him about her exposure to combat on the front lines, the exodus to Paris and to Saint-Nazaire, and her evacuation to England—leaving out the disaster of the *Lancastria*.

"Impressive." He flicked ash from his cigarette. "And now you're a driver for the Women's Auxiliary Air Force."

She shook her head. "Parachute packer."

"It's not as dangerous and daring as what you did in France. How do you like your current duties?"

"It's important work," she said.

"It is," he said, "but you didn't answer my question."

"I really need to go," she said.

A black sedan approached and stopped a few feet away.

"I need to leave, too, but hold on a second." He went to the sedan and retrieved a piece of paper and pen from the driver. He placed the paper on the roof of the vehicle and scribbled.

Tension spread through her neck and shoulders.

He returned and handed her the paper, which contained a name, Nicolas Bodington, and a telephone number.

"Who's this?"

"A friend," he said. "He's seeking candidates for a special role. I think you might be well suited for it. Tell him George sent you."

She looked at him. "You didn't mention what you do for the military, George."

"Intelligence." He tipped his cap and got into the back seat of the sedan.

Ruth, feeling dumbfounded, watched the automobile leave the airfield. She tucked the paper into a pocket of her uniform and got into the driver's seat of the lorry. She gripped the wheel to steady her nerves, started the engine, and sped away.

CHAPTER 58

LONDON, ENGLAND—
SEPTEMBER 24, 1940

Ruth exited a train at Marylebone station in Central London and traveled down a sidewalk. Clouds of smoke wafted over the city, and wails of fire brigade sirens filled the air. But Londoners, despite seventeen consecutive nights of Luftwaffe bombardment, were going about their morning routine. Proprietors opened their shops. Police officers patrolled the streets. Teachers headed to their classrooms. Bus drivers shuttled passengers to work. A deep admiration for the British people rose inside Ruth. *They're all going about their duty*, she thought, her shoes clicking over the sidewalk. *And so will I.* She quickened her pace and turned onto a side street.

Initially, Ruth was hesitant to call Nicolas Bodington. She'd worked with Lucette since her days at the cabaret, and—together—they'd persevered through dreadful times while serving in the ambulance corps. To Ruth, it felt wrong to explore another role without her friend. But her feelings began to change after she confided in Lucette about her unusual encounter with an intelligence officer named George.

"It was my leg that held you back from joining a British ambulance corps," Lucette had said, rubbing her sore knee. "I won't let it happen again. That man saw something unique in you, and you need to find out what the role is about. If you don't ring him—I will."

The following day, Ruth called Nicolas Bodington from a telephone box at RAF Croydon during her break. She'd expected to leave word with a receptionist and was surprised when he answered. She explained how she got his number, and when she inquired about the position, Bodington declined to provide details. He did, however, invite her to come to his office to talk. They agreed on a date and time, and he informed her that someone would contact a WAAF superior to arrange for her absence.

Fifteen minutes after leaving Marylebone station, she arrived at 64 Baker Street, the address given to her by Bodington. She paused at the entrance of the six-story, stone building with no signage. She smoothed her tunic and walked inside.

"Hello," Ruth said, greeting a silver-haired male receptionist, who was seated behind a desk. "My name is Ruth Lacroix. I'm here to meet with Nicolas Bodington."

The receptionist looked at a list of names. "He's expecting you. Third floor—room thirty-three."

"Thank you."

Ruth climbed the stairs and stopped on the third-floor landing to catch her breath. She located the room and knocked on the door.

"Come in," a man's voice said.

She entered, closed the door, and turned to a bespectacled military officer in his mid-thirties who was wearing an olive-colored uniform. "Hello, sir."

"Good day." The man stood from his desk and shook her hand. "Nicolas Bodington."

"Ruth Lacroix."

He gestured to a wooden chair beside his desk. "Have a seat."

Ruth sat and placed her hands on her lap. She suddenly felt awkward and wished that she had brought a clipboard and something to write with.

Bodington took his seat and removed an engraved metal case from his pocket. "Cigarette?"

"No, thank you."

Bodington placed a cigarette to his lips, lit it, and put away the case. He took a drag, flaring the ember. "I suspect that you're wondering what this is about."

"I am," Ruth said.

"Consider this to be an interview," Bodington said.

Ruth shifted in her seat. "What is the role?"

"First, let's proceed with some questions. If I'm satisfied that you meet the qualifications, I'll tell you about it." Bodington rested his cigarette on an ashtray and retrieved a file and pen from his desk.

"All right," Ruth said. "Ask away."

The interview began with basic questions—place of birth, education, work experience, and language skills. But soon, Bodington's queries turned personal.

"I understand that you lived with your aunt and uncle in Paris while you worked at Bal Tabarin cabaret."

She straightened her spine. *How does he know this? Maybe it's in my WAAF record.* "Yes."

"What is the political party affiliation of your aunt and uncle?"

"I don't know. They rarely spoke of politics."

"How about your parents?"

An ache grew in her stomach. "I'm not sure, but I do know that they voted for FDR to be president."

Bodington wrote on his paper. "Which areas of France are you familiar with?"

"I know Paris and the surrounding areas quite well. Also, my role as an ambulance driver required me to spend a good deal of time in many towns near France's border with Belgium."

He scribbled and retrieved a new piece of paper. "Have you ever gotten into a fight?"

She raised her brow. "What kind of fight?"

"The physical kind."

"Not since kindergarten," she said, feeling confused and annoyed.

Bodington puffed on his cigarette. "If you were confronted by a Nazi soldier, could you kill him?"

Ruth gripped her thighs. "Why are you asking me this?"

He flicked ash into a tray. "Merely answer the question."

She thought of Jimmie, and an image of bombs exploding on the *Lancastria* flashed in her head. "Yes."

"What makes you think you could fight the enemy?"

"People I care about were slaughtered by the German military." She looked into his eyes. "I despise them."

Bodington, his face stoic, lowered his head and scribbled on his paper.

Ruth's patience waned. "Sir, these questions are quite unorthodox. What are you trying to learn from this?"

"I'm evaluating if I can risk your life," he said, picking up his cigarette. "And if you have the guts to risk it."

Ruth's skin turned cold.

He took a drag and blew smoke through his nose. "Would you like to carry on?"

She swallowed. "Yes."

For over two hours, Ruth answered Bodington's questions. He set aside his notes and lit his fourth cigarette of the morning.

"I want you to work in occupied France," he said, turning his chair toward her. "Your role will be to organize resistance, and act as a liaison with London."

Ruth's heart thudded inside her chest as she fought to keep her composure.

"I'm a general staff officer for the Special Operations Executive—SOE—a newly created organization to conduct espionage, sabotage, and reconnaissance in German-occupied Europe. Assuming you successfully pass our physical and instructional training programs, you will be deployed to France by either sea or air."

Ruth took a deep breath, attempting to process his words.

He put down his cigarette and stood. "I'll give you twenty-four hours to make your decision."

As Ruth rose from her seat, horrid images of bombs falling on innocent civilians filled her head. A wave of vengeance flooded her body. She turned to him and said, "I can give you a decision now, sir. I accept—but I have two requests."

Bodington frowned. "We do not make concessions with candidates."

"Please, sir. Hear them out. I think one of the requests will be of help to you, and the worst that could happen is that you say no and rescind my offer."

Bodington rubbed his jaw. "Very well."

"The first request is that you grant Lucette Soulier, a parachute packer of the WAAF, an interview with the SOE. She's from Paris, and she experienced everything I did while working for the ambulance corps in France. I'm quite certain you will find her to be an outstanding candidate."

"All right. What is your second request?"

"There is a young French Jewish girl named Aline Cadieux in the Dankworth orphanage, which has been unsuccessful with finding her a private home in the countryside. She's lost her family and her father is missing in action. I'd like for someone of influence to contact USCOM, an organization to bring refugee children to America, and arrange for Aline's passage to the United States."

He shifted his weight. "That's quite a request."

"With all due respect, sir," Ruth said, holding her ground. "If the SOE is capable of deploying agents into German-occupied territory, it should have no trouble placing a girl on a boat to America."

Bodington smiled, as if he were impressed or amused by her pluckiness. "I think we can make that happen."

A wave of relief washed over her. "Thank you, sir."

"I will be in touch in a few days with plans for your training, and we'll take care of notifying the WAAF that you are being deployed to a confidential assignment. In the meantime, you are to tell no one, including Lucette and Aline, about your role or the SOE."

"Yes, sir."

Ruth shook Bodington's hand and left his office. She made her way to the train station, all the while knowing, with great certainty, that her life would never be the same again.

CHAPTER 59

LONDON, ENGLAND—OCTOBER 1, 1940

Ruth, walking with an eagerness in her stride, entered the front gate of Dankworth Hall and traveled down a stone walkway. Inside the building, she found the director of the orphanage waiting for her in the entrance hall.

"Good day," Mrs. Webb said, clasping her hands in front of her.

"Hello," Ruth said. "Thank you for allowing me to speak with her first."

The woman nodded. "I was quite surprised to receive a telegram from the British government, instructing the orphanage to release Aline to a representative of the United States Committee for the Care of European Children. I assume you had something to do with it."

"I did. I wrote several letters to USCOM. Are you having any luck with getting some of the children into homes outside the city?" she asked, wanting to steer the conversation away from how Aline was selected.

Mrs. Webb perked her head. "We have. A retired couple in Daventry has agreed to take in two five-year-old girls to live in their home."

"That is good news," Ruth said. But she felt terrible for the children who remained in the orphanage. The Luftwaffe had bombed London for twenty-four straight nights, and she expected

the raids to worsen before things got better. "I hope you are able
to find safe havens for the rest of the children."

"Me too," Mrs. Webb said.

"When will the chaperone for USCOM arrive?" Ruth asked.

"Tomorrow."

"May I see Aline?"

"I'll arrange for her to meet you in the garden," Mrs. Webb said.
"It'll give you some privacy."

Mrs. Webb led Ruth down a hall, through a rear door, and gestured to a stone bench in the garden. Ruth sat and the woman
disappeared into the building. A few minutes later, the rear door
swung open.

"You're here!" Aline said, running to her.

Ruth hugged her. "I am."

Aline slipped away and pointed to rows of green vegetable tops.
"Do you like our victory garden?"

Ruth smiled. "It's lovely. Did you plant the vegetables?"

"*Oui*. The children get to help the workers in the garden."
Aline scanned the rows. "We have potatoes—beets—radishes—
turnips—and winter cabbage."

"It's wonderful, and I'm proud of you."

Aline beamed.

Ruth patted the space next to her on the bench. "Have a seat."

Aline sat. "Where's Lucette?"

"She's working at the airfield and will be coming to see you
after her shift."

"Why aren't you at work?"

Tension spread through Ruth's chest. "I came to tell you good
news."

Aline sat up straight.

"I wrote to a special organization called USCOM that brings
refugee children—many who are Jewish—to America. You were
accepted into the program."

Aline's eyes widened. "That's so far away. How will I see you
and Lucette?"

"The bombings have gotten worse. It's important that you're
someplace out of range of the German planes."

Aline's bottom lip quivered. "I don't want to leave you."

"I don't want to be away from you either, but Lucette and I need to do our duty to aid the fight." Ruth placed a hand on her shoulder. "Someday, this war will be over, France will be free, and we'll see each other again. I believe that with all my heart."

Aline blinked her eyes, as if fending off tears. "Do I have a choice in this?"

Ruth slipped her hand away. "*Non.*"

Aline lowered her head. "Where are they sending me?"

"Maine." Ruth kneeled on the ground in front of Aline. "I've been in contact with my *maman* and dad. They've been accepted as a foster family for USCOM. My parents know all about you, and they want you to stay with them."

Tears welled up in Aline's eyes. "On their apple orchard?"

Ruth nodded. "You'll love staying with my parents—they're sweet and kind. There will be loads of trees to climb and apples to pick. Many people in Lewiston speak French, and you'll go to the same school that I did. You'll make lots of friends."

Tears fell down Aline's cheeks.

"Do you remember me telling you about our family dog?"

"Moxie," Aline said, her voice cracking.

She nodded. "I'm hoping that you'll help take care of her while I'm away. She'll need to be fed twice each day, have lots of walks around the orchard, and plenty of belly rubs."

"I will."

Ruth smiled.

Aline sniffed back tears. "What will happen to me if my papa doesn't come home from the war?"

"He will."

"But what if he doesn't?"

Ruth looked into the girl's eyes, filled with fear and uncertainty. "My parents said that you are welcome to stay with them for as long as you want."

Aline threw her arms around Ruth and hugged her. "*Merci,*" she cried.

Ruth's eyes blurred with tears and she squeezed her tight.

Aline's sobs gradually faded.

Ruth slipped away and wiped the girl's cheeks with a handkerchief from her pocket. They rose from the bench and meandered through the victory garden, while talking about Aline's new home and relishing their time together.

CHAPTER 60

LONDON, ENGLAND—OCTOBER 7, 1940

Ruth entered the bedroom of her flat and packed belongings into an old suitcase and travel bag that she'd acquired at a charity shop. She retrieved an envelope, given to her by Nicolas Bodington, that contained money and a train ticket to Arisaig, a remote village in the Scottish Highlands where the SOE training school was located. A meld of melancholy and restlessness churned inside her. She slipped the envelope into her travel bag and carried her things to the entryway of the flat, where Lucette was waiting for her.

"That was quick," Lucette said.

"I didn't have much to pack." Ruth adjusted the tunic of her WAAF uniform. "I'm wearing most of what I own."

"Traveling light is a good thing," Lucette said, as if trying to soften the mood. "What time does your train leave?"

"Five."

"You might be the last train out of London. They've come early the past couple of nights."

Ruth nodded. "I'm sorry that you were moved to the third shift."

"It's all right. I can't sleep during air raids, so I might as well be productive by packing parachutes." Lucette glanced at the luggage. "Would you like me to see you off at the train station?"

"No need," Ruth said. "You haven't slept; you should get some rest before your shift."

"Are you sure?"

"Yes." Ruth hugged her tight. "I miss you already."

"Me too," Lucette said, her voice quavering.

Ruth released her. "I will keep Paul in my thoughts and prayers."

"*Merci*." Lucette wiped her eyes.

"I wish I could tell you everything."

"It's all right."

"No, it's not," Ruth said. "I've never kept a secret from you, and I hate that I can't explain where I'm going, what I'm doing, or when I'll see you again."

"I don't like it either," Lucette said, "but I understand and accept that your role requires confidentiality. You were chosen because someone saw something special in you."

Ruth swallowed. "I'll always be proud of you."

"Me too." Lucette slipped a folded envelope from a pocket of her uniform, and a smile spread over her face. "I'll send you off with some good news. I received a telegram during my last shift—I've been instructed to attend a meeting in Central London this Friday with Nicolas Bodington."

Ruth smiled. "You'll do great."

"Do you really think so?"

"I know so."

Lucette tucked away the envelope and walked Ruth to the door. "Break a leg."

"*Merde*," Ruth said, using the customary expletive to wish a French dancer good luck.

Lucette grinned.

Ruth gave her a final hug goodbye, picked up her luggage, and left. Outside, she walked down the sidewalk. Her joy faded and a thorn of loneliness pricked at her heart. "I'll see her again," she whispered to herself, as if reciting an affirmation. She buried her apprehension and weaved her way through people—carrying blankets and pillows—who'd left early to find a good spot in an air raid shelter.

CHAPTER 61

LONDON, ENGLAND—OCTOBER 7, 1940

R uth arrived at the Liverpool Street station twenty minutes before her scheduled departure. In hopes of distracting herself
from her solitude, she purchased a paper at a newsstand and sat on
a bench. She scanned the front page and wished that she'd bought
a magazine when her eyes locked on a headline:

VICHY FRANCE PASSES ANTISEMITIC LEGISLATION

She felt sick to her stomach as she read the piece, which claimed
that France's new puppet government for Germany had enacted
laws that excluded Jews from most public and private occupations,
and allowed for the internment of foreign Jews. *Nazi Germany's
antisemitic plague has spread to France*, Ruth thought, gripping the
paper. She prayed for the safety of Colette and Julian, and hoped
that their medical profession would preclude them from suffering
the consequences of the laws. Unable to read any longer, she put
down the paper and took deep breaths to quell her nerves.

A woman and a girl, who was approximately nine years of age,
walked along the landing and stood near a large metal clock. The
girl leaned to her mother and wrapped her arms around her waist.

Ruth smiled softly and thought of Aline, who'd left with the
USCOM chaperone five days earlier. *She's likely on a ship and*

will soon be in America. She imagined the beautiful life that Aline would have while living with her parents in Maine, far beyond the reach of Luftwaffe bombing raids. She was eternally grateful to her parents for welcoming Aline into their home, and she was relieved that Aline would be safe, cared for, and loved. More than ever, she was determined to pass her SOE training and do her part, albeit small, to fight fascist cruelty and make the world a better place for children to live.

The crowd grew, and people milled around the landing.

Ruth glanced at the clock and saw that the train was running late. Minutes passed and talk spread through the crowd that the train might be canceled. Ruth, growing restless, got up from the bench and retrieved her suitcase and travel bag. She weaved her way through the crowd to the edge of the landing and peered down the empty railway track.

"Ruth!" a voice called from far away in the station.

She perked her head and struggled to see over the large number of people in the station. *It's someone else with the same name.* She relaxed and adjusted her grip on the luggage.

"Ruth!" a man shouted, closer and more discernible.

The timber of the voice sent shivers down her spine. Her heart thudded against her rib cage. *It can't be—*

"Ruth!"

She shot forward. "Jimmie!"

"Ruth!"

She labored through the throng and, as she passed a group of businessmen with briefcases, Jimmie's face emerged from the crowd. Her body went weak, the luggage slipped from her hands, and she collapsed onto her knees. Tears flooded her eyes, and she felt him scoop her into his arms.

"Oh, darling," he cried.

"Jimmie," she sobbed. "You're alive."

He covered her face with kisses.

She pressed her lips to his and drew him tight.

The crowd stepped back, creating a circle around the couple. Eyes of people fell upon them. An elderly woman smiled and looped her arm around her husband's elbow.

Jimmie gently placed his hands to her cheeks and looked into tear-filled eyes. "I'm so sorry it took me so long to return home and find you."

"You're here now," she cried. "That's all that matters." Tears streamed down her face. Waves of emotion flooded her body.

Together, they wept, oblivious to the hundreds of Londoners who surrounded them.

He kissed her tears.

She clutched the tunic of his uniform and pressed to his chest.

An air raid siren sounded.

People shuffled down the landing, and Londoners, coming from nearby neighborhoods, began to enter the train station.

Ruth slowly released him. "We need to go."

He stood and helped her to her feet, and then picked up her luggage.

Ruth clasped his arm, absent a cast and appearing to be fully healed. She led him through the surge of people making their way to the underground section of the train station. They traveled down flights of stairs and entered a tunnel, which was a disused section of the Central Line extension.

"There," Ruth said, pointing to an empty spot at the back of the tunnel. She squeezed between people, who were putting down blankets and pillows, and sat on the concrete landing with her back against the wall.

Jimmie put down the luggage, sat, and wrapped his arm around her.

"I can't believe it," Ruth said, filled with joy. She leaned into him. "I watched the ship go down, and I thought you didn't make it out. I searched for you in the water—on the evacuation ship— at the port in England. I thought I lost you." Tears of happiness welled up in her eyes.

"I'm so sorry." He kissed her hair. "I wish I could have found you, or gotten word to you. I'm so happy you're alive."

"The life jacket saved me." She eased up and looked at him. "What happened?"

He drew a deep breath and peered at the arched ceiling of the tunnel, as if he were sifting through his memories. For several minutes, he told her about his struggle to get to the hull of the *Lancastria*, the reluctance of most of his ground crew members to disregard orders and come topside, and the explosion that occurred while he and some of the men began their ascent.

"I was the only one to get to the stairway landing," Jimmie said, his voice somber. "The hull rapidly flooded. My friend Horace and the other members of my squadron didn't get out, nor did the hundreds of ground crew who were ordered to go to the hull."

"Oh, God." She placed a hand to his cheek. "I'm so sorry."

He nodded. "I was overcome by water, and I swam through a submerged passage in search of a way out. As my body was giving out, a man grabbed me and pulled me into a compartment with an air pocket. We escaped through a porthole."

Ruth shivered. She pulled him tight.

"I floated on a piece of wood debris from the ship's deck, until French fishing vessels joined the destroyers and trawlers that were rescuing survivors. I was taken aboard an oared fishing boat that was rowed by an elderly Frenchman and a boy. They took me to shore and found a doctor to tend to my arm that I reinjured in the escape. By the time I got to Saint-Nazaire, the evacuation was over."

Ruth drew a jagged breath.

"I met up with several BEF soldiers who failed to make it out of the port. We made our way south through France, Spain, and to Gibraltar, where we boarded a British ship to England. I got back a few weeks ago and learned from Nora that you were alive. I contacted ambulance units but couldn't find you, so Nora and I wrote letters and made telephone inquiries to each of the women's branches of the British military. This morning, I discovered that you were a member of the WAAF and acquired your address, but no telephone number. I couldn't wait to see you, so I talked my squadron leader into giving me a day of leave. I went to your apartment and found Lucette. She told me you were on your way here to board a train."

"Thank goodness my train was late," Ruth said.

People—carrying blankets, pillows, lamps, and torchlights—

flooded into the tunnel and squeezed into spaces. A muted sound of air raid sirens echoed through the underground shelter.

"It was wonderful to see Lucette," Jimmie said. "I'm so glad she's okay."

Ruth nodded.

"How's Aline?"

She told him about her parents becoming a foster care family for USCOM and arranging to bring Aline into their home.

He smiled and held her tight.

A rumble of bombs came from above. Lights—mounted on the sides of the tunnel—flickered and went out. People turned on electric torches and lit oil lamps, producing a dull glow and inky shadows over the subterranean refuge.

"Are you back with the Seventy-Three Squadron?" Ruth asked.

"Yes, we're temporarily stationed at RAF Castle Camps. Next month, we're being deployed to a base in Africa."

She clasped his hand and intertwined her fingers with his.

"Are you being redeployed to another WAAF location?"

She drew a deep breath. "No."

"Where are you going?"

She looked into his eyes. "I've accepted a confidential assignment. I want to tell you about it, but I was sworn to secrecy. I promise—someday, I will tell you everything."

"It's okay." He caressed her hand with his thumb. "Whatever duty you've chosen, I'm quite certain you are doing the right thing. I'm in awe of your spirit and courage."

She released his hand and hugged him.

He pulled her close.

She felt his heartbeat against her chest. "I wish we had more time."

"So do I," he breathed.

She closed her eyes. "But we're here together now."

"We are."

A bomb blast shook the ground. Tiny bits of mortar fell from the ceiling and into Ruth's hair, but she made no effort to shake it away. She clung tightly to Jimmie, refusing to let him go.

As hours passed, the Luftwaffe conducted wave after wave of mass air attacks on London. Electric torches were eventually turned off and lamps were dimmed. Children were tucked into blankets and people curled on the ground to rest, but Ruth and Jimmie remained awake. Nuzzled together in an unbreakable embrace, they whispered their hopes and dreams of a life together.

Chapter 62

London, England — October 8, 1940

The all-clear signal sounded, stirring the hundreds of people in the tunnel. Ruth opened her eyes and sat up. She felt Jimmie place his arm around her and kiss her cheek.

Her skin tingled.

"Good morning," he said.

She smiled. "Good morning. I must have dozed off. How long did I sleep?"

"Not long," he said. "Is there any way to delay your departure for your assignment?"

"I'm afraid not. I was expected to leave last night, so I'm already late on my travel to my post. How about you?"

Jimmie shook his head. "I'm required to report back to RAF Castle Camps by noon." He helped her to her feet and gathered her luggage.

They followed the mass of people, who were carrying their belongings, out of the tunnel. They climbed the stairs and made their way to the landing where Ruth's train had arrived and people were beginning to board.

"I guess this is it," Jimmie said, placing her luggage near the entrance steps of the train.

A surge of sadness flowed through her. "I don't know when, or if, I'll be able to write to you."

"It's all right. I understand." Jimmie drew a deep breath and looked into her eyes. "If we should never see each other again—"

"We will," she said, clasping his hands.

He squeezed her fingers. "I want you to know that I believe you came into my life for a reason. You've made me a better person, and you've created an indelible mark on my soul that will be with me always."

Tears welled up in her eyes. She leaned in and hugged him.

He wrapped his arms around her and lowered his cheek to her hair. "You have my heart."

She pulled him close. "And you have mine."

A train whistle blew.

Ruth raised her chin, his lips met hers, and they kissed long and deep. She felt his body slip away, and she gathered her luggage and stepped onto the train.

Ruth made her way through a carriage and sat at a window seat. She looked at Jimmie, who remained standing on the landing. A whistle blew and the train jerked forward. She kissed her fingers and placed them on the glass.

Jimmie smiled and put a hand over his heart.

A tear fell down her cheek. The train chugged over the tracks, and she watched him disappear.

Conflicting emotions surged through her. She was overjoyed that Jimmie was alive, yet gutted to leave him. *Our obligation to serve Allied forces comes first*, she thought with her vision blurred with tears. Her sense of duty did little to quell her anguish, and she knew, deep down, that the chances of survival for a pilot and intelligence agent—assuming she passed her SOE training—were stacked against them. She resolved to carry on the fight for freedom, regardless of the risk, and return to him after the war. *We found our way back to each other once—we will do it again.*

Ruth leaned back in her seat and wiped her eyes. She gazed out the window at the skyline of London, scarred with destroyed and damaged buildings. The train chugged away from the city center, leaving the destruction and howls of fire brigades behind.

"Tickets!" a train attendant called.

She straightened her back and smoothed her skirt.

The attendant—wearing a black suit with brass buttons and a cap—examined and punched passenger tickets as he made his way down the aisle of the carriage.

Ruth retrieved her travel bag, reached inside, and froze. A smile formed on her lips, and a warmth of hope enveloped her as she removed a tattered, oil-stained Piglet.

AUTHOR'S NOTE

While conducting research for *Fleeing France*, I became fascinated by Operation Aerial and the tragedy of the RMS *Lancastria*. The goal of the operation—which took place from June 15 to 25, 1940—was to evacuate Allied troops and civilians from ports in western France, following the collapse of Allied military forces in the Battle of France. The mission was a huge success, rescuing 191,870 soldiers and approximately 40,000 civilians, but it came at a great cost. The *Lancastria*, a British ocean liner requisitioned for the operation, was sunk by a German air raid off the coast of Saint-Nazaire on June 17, 1940. The ship was loaded far beyond its capacity of 1,300 passengers, and it is estimated that between 4,000 and 7,000 people perished in the sinking of the vessel. The *Lancastria* is the largest single-ship loss of life in British maritime history, and more people were killed in the sinking of the *Lancastria* than the *Titanic* and *Lusitania* disasters combined. Due to the enormous loss of life and potential wartime implications, British Prime Minister Winston Churchill issued a D-notice to suppress news of the tragedy from being released to the public. According to the British Official Secrets Act, the government's report on the *Lancastria* cannot be released until the year 2040. Also, I was surprised to learn that the French government placed an exclusion zone around the wreck site of the *Lancastria*, but the United

Kingdom has yet to make the site an official maritime war grave because the wreckage lies in French territorial waters. The secrecy surrounding the *Lancastria* served as inspiration for writing the story, and it is my hope that this book will commemorate the thousands of soldiers and civilians who perished in the disaster.

During my research, I became increasingly captivated by the brave women who volunteered to drive ambulances for France. There was no women's section in the French Army of 1939–40. However, several hundred women served as civilian volunteers in auxiliary ambulance sections, attached to the army in the field. It is difficult to imagine how dangerous and difficult it was for the drivers to perform their duties under the rampage of the German military. After the fall of France, many of these women drivers served in the French Resistance, and some went on to become spies in Britain's Special Operations Executive (SOE), including an American named Virginia Hall and a New Zealander named Nancy Wake. Hall and Wake, both of whom accomplished valiant feats of espionage in German-occupied France, provided inspiration for creating Ruth Lacroix's character. I like to imagine that Ruth's experience in a French ambulance corps during the Battle of France provided her with the motivation and skills needed to be a stealthy spy.

In addition to the women ambulance drivers, I was intrigued to learn about the No. 73 Squadron RAF, a real group of fighter pilots who were equipped with Hawker Hurricanes and deployed to France at the outbreak of the war. Edgar "Cobber" Kain, Newell "Fanny" Orton, James "Hank" More, and Peter Ayerst were real pilots of the squadron who make appearances in the book. There were multiple leaders of the No. 73 Squadron during the timeline of the novel, and I used Hank as the sole squadron leader for consistency. Cobber was the RAF's first flying ace of World War II, and he was killed when he crashed his Hurricane while performing low-level aerobatics for his squadron mates, who were gathered at the airfield at Échemines to bid him farewell for his flight back to England. Fanny, another flying ace of the squadron, was wounded in a dogfight in the Battle of France, which is included in the book. Although Fanny survived the timeline of the novel, he was shot down and killed in September of 1941 on the Channel Front. Of the four real pilots of the squadron who appear in the book, Ayerst—who lived to a splendid age of ninety-three—is the only one who survived the war.

There were several Hurricane squadrons in France during the onset of the war, but I chose the No. 73 Squadron because of its ties to the *Lancastria*. Approximately forty ground crew of the squadron perished in the sinking of the vessel. I used Jimmie's friendship with Horace, a ground crewman, to provide readers a view of the approximate eight hundred men who were ordered to remain in the hull of the ill-fated ship.

While conducting research on RAF pilots of World War II, I learned that many aviators were quite superstitious and often carried a good luck charm, talisman, family photo, or religious medallion while flying missions. I wanted to give Jimmie a symbol of hope, so I imagined that his sister, Nora, who fought to regain her ability to walk after contracting polio, would gift him something special for inspiration. As a child, I loved the book *Winnie-the-Pooh*, and I couldn't resist endearing him with a tiny stuffed Piglet, a timid character who endeavors to be brave and overcome his fears.

Prior to doing research for the book, I knew little about the Phony War, an eight-month period after France and Britain declared war on Nazi Germany. During this phase of the war, there was little military conflict, with the exceptions of air skirmishes and a French invasion of Saarland, Germany, from September 7 to 16, 1939. In the Saar Offensive—a now nearly forgotten invasion—French troops suffered approximately two thousand casualties before retreating amid a German counteroffensive. In the book, Ruth's cousin, Marceau, was killed during France's invasion of the Saarland. I used this event to launch Ruth into serving in the war, and I thought that readers might enjoy learning about this little-known event. Who knew that France invaded Germany?

The Battle of France lasted approximately six weeks and, prior to conducting research for the book, I was of the mindset that the French military was far inferior to that of the German Army. While Hitler's military was superior, especially his Luftwaffe, the

French Army was a million strong with five million reservists. Also, France had large and formidable battalions of tanks, and its air force had a sizeable fleet, although many of the aircraft were outdated. My research indicated that most French soldiers fought courageously, and it was catastrophic actions of senior French military leaders—such as poor communication and military tactics, and the assumption that the Ardennes Forest was impassable for German Panzer tanks—that led to the swift fall of France.

It was heart-wrenching to learn about the massive exodus of French civilians during the German invasion. In the summer of 1940, between six and ten million French fled their homes. It was my intent to provide readers with a personal story of the hardships faced by refugees, so I created a subplot with Pierre and his granddaughter, Aline—French Jews who suffered the loss of family members and were determined to never live under German occupation. During my research, I encountered many stories of children who were orphaned during the invasion of France, and I imagined Ruth and Lucette coming to the aid of Aline to provide her a home where she would be loved and cared for. The United States Committee for the Care of European Children (USCOM) was a real organization that was established in June of 1940. First Lady Eleanor Roosevelt was the USCOM's chairwoman, and the organization rescued more than three hundred refugee children, most of them Jewish, from western Europe.

It was an honor and pleasure to research the rise of Winston Churchill from First Lord of the Admiralty to prime minister. I spent many enjoyable hours reading and listening to his speeches, as well as scouring over reports of his interaction with Prime Minister Chamberlain, members of the Anglo-French Supreme War Council (SWC), and General Hastings "Pug" Ismay—Churchill's chief military assistant. Although Churchill was a hands-on leader who engaged directly with his Chiefs of Staff, I used his close relationship with Ismay to provide readers a view of the events taking place during the French Campaign. I strived to display Churchill as a confident wartime leader who inspired hope in the darkest of times. Also, it was my endeavor to show Churchill's reasons for keeping the sinking of the *Lancastria* a secret.

During my research, I discovered many intriguing historical events, which I labored to accurately weave into the timeline of the book. For example, on June 3, 1940, the German Luftwaffe bombed Paris and its suburbs for the first time. The Luftwaffe's primary target was the Citroën automobile factory, but a bomb also struck a school. The air raid on Paris killed 254 people, including 195 civilians. The German invasions of Denmark, Norway, the Low Countries, and France are depicted in the story, and I strived to provide accurate dates of unfolding events. I was surprised to learn that Churchill visited France during the conflict, and I included his meetings with the Anglo-French Supreme War Council in the story. In addition to Operation Aerial and the sinking of the *Lancastria*, I included mention of lesser-known military plans—Operation Wilfred, a British naval plan to mine the sea passage between Norway and its offshore islands; and Operation Royal Marine, a plan to float fluvial mines down rivers that flowed into Germany from France. The No. 73 Squadron RAF moved many times during the Battle of France, and I used the airfields reflected in my research. On November 8, 1939, Cobber Kain shot down a German Dornier Do 17 bomber, the first aerial victory of this war, and I thought it was important to include this event in the story. Also, Ruth is recruited for Britain's Special Operation Executive in late September of 1940, a few months after the creation of the organization. Although most female agents were recruited later in the war, I accelerated the timeline of Ruth's enrollment into the SOE to align with Jimmie's escape to England. I attempted to accurately reflect the timeline and locations of the Germany military invasion, specifically the advancement of Panzer tank divisions through France. Additionally, I strived to precisely depict various types of RAF and Luftwaffe aircraft. Any historical inaccuracies in this book are mine and mine alone.

Numerous historical figures make appearances in this book, most notably Winston Churchill. It is important to emphasize that *Fleeing France* is a story of fiction, and that I took creative liberties in writing this tale. In addition to Churchill, British Prime Minister Neville Chamberlain, French Prime Minister Paul Reynaud, General Ismay, General Weygand, General Gamelin, Marshal

Pétain, Cobber Kain, Fanny Orton, Hank More, Peter Ayerst, and Nicolas Bodington appear in the story. Also, the Bal Tabarin was a real cabaret in Paris during the war. I created a fictitious casting director named Fermin to develop tension for Ruth to quit her singing job and join the ambulance corps. In real life, Pierre Sandrini was a producer and co-owner of the Bal Tabarin, and I discovered during my research that he saved the lives of four Jewish employees during the war.

Numerous books, documentaries, and historical archives were crucial for my research. *The Fall of France: The Nazi Invasion of 1940* by Julian Jackson was incredibly helpful with understanding the events that led to the defeat of France, and the exodus of refugees fleeing the country. *Operation Aerial: Churchill's Second Miracle of Deliverance* by David Worsfold and *The Sinking of the Lancastria: Britain's Greatest Maritime Disaster and Churchill's Cover-Up* by Jonathan Fenby were exceptional resources for understanding the details of the evacuation operation and the *Lancastria* disaster. Also, the 1939 newsreel *Paris Dances* included the actual film footage of Bal Tabarin, which was a tremendous resource for writing the scenes with Ruth working as a cabaret singer.

It was a privilege to write this book. I will forever be inspired by the courageous service of the women of the French ambulance corps, and the RAF pilots who were deployed to France. I will never forget the thousands who died in the sinking of the *Lancastria*, and I'll always remember the millions of French citizens who fled their home in the wake of the German military invasion. It is my hope that this book will pay tribute to the men, women, and children who perished in the Battle of France.

Fleeing France would not have been possible without the support of many people. I'm eternally thankful to the following gifted individuals:

I am deeply grateful to my brilliant editor, John Scognamiglio. John's guidance, encouragement, and enthusiasm were immensely helpful with the writing of this book.

Many thanks to my fabulous agent, Mark Gottlieb, for his support and counsel with my journey as an author. I feel extremely fortunate to have Mark as my agent.

My deepest appreciation to my publicist, Vida Engstrand. I am profoundly grateful for Vida's tireless efforts to promote my stories to readers.

It takes a team effort to publish a book, and I am forever grateful to everyone at Kensington Publishing for bringing this story to life.

I'm thankful to have Kim Taylor Blakemore, Tonya Mitchell, and Jacqueline Vick as my accountability partners. Our weekly video conferences helped us to finish our manuscripts on time.

My sincere thanks to Akron Writers' Group: Betty Woodlee, Ken Waters, Dave Rais, John Stein, Rachel Freggiaro, Marcie Blandford, and Corry Novosel. And a special heartfelt thanks to Betty Woodlee, who critiqued an early draft of the manuscript.

This story would not have been possible without the love and support of my wife, Laurie, and our children, Catherine, Philip, Lizzy, Lauren, and Rachel. Laurie, you are—and always will be—*meu céu*.

FLEEING FRANCE

ABOUT THIS GUIDE

The suggested questions are included to enhance your group's reading of Alan Hlad's *Fleeing France*.

Discussion Questions

1. Before reading *Fleeing France*, what did you know about the fall of France in World War II? Were you aware of the Phony War? What did you know about the millions of civilian refugees who fled the conflict?

2. What are Ruth's aspirations while working as a cabaret singer in Paris? How does the death of Ruth's cousin motivate her to serve in an ambulance corps?

3. Why do you think Jimmie joined the Royal Air Force? How does his relationship with his sister, Nora, shape his service as a fighter pilot?

4. Describe Ruth. What kind of woman is she? What attributes did Ruth possess that made her well suited for the French ambulance corps and the British Special Operations Executive?

5. While fleeing the German military invasion, Ruth and Jimmie fall in love. What brings them together? Why does their relationship develop so quickly? At what point do you think Ruth realized she loved Jimmie? How is the war a catalyst for their affection? What are Ruth and Jimmie's hopes and dreams?

6. Describe Lucette. Why do you think Ruth and Lucette formed a strong friendship?

7. Describe Pierre and his granddaughter, Aline. Why is Pierre determined to prevent Aline from living under German occupation? Is there anything Ruth could have done to save Pierre?

8. Prior to reading the book, what did you know about the sinking of the RMS *Lancastria* and the order by Winston Churchill

to conceal the news of the disaster? What did you know about the Luftwaffe bombing raid on Paris in June of 1940?

9. Have you ever had a good luck charm? Why do you think some people believe that special objects can bring safety or good luck? What did Piglet represent to Jimmie? Why do you think Jimmie left Piglet in Ruth's luggage?

10. What are the major themes of *Fleeing France*?

11. Why do many readers enjoy historical fiction, in particular novels set in World War II? To what degree do you think Hlad took creative liberties with this story?

12. How do you envision what happens after the end of the book? Do you think Ruth and Jimmie will reunite after the war? If so, what do you think their lives will be like?

Visit our website at
KensingtonBooks.com
to sign up for our newsletters, read
more from your favorite authors, see
books by series, view reading group
guides, and more!

Become a Part of Our
Between the Chapters Book Club
Community and Join the Conversation